THE EMBRACE OF THE GODDESS

They came at her as she rounded the bend, twin shadows that formed themselves into two men. They were
armed with daggers already raised high as they leaped
toward her. The blades glistened darkly, as if her blood
already stained them.

Their faces loomed at her, caught up and revealed in
fragments of shadowy light. She had a jumbled impression of beards, gleaming eyes and grim smiles.
Their expressions laughed at her. She would not escape
them. She knew it, and so did they.

You know no such thing.

The voice boomed through Sirona's being, each
word bursting in her head like a crack of thunder. An
awful force came searing out of her. The presence of
the Goddess swamped Sirona, washing her in strength.
Here was a force that had lain banked within her. Now,
for the first time, it was surging to life, burgeoning up
within and without, surrounding her like a great glowing shield.

The two men stopped in their tracks. The strength
that bathed her was not of this world, and too late,
they now saw that . . .

Other Books by Sarah Isidore

The Daughters of Bast
THE HIDDEN LAND
SHRINE OF LIGHT

THE DAUGHTERS OF BAST

The World Tree

SARAH ISIDORE

An Imprint of HarperCollinsPublishers

This is a work of fiction. Names, characters, places, and incidents are products of the author's imagination or are used fictitiously and are not to be construed as real. Any resemblance to actual events, locales, organizations, or persons, living or dead, is entirely coincidental.

EOS
An Imprint of HarperCollins*Publishers*
10 East 53rd Street
New York, New York 10022-5299

Copyright © 2001 by Sarah Isidore
ISBN: 0-380-80320-8
www.eosbooks.com

First Eos paperback printing: November 2001

Eos Trademark Reg. U.S. Pat. Off. and in Other Countries, Marca Registrada, Hecho en U.S.A.
HarperCollins® is a trademark of HarperCollins Publishers Inc.

Printed in the U.S.A.

10 9 8 7 6 5 4 3 2 1

To Ely . . . walk with Bast, little one

Prologue

In the courtyard of the great temple the cats slept. Once they had hunted and made love, washed themselves and purred in a great concert of sound, all under the benevolent eye of their Goddess.

Now the liveliness that had lasted for ages beyond counting had been replaced by this profound slumber. The cats lay in multicolored heaps: calico and black and ginger and white and stripes and silver all tumbled together. They slept. And they waited.

Above them the pink stones of the great temple no longer glimmered. Once those stones had been as bright as the cats that scampered beneath them. Now they were dull, the life leached from them, as though they, too, were sleeping. The chambers the stones enclosed were silent, and the most silent of all was the sanctuary where the Goddess Herself sat upon Her gold-and-silver throne.

Long and long had She reposed in Her ancient sanctum. Her wondrous eyes were closed, though, unlike the cats in the courtyard, She did not sleep. Never had She slept. Grieved, yes; called out and wondered, that, too. But slumber had been a gift She had given Her cats and not Herself. It was a luxury She could not afford. She, too, must wait; but She must be awake, so that She would know when the waiting was over.

She stirred upon her jeweled throne. Her enormous eyes, as luminous and glowing as twin emeralds, opened.

She smiled.

I

THE MAN WAS AS DARK AND WET AS the night.

Huddled in his cloak, he stood beneath the limbs of a giant spreading oak and waited. Just beyond the outstretched branches the track meandered through a meadow dank and dripping with rain. The man shivered and drew the folds of the cloak tighter. The odors of wool and sweat and damp wafted about him. Yet the material could have been far wetter. Gratefully, the man glanced up at the sheltering oak tree. Oaks such as this were becoming more and more unusual. Mighty Carolus the Great, the ruler of Christendom, was determined to destroy the sacred groves of the pagans, and he was making sharp inroads on these trees, which had stood from the beginning of time.

The man's gaze shifted away from the dense canopy, back out to the meadow. Suddenly he stiffened, his eyes straining through the gloom. A figure, whose shape was all but obscured by its heavy cloak, was striding down the track. Its steps were firm and swift, the folds of the cloak flapping about its ankles. The man uttered a soft exclamation. There, she was coming at last.

Of course, it was impossible to tell whether the person wrapped in the heavy mantle was male or female, but the man was certain it was the latter. After all, who else would venture forth on a night like this, when the old gods were sure to be abroad, save for a wisewoman familiar with the ways of the Old Ones?

As the figure made its purposeful way through the meadow, the man left the shelter of the oak tree and hurried out to intersect its path. He had scarcely taken two steps before the cloak-muffled shape swung about to confront him. Her voice: female—just as he had suspected—but sharp and filled with an authority he had seldom heard in any woman's voice, snapped out at him.

"Stay your distance, stranger," she ordered. "I know not who you be."

The man extended his arms and opened his hands to show that he held no weapons. "I mean you no harm, woman," he called in as reassuring a tone as he could manage. "I would only speak with you a moment. It is most important."

"It must be," she observed dryly, "for you to be out here. A man who spends the dark of the night standing under a tree is either up to no good or driven by an urgent purpose."

"Rightly spoken." The man shivered both from the rain and the realization that the woman had known he was there. "And it is the purpose that drives me. May I draw nearer so that I need not go on shouting?"

She watched him a moment, then freed a hand from her cloak and granted him permission with a curt gesture. "Whatever you wish to speak of, do it quickly," she warned. "I am on my way to someone whose need is, for certain, far greater than yours."

The man's expression turned grim at her words. A sharp reply sprang to his lips, but he corrected himself at once. This was a matter that must be handled with wisdom and subtlety. Both words and face must be carefully controlled. He came closer to the woman. During the wait his eyes had grown accustomed to the dark, and, in spite of the wind-driven rain, he could dimly make out her features.

She was young, younger than he had thought she would be. Her deep brown hair hung in three neat braids on either side. Her eyes gleamed at him, impossibly dark one moment, then strangely light as the gusts of wind shifted. He glanced away uneasily and cleared his throat to begin. "There is magic abroad this night—"

The woman raised an impatient hand, cutting him off. "I am a wisewoman, not a sorceress. Healing is my province. I am on my way to bring a baby into the world, and the mother is going to have a difficult time. The workings of magic do not interest me."

"But they must," the man hissed. A single spear of moonlight glanced through the clouds, setting both their wet faces agleam. "I know what you are."

"Do you?" The woman's gaze grew as cold and piercing as the moonlight. "And precisely what am I?"

The man quailed at her tone. Yet he could not back down. There was no choice in the matter. Too much was at stake; not to mention that the one who had sent him on this mission could be even more fearsome than the woman before him. "You are not"—he made the sign of the cross—"you are not a Christian."

The woman's laughter was dry and genuine. "Indeed, I am not. But what has that to do with magic?"

"Everything!" Impatience melded with apprehension. The man glared at her. The admonition he had given himself to speak with care was deserting him in the face of her irreverence. "Any person who has not accepted God's grace is in league with demons and other forces of evil."

"I thought," said the woman in a tone as dry as her laughter had been, "that we were speaking of magic."

"They are one and the same. And that is why I have been waiting for you on this accursedly foul night, when I could instead be sitting before a warm fire with a flagon of mulled wine. You are a priestess . . . lady." Grudgingly, the man added this title of respect. He had a favor to seek of this woman, he reminded himself; angering her would not help him in achieving it. "The blood of Druids runs in your veins. Everyone in this province knows it."

The woman sighed. "I do not practice the rites that those before me did. Everyone knows that as well."

"Still," the man insisted, "you have powers—abilities that others do not. I would have you use those abilities."

The dark-light eyes watched him narrowly. "In what way?"

The man drew in his breath. Now was the moment where absolute delicacy was called for. The request must be made in such a way that she would listen and not dismiss it out of hand. "The birth you attend this night . . . it must not end well. The mother is having a difficult time, you said so yourself—"

He allowed his words to trail to a stop, aware that she would draw her own conclusions. He saw that the woman was staring at him. Indeed, she was staring so intently that he had to drop his eyes.

"I give life," she said sternly, when his gaze had fallen away from hers. "I do not take it."

"But when a woman is brought to bed and the birth is too hard the baby is not likely to live in any case. It happens often enough. My wife has lost two that way, and my first concubine died in childbed, along with the babe."

"Yes, it is common." The woman's stern tone had not changed. "Common enough without me helping it along."

"Come now." The man's voice grew subtly more threatening. "You have helped other women to sin against God. All wisewomen have. You are the keepers of secrets: of your sex and of the power of the old heathen ways. I know you worship Brigando, the pagan goddess, she who turns women away from the paths that the one true Lord has decreed for them—"

The woman stepped forward, forcing the man to take a hasty step back. "You do not know who I worship," she said in a low voice that pushed him back yet farther. "But I will tell you this: I am no Christian. The paths of women were formed long ago, ages and ages before your Lord was even a whisper in the ear of some priest. The Ancient Harmonies guide the lives of women, and the Harmonies guide me in my healing of them. No male—God or man—may say otherwise."

"Blasphemy!" Instinctively horrified, as well as angered, the man crossed himself. "To speak against the true faith is to bring down the wrath of our Savior himself."

"Well, then." The dryness returned to the woman's voice, and she turned around. "If my speech displeases you, there is no need for us to speak further."

"Wait." The man swallowed a frustrated oath. He was

botching this miserably. The situation had to be salvaged, and quickly. "In truth, I meant no offense." Rain splattered his face, obscuring the winning smile he pasted on his lips. "Lady, may we not start over?"

The wisewoman was already walking away. "There is no time," she called back over her shoulder. "I must be on my way."

Desperation drove the man after her. "You go to attend the Lady Bathilde this night," he rapped out.

She slung him a sidewise glance. "What is that to you?" Her voice had turned as hard and cold as the rain.

"The babe must die; the Lady Bathilde, too, if you can manage it. You will be paid well for your trouble. In gold, not silver, and more gold than you have ever seen, or will see, if you continue in this meager existence as a wisewoman." The words tumbled over each other. It was not how he had planned it, but the offer had to be made before he lost her attention completely.

"Lady," he called sharply. "Hear you my words?"

"I hear you." The woman paused briefly in her long strides. "Has your Savior instructed you to ask murder of me?"

The man's eyes narrowed. He crossed himself again, this time without concern that he might offend her. "The priests were right," he snarled. "You who hold to the ancient demons that were once gods are indeed evil—"

"I, evil?" The wisewoman's laugh was sardonic. "Evil is a woman ripening with a babe when she will not survive another birth, or becoming pregnant when she already has too many mouths to feed. Evil is when a young girl's belly swells because some lout has forced himself on her. I help women in such circumstances. To not help them is where the evil lies."

The man was trembling with anger and a touch of fear. But he now understood why his comrades had been so insistent on choosing this particular wisewoman. Priests' warnings or no, her power was incontrovertible. "You are the only one who can commit the deed," he insisted.

"You misjudge me," the woman said harshly. "Murder is

a violation of the Ancient Harmonies. This woman desires her life and her child. It is my calling to help her, though in the end, the result must be as the fates will."

"And what if the fates have decreed that she and the babe die? All you need do is help it along."

Suddenly the woman was standing closer. The man had not seen her move, yet all at once she was right in front of him, looming far too near for his comfort. He stepped back, but her eyes followed. They pursued him. They burned in the night, flickering from dark to light, light to dark, so swiftly it was like staring into flames in a darkened room. Those eyes were far too bright and dancing for the eyes of a normal woman, a Christian woman.

"I would not," she said in a low terrible voice, "commit such an act if all the mountains of Saxony turned to gold and glittered before me."

But the man was scarcely listening. His ears had closed at the sight of those strange flickering eyes. "You do have powers," he croaked. "Begone from me." He crossed himself frantically. "Begone."

The woman's smile was cold. "That was my intention."

She swung back along the track, disappearing into the rain and darkness.

The man's curses followed her on the wind.

The wisewoman hurried through the storm. The wind was at her back, pushing her along. She welcomed the push of the wet, powerful hands. There was little time, and too much of it had been wasted on that man and his unholy demands. The conversation he had engaged her in so unwillingly was deeply troubling. It could not be ignored, but for now other matters must take precedence.

The steady rain had made the track even muddier than was its normal wont. The muck clung to the woman's feet as she made her way steadily toward her destination. She knew by the track's widening that she had entered the lands that had once been held by Erchinoald, the Count of Estrancia and the Lady Bathilde's departed husband, but which were now his widow's. The woman quickened her strides as the heavy stands of trees gave way to small fields and vine-yards and cleared pastures bounded by rough fences of piled stones. Tenant villages belonging to the manor lay along the track: small clusters of wooden huts with thatched roofs arranged around a central gathering circle. The homes were dark save for the weak glimmer of banked hearth-fires. The woman passed them one by one, glancing only briefly at the curls of smoke that drifted out from the in-evitable cracks in wood and thatching.

The manor lands were extensive and prosperous, as befit-ted the lord who had owned them. Thick woodlands of beech and oak provided timber and charcoal and sheltered wild game, as well as herds of semi-wild pigs that roamed through the spring and summer, fattening until the time came to slaughter them in the fall. The partitioned fields, farmed by the bond peasants who lived in the villages, looked barren from the winter's long passing, but soon they would be heavy with barley, rye, wheat, and spelt. The live-stock had been taken to their huts for the night to protect them from wolves, but their presence lingered on the rain-drenched air. Odors of cattle and sheep wafted to the wise-woman, mingling with the earthy grass smell of their pastures.

Eventually, a shape loomed up against the night, darker than the darkness. The manor lay ahead, bounded by the demesne, the lady's lands, cultivated by the house servants for the use of the manor and its inhabitants. The woman quickened her pace still more, until she was nearly running as she went through the fence that enclosed the curtis, or manor enclosure.

A gate made of stone formed the entrance, together with a platform from which commands were proclaimed. Nearby was a wooden chapel large enough to accommodate the manor folk as well as the lord and his family. Inside the enclosure itself at least twenty single-room huts to house the manor folk nestled together. A large stable, a round bakehouse, two barns, a kitchen, and three poultry houses bordered them. At the center of this network of workshops, stables, and outbuildings, the house itself reposed. It was

built of stone—an exception and a rarity in these times—
and was very large.

The great entry doors were unbarred, and a lone figure
holding a lantern huddled beneath the shelter of the eaves.
The candle inside the container swung crazily as he lurched
into the rain to meet the approaching woman.

Panting, she drew up, recognizing the man as the
manor's chief servant. "Seneschal," she began, "I am
Sirona, the healer—"

"At last!" The seneschal cut her off, impatience and fear
and worry all mingling in his angry voice. "I was beginning
to fear you would not come at all, and with my lady screaming in agony as she struggles to birth the son of my poor
lord—may Jesus and all the Saints bless his departed
soul—"

The wisewoman called Sirona swept past him. She had
seen this type of anger too often to be troubled by it. "I am
here now," she threw over her shoulder. "All will be well."

The head servant leaped after her. "Wait, I must escort
you!"

"I can find the way."

And she did. Great manor house or peasant's hut, the
physical circumstances for bringing children into the world
were much the same. There was no private space for giving
birth. Women labored in the central chamber of their home,
whether that be a great hall or the single room of a thatched
hut. In the case of a high-ranking noblewoman like
Bathilde, the lone concession to privacy would be the enclosed bed box she had once occupied with her husband.

"Still," the seneschal insisted, "I must lead you."

He was a red-faced man, large with good living and
puffed even larger with the importance of this night. He
forged ahead of her, the lantern throwing off shadows
against the stone walls. Sirona caught a glimpse of the
Royal Hall as the servant led her on, especially constructed
to entertain Carolus, should the King and his retinue honor
the manor with their presence. Beyond it was the central
hall, where her patient was waiting.

Sirona frowned. So far, she heard none of the sounds that

attended a happy birth: no laughter or singing, no excited chatter. Hushed voices drifted to her ears, broken by periodic groans. All of it was confirmation that here was a labor where things were not progressing as they should.

The seneschal paused in the entryway, swinging the lantern aside to let her pass. His self-importance had deflated. Birth was women's business and no place for a man. "I cannot accompany you farther—"

"Of course, you can't." Impatiently Sirona brushed past him into the vast firelit hall.

A collection of faces turned toward her at once. Their features were burnished by the glow of torches, oil lamps, and flames dancing in the central hearth. Her patient was, of course, not alone. No woman who gave birth ever was. Friends and relatives surrounded the common born and servingwomen and attendants clustered around the highborn.

The faces that surrounded the Lady Bathilde were all female; in addition to the seneschal, all the other male house folk who normally filled the place had been banished. Servingwomen and slaves hovered about their mistress, whose great oaken bed box, with its elaborate carvings, was situated near the warmth of the great hearth-fire. Some of them were trying to tempt the pregnant woman with soothing teas, while others huddled together whispering. Relief, anxiety, and impatience washed over all their faces as Sirona strode toward the bed box.

"Lady," one of the women said. "The wisewoman has come."

"Ah," the noblewoman responded, "so you have got here at last."

Bathilde's voice was gruff and surprisingly strong. She lay in the bed, propped up by bolsters and cushions, her belly so large it seemed as though it were trying to touch the broad-timbered beams of the ceiling. She was a vigorous woman with black hair and even blacker eyes.

Her beauty was compelling; she had entered this very house as a Saxon slave and had quickly caught the eye of Erchinoald, its lord. And Erchinoald was no minor lord. He was an *iudex*, appointed by Carolus himself. Such men were responsible for administering the royal estates. In the name of the king, they judged law cases and supervised the running of the several manors that comprised each estate. This important nobleman had taken Bathilde as his concubine, only to grant her her freedom, and then marry her when his own lawful wife died.

It had been an astonishing triumph for one who had started as a slave. There were those who whispered that it had not been Bathilde's beauty alone that had won her the position of noblewoman, that she had taken more than a hand in the death of Erchinoald's first wife. However, such rumors could never be proven, and as the years passed few dared speak of them aloud.

Now there were strands of gray in Bathilde's thick dark tresses and lines in her fine-featured face. She was older than was considered wise for the rigors of childbirth. Yet that had not excused her from a wife's duty. The living children she had borne her husband during their marriage were all female: two boys had died before the age of two. It had been her husband's hope that this babe would be the son and heir he needed to hold his lands and carry on his name.

Bathilde raised a hand. Heavy jeweled rings encircled her fingers, though unlike other women of her class, her hands were veined and callused from years of hard work. All women—noble or not—worked, but Bathilde had always taken intense interest in every facet of the running of the manor. She had never been one to disdain the tasks commonly vouchsafed to lower-born women, and she had not forgotten her days as a slave before she caught the eye of her lord, when she had cut and toted floor rushes, carried wood, tended fires, washed, and cooked.

"Leave us," the noblewoman said. She gestured at the women gathered around the bed. "I would be alone with the wisewoman."

The servingwoman who had announced Sirona's presence cast a worried look at her companions. "Lady"—she included Sirona in her concerned glance—"is this well-done of you? The wisewoman will require assistance—"

"She will have it," Bathilde said irritably. "But for the moment, I bid you leave. The babe will not come quickly, and we all know it. There is time for me to have a little privacy."

The women could not gainsay her; she was the mistress, after all. Silently they flurried from the hall, heading, no doubt, into the questions of the waiting men. Sirona went to the bed. Her practiced gaze told her much. Her hands told her even more as she set about examining Bathilde.

"I will prepare teas and a poultice," she told the woman after a few minutes of feeling and kneading. "But I fear the baby may not be positioned well. I will have to do a great deal to move it."

The dark eyes watched her calmly. "Well, that is why you are here, is it not? I would have no less than the most skilled of wisewomen to attend me."

Lady Bathilde had recently become a widow. Her husband had died beneath the tusks and hooves of a wounded boar: an all-too-common occurrence in the sport of hunting that was a nobleman's most popular pastime. Erchinoald's death had left his wife with both child and power. Widows occupied a unique position; they enjoyed a recognition denied to their married sisters, even to the point of being allowed to act with the independence of men—at least until any sons they had borne had attained the age of majority.

Still, it was a sad business, bringing a babe into the very world its father had so precipitously left. Sirona thought of this as she tested the kettle of water that had been placed to boil near the hearth. Fortunately, this child would be born into a world of wealth and privilege. Sirona remembered too many other births: births held in small dark huts, where the mother wailed, not only with the pain of labor but with terror at how she would feed her growing brood with a husband dead from illness or some other ill-fated accident.

"You are not married." Bathilde's voice broke in on the wisewoman's reverie. The noblewoman was studying her. In spite of her travail, the black eyes were sharp and thoughtful.

Sirona opened the pack she had brought with her. Carefully, she measured out a number of herbs, spread open a clean piece of linen, and busied herself with making the poultice. "No, lady," she said after a moment. "I am not."

It was a question often asked, and one she had grown used to answering. Women were supposed to marry, to place themselves under the *munt*, the protection, of a man. The importance of such bonds went back much farther than the advent of Christianity, but where a priestess of the old days could remain independent, or not, as she chose, the only women exempted from male attachment these days were either nuns or prostitutes. As for wisewomen: there were folk who viewed even married ones with suspicion; those who remained single were even more suspect.

Bathilde sighed, her hands smoothing over the grotesquely swollen mound of her belly. "Once I would have said that such a state went against God's plan. I would have asked how your father could have erred so in not finding you a suitable husband. Ah, but now"—her heavily ringed fingers tightened over the mound of her pregnancy— "now I wonder if your path is not the better way for a woman to follow."

Sirona smiled. "I have attended many women," she said in the gentle patient voice she cultivated for such occasions. "Noble or common born, there is a time in the bringing of every child when the mother speaks as you do, lady. Indeed, I have heard women curse their husbands and all men besides, into the depths of the Christian hell, when the worst pains are upon them."

Finished with the poultice, she moved toward the bed box. Still smiling with professional reassurance, she pulled back the covers and reached to move her patient's hands aside, so she could apply the soothing dressing.

Bathilde stopped her.

"Heed me." The noblewoman's voice was harsh. "I do not speak out of the haze of childbirth. I am no young doe about to drop her first fawn. What I am is a new widow about to deliver a child into a world without a powerful father to protect it, assuming I survive the birthing, that is."

Bathilde gasped as pain seized her. Her hands left her

belly, clutching at the knotted sheets at each side of the bed. Sirona's firm hands helped her through the contraction.

"You will not die," the midwife said, and her voice was as firm as her hands. "That is why I am here, to see that you do not."

"Is it?" The keen look returned to Bathilde's eyes as the pain released her momentarily from its grip. "There are those who desire my death, and that of this child. And they would pay handsomely to see it done."

The woman's tone caught at Sirona. Shocked, she faltered in her work of kneading Bathilde's belly. Steadily, the noblewoman returned her gaze. Her black eyes were suddenly bottomless.

2

THE TWO WOMEN STARED AT EACH other.

"Once I followed the old ways," Bathilde said softly. "But when Erchinoald offered to free me and make me his wife he said that first I must become a Christian. He told me that Carolus requires from all his lords that the women they take to wife be baptized. Who was I to gainsay him? I was being asked to choose between freedom and noble position, or continued slavery."

Her wide mouth twisted in a wry and bitter smile. "It was a simple choice. I became a Christian. I renounced the ancient gods. I stood naked in the baptistery of the church while the priest poured water over my head. I took the Christian name he gave me. But in my heart, I never truly abandoned the old gods, and in return, the gods did not leave me. Neither did the gifts of power they had given me."

She paused, watching Sirona's suddenly still face. "You, Wisewoman, have powers, as well. I see them. And I see what happened to you on your way here to attend me this night."

"You must rest, lady." Sirona determined to regain control of the situation, not so much for herself, but for the sake of the mother and child. "You must concentrate your strength on bringing this babe. Talk can be saved for later."

"No." The weakness of exhaustion was beginning to fight with the strength in the other woman's voice. "I must know if I can trust you, if I can entrust the life of my child to your care. Tell me what I saw was true."

Sirona met her gaze. "It was. A man was waiting for me

15

on the track. By his speech I knew him as noble, though it was too dark and rainy to tell more."

"He wanted you to kill me." Bathilde's eyes stabbed at her. "Answer me, Wisewoman. He offered you gold, did he not? A great deal of it." She chuckled hoarsely. "He would have to. I am the widow of an important man." She chuckled again. "So much for the law protecting widows from the importunate acts of men during the thirty days of mourning."

"I refused him," Sirona said harshly. "He could have offered me *solidi* enough to drown all of Saxony beneath its weight, and still I would have refused. I am a healer, not a hired assassin. My task is to save lives. I do not take them."

The black eyes softened and grew tired, regaining the blurred inward focus of a woman in labor. "So you are," Bathilde murmured. "A healer, indeed."

"And since I am," Sirona went on, "you must heed me when I say it is time to return to the business at hand. A baby is coming. That and only that is what matters now."

The noblewoman's nod of assent twisted into a grimace and then a cry of agony as another pain clutched her. Hard upon that one followed another. Throughout the contractions Sirona was busy, her strong hands kneading and probing, her voice soothing and urging at once. When the pain had faded she felt Bathilde's swollen abdomen, pressing her ear against the tight skin to listen to the baby's heartbeat. She frowned.

The ease of childbirth was dependent upon three factors: the condition of the mother, the size of her pelvis relative to the baby's head, and the position of the baby in the womb. In the case of this patient, all three factors had their problems. Strong though she was, Bathilde was not a young woman, and she had just suffered the loss of her husband. Even worse: Sirona's examination had shown her that this was an unusually large baby that had got itself in a most unfortunate position to be born. Just as she had warned the noblewoman, this delivery would not be easy.

With the contraction easing its grip on her once more, Bathilde looked up at Sirona. The dark eyes were knowing.

"You are worried, Wisewoman. Your face ill conceals it. I expected you to be better schooled when it comes to revealing such things."

Sirona smiled. "With some women honesty is the better course. You, lady, I judge as one of those." Her smile faded. "Your ordeal will be great; I'll not hide that from you. But there are teas to strengthen the contractions when the time comes, ointments to soothe and soften you, and, if the pain grows too harsh, drinks to put you into a twilight sleep."

"Sleep." Bathilde's grimaced. "The priests say that it is a sin to ease the pain of a woman's labor. They say that God wants us to suffer, as punishment for Eve driving Adam from the Garden of Eden."

Sirona straightened up from the bed. "That is nonsense," she said briskly. "And you, who told me you never truly abandoned the old ways, should know it. This is not men's business, priests or otherwise. In any case, no priests are here to see what you either have or do not have."

The labor pains began again, and they went on and on. Sirona went to the entryway and called out for the serving-women to come back in. Hovering just out of earshot, they saw her figure limned in the entrance and ran to help. They bustled around the bed box, hurrying to obey the wisewoman's orders. They brought more water and heated it over the fire so herbs of wallflower, lady's mantle, and ergot could be brewed. They watched as Sirona applied ointments to soften the pregnant woman's cervix. Their faces were grave. There was not one among them who did not know the fierce tearing pains of giving birth; indeed, they had assisted at many deliveries.

But a normal birth was one thing; prolonged labor due to an awkwardly positioned baby was another entirely. In such a case, the woman's age-old task of waiting for the pains to bear fruit would not work. Inaction meant death for the woman and probably for the infant as well. Intervention was required—intervention from a wisewoman who possessed knowledge and skills beyond those of an ordinary midwife.

Sirona straightened from her latest examination. "The

child is lying straight across the womb," she said to the women. "Your lady will not be able to push it into the birth passage by her contractions alone. Continuing to try will eventually kill them both."

"You can save them?" asked one of the women. She crossed herself as she spoke and her companions followed suit.

Sirona watched the gesture impassively. "I hope so. I will have to manipulate the child—with luck I'll be able to do so from the outside. If I have to put my hands within her, it will increase the risk of her suffering a corruption inside her womb."

Under the eyes of the watching attendants, she set once more to her task. This time her hands had another purpose beyond ascertaining the child's position. It was hard work, and painful for the mother. But Bathilde endured, knowing it was her babe's only chance. Suffering contraction after fruitless contraction, she gasped and screamed through each one, followed by ceaseless careful manipulations by the strong fingers of the wisewoman.

At length, Sirona moistened a square of linen cloth and gently washed the face of the mother-to-be. "Have courage, lady," she murmured. "I think I have positioned the babe so that all your efforts will soon bear fruit. You have been strong. Now stay strong for just a little while longer."

Bathilde made a choked, exhausted sound that could have been a snort. She was gaunt and worn; her hair hung in wet strands, and her face was so gray she might have passed for a corpse. "I have never lacked in either strength or courage, Wisewoman." Her voice was the merest whisper; yet determination hardened it like an iron blade. "Such qualities are not the sole province of men."

Sirona smiled. "Indeed not. And who would know it better than I? No king or warrior ever been born could give birth with the courage of the most humble peasant woman."

"Or slave." Bathilde's sunken eyes turned distant. A brief silence hung between the two women as the logs popped and hissed in the hearth. "He took me as his concubine," Bathilde said suddenly. "But then you know that." Her haggard face took on a wry expression as she glanced at her listening women. "Everyone knows that."

Sirona watched her. An image wafted across her inner eye: Bathilde as a young girl, a slave, rippling with beauty and desire and ambition. In truth, it was a potent combination, one that would have been difficult for any man to resist. Erchinoald would have been no exception.

"Aiiee!" The cry of a servingwoman shattered the image of a young Bathilde into shards and fragments. "May the Savior protect us, look!"

All eyes, even Bathilde's, swiveled in the direction of the servant's trembling finger. Silhouetted in the hall entrance was a cat. Large and black, he sat motionless, staring fixedly at Bathilde and Sirona. The firelight from the hearth seemed to leap out at him so that the white patch on his chest glowed, and his eyes blazed as bright and orange as two suns.

The sight of him sent a flurry of hands into making the sign of the cross. "A demon," choked another woman. "The devil has sent him to curse the babe in its mother's womb."

"No, no," Sirona broke in. Hysteria had appeared in the air as suddenly as the cat, and she strove to keep it at bay. "Heed me." She forced professional calm into her voice. "A black cat is a sign of good luck." Her soothing tone belied the impatience burgeoning within her. She was stating the obvious, and here at this difficult labor the last thing she needed was a flock of panic-stricken attendants.

Everyone knew that black cats were lucky, as lucky as white cats were not. To see a white cat was to be visited by a harbinger of ill fortune. At least, that was how it had always been. But in recent years Sirona had begun to notice a change in people's attitude. The Christian priests spoke with increasing strength against cats of any color. They claimed the creatures were evil, possessed of dark and unholy powers given to them by the dispossessed old gods. Slowly, folk were beginning to believe what the priests said. The fear and revulsion in the faces of these women confirmed it.

"Black or white, it makes no difference," the first woman

quavered. "Such a beast will suck the breath of life from the babe and its mother. I knew it was ill done not to have a priest here. Only a priest can protect us. Only a priest—"

"Priests," Sirona said coldly, "are men. And men have no place at a birth. You know that."

The cat flicked a long black tail and stood up. The movement sent a new wave of fear through the women. But in the midst of their cries and gestures Sirona flung herself back to Bathilde, who was in the grip of another contraction. "Help me," she shouted over her shoulder. "Would you have your lady die while you dither over a cat?"

Guiltily the women sprang to the noblewoman's bed. Bathilde's shrieks overrode even the intensity of their superstitious dread. It seemed to take forever before the pangs eased off. Gray-faced and ashen, Bathilde lapsed into stillness, so motionless in the rumpled, dirtied bedcoverings it seemed to the worried attendants that death had finally taken her. Nervously, one of the women crossed herself and glanced over her shoulder.

"Praise be to the Holy One," she gasped. "The demon is gone."

Sirona looked up. It was true; the cat had vanished as suddenly as he had appeared. As the servingwomen murmured about what this could mean she turned back to her patient. Bathilde's eyes had opened. Dark-shadowed and hollow, luminous and burning with agony, they looked up at the midwife.

"What"—the noblewoman's voice was querulous and faint—"what demon is she speaking of?"

Eagerly the attendant leaned forward to answer her. "Lady, the devil sent one of his minions here to menace you and your child. But our mighty Lord in all his power caused the creature to flee. You are safe now."

"There was a cat," Sirona said bluntly, and directed a glare at the attendant, warning her to be silent. "It was here for a moment, and now it is gone. You need not be concerned."

Bathilde's eyes continued to question her. " "Of course not," she whispered. "If it was a black cat. Was it?" At

Sirona's nod, she sighed and closed her eyes. "Good. Then it came to bring me luck."

"No, lady," another attendant began, but fell silent at another sharp look from Sirona.

Bathilde's harsh weak voice broke apart the silence. "All of you," she ordered her servingwomen. "Thanks to this good woman's aid, my time draws near. Leave me to her hands. She will summon you when the babe arrives."

The women cast concerned looks at Sirona, but she nodded reassuringly. "Go," she whispered. "I will help her to the birthing stool."

With the women gone again, Bathilde shifted in the bed. "He made a *Kebsverhaltnisse* with me," she said, referring to the word for the relationship between a nobleman and a slave. "But it was not enough. How could it be?" She bared her teeth in a grim smile. "Before I was taken into slavery I was as wellborn as Erchinoald. Never would I be content with being some man's *Friedelehe*, his bed partner, while his lawful wife ran his estates and shared in his power. No, Wisewoman, I had plans. I have always had plans."

"And those plans include your children." Sirona did not wait for Bathilde to answer. "As a concubine your children would be provided for, but they could never inherit their father's noble position."

"Precisely." Bathilde's dark exhausted eyes blazed black. "And for this child, in particular."

"Why this child?" Sirona's question was distracted. She knew the pains were gathering again. She could sense the heaviness of the next and most difficult stage of the labor hovering about the mother; she saw the hard fingers of a new contraction in the noblewoman's suddenly tightened features.

Bathilde cried out. Her voice was hoarse, strained ragged from earlier efforts. She hauled on the knotted sheets at either side of the bed with whitened fingers. Sirona comforted her until the contraction released its grip.

But Bathilde needed no comforting. She was bent upon her goal, and there would be no swaying her from it. "This babe will live," she said through clenched teeth. "And so

will I. With your help, he will enter this world and stay
within it, unlike my other sons before him."

There was power in her voice. Sirona felt it as strongly as
Bathilde felt her birth pains. "You have seen this," she said,
and it was a statement, rather than a question.

"I have." Bathilde's eyes burned blacker than ever, and
deep, as deep as the sea on a moonless night. "And I will
tell you what else I have seen. My son will sit upon the
throne of Saxony. And I—I will be queen."

Sirona looked at her. Off in the distance, she thought she
heard the distinctive sound of a cat's miaow.

It has begun.

The words were somewhat garbled, for the black cat was
purring as he spoke. But the one whom the cat had addressed understood him perfectly.

At last, the Goddess said. Her voice was deep and musical, chiming with melodies older than time. *I knew she
would be the one I had waited for.*

The cat considered. *Perhaps,* he replied. *And perhaps
not. Remember, Mistress, she does not worship You; not like
those who came before her.* This time, his words were as
clean and sharp as his claws.

The Goddess looked at him out of depthless green eyes.
*She is still My daughter, Mau. And in her devotion to the
healing arts, she worships Me. I am the source of her gifts.
She has placed her feet upon the path that will bring her to
a full knowledge of Me. Thus will I return to the world of
mortals.*

The cat twitched his whiskers, his way of indicating that
he was still not convinced. *Well, in any case, the baby is
coming. The Goddessless ones sent a man to pay her for
seeing to it that the babe would not be born, but she refused*—he let out a faint purr—*and quite eloquently, too, I
must admit.*

Of course. Satisfaction thrummed in the melodious
voice. *As I told you, Mau. She is the one. Went you to the
hall?*

I did. Once more Mau stopped purring; his whiskers

went straight and stiff. *The place was filled with foolish Goddessless women who shrieked at me and made the sign of their god to drive me away. Your daughter did not, of course, and neither did the babe's mother, although as one might expect, she had too much else occupying her to pay attention to me, or much of anything else.* He licked a spot on his chest. *Humans make birthing into such a complicated business,* he added reflectively. *In any case, I made certain that Your daughter had seen me. Then I left.*

Well done, the Goddess said. Her enormous feline features shone with approval. *I can feel new life stirring within Me already. Now I have another task for you, my faithful one. Go to the shrine of Freyja, to Irminsul, where Her World Tree upholds the world. She will be waiting for you. Tell Her what is happening in the hall of the mortal noble-woman.*

Does She not already know? asked the cat in surprise. *The woman bearing the child is one of Her daughters, after all.*

The Goddess shook Her great head. *Freyja's powers are incomplete. They are not as torn and scattered as Mine are, for there are still those who speak Her name, but She does not have the strength and knowledge that She once did. You, Mau, must be the go-between for Us until We are both stronger.*

What would You have me tell Her about the baby? The cat stood up in preparation to depart. His long dark tail flicked softly against his flanks.

Tell Her, the Goddess said, *that the baby will be born, that his mother seeks Her, and that My daughter is coming back. Tell Her that the ancient powers are stirring at last, and not again will they go to sleep.*

The cat swung around and loped toward the silver doors of the sanctuary. They swung wide at his approach. He darted through and set off down the hall. Long had these wide corridors been silent, but now, for the first time in these endless days of being forgotten, the cat's sensitive ears picked up the tingling notes of music. Far off they were, barely audible even to his keen hearing, but after so long a period of silence the tiny weak notes rang deafening as cymbals.

Outside, a subtle change had taken place in the pink stones of the temple. A faint glimmer had begun to suffuse their dullness. The cat glanced at them as he went past, and his orange eyes glowed.

"The babe lives."

Count Haganon stiffened at the words. He was a man whose bulk loomed over others. He fancied himself a handsome man, despite the fact that his round features had grown florid from a diet rich in meat and wine, and his pale reddish blond hair was thinning over his broad skull. Resolutely, Haganon chose to ignore these changes. Instead he took pride in his tall, massive body, striving always to hold himself as though his thinning hair and bulging belly did not exist.

Anger made him seem even larger on this morning, a fact the noble was fully aware of. He paced back and forth in front of a crackling, newly laid fire that sent smoke wafting up into the rafters. Haganon moved as restlessly as the smoke. The fury that possessed him made him appear enormous. The night storm had passed on, leaving in its wake a daybreak agleam with pale gray light. But in the hall of Haganon the storm still raged. Its darkness was evident on the count's face as he wheeled to confront the man who had just spoken.

"And it is a boy?" Haganon's voice was deep and harsh. His pale brown eyes seemed to crackle like the logs.

The man who had brought the morning's tidings was the same noble who had sought to purchase Sirona's aid. He had difficulty meeting Haganon's gaze as he gave his answer: a silent nod of assent.

Five other nobles were gathered around the fire listening to this conversation. At the man's nod, glances varying from anger to shock and dismay flew between them. "This was not supposed to have happened," one of the men said.

"Indeed not." Haganon's voice was growing louder. He thrust a meaty fist toward the hapless noble. "*You* were to have prevented it, Ebbo. Why else did we send you to way-lay the wisewoman and buy her services?"

"I tried." The noble Ebbo was becoming angry himself. "All of you can stand here and accuse me, but none of you were there. If you had been, you'd have gotten no further than I did. The woman is evil. *Maleficia* fills her like sour wine in an old jug, and it is as old and powerful as the an-cient demons themselves."

His eyes stabbed at the other men. "Every man here knows me. I have stood against wounded boars; my spear arm has slain charging bears. I have fought in battle and bloodied my sword as any warrior. But I say this"—he shuddered as he recalled the woman's dark eyes burning at him with that eerie light—"there are some things better left untampered with. And that creature is one of them."

Haganon let out an oath. "Of course, she is!" he roared. "That is why I chose her." He strode close to the fire and glared into the flames. "Bathilde, that slave whore who made herself a noble, is too strong for some mere herb woman to dispose of. The task required another woman with *maleficia* equal to hers."

He swung around, fixing first Ebbo and then the other nobles with his light brown gaze. "Very well. She refused and Ebbo failed. Now she must die."

There was a long silence.

"Haganon," a white-haired noble said at last. "That may not be wise. Ebbo has said the woman is *maleficia* and I be-lieve him. Such things are better off not meddled with. I have lived a long time and seen a great deal, and if there is one thing I've learned, it's that women like that are better left alone."

"Are you saying that she cannot be killed, Aelisachar?" Haganon spit out the question, daring the older man to re-ply.

Steadily, Aelisachar returned his gaze. "I am not," he said, and crossed himself. "All men and women can be killed. But how easily may such a thing be accomplished, and at what cost?"

Haganon pondered this. "The risk may be great, indeed,"

he conceded in a grudging tone. "Yet the risk of leaving her alive is greater. She talked with Ebbo. She knows that there are those who wanted the woman and child killed. It does not require the learning of a scholar to grasp that unless she is in our control, she possesses too much knowledge to live."

Speaking the words aloud was enough for the burly nobleman to make up his mind. "Yes," he told himself, as well as the others. "It shall be done." He paused, waiting for his companions to voice their approval. It did not come. Ebbo and Aelisachar exchanged glances. The other nobles were silent. *A bunch of weak-livered women,* Haganon thought disgustedly.

"I see." Anger coursed through him, turning his light brown eyes as pale and icy as trees in winter. "Since all of you are afraid, I will have to arrange the woman's death myself."

"Haganon is correct."

A new voice spoke from the far end of the smoky hall. The men turned to face the speaker, and he smiled at them. He was a lean man, dressed in the garb of an abbot. Content to listen, he had been standing by a trestle table sipping from a goblet of morning ale, but now he stepped forward out of the shadows.

"God Himself will look with favor on the deed," he continued. "The woman is not a Christian, and she is indeed *maleficia.*"

Seeing the dubious expressions on the faces of Ebbo and Aelisachar, he nodded sympathetically. "Oh yes, I understand the danger, and even more do I understand the sadness of taking a life. But know you this: the true faith can never succeed in this heathen land while the priests and priestesses of the pagan religion still live. They must be rooted out the way a farmer tears out weeds before they choke the growth of his young sweet crops. God is the farmer, and we are His fields. In his zeal, Haganon is acting in God's stead. He will be rewarded for sending this woman from the world of decent men."

Haganon jerked his balding head in grim satisfaction.

"Thank you, Abbot. As always, you speak with the wisdom of our holy cause. In sending you to aid us, the Lord blessed us, indeed. And you, my friends," he added, favoring each man with one of his cool glares, "will soon see that the power here does not belong to that witch, but to me."

"No," the abbot broke in sharply. "The power is God's. All power, here and everywhere else in the world and in Heaven, belongs to the Lord."

He crossed himself, and, piously, the nobles followed suit. Only Haganon hesitated. It was only the merest pause, so slight that not even the abbot marked it. But as his hand made the symbol of Christian faith, the look in Haganon's blazing eyes belied the gesture.

The power is mine, he silently told himself. *Mine.*

3

IN THE END, A SON HAD INDEED BEEN born to the Lady Bathilde. He was strong and lusty, as none of her other boys before him had been. He emerged into the world, squashed and rumpled from his difficult journey through the birth canal, and filled with anger at having been disturbed. His furious squalls resounded through the hall, and the women beamed at the sound.

But none of them beamed more than the mother herself. Bathilde held her son close against her breast, smiling with a fierce exultant joy. She was utterly exhausted, barely able to lift her head while her women cleaned her, but none of that mattered. She had borne a living son. Ambition glittered in her heavy-lidded dark eyes. This particular battle she had won.

According to ancient custom, the baby was washed with salt, his tiny mouth cleansed with honey, and then swaddled, each tiny limb carefully bound, then wrapped with cloth. The binding would protect the child from deformity and illness, preserving the straightness of the limbs and the proper placement of each organ. Or so it was believed.

Sirona watched the process and sighed. She had given up seeking to persuade against the custom. Her own ancestors had not swaddled their infants, allowing nature alone to determine the baby's shape, and their children had grown up straight and strong. But the nobility, in particular, insisted on swaddling; Bathilde, especially, would have no less for her precious son.

A wet nurse took over the feeding of the infant, though Sirona stayed on over the next several weeks, mostly to attend to the new mother. Ailments such as childbed fever were a risk after any birth, and even more common after an ordeal as difficult as what Bathilde had endured. At dusk, toward the end of the third week, as the bells for vespers tolled in the distance from the village church, Sirona went to the bed of her patient.

Propped up with freshly cleaned bolsters and cushions, her unbound hair streaming over her shoulders, Bathilde smiled at her. In the space of these weeks she had already regained a good deal of her strength. The gaunt bones of her face were becoming blurred with a healthy glow of flesh, and her dark eyes were bright with life and purpose. Her milk-swollen breasts pressed against the linen of her bed-shift; soon they would have to be bound to stop the milk. Highborn women did not nurse their own children.

"Well met, Wisewoman," the noblewoman said warmly. "Have you come to tell me how my son thrives?"

"He thrives, indeed," Sirona answered, with a smile of her own. "And so does his mother. In truth, you are both so healthy that there is no reason for me to stay any longer."

Bathilde's smile stiffened into a frown. "I would that you remain here," she said gravely.

Sirona chuckled. "Many women wish that; having borne before, you should know it. It comforts a mother to have the wisewoman near. But my task is done, lady. Your babe is in the world and you are fast regaining your strength. It is time for me to return home."

The noblewoman's expression did not change. "I am not some fearful peasant woman with her first child. You are in danger, Wisewoman. I told you that before. But now the danger has grown greater. You refused to help those who wished to prevent this birth. Because of your skills my son came into the world, and instead of death, both he and I flourish. How much greater do you think the anger of those men will be toward you because of what you have done?"

"I do not think," Sirona said gently, "that I am as important to them as you think I am."

"Indeed? You are wrong, my girl. And that is why I would have you join with me."

"Join with you, lady?" A tingle went through Sirona. Apprehension rippled along her nerve endings, whispering and warning of what the noblewoman would say next.

Bathilde pushed forward from the pillows. Her dark eyes, still hollow from the ordeal of childbirth, blazed with intensity. "Heed me, I do not speak of this lightly. I have found my path back to the old gods, but you, Wisewoman, you have never left it. Your way has ever remained clear. You have remained faithful to your Goddess, and She has rewarded you."

"There are those," Sirona said dryly, "who would not view it so. These days the church decrees the meaning of faith, and according to the priests, there is no room in those decrees for the Ancient Mothers."

"The church." Bathilde made one hand into a fist. "I have done with listening to the church and the men within it. This religion of Carolus the Great and his priests speaks to men, not women. Oh, women have their place, 'tis true, but it is not a place of power."

"And yet," Sirona pointed out mildly, "that has ever been the way of the tribes in Saxony, far beyond the time when Christ became known."

The noblewoman stared at her. "Not always. There was a time when women had power, great power, given to them by the Mother Herself." The dark eyes were piercing. "You know this. With me, you need not pretend otherwise."

When Sirona said nothing, she went on with greater force. "I need a woman with your gifts. The Saxons have departed from the ancient ways, and until they return we will never be free of foreign kings and their rule. In our sacred enclosures we were strong, but Christianity has taken away that strength. The time has come to regain it."

Her voice grew louder. "I have had dreams and visions, Wisewoman. They speak to me of days past and of days to come. Let Carolus rule over Gaul. Saxony belongs to us and to the old gods and goddesses. We must take it back again. It is a holy task, one that I, and the son I bore with your help, will take on."

Her black eyes burned past Sirona, gazing at some sight

only she could see. "The nobles I have spoken of will continue to oppose us," she muttered. "They see their future as lying with Carolus and his church. I am a threat to them, because of my power, and of what I can set loose in Saxony."

Sirona sighed. She had heard such talk before. Any person living in these lands was familiar with the refrain of rebellion. The Saxon tribes were a warlike folk; they always had been. But so, too, were the Franks, and under their king, Carolus the Great, the power of the Carolingian dynasty had reached its apex.

Carolus had long coveted the lands of Saxony, but for reasons that went far beyond the mere acquisition of territory. The Frankish king was a devout Christian and an even more devout missionary. He was determined to convert the whole of Saxony to the true faith, regardless of how much force the undertaking of it required. And force was required, indeed, for the Saxons were as stubborn as they were warlike, and they were loath to be swayed from their own ancient religion.

Great had been the bloodshed and greater still the resistance. Carolus had succeeded in spreading churches and priests across Saxony, but he had not succeeded in quelling the hearts of its people. Periodic rebellions cropped up whenever Frankish vigilance eased. Sirona recognized the zeal she saw burning in Bathilde's eyes; she had seen it in the eyes of others. But she also remembered the conversation she had held with Bathilde during the long travail of birth. Bathilde's dreams and visions were speaking to her of more than a return to the ancient ways. More was driving this slave-turned-noblewoman than a desire to see the revival of the old religion.

"You talk of the old ways," she said. "But in truth, lady, what you are really speaking of is politics, and power. I have no interest in involving myself in either. Such matters are not within my province. I deal in healing. That is the source of my power, and always has it been. I bear no love toward the church; how can I, being what I am? No one would be pleased than I to see the ancient Shining Ones honored openly once more. But I cannot help you. You are bent upon a bloody undertaking, lady. It will lead to killing, to death upon deaths, and as a healer, I cannot be a part of it. I am sorry, lady. I have no help to give."

"You are wrong," Bathilde snapped. "Your help is essential."

"How?" The soles of Sirona's feet twitched. The rushes scattered across the floor seemed to be moving, as though the earth itself were shifting in anticipation of what Bathilde's answer would be.

"Speak to your Goddess. Petition Her for Her help. She will not refuse you. I need Her. Driving the Franks from our land will not be easy. It can only be done with a tool that the Christians despise. We both know what that tool is. Magic."

"I cannot." Sirona stepped back from the bed. "I have no more love for the Franks than for the priests and their churches. But you misjudge me, lady. Magic is not my tool. I do not possess the powers you think I do."

Bathilde leaned back against the pillows. "Oh, you possess them, Wisewoman. Refuse to see it, if that be your will, but I know better." She closed her eyes a moment, then opened them wide, staring at Sirona. "Seek your Goddess, child. Accept the gifts of magic She has given you."

Footsteps whispered across the floor rushes. Both women looked up and fell silent. The wet nurse had entered the hall. In her arms she was carrying the swaddled bundle that was Bathilde's son. She was a large woman with a kind face and ample breasts, against which the baby nestled contentedly. Her smile was as wide and warm as the rest of her as she approached the bed box.

"Your son thrives, lady," she said happily. "He nurses with the lustiness of a child twice his days. Now that he has fed, the little mite sleeps. It is my joy to bring him to you."

Bathilde's face softened. Stretching out her arms, she waited impatiently for the infant to be laid within them. "Ah," she crooned. "How fares my son this day?" The baby's tiny features twisted into a yawn. His eyes, milky blue as the eyes of all newborns were, formed sleepy slits, then dropped shut. His mother held him close. "Growing strong, are you? That is well, very well."

Sirona was grateful for the interruption. Although the conversation between her and Bathilde would obviously not be continued in the presence of the nurse, the weight of the words that had been spoken still pressed upon her. Bathilde's zeal and ambition coiled about the great hall, as relentless as the noblewoman herself. It was a heavy burden, and now she had laid that burden upon Sirona.

But she did not want it, Sirona told herself angrily. This was not her business. Her business was done. It was time to go home. Under the wet nurse's beaming gaze she spoke to Bathilde. "I will prepare to take my leave of you, lady. You are recovering well, and"—she smiled at the nurse—"with the care of this fine woman your babe will continue to flourish. There is no need for me to stay longer."

Bathilde's distinctive features grew cool and expressionless. "Very well," she said, drawing the mantle of her position about her. "I will arrange for your payment." She paused, and her dark eyes warmed. "It will be generous. You deserve no less for the great service you have done me."

"I have only done as my calling bids me." Sirona spoke firmly. There was meaning beyond meaning in her words. The good-natured nurse standing beside the bed nodded and smiled, having no idea of anything other than the words she had heard.

But Bathilde understood. "Depart on the morrow, then," she said, and added for the benefit of the nurse, "and may the blessings of the Holy Ones go with you."

Taking her mistress's words as those of a good Christian, the nurse crossed herself happily. Sirona inclined her head, turned, and walked out of the hall.

Bathilde watched her, then made a brusque gesture at the nurse. "Leave us. I would hold my son for a time. Return when the sun is low."

Alone in the hall, Bathilde pressed the infant possessively close. The baby let out a squeak of protest, but went on sleeping. "You'll be back," the noblewoman said softly, as though she could still hear the wisewoman's footsteps. "When the nobles try to kill you, then will your heart be changed toward this holy undertaking."

Sirona left the manor as the gray light of a new day spread over the manor house. The weather had cleared over the time of her stay. Every morning had dawned clear and cold, with crisp biting winds and skies tinted pale blue with frost.

But on this morning the clouds had returned. Leaden and heavy, they pressed down over the trees. Off to the west, in the far distance, there was a faint line of black tinged with red. The air was sweet with the odor of baking bread from the kitchen buildings, and yet the fragrant air also carried the smoky damp smell of a coming storm.

Sirona sighed. Thus had it smelled on the night she had set out to attend Bathilde. It would surely be raining by the time she reached home, almost as if the gods had decreed that she must arrive here in dark and rain, and leave in the same way.

The narrow track stretched ahead to the village. It was pocked with ruts, but the clear cold weather had hardened the mud and made easier going. Her braids bouncing on her shoulders, Sirona strode briskly in an effort to push away her fatigue. She had rested poorly the night before. During her stay in the manor she had slept in the great hall along with Bathilde, her attendants, and the personal house servants, on a pallet that had been made up especially for her in a favored spot by the fire. But last night sleep had doggedly refused to come. She had tossed and turned on her pallet, keenly aware of the mistress of the house lying nearby in her ornate raised bed.

Now that the women's business of birth was over with, the men had returned to their accustomed places and the hall was crowded with prone bodies. Smoke from old fires hung heavy in the air. Around Sirona the familiar sounds of the sleeping manor had resounded: snores, groans, the rustling of dried rushes, whimpers from a dreaming hound, the feeble crackle of the banked hearth-fire. The baby wakened several times, uttering fretful cries of hunger, and the nurse hushed him drowsily and quieted him with her breast.

Though her son lay with his nurse, Bathilde had wakened each time the babe did, though indeed, she was not truly sleeping. Sirona sensed it. She could feel the noblewoman's awareness emanating from the carved bed box, and Sirona's own awareness put that consciousness into words. The conversation between them was not finished. Bathilde lay there silently reminding her of it.

It had been a long night. Sirona had welcomed the dawn.

The payment given her was as rich as Bathilde had promised. Too rich, Sirona protested, when she felt the heaviness of silver denaris crammed into the leather sack the seneschal handed her.

The plump man had shaken his head, stepping back when Sirona tried to give it back to him. "It is my mistress's wish," he explained. The reserve of his office suddenly parted to reveal a rather embarrassed smile. "In truth, you deserve it, Wisewoman. You brought life to this house instead of the death we all expected." He did not add what would have happened had Bathilde died. The manor and its holdings would have reverted to the Frankish king, and the future of the seneschal, as well as all the other servants, thrown into question. The heavyset man's gratitude was utterly genuine.

So Sirona had accepted the bulging sack. The coins swung from her girdle, clinking heavily with every step. Man or woman, it was not wise to travel these roads alone, even less wise when one was weighted down with silver. She wished now that she had asked for an escort. The seneschal had not offered one, and Sirona strongly suspected that his mistress had ordered it so. If there was danger waiting for her, Bathilde obviously wanted the wisewoman to experience it, to see that her warnings were correct.

Regardless, Sirona thought with a grim smile, of what the consequences might be.

Ahead of her the track began to curve and narrow. It was a spot Sirona was familiar with. There were many such places along this road, places where someone who meant her ill could hide and await her passing. But the alternative meant striking out across the fields, and then through the trackless forest. It was a plan that contained even more risks than continuing on her present course.

She strode on, her eyes searching the growth that lined both sides of the path. Willow thickets grew densely. She heaved a sigh of relief as she passed them. Interspersed among the thickets were places where tall stands of oak and hawthorn and beech stood. It was safer when passing those stands; there were openings enough between the trees so that one could see possible attackers.

A stand of hawthorn gave way to more thickets. Willows crowded both sides of the road, and the narrow trail thinned still more, seeming to lose its way in the shadows beyond. Sirona's muscles tensed. She halted. Her eyes probed the dark brush for signs that did not belong there: a human arm or leg, light glancing off a woolen tunic or a drawn blade. She saw nothing, yet the powers she only used for healing eddied up, speaking to her in ways they seldom did.

The warning was clear, yet what could she do? If danger awaited her, it would follow her even if she turned back the way she had come. She took a step forward, then another.

4

THEY CAME AT HER AS SHE ROUNDED a bend where the trees grew so thick their bare limbs overhung the faint track, practically obscuring it. Twin shadows that formed themselves into two men. They were armed with daggers already raised high as they leaped toward her. The blades glistened darkly, as if her blood already stained them.

Something pushed Sirona violently aside. Her foot struck a half-buried root, and she fell, awkwardly and hard. It saved her life. The daggers sliced through air, slashing at the place where she had stood. Instinctively, she rolled, bringing herself into the thick brush, then springing to her feet.

But the men followed. Their faces loomed at her, caught up and revealed in fragments of shadowy light. She had a jumbled impression of beards, gleaming eyes, and grim smiles. Their expressions laughed at her. She would not escape them. She knew it, and so did they.

You know no such thing.

The voice boomed through Sirona's being, each word bursting in her head like a crack of thunder. An awful force came searing out of her. Perhaps it was the confidence in the faces of her attackers, the realization that they meant to murder her that had set it loose. Whatever the reason, the presence of the Goddess swamped Sirona, washing her in strength. On some level she had always been aware of Her presence, but this was different. Here was a force that had lain banked within her. And for the first time it was surging to life, burgeoning up within and without, surrounding her like a great glowing shield.

The two men stopped in their tracks. Their hard faces,

frozen into the anticipation and excitement of killing, altered. Their eyes widening, they almost, though not quite, took a step back. Although Sirona could feel the power washing through her, she could not see it. These men could. The strength that bathed her was not of this world, and, too late, they finally saw that. One of them—the shorter of the two—was clearly aghast; he thrust out his free hand at her, the fingers formed into the sign against evil.

The attack and Sirona's response had taken no more than a few heartbeats. In the next heartbeat, before the men or the power enfolding their target could react, another figure darted through the gloom. It formed itself into a man. He let out a furious cry and hurled itself at the attackers. Pandemonium ensued. The dark place beneath the trees became a whirl of shouts and bodies and flashing weapons.

The newcomer was armed with a heavy oaken staff that he wielded with savage skill. His arrival shattered the links of the power that had surged up in Sirona. She staggered, suddenly bereft. But the sensation of loss was a luxury she could not afford; necessity dictated an instant recovery. She snatched up a fallen branch and laid it alongside the head of one of the men. He, too, staggered. Combined with the fury of the stranger it was enough to end matters. Both men broke off the attack and abruptly fled into the willow thicket.

Their bodies crashed and tore through the underbrush. The loud, careless sounds quickly faded, leaving a silence that was louder than the assault had been. Panting, Sirona and the stranger looked at each other.

"Are you harmed?" Leaning on his staff, the man gulped in breath after shaking breath. His eyes swept over her, searching for injuries. "Did either of those bandits cut you?" he demanded.

Sirona looked down at herself. "I—I believe not." With the danger over, all the sensations she could not react to before came sweeping over her: the voice of the Goddess, the terrible and yet welcome surge of power, the heart-pounding need to defend herself. "Thanks to you, stranger," she added belatedly.

The man dropped the staff and sank down, sitting back on his heels. "Well, the thanks should not be entirely mine," he said in a steadier tone. "The Holy One, blessed be His name, led me to this place." He regarded her thoughtfully out of blue eyes nested in wrinkles of humor. "Bandits and cutthroats haunt these ways. They are no place for an armed man, much less a woman. You must be an exemplary person to merit the protection of God Himself."

Sirona blinked at him. Clearly he was not aware of what had truly stopped the two men. Perhaps he had been too caught up in the need to protect her to see; or perhaps his god would not allow him to see.

Slowly, she pushed herself to her feet. Instantly the stranger jumped up to help her. His touch was light and respectful; he watched anxiously as Sirona felt herself over. A careful exploration revealed that no bones were broken, no limbs sprained. "I think your god would have little reason to protect me, good traveler," she said, chastising herself for the wisdom in saying this even as she spoke. "I am not a Christian."

To her surprise the man laughed. "Neither am I, good woman."

"But"—Sirona looked at him in bewilderment—"you speak of one god. If you are not a Christian, then what are you?"

"Why, lady," the man said with a wide gentle smile, "I am a Jew."

"A Jew?" Sirona gave her benefactor a long perusal. He looked no different than any other lone traveler she had seen crossing the rough tracks from village to village, and there were few enough of those, particularly in the season of cold and rain. "I have never seen a Jew."

The man's chuckle was as gentle as his smile. "You have seen one now. What think you of me?"

"I think," Sirona said slowly, "that you look like a good-hearted man who was willing to put himself at risk to help a stranger. And," she added, "since you are a stranger, you must be a merchant."

The man chuckled again. "Indeed. And that is what I am.

My nephews and I were on our way to the manor of Erchinoald with trade goods. A storm is brewing up in the west; the clouds are chasing after our mules, and they are as black as a demon's soul. I had hoped to sit out the weather by the manor's fire and conduct some business as well."

"Then you have not heard." Of course, he would not have known of the lord's death, Sirona told herself, not if he had recently come down the western roads. She brushed leaf mold off her tunic. "Erchinoald has died. He met his death in a hunting accident. His wife the Lady Bathilde now rules the manor in his stead."

"Be that so?" The merchant gave her an interested glance. "I am sorry to hear of it. Yet I would still seek shelter at the manor, if this lady welcomes us. What sort of woman is she?"

A woman who had predicted the attack I just suffered, Sirona thought grimly. Aloud, she said, "A strong woman with a will as great as that of any man. And she is brave, as all women are brave. She gave birth but three weeks ago to a healthy son." She paused. "It was a birthing as difficult as any I have attended."

The merchant's gaze increased in curiosity. "Are you one of her ladies?" he asked. Other questions swirled in his merry eyes: such as what she was doing out on this forest track alone if she was indeed one of Bathilde's attendants, and why those men had sought to kill her, rather than raping and robbing her first, as was the tragic though customary practice in such attacks.

Sirona shook her head. "I am a wisewoman. Bringing babies into the world is my business, as trading is yours. In births as hard as the Lady Bathilde's was, it's not uncommon for both mother and babe to die. That did not happen, and the reason it did not was due in large part to the lady's courage."

"I see." The merchant muttered some words softly under his breath in a tongue Sirona had never heard. "It is a blessing," he explained at her uncomprehending look. "A wish for my god to bring comfort and solace to this poor woman who has lost her husband and the father of her child." He looked past her, and his merry eyes were sad. "Life and death are forever twined together in this world. What the Holy One, blessed be He, would take away in one breath He gives back in the next."

Sirona stared at him. He spoke of a single God as the Christians did, but the words themselves sounded astonishingly like the teachings of the Mother. Unknowingly he had described the great circle of life, where death and rebirth blended seamlessly into one another.

"The Lady Bathilde will surely appreciate your wishes," she said. "And I am certain that she will give you shelter in her house." Even had he not helped her, Sirona knew he would be welcomed. In a land where news was scant and folk isolated, traders, with the gossip they carried, were always an eagerly sought-after diversion.

The merchant smiled. "Let us go, then. My nephews are waiting with the mules. This is only their second trading journey with me, and they will grow anxious if I do not return quickly. You must come along, lest more bandits like those men be waiting elsewhere along the road. This track is far too dangerous to travel alone. When the lady of the manor learns what has happened she will surely send a man-at-arms back with you so that you may arrive wherever you are bound in safety."

Bathilde would also remind her that this was precisely what she had warned of, Sirona thought. She said, "I will go back with you, good trader, if only to show you the way. It's the least I can do after the aid you have given me."

The merchant retrieved his staff. "I am called Isaac," he said as they started back to where he had left his mules. "What is your name?"

"My name is Sirona," she told him. "But few call me that hereabouts." He glanced at her curiously, and she went on. "They call me by what I am. The wisewoman."

"Ah." Isaac nodded, and they went on in silence to where the mules and the trader's nephews waited.

Above them the sky had grown darker.

"I told you we should not have used daggers!"

Panting, the man who spoke thrust out the words as furi-

ously as he had stabbed with his dagger. He was short and
squat, but powerfully built and deceptively quick on his
feet. He glared sideways at his companion as they jogged
along, making a wide circle to get back to the track. They
had forced their way through the willow thickets and were
now jogging in and out of birch tree groves. The trees' thin
peeling trunks glinted palely in the early-gloom, hollow and
white in the darkness of the approaching storm.

The second man glared back. He was far taller, strongly
built as well, although, despite the length of his legs, not
nearly so quick on his feet as his fellow assassin. "It would
have made no difference," he pointed out. "No matter what
sort of weapons we used."

"Hah!" The first man let out a resounding snort. "God's
bones, it would not. A well-placed arrow, and the creature
would be dead. She would have had no chance to use her
unholy powers. We would have accomplished what we set
out to, and been safe from her *maleficia*." He paused as he
remembered the eerie glow surrounding the woman in the
moment before the stranger crashed in upon them. He shuddered and once again made the sign against evil.

"So say you," the taller man said darkly. Muttering an
oath, he wound his long body awkwardly between the
closely growing birch trees. "But the woman's magic could
have prevented the arrow from finding its mark as easily as
it did the daggers. And at any rate, it was not *maleficia* but
that stranger who saved her, blundering up with that blasted
staff the way he did."

The short man was still holding his bared dagger. Glancing down, he growled a curse of his own, and sheathed it.
"After all the denaris Count Haganon promised us for the
deed, he will be most displeased to hear of this. And by the
Savior's holy cross, I do not want to be the one to tell him."

"You won't," the taller man said shortly. "Neither of us
will, because we are going to follow the woman and finish
the task we were hired for." He set his jaw. "I care not how
much magic the witch possesses. I plan on collecting my
share of that silver."

They passed through the last of the birch groves, plowed through more willow thickets and underbrush, and came at last onto the faint line of the track. The clouds had moved closer. Under their lowering stare the beaten earth of the muddy track seemed even more insignificant, barely a road.

At the edge of the trees the tall man stood for a moment to catch his breath. "They will have gone to seek shelter from the storm," he panted. "And what place is closer than that which she has just left? The manor, of course."

Frowning and not at all winded, the other assassin regarded him. "Be that wise? They will surely tell the Lady Bathilde of what happened, and she will see to it that the woman is closely guarded. We'll not get close to her."

"Perhaps. And perhaps not." The tall man's teeth glinted through his neatly trimmed beard; they were stained brown, and two were missing. "Christ's bones, man, you're as superstitious as a peasant. An opportunity will present itself, and if it doesn't, we'll make one. After all, opportunities are our business, are they not? Now stop whining and let's be on our way before the weather turns foul."

But the short man was not through. "To where?" he grumbled. "Think you that we can just ride up to the gates and be welcomed in, especially after she arrives with her tale of being attacked by two men on the road?"

A loud whinny rang through the heavy air, almost drowning out his last words. Two horses were tethered well off the track, hidden in the brush and a stand of young elm trees. They shifted restlessly, tugging at their reins as the men approached.

"It's a blessed miracle of the Virgin that the beasts were not stolen while we were rolling about slicing uselessly at the air with daggers," the man went on.

His tall companion cast him a jaundiced look. "You're the one who is useless, Waldo. You've not been yourself since we started on this mission."

Waldo sighed. "I know it. But something is not right about this. We're the ones in danger, not her. After what I just saw, I feel that in my bones."

"Your bones." The tall man laughed. "You've never let that stop you before, particularly not when there was this much silver involved."

Waldo glared at him. "This time," he said grimly, "we are hired to kill a woman. I mislike the entire thing, Lupus. It's a bad business, killing a woman. We've taken the lives of many, I'll not deny it, but never before a woman, especially one who has powers. It doesn't sit well with me. It hasn't from the first."

They reached the horses and began to untie the tightly knotted reins.

"She is not a woman," the tall man called Lupus grunted as he freed his gelding's reins from a hawthorn branch. "At least," he amended, "she is not a woman as others are. You saw that for yourself. She is evil." He crossed himself with his free hand. "The abbot said that to send her from the world of decent Christians into Purgatory is a holy act. God will reward us for doing it."

"Will He?" The short man let out a bark of laughter. "Lupus, your faith is silver like the moon. It waxes and wanes with the number of denaris you are offered. You care nothing about God's reward; it's Count Haganon's that interests you."

Lupus glanced over at him as he swung up into the saddle. Coming from another man, such words would have provoked a violent reaction, but these two knew each other too well. Indeed, the tall man let out his own rueful laugh.

"You have the truth of it, my friend," he agreed. "The money is what I want. And so, I thought, did you. Tell me: what has caused you to lose your belly for this job? The woman has power, I know, and it took me off guard, too. But I'm over it now. Why aren't you? Are you so greatly afeared of killing her?"

Waldo mounted his horse. "I fear the anger of the old gods. You are not a Saxon, Lupus, but I am. The gods of Saxony are powerful, for all that Christianity has been forced down the people's throats by the soldiers and priests of Charles."

"Forced?" Lupus asked dryly. "You are baptized yourself."

"That is true," Waldo said. "I am a Christian, but religion has never concerned me much. It does now, though, and it's not the Christian religion I am speaking of. This is an old land, my friend. There are forces here that no amount of holy water can wash away. A wise man knows better than to meddle with such things."

He looked down at his horse's neck. "It is unfortunate," he added in a quiet voice, "that I am not wiser."

The two men turned their horses' heads toward the track. The animals went forward eagerly; they sensed the ominous change in weather and were as anxious to find shelter from it as their riders. Lupus looked up at the sky as they rode. There was scarcely any more light in the open track than there had been in the heavily grown thickets. The winds rose, and the clouds were boiling up steadily from the west, lowering and thick, pressing down on the heads of anyone outside like enormous hands.

It was almost, Lupus found himself thinking, as if the gods Waldo spoke of were gathering. And they were angry . . .

"Blast." He shook himself free of these unnerving thoughts. "Your superstitions spread as quickly as a fever. You've even succeeded in putting me on edge." He shook himself again, crossing himself for good measure. "Christ is more powerful than any god of the pagans. You know that."

Waldo rode in silence for a space. "What I know," he said at length, "is that we are in Saxony, where the gods still live. If they have taken this woman under their protection, they will not look kindly at our trying to kill her."

"We have to," Lupus said shortly. "We've already given our word by accepting partial payment." His tone indicated that as far as he was concerned, this was the end of the matter.

But not for Waldo. "We should depart from here," he muttered, more to himself than his companion, who, in any case, did not answer. "We have been given one warning. We'll not be given another. What will we bring down upon us if we continue?"

And yet, despite his misgivings, Waldo did not turn around. Indeed, he was not the wisest of men. Side by side with Lupus, he kept riding down the track, toward the manor of Bathilde.

5

IF **B**ATHILDE WAS SURPRISED TO SEE Sirona return, she did not show it.

Ensconced in her bed, propped up by bolsters and cushions so that she almost appeared enthroned, she calmly regarded the wisewoman and the traveler who accompanied her.

"So, Wisewoman," she said, as if she had never warned Sirona, "you have returned to us."

Sirona met her gaze. "Not by choice, lady. I was attacked on the road. It would have gone ill with me, were it not for the aid of this good man."

Bathilde turned to the trader. "You have my great gratitude, stranger. This wisewoman is a skilled healer. My babe and I live because of her knowledge. The loss of her would have been irredeemable."

Isaac gave Bathilde a deep bow. "I only acted as was my duty," he said with an oddly touching sincerity. "To help another person in need is a holy act."

"Indeed." Bathilde studied him. "Forgive me for not receiving you properly," she said with a dignity that belied the fact that she lay in bed. "It is not seemly to appear to a stranger this way, but as the wisewoman has no doubt told you, these are unusual circumstances."

Isaac bowed again. "She did, lady. And while I rejoice at the birth of your son, I grieve at the loss of your lord."

Bathilde inclined her head. "It was a terrible loss, in truth. Were it not for his untimely passing, I would be in confinement after giving birth, as befits my rank. But I am forced into receiving guests, just as I, a mere woman, am forced into ruling over this manor in my husband's stead."

Sirona hid a smile. Briefly she wondered if Isaac saw the

strength in Bathilde that contradicted her words. If he did, he gave no sign of it. He was a trader, after all, and traders were as skilled at diplomacy as they were at bargaining. Perhaps more so.

"I would not willingly add to your burdens, lady," Isaac went on gallantly. "But my nephews, my animals, and I are in need of shelter. The weather threatens foul, and I hoped you would let us bide in the warmth of your manor until it clears." He smiled. "In return, I can promise you news, as well as many delightful and rare goods to look at, and perhaps acquire, if you are interested."

The servants clustered around the fire murmured in excitement, and Bathilde returned Isaac's smile. "When are a trader and his goods not welcome? You may stay with us as long as you like." She gestured to the seneschal. "Arrange accommodations for his men and see to it that the beasts are stabled and fed. You will want to go with him, I assume," she said to Isaac. "To supervise the proper unloading of your goods."

It was a request, rather than a question, but Isaac welcomed it. "I will," he said. "For my nephews are somewhat inexperienced, and certain items among the packs are fragile and must be handled with care." He offered Bathilde a final bow. "My lady is kind and generous. All that I have heard about you is true. Indeed, it is more than true."

"Is it." Bathilde cast a look at Sirona.

The seneschal, who had been struggling to maintain his air of self-importance, despite his own excitement at a trader's visit, motioned to Isaac to follow him out into the curtis, where his train waited.

"Go with them," Bathilde called to the servingwomen by the hearth. "Help our guest with his belongings and goods." She nodded to the wet nurse. "You, too, Begga. Give the child to me."

"Thank you, lady!" The wet nurse grinned delightedly, laid the swaddled infant in his mother's arms, and hurried after the others.

It was not a command their mistress had given the nurse

and the other servants, but a gift. Chattering eagerly, the women ran to take advantage of it. All of them were anxious to gain a first glance at the rare treasures that lay hidden within the visitor's packs. Traders were rare enough at any time, and with the harvest season fast approaching and folk soon to be too busy to do anything but bring in their crops, they were rarer still. Each servant was already calculating what she could barter or buy from among the treasures that were contained in the merchant's hoard.

Alone in the great hall, as she had meant them to be, Bathilde held her sleeping baby and stared at Sirona. Yet she did not speak. Several moments stretched between them. Then Sirona broke the silence.

"You do not chastise me, lady" she said, and though she tried, she was not quite able to keep the sharpness from her tone. "You should; you warned me of this, after all."

Bathilde looked at her sadly. "I take no pleasure in it, Wisewoman; believe me I do not." Her dark gaze grew more intent. "What happened?"

Sirona shrugged. "Two men leaped out at me on the track. They were armed with daggers." Her aplomb wavered. "They meant to kill me."

"But they did not."

"Thanks to the trader and his oaken staff. He happened upon me just in time and managed to drive them off."

"And you are certain it was the merchant alone who saved you?" Bathilde watched her steadily.

"He told me that his god brought him." Sirona frowned. "Though I have no idea why his god would wish to help me."

Bathilde made a disgusted noise in her throat. "His god had naught to do with it. You"—she leaned forward, fixing Sirona with her stare—"you saved yourself. Why do you deny it?"

"I deny nothing," Sirona snapped.

Bathilde settled back against her bolsters. "How he sleeps," she murmured, looking down at the babe. "Such a delight they are, when they are new like this. They sleep so much and awaken only to eat." A slight smile touched the edges of her mouth. "We must enjoy it while we may. Soon enough, he'll be keeping us all awake with his crying."

She looked up at Sirona. "You are sleeping, too, Wise-woman. Or rather, the powers within you are sleeping. But they are beginning to awaken, and that frightens you."

"Lady." Sirona spoke tightly. "I am frightened of you, and of what you have started. I did not wish to be a part of it. I do not. Yet here I am, back in your hall after having my life nearly taken from me in a cause I have no stake in."

"Ah, but you have a stake in it," Bathilde reminded her. "Whether you will or no. It began when you refused to kill me."

"Not only you, lady. I will not take any life. I have told you that. My calling forbids it."

Bathilde gazed at the younger woman in silence. A beat of silence passed, and she sighed. "I did warn you, you know," she went on gently. "But you need not be afraid. Your gifts are growing, just as this babe is growing. What has happened will continue to happen."

"And what will continue?" Sirona demanded. "That more attempts be made on my life?"

Bathilde's dark eyes grew distant. Sirona stared and watched them take on that farseeing look that spoke of a knowledge guided by magic. Her voice was still gentle. "Must I speak of what you already know?" she asked softly. "I am not the only one here with power."

Sirona stood looking at her. A gust of wind rattled through the hall entrance, causing the hearth flames to leap and the baby to stir. Noises drifted in from the commotion outside. The mules were being unloaded, accompanied by loud, eager voices, the high-pitched ones of women and the lower tones of men. Exclamations and questions rang out, followed by laughter from Isaac and his cousins. Sirona had met those nephews; they were friendly and eager as puppies, with some of that same clumsiness. They had been fascinated by the attack upon her, jealous that Isaac had forced them to stay behind with the mules and miss it.

Sirona's glance went to the swaddled little bundle as it let
out a fretful mutter. "You liken magic to babies," she said at
last. "The two are not the same."

"Are they not?"

"No, they aren't. Babies are simple; give them love and
food and care, and they will grow as the Great Mother
meant them to. Magic is another matter entirely. It is complicated, it takes control of you, rather than the other way
around."

Bathilde laughed. The sound of her mirth bounced
through the hall, and suddenly she appeared as young as
when she had first attracted the eye of her lord. "So do
babes, my girl, so do babes. With all the children you have
brought into the world, you, as a wisewoman, should know
that better than any."

"But we are not speaking of babes, lady." Sirona regarded her unsmilingly. "We are speaking of magic. I am
content with my gifts of healing. I need naught else." She
shivered, recalling the attack on the road. The men's faces
loomed in her mind's eye; her muscles tightened in memory
of the force that had surged unbidden into every thread of
her being. "Especially," she added, "not the complications
that the gifts of such magic would bring."

"You are indeed afraid." Bathilde's voice was sad. "You—"

Sirona put up a hand, cutting her off. It was the height of
unseemliness to interrupt a person of Bathilde's rank, and
Sirona well knew it. But for the moment, she found it hard
to care. The conversations Bathilde had engaged her in had
already gone well beyond the bounds of seemliness.

"I will stay the night, and I thank you," she said firmly.
"As it would be madness to venture out again with a storm
coming on. But at first light tomorrow, I will set out for
home again. If you care for my safety, you will send a
man-at-arms to accompany me so that this time, I arrive
safely."

Bathilde said nothing. A new ripple of anger coursed
through Sirona at the noblewoman's silence. She gestured
at the sleeping baby. "For sake of the debt you owe me, I
ask this boon. Will you grant it?"

"I will." Bathilde spoke reluctantly, then, all at once she smiled. "If it comes to that."

Her smile faded, her handsome face grew sober. "You cannot stop this, Wisewoman," she said. "Any more than I can stop this one"—she laid a tender hand on the infant's vulnerable skull, so soft and darkly fuzzed—"from getting too big for his swaddlings."

Sirona did not answer. She inclined her head in a respect-ful nod and turned to leave. She wanted this talk to end. She didn't want to think about power and magic and men leap-ing out at her from dark thickets. She wanted to be home in her cozy hut, preparing herbs and tinctures, doing all the fa-miliar and safe tasks. Above all, she had no wish to be drawn into the fierceness of this noblewoman's desires.

But as she walked toward the hall entrance, she felt driven to turn around one last time. "I wish you well, lady," she said. "It is simply that I cannot follow you down the bloody path of what you seek to accomplish. I know my place in the world, and what you would have me be goes against that."

She hurried out before Bathilde could answer.

Wisewoman.

The voice coiled about Sirona's head, a sibilant whisper inside her head. Half-asleep, groggy and exhausted from the rigors of the day, her eyes forced themselves open. Rain beat like thunder about the manor. The storm had arrived before nightfall, drowning out the bells for vespers, bring-ing the rain, and a wind that howled as though it were a liv-ing thing, as if it were a woman giving birth.

Sirona's heart sprang, threatening to beat through her chest. Had the assassins slipped into the manor seeking to complete their task? But at the same moment the thought came to her that if they had, they would hardly call out her name before they struck. And, adding its reassurance, was the stillness in the hall. All around her the dense, smoky air was murmurous and peaceful. The house folk lay asleep, snoring and twitching through the storm, men, women, couples, children, dogs, all scattered on the rushes throughout the hall. Not one of them had opened an eye or even stirred at the sound of the voice.

The whisper came again. *Wisewoman, awake.*

Fully alert, Sirona grasped why it was that no other person had stirred at the sound of the voice. This summons was meant for no ears but hers. The speaker was addressing her by means of an enchantment. The sibilant words coiling through her mind vibrated in her head alone; no one else could hear them.

Cautiously, she rolled over on her pallet. Before her sat a cat. His body was scarcely visible in the dim light from the banked hearth-fire. His eyes glowed orange in the brief shards of light from popping embers, and the patch of white fur on his chest glimmered bright as a piece of the moon. Sirona stared. This was the very cat that had appeared on the night that Bathilde had given birth.

As she returned her gaze from those huge orange eyes, the cat rose to his feet. *Come with me*, he said.

Why? Who has sent you? The questions swirled through Sirona's mind. She did not voice them aloud; somehow she knew the creature could hear her. Nonetheless, he did not answer.

Be quick, was all he said. *I will be waiting at the manor door.* He glided off between the pallets of the other sleepers, into the shadows toward the doorway of the hall.

Sirona looked after him. Leave the safety of the crowded hall with its quiet sounds of snoring, grunts, and sleepy murmurs, and the familiar odors of smoke and farting, to follow this magical being through the recesses of the deserted house? One would have to be gripped by madness to do it. Yet, even as she thought this, she was pushing the fur coverlet aside and clambering up from the pallet.

Her bed was near Bathilde's closest attendants, in the favored guest spot beside the fire. But like everyone else, Sirona slept naked, and away from the warmth of the cloak she had wrapped about herself and the extra hospitality of a wolf-fur coverlet, she shivered in the night chill. Scrabbling around for her linen undertunic, she pulled it over her head. She followed it with her long tunic, secured her girdle with a hastily tied knot, and knelt to yank on the soft boots she favored over the more customary shoes worn by women. At last she grabbed up the thick coverlet of wolf fur and wrapped it about her shoulders.

No one had awoken at the rustlings she had made while dressing, not even the dogs. The realization made Sirona shiver again, and not with cold. Perhaps the fierce drumming of the rain drowned out her own small noises; or perhaps not. Mayhap a spell had been placed on the house folk, enabling the cat to make his visit unseen and undetected. But if that were true, would it not indeed be wiser to stay here?

She shook her head, at herself as much as at the appearance of the cat, and started to move past the scattered pallets of the house folk. Still, none of them opened an eye. A spell must indeed have been laid upon them, and perhaps upon Sirona as well, for it seemed to her that she was treading as silently as the cat had. Soft-footed as the creature that had summoned her, she padded through the entryway and out into the silent corridor.

It was very late. The flames from the night torches set in their niches along the stone walls had burned low, casting wavering shadows that seemed to follow her with an eerie awareness as she slipped past. Sirona had the uneasy sensation of being watched. Yet when she swung around to search the dim corridor, no menacing figures revealed themselves, and no figure of a cat either. She steeled herself against the feelings and went on toward the entrance of the manor.

The front doors of the house were massive, made of carved oak thick enough to withstand all but the most determined invaders. They were also barred, as they were every night at sunset. Sirona walked over to stand before them. Here the fury of the storm could be felt more clearly. In this chilly spot the wind and drumming rain took on a closeness that the comfort and smoky warmth of the hall protected against.

Sirona stared about with a prickle of impatience. Did the creature expect her to pass through the doors? He might be able to accomplish such a feat, but spell or no spell, she certainly could not.

"Cat," she said. "Be you here?"

No one was about—at least, no one mortal—but she found herself speaking softly all the same. The wind promptly swallowed up her words, and she was about to repeat them, when a voice answered her.

"I am here," the cat said.

Suddenly she saw him. He was sitting in front of the barred doors, his tail curled with exquisite care about his paws, arranged as only a cat can manage. The fine hairs at the back of Sirona's neck stood on end. She had stared at that very spot not a moment ago, and nothing had been there.

"I have been waiting for you," the cat said. "By the Sacred Ankh, it certainly took you long enough."

His voice was clearly audible above the wind and rain. No longer was he sending his words out to whisper in Sirona's head. He was speaking to her as any man or woman would. His was a light voice, yet oddly penetrating. The words were accented in a way Sirona had never heard before, although—and she found herself holding back a sudden burst of nervous laughter—what else could one expect from a talking cat?

She swallowed, then swallowed again. "I am here," she got out, hearing the shaking in her voice. "What do you want with me this night?"

The long black tail gave an impatient twitch. "I do not mean only tonight. My wait has been far longer than that. And so has Hers."

"Hers?"

"Of course." The tail twitched again. "Seek you to tell me that you do not know who I mean?"

Sirona was silent. She heard once again the voice that had boomed through her head when the men attacked her. It was only in her memory, but the presence and power of it was as real as it had been that morning. She shivered, gripped by the memory of that mighty tone and the words it had spoken.

The cat shifted his front paws at Sirona's silence. She could have sworn she heard the creature sigh at her obtuseness. "I am speaking," he said with exaggerated patience, "of the Goddess. The Lady of Silver Magic. The Ancient Mistress. She, Who has given you your gifts."

"I know that," Sirona said with quick anger. "She was the Goddess of my ancestors. I honor Her, as is right and proper, as I honor all goddesses. But the ancient foremothers were priestesses. My mother was not one, nor her mother before her. I am no priestess either. We are healers, me and mine. I have not forgotten your Lady; indeed I could not do my work without Her blessing."

"But"—she hesitated, feeling suddenly and unaccountably ashamed— "the foremothers had a bond with Her that only comes to priestesses. They belonged to Her," she found herself confessing, "in a way that I do not."

The cat's great orange eyes glared. "You are of the Goddess as much as they were," he snapped in his dry cutting voice. "You always have been, even if you are too foolish to know it. Think you that She bestows Her gifts upon anyone? That it is enough to say you honor Her and all goddesses, when you regard them as nothing more than tools to do your healing?"

His voice was growing angrier and angrier, turning into a peculiar combination of human speech and feline spitting that hissed more loudly than the rain whirling down overhead. Sirona listened in bewilderment. Yet she understood him. Better than she might have wished, she thought ruefully.

"I meant no offense, magical one," she started to explain. "Against you or Her—"

The cat stood up. "You cannot offend me," he said more calmly. "You are but a mortal, after all. And my Mistress is far more patient than I; for She is a Goddess. But you will find that out for yourself soon enough."

"What do you mean?" The hairs at the back of Sirona's neck lifted again. Unease tingled through her, mingling with an odd sense of excitement, perhaps even eagerness.

"The Goddess would speak with you," the cat told her,

adding with another hiss of irritation, "Why else would I be abroad on a night like this? Magical or mortal, any self-respecting cat does his best to avoid rain." His fiery eyes slitted, as if he were remembering other missions on other stormy nights. "Sometimes, however," he added, reflective and resigned at once, "it cannot be avoided."

Sirona could not take her eyes from the sleek black form and glowing orange gaze. "I don't understand," she said slowly.

"Is it not obvious? My Mistress wishes to speak with you, and I am to bring you to Her."

Sirona drew back. "I cannot. I"—she struggled for words, feeling her odd sense of excitement evaporate into apprehension. "What would happen were I to be missed? There would be a terrible outcry. That good trader who helped me might well be blamed . . ."

She trailed off into silence. It did not sound very convincing, even to her, and by the irritated twitching of his tail, the cat clearly agreed. "Do you even remember the name of the One Who gave you your gifts?" he asked dryly. "Your ancestors knew it well. They worshipped Her for all the days they lived in this mortal world. They honored Her out of love, not the duty or fear so many mortals feel they must show to honor the Christian God nowadays. Those women were the Goddess's daughters, as you are Her daughter, although you ill behave like it. Her name," he went on, before Sirona could answer, "is Bast."

Stung, Sirona snapped, "I know Her name, magical creature. I have always known it."

"Do you? Then show Her."

"By coming with you."

It was a statement, rather than a question, and Sirona knew what the answer would be. The cat sat down, wrapping his tail about his paws again. A pink tongue flicked out. He licked his chops several times, revealing long fangs, white as polished pearls.

"Shall we go?" he said.

Sirona looked away from the orange eyes. She stared down the darkened corridor. The torches had burned lower, leaving the manor deeper in shadow than when she had passed through it. But she knew she could find the way back. She could turn away from this being from the world of magic and return to the hall. Safety lay there, with Bathilde and her sleeping folk: a dubious safety, in truth, but was that still not better than following this cat who spoke human speech off into the unknown?

Even as these thoughts went through her mind, Sirona turned her gaze back to the cat. Slowly, she tightened the folds of her cloak about her shoulders. "I think it may be madness to go with you," she told him. "Yet for the sake of the ancestors, those mothers who came before me, I will come. I pray," she added grimly, "that my decision is not a misguided one."

"It isn't," the cat replied in his flat voice. "The madness would be in going back to that hall." He leaped to his feet and stretched. "Come, stand next to me," he instructed. "And do not trouble yourself. We'll be back before that kindhearted trader knows you've been gone."

Sirona did as he bade her. The cat brushed against her ankles. His upraised tail flicked at her knees. He opened his mouth and yowled. An unsettling combination of speech, both the meowing of a feline and the words of a human, came pouring forth.

> *"Soul of the Night, heed me.*
> *Moon-Mother, heed me.*
> *Wind-Woman, heed me.*
> *Speed us from this world.*
> *And bring us to my Mistress.*
> *Do this now!"*

6

THE NIGHT ITSELF CAME SWIRLING
into where Sirona and the cat stood,
and with it burst the full power of
the storm. The oaken doors and
stone walls were nothing against
them—they were built of mortal
stuff, meant to withstand mortal
threats. The storm winds were
forces from another world. The cat had called them up, and
they came swooping to his call. Howling, they surrounded
the two figures, buffeting woman and animal, then sweeping both up and carrying them away.

Sirona's clothing billowed and spread about her like a
pair of wings. Her hair, unbraided for sleep, snapped across
her face like ropes. Instinctively, her feet struggled for the
solidity of the ground and found only air. She felt herself
rising, lifted higher and higher by this implacable power
until she was outside, caught in the wildness of the night
storm. The fur coverlet went whipping away, leaving her in
just her tunic. Helpless, utterly at the mercy of the cat's incantation, and yet exhilarated beyond imagining, she took
flight.

It was a sensation beyond any dream or vision. She
should have been terrified; somehow she was not. The
power bearing her along was massive, as impersonal as the
night and storm itself, and yet there was no harm in it, at
least to her. Within the howling, swirling motion she floated
in a space of serenity, staring down at the dark rainswept
world below, as though she were a bird flying to shelter. She
was aware of the cat beside her. She sensed his presence,
but when she tried to turn her gaze to see him she could not.

Her feet touched solid ground, so suddenly that she staggcrcd and almost fcll. The wild sensation of flight was gone. They had arrived. But to what place had they come?

Dazedly, she waited for her vision to clear. She blinked in awe. She was standing atop a mountain, and the whole world seemed to be made of sky. Pale as beaten silver, it loomed overhead, stretching off into the distance in layer after layer of luminescence. Sirona looked down. Her feet were resting upon a layer of grass softer than the thickest fur she had ever felt. The living mat shimmered beneath her gaze, slightly darker than the sky, but still gleaming like tarnished silver. She looked up again and found herself staring at a towering edifice of pink stone.

Intuitively, Sirona knew that it was a temple, though it was like none she had ever seen. The temples in her world—what was left of them—were aging ruins, piles of stones and fallen columns, much of which had been looted to build churches. But this temple was different. It soared up into the multicolored sky, all arches and spires and oddly fluted columns as graceful and elegant as leaping cats.

Sirona felt an odd tightening in her chest. Holiness enveloped the place, striking at her as no church ever had. The strange building beckoned, calling out in voices that thrummed from within rather than without. A yearning leaped up in her to go there, to explore what lay behind those spirals and columns. And at the same time the yearning made her uneasy. The path that had begun in the sleeping hall of the manor house continued toward that temple. Perhaps it ended there, and perhaps it would take her on to other places she did not wish to go.

"It is beautiful," she breathed, enchanted despite her uneasiness.

"Once it was more so," said the cat.

In spite of the fact that he was the source of what had brought her there, Sirona had momentarily forgotten about the cat. She started at the sound of his light, dry voice.

He did not appear to notice. His bright gaze was fixed on the temple, and he seemed to be speaking as much to himself as to her. "This is the house of my Mistress, and once it shone brighter than the sun. The power of more centuries than you will ever know was alive in those stones. They glowed with a light that may only come from true magic."

He fell silent, and Sirona tore her gaze away from the temple to look at him. "What happened?"

The animal made what would have been a shrug had he possessed human form. "Time happened. And change. A new religion came into the world, a religion that shows no favor toward what came before. Mortal folk forgot the ancient ones they used to worship, and as their memories grew dimmer and dimmer, so did the power of those old gods and goddesses dim, as well. You should know that." His eyes narrowed. "Yes, you should know that, indeed. You who insisted to me that magic has no place in your life."

Sirona could find no answer to that. Magic had a mind of its own. When it decided to enter one's life it carved itself a place regardless of how a mortal felt about it. Sirona had just learned that lesson for herself, and most powerfully; she had no desire to open herself up to it any further.

The cat's voice grew more cheerful. "But look you, the stones have begun to glow again. Only a small bit, but their light will get brighter."

Sirona stared. It was true. Even as she looked a faint glimmer had begun to suffuse the graceful lines of the stone temple. They gleamed softly, as though a myriad of tiny suns was slowly coming to life within their depths. The beauty of the temple deepened. Yet, instead of being entranced by it, Sirona felt a wave of apprehension.

"And why is that?" she demanded. "If they have been dull for so long, what has caused them to start glowing now?"

The cat growled deep in his throat. "You truly do need educating, don't you? Because, mortal woman, *you* have come! Hurry now. She is waiting."

Sirona's eyes widened. Caught up in the wild journey and the splendor of this realm, she had all but forgotten the purpose behind the cat's appearance and everything that had followed. But how could she have forgotten? Of course everything would lead to the Goddess.

"In the temple?" she whispered stupidly.

"You will not be the first of your line who has gone there."

"But—"

The cat lashed his tail and trotted off.

Sirona stumbled after him.

They went along a path that glimmered as silver as the sky and passed into a vast courtyard. Sirona's steps faltered again. Regardless of what she saw she would have had to stop in any case, for her way was blocked. By cats. Scores and scores of them, so many they were beyond counting. She stared at them, and they stared back, hundreds of eyes glittering in shades of green and yellow and orange and blue. In the midst of fur and eyes and waving tails she immediately lost sight of her guide. The courtyard cats seemed to know this and made a path among them. The sound of their purring rumbled in the air like thunder.

Sirona saw the cat. He was standing in the space the other cats had created for him, and even as she looked, he began to change. Already large for a cat, his body lengthened and grew until he was taller and longer than it was possible for any cat to be. The white patch on his chest disappeared. His black fur lightened, becoming a deep shimmer of silvery brown. Only his eyes remained the same, huge and orange and filled with knowledge.

"Oh," Sirona said softly. "Oh."

"This," the creature said calmly, "is my true appearance."

Sirona's eyes drifted over him. Surely she was in a dream, and this being had appeared to her out of that dream. "You are beautiful," she said slowly.

"I know." There was nothing smug about the cat's reply. "Come," he went on. "We will go this way."

Sirona went toward him. The gathering of cats watched her, packed in masses of fur and glowing eyes on either side of the path they had created. They still purred, and as she approached her guide the purring grew so loud that though she wanted to speak, she could not be heard. An archway gilded in silver and gold led into the temple's inner recesses. Sirona followed the cat through it, and only then did the deafening thunder of purring begin to fade so she felt she could be heard.

"What are all those cats doing out there?" she asked. They had begun walking down a wide corridor lined with pink marble. Her voice echoed eerily, the words bouncing back at her from the smooth tiles. "Where did they come from?"

"They have always been here." The cat's voice did not echo as Sirona's did; it sounded deeper, like the beat of a gong. "They are the children of Bast, and the guardians of Her temple."

"And do they ever leave?" Sirona thought of the cat's appearances in her own world. "As you do?"

"That is not their purpose. If anything, their numbers will only grow as the new religion does."

Sirona flinched at the sudden darkness in the cat's voice. Ill versed in magic she might be, but she recognized the sound of portent when she heard it, especially in a place such as this. She said, "The priests do not favor cats. They call them demons. The sadness is that people are beginning to believe it." She paused, thinking of the cats outside, remembering the servants' reaction to this particular cat when he had appeared in Bathilde's hall the night of the birth. "Someday, the Christians will begin to kill cats, won't they?"

Sudden respect shone in the orange gaze the cat turned upon her. "You're quick," he said. "By my claws, there may be hope for you after all."

Sirona glared, but whatever reply she might have made went unuttered. The doorway to a chamber had opened up before her. They were huge doors, carved from gleaming mahogany, inlaid with gold and silver and rimmed with precious gemstones that danced in a thousand tiny multicolored flames. Music touched Sirona's ears. It was unfamiliar music; the notes issued from strange drums and cymbals and stringed instruments. The melody was faint, a subtle drift of sounds, accompanied by even fainter voices. Straining to listen, she did not realize she had come to a stop until the cat spoke to her.

"We are here." He gave a quick, almost kittenish, leap through the entrance. "Come in." He glanced back over a shimmering silvery shoulder. "Do not be afraid."

"I'm not."

This was not quite true. Sensations were rippling through Sirona in steadily building bursts: anxiety, trepidation, uneasiness, and yes, fear. But it was not the fear that some harm might come to her; rather it was the sense of what would happen *after* she left this place. That was the source of her misgivings, and it should have been enough to drive her away, to send her scurrying back down the hallway like a terrified mouse fleeing the claws of the creature that had brought her there.

But she did not flee. A vast presence was inside that chamber, as encompassing as the night sky. It held her, as the moon holds the dark sky when it is full; and, entranced by it, her misgivings seemed small, insignificant.

Incense wafted through the open doors, heavy and sweet, its odor clinging to her nostrils. Through the pale wraiths of smoke she saw the cat staring at her from just inside the chamber. His eyes were very wide. He looked at her for a moment, then glided farther into gilded shadows of the great room.

"I have brought her," he announced to the presence inside the chamber. "If she will decide to come in."

Let her enter, then, a deep ringing voice said. *In her own time.*

The words resonated through Sirona's being like the tolling of bells from the Christian churches. She listened to them with a strange feeling of joy. That same voice had addressed her when the assassins attacked, but now it was gentle and welcoming, drawing her forward as inexorably as the moon moves the tides.

An enormous throne sat at the farthest end of the room. Made from the purest gold, it was a seat Charles the Great himself would have been envious of. Symbols were carved into its base, inlaid in silver, odd figures and depictions of events that flitted across her vision in an unfamiliar tapestry. But it was the figure upon the throne that dimmed the glittering throne and its symbols into pale insignificance.

Sirona's dazzled eyes told her it was a woman. In the same instant she realized her eyes were mistaken; it was a cat, an impossibly giant cat. But unbelievably, her perceptions changed again. The strains of drums, harps, and cymbals grew closer, the outlines of the figure seemed to dance in time to the music. They wavered, shifted, and suddenly coalesced into a sight beyond any dream or spell of magic.

Sirona stared up at the figure in frozen stillness. She was nearly blinded by disbelief and a terrifying sense of recognition. Here was the Goddess of her ancestors. Bast, the mighty deity Who was part woman and part cat. Sirona knew of Bast, in her soul, and in the stories she had heard all of her life, but she had never expected to see Her. The female body of the Goddess was garbed in a garment of linen so sheer each vast curve glowed with a clarity of its own. Her feline head was bathed in a shimmer of silver light. The enormous green eyes gazed steadily at the mortal woman, welcoming and enigmatic at once.

Come closer, child, She said.

Sirona obeyed, scarcely realizing she was doing so. As she moved toward the throne, the light about the Goddess's head brightened. The shimmer was startling; it spread down toward the curve of gossamer-clothed breasts even as Sirona watched. The cat, who had been sitting at the base of the throne, sprang to the arm of the throne and began washing himself contentedly in the glow.

You wish to know why I have called you.

Sirona searched for her voice. Finding it, she winced at how thin and weak it sounded in this vast, otherworldly place. "Lady," she whispered. "I think I know."

Do you?

The cat stopped his grooming and looked up.

"You want me to stop being who I am." It came out more harshly than she had intended, but she continued anyway. "You sent Your creature to bring me because I would not seek You out myself."

The great cat face was beautiful. There was ageless wisdom in the gaze it bent upon Sirona. *And what,* the musical voice asked gently, *do you think you will stop being because you have come to Me?*

"I am content with what I am—with what I thought You desired of me—a healer, as my mother and her mother before her, taught me to be."

Sirona fell silent before the enormous figure on its gold-and-silver throne. In this place of power and holiness, before this ancient and mighty Goddess, her fear coalesced, took on the solidity of speech. There was no way to hide from the knowledge in those all-seeing eyes. Suddenly she did not wish to; it was a profound relief to shout her fear aloud.

"I know there are other powers within me," she cried. "But I do not want them. I have never wanted them."

Yet you honor Me for the gifts of healing I have given you. Have you no desire to experience My other gifts? The power of true magic?

There was kindness in Bast's voice, and a note of genuine curiosity. She was a Goddess. She could have looked into Sirona's heart to see the answers to Her questions, but She did not. Something like love moved in the mortal woman's breast at that gentle regard for her private thoughts.

"Lady," she said, trying to explain, "the magic would make me into something else, something I do not wish to be."

What? the deep rich voice asked her.

"A warrior." Sirona realized the truth of it as soon as she spoke. "I fight my battles for the sick and the dying. If—if I take Your other gifts, I would be drawn into a great battle that will soon fall upon my land. And it will be a real battle, filled with blood and death, all brought upon mortal folk by the hands of other folk."

She went silent again. The history of the foremothers had grown blurred by time, detail after detail losing itself with each succeeding generation. But Sirona's mother had done her best to pass on what she knew to her little daughter. The stories of fierce women were a part of Sirona: women who walked with goddesses, who fought with swords and magic rods, who kept sacred shrines and defied evil, whether mortal or immortal. When had it come about, this knowledge that she would not—could not—be like them? Whatever had driven those heroic ancestors was not in her. And, truth be told, she did not want it to be.

Child, the Goddess said with deep compassion, *what is coming will come regardless of whether you accept or refuse that which is your birthright.*

Sirona stared up at that enigmatic face, at those astonishing feline features with their unknowable wisdom. "You want this, don't you? You want Bathilde to start a war to bring the old gods back, even though they are not the gods of your land, the country my mother told me of, called Egypt."

Sirona's mother had actually told her very little about that far-distant country that was the origin of this ancient Goddess. But it was not her fault; she had told her daughter all that she remembered. That knowledge, too, had faded over the ages, but Sirona had grown up with a vivid impression of a desert land baked by heat, ruled over by a merciless sun, the only respite the broad expanse of a great river. It was a strange land, that country, as strange as the Goddess Who had sprung from it.

Egypt is not its true name, Bast corrected gently. *That was a name given to it by foreigners. The land's true name is Kemet. It means the Black Land, for when the Mother of All Rivers floods every season in her sacred time, she turns the land black with her riches: soil which will nurture grain for the people.*

The cat let out an irritated little growl. "Enough of this," he said to the Goddess. "Did You summon the girl here for a history lesson? You can command her, You know. Why all this coddling? She belongs to Veleda's line, and in her own way, she's as stubborn as all the rest. She may not listen to reason, unless You show her Your own power."

Bast looked at him. *I have no need to command her, Mau. She is My daughter. She will make the choice for herself, when the time comes.* The great eyes turned their gaze upon Sirona. *And for that to happen, you must grow angry. There is no anger in you, child. Usually, that is a thing to be desired, particularly in the case of mortals, but not always.*

Sirona looked at Her. Words sprang to her lips so sharply she briefly forgot that she was addressing a Goddess. "So You intend to make me angry? Will You send other men to attack me? And then protect me from them to show Your strength? I warn You, Lady. That will only succeed in making me angry at You!"

She caught herself at once. She was challenging a Goddess, and in a most appalling fashion. She could very well succeed in making Bast angry with her. If that happened, the Goddess could blast her on the spot. Indeed, it would hardly be surprising if She did.

But the Goddess's calm demeanor remained unchanged. *I did not send the first men,* She said. *And I will not send others. But when they come, and they will, I will not protect you. You must protect yourself. Only then will you see.*

A shiver went through Sirona. "See what?" she asked, not caring if it sounded more like a demand than a question.

But it was the Goddess's turn to be silent. The light about her face and upper body began to dim. The change was subtle. Slowly, the shimmer lost its brightness, leaving the glorious form upon its golden chair. Bast looked at Her visitor, and the long green eyes were sad. Sirona felt a painful heave in her breast. Somehow, the dulling of the light about the Goddess had to do with her. She sensed it, though she knew not how.

The cat leaped from his place on the arm of the throne. "Come," he said to Sirona. "It is time to return." He trotted toward the open doors of the sanctuary, not looking back, obviously expecting her to follow.

Sirona hesitated. She looked up at Bast, but the Goddess did not return her gaze. The enormous cat face with its ageless eyes had taken on an expression as distant as the desert land Sirona's mother had once told her of.

"Lady," Sirona began. She did not finish. The remoteness in the Goddess was daunting. All at once she was keenly aware of the fact that she was a mortal facing an ancient deity. In any case, what more was there to say? Feeling oddly bereft, she turned and followed the cat.

Silently, the two walked down the corridor, guided by the faint glimmer of the pink walls. The cat was grimly uncommunicative. He was angry with her, Sirona knew. He marched stiffly ahead of her, his whiskers straight out, his tail whipping against his flanks with every stride. Following along behind, she could not see his eyes, but she could well imagine that they were slits of glowing orange displeasure.

"Well, what did you expect?" she finally burst out. "I told you from the first moment you came to me that I wanted no part of this."

The cat stopped. "All mortals are fools," he said shortly. "But you are perhaps the most foolish of all. Don't you understand that She wants to help you? And aside from that, She needs you."

Sirona stopped, too. "How?"

"Did you not see the light about Her? How it brightened as you came, and how it dulled when you left? That was because of you, mortal girl; you and no other." The cat sprang forward, his tail lashing even more angrily.

Helplessly, Sirona went after him. "Cat, She is all-powerful, a Goddess! She needs my help no more than She needs the help of any mortal."

"She is a forgotten Goddess." The cat glared back over a furry shoulder. "Where are Her worshippers? Once there was an entire city named for Her. Temples and shrines dedicated to Her were everywhere. At the time of Her yearly festival the Nile would be overrun with the faithful traveling to worship in Her city. But they are gone now, all of them. Her city lies in ruins, and Her temples are crumbling to dust. No one speaks Her name. No one offers up prayers and petitions for Her help. We cats, who were once treated as Her sacred children, are beginning to be called demons. Yes, My Mistress is forgotten, indeed, and now, thanks to you, She will continue to be."

"That is unjust," Sirona protested. "Is it my doing that Christianity has driven out all other gods but its own? I am sorry that Her worshippers are gone, but it is not my fault."

She hesitated. Memories cascaded through her, vague and yet terribly potent. Some were stories her mother had told her; others seemed to come from minds other than hers, as if she were suddenly viewing the lives of her foremothers. She seemed to glimpse other women walking through these halls; for an instant she thought she saw Veleda, the ancient mother, the originator of all who would come after her. Many other names had been forgotten in the intervening centuries, but not hers. Veleda had passed through this temple; she had been only a girl then, untried and unfamiliar with this Goddess from another land. Yet she had picked up arms in defense of Bast, and of so much more.

Sirona flinched. Guilt pricked at her, unfamiliar and annoying. She was inadequate to follow in the footsteps of those who had come before. Bast should not have called her to this magical place in the Otherworld. A wave of sadness poured through her, swiftly followed by anger that she should be feeling these things at all. She wanted to go home, to put this night and its magic behind her.

The cat had slowed his pace. With Sirona behind him, he came out into the courtyard. The cats gathered there were no longer purring. They had drawn together in close-curled heaps and lay silent, regarding Sirona out of scores of sleepily blinking eyes. The light that had burnished the pink stones had dulled, as had the light in Bast's inner sanctuary.

"Look about you." The cat glared around him as he spoke. "Gods and Goddesses need mortals. They always have. The prayers and devotions of humans give them their power, give them their very life. Take that away, and they fade, as the light in these stones is fading. When people cease to remember them, they cease to remember themselves. Eventually, they will go to sleep, just as these cats around us. The same cats," he added bitterly, "that were beginning to wake up when you came."

"Are you saying"—caught up by the hush in the courtyard Sirona spoke in a low voice, involuntarily seeking not to disturb its drowsy inhabitants—"that *She* will go to sleep?"

"Others have. Bast's own Sister, for one, though in Her case, that may not be a bad thing. But there are so many more besides. The Black Land had many deities, more than I could describe to you in a long winter's night. So did Veleda's land and the lands of her other daughters. So does your land of Saxony. But people no longer speak the names of the ancient ones. They have stopped praying and leaving offerings. The strongest god or goddess cannot long keep their power in the absence of memory."

He turned his glittering eyes on Sirona. "My Mistress has only stayed awake this long because, even in your poor way, you still remember Her. The other Shining Ones have no one."

Sirona clutched her arms about her. She shivered, and for the first time remembered that the heavy wolf-fur coverlet had been snatched away by the wind the cat had called up to carry them there. "But if I were to worship Her as She wishes," she said desperately, "what would it accomplish? I am only one soul, cat. One very mortal soul."

The cat watched her for a moment, then opened and closed his eyes in a slow blink. Flicking his tail, he turned away. His light voice floated back to Sirona. "Mortal you are, indeed, but you give yourself poor credit. Your honoring of my Mistress is weak, but it has kept Her awake thus far. How much stronger will She be if you stop being afraid of becoming what you are?"

He began picking his way through the sleepy clumps of fur and eyes, clearly unconcerned as to whether she answered him or not. At the edge of the courtyard, where the path out of the temple compound began, he stopped, waiting for her. Keeping her arms tight across her breasts, Sirona stepped through the cats and hurried toward him. Infuriating and unsympathetic as he was, this shimmering silver-brown creature was her only key to returning to her own world.

And yet this might all be a dream. She would open her eyes to the smoky darkness of Bathilde's hall, would find herself surrounded not by sleepy cats, but by the reassuring shapes of sleeping mortals, each of them wandering his own dream world. Of course, even if this were a dream, that did not negate its reality. No magical powers were required to be aware that sleep was the time when one could cross the boundaries between worlds. Everyone knew it, including those who professed themselves Christians.

But somehow, despite knowing all this, Sirona still wanted it to be a dream.

"Well, it's not," the cat said as she came up to him. "And it would not change anything if it were."

Sirona stared. "Can you see all of my thoughts?" she demanded.

The cat gave his feline version of a shrug. "Only the important ones."

Sirona's stare hardened into a glare. But there was no time for anything more. The wind that had brought them was springing up once more. Howling, it surrounded woman and cat, enfolded them in its dark wild arms, and bore them both away.

They landed hard, or at least Sirona did. The wind dumped them unceremoniously to the ground so that she tumbled to her hands and knees. The cat bounced lightly, recovered himself with a graceful spring, and instantly began to wash himself.

They had returned to the same spot inside the manor. The wind had died down, though the rain still pounded at the stone and timber of the great house. But another sound rose above the rain. Words hissed out in a terrified whisper, spoken in a language Sirona did not understand. Still in the act of scrambling to her feet, she jerked her gaze upward.

Isaac the trader was standing there. The wolf-fur coverlet was clutched in his hands. His friendly guileless eyes were huge with fear.

7

THE GIANT LIONESS HAD BEGUN TO
awaken. Slowly her head moved.
The eyes, yellow as desert sands,
opened drowsily; they drooped shut,
then opened again. Her long body
was as tawny as her eyes, the pelt
golden and gleaming, taut with layer
upon layer of bulging muscle. Slowly,
as the slanted yellow eyes stayed open, that powerful body
now stirred with lazy sleepy grace.

Long and long had the Goddess Sekhmet been asleep, so
long that it seemed as if there would never be anything else
than sleep. It was not an unpleasant state to be in. The
countless centuries of her ancient life could spin themselves
before Her. She could relive the glorious days when She
was worshipped and feared. Her victories could be tasted
with the sweetness of new blood; Her defeats reordered so
that they, too, became victories.

At first, the Lion-Headed Goddess did not know what
had awakened Her, nor was She at all certain that She
wanted to be awakened. With sleepy irritation she glared
about her. The spot in the tall grass where she had made
her bed had been pressed flat by the weight of her body and
the long ages it had lain there. The flat hot plains of her
sunburned realm stretched beyond her. Herds of beasts
roamed there, pulling up large mouthfuls of the tall dry
grass. The animals knew the lioness had awakened. They
paused in their grazing, lifting heads that were striped
black and white, dappled with cream and fawn, or crowned
with spiraling horns, to stare at the queen of their realm.
Regarding the lioness briefly, they soon dropped their
heads back to the waving grasses. The lioness might be

73

awake, but she was not hunting; at least, she was not hunting them.

They did not lift their heads again, not even when the great cat began to rise. She stretched, and then stretched again. For several minutes she lost herself in the luxury of movement, of lowering her giant head to her enormous forepaws, raising her hindquarters into the air, and elongating every muscle in her golden body. It had been a long sleep. There was a lot of stretching to be done.

At last, the lioness sat down in the flattened grasses that had served as her bed. Her sun-bright eyes were wide-open now, and they perused the distance with a hard, searching stare. She seemed to be looking beyond the plains and the herds of animals grazing there, beyond the flaming sun that hung scorching in the pale sky. Pulling her whiskers back, she bared her fangs.

"It is time," she said in a deep, rolling growl, "that I resumed my other form."

No sooner had the words been spoken than the lioness began to change. The lithe cat body blurred, broke apart, and shot upward. Her head remained the same, but the rest of her turned startlingly different. From the neck down, the lioness now possessed the form of a woman, powerfully muscled and clad in a tight-fitting garment of sheer red linen. In one great hand she clutched a bunch of arrows. As if rejoicing at the change, the sun bathed her in its glow, covering her with a pale light that burned strangely red.

The Goddess exulted in the transformation. Raising Her arms high, She let out a roar so deafening that most of the grazing beasts startled and fled. This was Her favorite form. Far too long had it been since She had taken it.

Still burning in the sun's glow, the newly transformed Goddess set off down a narrow path through the high grasses. Each step She took landed on the hard ground with an impact like thunder. The steady rhythm created a drumbeat of purpose, ominous and impossible to stop. As the hoofed and horned animals of the dry plains watched, the Goddess strode determinedly out of Her realm.

* * *

The trader was terrified. And with good reason, Sirona thought in consternation. How often did one see people materialize out of the air? Belatedly, with increasing alarm, she realized that Isaac was not alone. Two of his young nephews were cowering behind him, their faces showing the same terror as their elder's.

"Isaac," Sirona began, though only the old gods knew how she could possibly explain what he had just witnessed.

"I—I woke up." The trader was stammering, scarcely aware of what he was saying. "My nephew and I had to relieve ourselves, and I saw that your sleeping place was empty. I—I took this"—he held up the fur covering as though it were a shield to protect him against her— "to bring to you. I feared you might be cold . . . cold . . ."

"Isaac," Sirona said again. "Please, I know you are afraid, but there is no need. Let me explain."

That should be interesting, the cat said. He had left his otherworldly shimmer behind in the temple of Bast. Black once more, he had returned to being an ordinary cat, save for his eyes and, of course, the fact that he had just spoken.

"Be still," Sirona snapped at him. Too late she realized by the look on Isaac's face that while he could see the cat, he could not hear him as she could.

As she expected, that only made matters worse. The trader's reaction was immediate. He flung the wolf skin at her. "Begone," he shouted hoarsely. "Out into the night with the other dark and unholy things cursed by God. Begone, I say!"

In another moment he would awaken others with his frenzied cries. Blindly, Sirona swung about to the outer doors. Never would she able to lift the heavy bars by herself. The panicked trader would continue shouting at her to leave until others came running to see what the matter was.

Astonishingly, the trader was suddenly beside her. "I will help you," he raged. "If only to see you gone. Help me," he roared at his nephews. "Help me with these bars, so we can get her out!"

The two lads were in utter terror of Sirona and her magical appearance. But Isaac's voice spurred them into action.

Leaping forward, they helped the trader shove up the bars
holding the great doors shut against the night. They pulled
the heavy doors open, the slabs of oak responding to the
pressure with groans of protest. Cold air rushed in, and with
it, bursts of rain. The wind had risen again.

"Out," Isaac bellowed. "Out! And take your demon creature with you."

Sirona had no choice. She ran out into the pelting rain,
sensing rather than seeing the cat dart out ahead of her. Behind her, the trader and his helpers began to shove the doors
shut. Shivering, Sirona stared back at them. She yearned to
return to the faint oblong of light from the guttering torches.
If only there were words she could grab hold of, an explanation that would convince them she was harmless. But her
lips stayed closed. Nothing she could say sprang to mind.

All at once, she was startled by a loud hiss from the cat.

"So," a harsh male voice said. "She has come out to save
us the trouble of getting into the hall to find her. Very accommodating of the wench."

Sirona spun around.

The two men who had attacked her took shape out of the
rain-drenched darkness. They must have slipped in before
nightfall and sheltered in one of the outer buildings while
they waited an opportunity to finish their task. One of them
grinned at her, his teeth briefly glinting in the thin stream of
light that seeped out through the heavy doors Isaac and his
youths were struggling to close. But the other man did not
smile.

"Hurry," he said gruffly. "Pull her away from the doors
and let us get this over with before those inside see us."

The cat's hiss deepened to a snarl. *Are you going to let
them kill you?* He spit the words into Sirona's mind and
darted ahead of her. Swift as a shadow detaching itself from
the night, he leaped up and whipped out a paw armed with
five dagger-sharp claws. Instantly, the taller of the men
screeched in pain.

"Mother of God!" Simultaneously he clutched at his
thigh and kicked futilely at the dark shape. "She has a demon with her!"

"Yes," a deep, rolling voice said. "She does."

A new light suddenly spread over the two men, Sirona, and the cat. It was lurid, bloody and bright, deadly as the knives clutched in the hands of the assassins. But it was what that light contained within its unnatural glow that held them all transfixed.

A huge figure was hurling up through the spears of illumination and darkness. Sirona's incredulous mind identified it as Bast, but this Bast was different. Her head was wider, her features more coarse. Her eyes were not green, as Sirona remembered. They had turned bright yellow, and they burned with a narrowed intensity fixed solely on the two men. That gaze was terrible; it lacked every shred of the vast wisdom and compassion Sirona had seen in the deep eyes of Bast.

The crimson light burst into flames. They writhed about the enormous form, revealing it as the body of a woman. The scarlet garment She wore blended together with the flames, so that it seemed as though they emanated from the Goddess Herself. Incredibly, She laughed. It was a thunderous, horrific sound, but laughter nonetheless.

Speechless, the two men staggered back. The daggers dropped from their nerveless fingers. Their thoughts were as befuddled as their reflexes, and as astounded as Sirona's, but with one difference. They knew the appearance of this thing was directed at them. And through the welter of confusion and dread, one thought sprang uppermost into their minds. They had better flee for their lives.

Both of them stumbled about—Sirona, and the task that had brought them had been completely forgotten—and broke into a clumsy run. Terror quickly erased their clumsiness, giving their legs a wild, desperate fleetness. Still laughing that thunderous roar, the Goddess watched them go. When they had fled far enough to think themselves safe, She raised a hand. Her gesture was almost lazy as She pointed at the two mortals racing away from Her.

Two fiery lances shot forth from Her fingers. Composed entirely of flame, they sliced through the rain, straight as flung spears, heading unerringly for their targets. The men rediscovered their voices in a burst of screaming as the flames found their mark. The shrieks of agony were piteous. Sirona winced, despite the fact that these men had intended to murder her. Instead they were dying, and the sounds of it battered her ears.

Abruptly there was silence. Only the steady beat of the rain continued. The heavy drops spit down on the heads of Sirona, the cat, even the Goddess, though the flames curling about Her were unaffected by the weather's seeming attempt to drown them. Nothing remained of the two men. If there were ashes from the flames that had consumed them, they would never be visible; the rain was washing everything away too quickly.

The Goddess lifted Her giant head to the sky and laughed again. "Rain," She said in Her mighty voice. "Long has it been since I have felt it."

The cat sat down. "You should not have done that," he said. His voice was vastly irritated.

The Goddess lowered Her head to stare down at him. "And why not? They were about to slay her, were they not? What were *you* going to do about it? Scratch them again, while you waited to see if she would use her powers? You should be thanking Me, little cat. But no, you have not changed one bit through the ages. As ungrateful as ever."

"And You," retorted the cat, "are as heedless as ever. You come leaping out of Your realm, immolating mortals right and left without giving the slightest thought to the consequences. I should not be surprised, I suppose. You are just as You've always been."

"Those mortals needed blasting. And I did not see My Sister doing anything about it." The Goddess raised Her massive arms in a luxurious stretch to the dark, rainy sky. A deep rumbling poured through the night, and Sirona realized that this astonishing being was purring. "Ah," the deity sighed, finally lowering Her arms. "It is good not to be asleep, even better with some blood to thoroughly wake me up."

Amazingly, in spite of the Goddess's savagery and terrifying appearance, the cat did not seem in the least afraid. "I preferred You sleeping," he said sourly. "Why do You not go back to it?"

The Goddess bared her fangs in what could either be a smile or a snarl. "Ah, no, my little cat. I am awake now, and awake I shall remain. Changes are afoot at last, and I intend to be part of them. My Sister has finally grown some wisdom. It's taken Her too long, but there's no point in arguing about that now. Better late than never, I say."

The cat bared his teeth back at her. "You should not be speaking of wisdom, You Whose interference far outweighs any of Your own. Do You have any idea as to what was actually going on here?"

"I know"—the Goddess turned her flaming yellow gaze on Sirona "—that this one is a daughter of My Sister's priestesses. But she is no priestess herself. Why is that?" She suddenly demanded of Sirona. "Why do you refuse your gifts?"

"And what difference does that make to You?" the cat snapped, before Sirona could answer, if indeed, she could have found words to do so, which was unlikely.

"Oh," the Goddess said with surprising mildness, "it makes a great deal of difference to Me. You see, for the first time since Great Ra asked Me to rid the world of evil mortals, I believe We are all going to be allies."

Her thundering laugh roared out again. The flames shot higher, enclosing Her towering form entirely. The magical fire suddenly yielded to the rain. The flames sizzled and popped. When they had disappeared, so, too, had the Goddess.

Sirona stared and stared at the spot where She had stood. There was no sign that the fantastic being had ever been there. Of the men She had slain there was no sign either. It was as if all of them had been nothing more than a dream, a dream wiped clean by gusts of wind and rain. The sleeping folk within the hall had not heard any of what had transpired. The buffeting anger of the storm had covered the men's screams, and if any person might have stirred, Sekhmet's laughter would have sounded no different than thunder.

But Isaac and his nephews had not been asleep. In the act of closing the doors, the trader had suffered a change of heart. Through the wavering light he had seen the two men; he had heard them speak, their voices cool and confident. The woman would be attacked again, and this time, killed. No matter what she was, there must still be some humanity in her. Would God want him to stand by and witness her being murdered, or even worse, close the doors in the face of her death?

Isaac had started out into the storm. Ignoring the horrified exclamations of his young companions, he had gruffly ordered them to follow him; between the three of them they could certainly drive the assassins off a second time. But the youths had refused. Instead, their voices had only grown louder, and more terrified. Isaac had finally seen why. When he had, no force on earth could have moved him from the relative safety of the half-shut doors.

He would never know why he and his nephews did not close the doors all the way and run back to the great hall to arouse the house folk. Perhaps it was the very horror of what they were seeing that held them motionless and transfixed. Or mayhap it was pure common sense: the wisdom not to interfere in these clearly supernatural events.

Whatever the reason, the apparition was now gone. The woman stood alone outside the hall. She was huddled in upon herself, her arms wrapped across her chest. Her attitude did not belong to one who had the power either to call up such a horrifying specter or send it away. Isaac discovered that he was trembling violently. If he was shaking so badly, how much worse must her shivering be, out in the rain as she was. Slowly, he stepped back from the doorway. Bending down, he picked up the fur coverlet and started forward again.

"Isaac," one of his nephews gasped, "what are you doing?"

Isaac did not reply. He pushed himself out a small way into the narrow oblong of light. "Woman," he called, not entirely surprised to find that his voice was little more than a croak. "Here, put this on."

In spite of his croaking voice she heard him. She turned to face him. "You would offer me warmth?" Her voice was as hoarse and croaking as his. "After what you have just seen? Do you not think me more evil than ever?"

Yes, Isaac told himself. The aftermath of terror roiled through him, mingling with an angry confusion. He should think that. Why didn't he?

"I should," he said aloud. "But when I bade you leave the manor I did not know those men would be waiting for you outside."

She was staring at him through the rain. With that unholy apparition gone the light was poor. The woman's face was only an oval shadow, her eyes glinting as vague pools of darkness, but still, Isaac could not meet her gaze. "I—I could not see you attacked," he muttered, not even sure if she could hear him. "They would have killed you, and since it was I who threw you out, I would have been a party to murder. Our laws forbid that."

The woman stepped toward him. Gingerly, Isaac held the fur out to her, and with equal tentativeness, she took it. Wrapping it about her shoulders, she continued to stare at him. "You say this," she asked in a low voice, "even after what you have seen?"

Isaac's eyes jerked up to Sirona's face. "What did I see? In the name of Blessed Jehovah, what did I see? Ah!" The cat had moved into the shifting light to stand beside her, and the trader's fear burgeoned up anew. "The demon is still with you!" he cried. "It was *he* who summoned that monstrous thing!"

Oh, by the dugs of Hathor, said the cat in disgust, though only Sirona could heard him. *As if I would have anything to do with bringing* Her *here.*

From behind Isaac his two young nephews were already reacting. One was pulling frantically at his elder nephew's sleeve, while the other struggled with the doors. "Isaac," the latter begged. "Get you back inside. Let us shut these doors on her before more unnatural things come to haunt us. Please, Isaac. In the name of the Blessed One!"

Their fear was as heavy as the rain. Sirona watched their

reaction. So much had happened that she could not say whether his fear came from the fact that he still thought the cat a demon, or that he had seen the cat conversing with the Goddess. She was afraid herself, and she could not say which of those factors was influencing that terror the most.

"I do not know what you saw, Isaac," she said. "Truly, I do not. I am as afraid as you, yet there is one thing I can tell you. This cat is as new to me as he is to you. But I do not think he is a demon."

The trader stared at her for a long moment, standing firm against the anxious tugs of his nephews. He motioned at her with a quick gesture. "Come inside," he said abruptly. "Before that horror returns."

"Uncle, are you mad?" One of the youths pulled at Isaac even more wildly. "You made her go out!"

"And now I am telling her to come back in." Isaac motioned to Sirona again. "Hurry. The Holy One, blessed be His name, does not want you out here. As for the rest . . ."

He paused. Once again his face wore the look of a man who has seen beyond his ability to understand. Slowly it passed. "Well," he finished grimly, "I will simply have to pray and ask the Lord's guidance. In the meantime, the rest of you must return to the hall and try to sleep for what remains of the night."

He jerked free of the youths, slanted fierce glares at both of them, and stepped aside so that Sirona could enter. Without warning, the cat swept in front of her, his furry side brushing against her leg. His orange eyes blazed up at her face. At the sight of him, the youths leaped back with cries of fright. Even Isaac flinched.

Do not go back inside. The cat's light voice sounded in Sirona's ears. *This is no time for sleep. It is necessary that we talk.*

The trader was staring. He had not heard the cat, but caught up in what had occurred only moments ago, it was all too easy to sense an unholy magic in this animal, whether it was there or not. "You say this creature is not a demon," he said. "I am not so sure. I must pray, and until the Lord has spoken to me, only you may enter this house. I cannot take the chance of bringing evil into this place where we have been offered shelter."

Behind him the young men exchanged glances of immense relief and nodded. "Then let us close the doors, Isaac," one of them urged. "Quickly."

"Yes, yes," the other said. "At once! That cat must not come in here, and neither should she. She is a sorcerer—"

Isaac cut him off with another glare. He looked back at Sirona, and she could see the welter of emotions struggling across his face. Sirona knew almost nothing about Jews, save for the fact that Isaac seemed a good man. But his actions this night showed that Jews must be little different from other folk.

To Isaac and his nephews, evil was a force as tangible as the wind or the sun. In their world, as in everyone else's, good and evil strove constantly against each other, with magic a clear manifestation of both. And from the way the two lads tried desperately not to look at her, it appeared that Jews viewed women with the same suspicion Christians did: as possible *stria*, witches, though after the events of this night, she could hardly blame them.

Isaac broke in upon Sirona's thoughts. "Will you come inside?" the trader asked. "Leave the cat in the darkness where it belongs and return to the mortal warmth of a fire made by men and not that dread creature of magic."

She sensed that he was testing her, trying to see on which boundary of good and evil she would set her feet. It was not that simple, but she did not know how to tell him so. The eyes of the cat were resting on her face. They felt as warm as two small flames. "I cannot," she said awkwardly. "I must seek some answers to what happened here. Until I do, I dare not enter Bathilde's house, lest I bring the danger inside with me."

Isaac studied her as closely as the wan light would permit. Admiration slowly warmed Isaac's pale drawn features. "You are wise," he said softly. "And brave. You understand, don't you?" The trader's voice took on a note that was almost pleading. "Why I must shut the doors now?"

"I do."

He nodded. "Take shelter in the stables or the bakehouse or kitchen. Whatever the evil was that visited will lose its power with the dawn, as all evil does. Perhaps you will have your answers by then. The house servants will be up, the doors will be opened, and I—I will say nothing to anyone until you speak to me." He stared warningly at his nephews. "And neither will they."

Sirona felt a twinge of gratitude. "I will come back in the morning," she said. "And Isaac," she added, "I thank you."

He looked back at her over his shoulder. His expression was baffled and wary and frightened all at once. "I will pray for you," he said.

The heavy doors protested as they were pushed shut.

Sirona drew the wolf fur closer. She remembered again that it was raining. The coverlet was soaked through, but still of some comfort—at least, it was real. She stared forlornly at the great doors, wishing that she had never heard of Bathilde or Bast.

The cat was staring at the shut-up manor as well. He stood motionless, glaring at the barred doors with narrowed eyes, as if the gnarled wood had transformed itself into a clear glass reflecting where the intruding Goddess had stood. "Now why did She awaken?" he muttered to himself. "Why tonight, of all times?"

Sirona twitched the fur closer. The rain always seemed to be falling harder on this strange night. It was hissing unpleasantly in rivulets through her hair and down her cheeks. "If you must talk," she said with weary impatience, "let us at least take shelter as the trader suggested. We can go into the kitchen house. It will be warm and dry there."

The cat purred. "You are thinking like a cat," he said approvingly. He led the way, thus proving to Sirona that she was indeed thinking like a cat.

As in all great houses the kitchen was a separate building. Fires were a constant hazard and all too common in a time where every woman did her cooking over fires. Peasant women had no choice but to prepare their families' meals in the open hearth of their wood-and-thatch huts. The wealthy had the luxury of having their food cooked in structures set well apart from the house, so when the inevitable fire did break out they and their goods would be protected from harm.

The kitchen house of Bathilde's manor was quite large; it had to be, to prepare the food for a big household. The leftover odors of roasted meat and fish, of boiled peas and beans, and new-baked bread, smacked Sirona like a dozen hands as she entered. Andirons, chains, and pothooks hung in carefully ordered disarray about the huge hearth. Iron and leather cauldrons sat empty, waiting to be filled with the next day's menu. Near them were heaping salt bins and wide arrays of wooden utensils, all neatly arranged and waiting for the cook, as the cauldrons were. An enormous buffet of rough-hewn oak sat in the center of the kitchen, crammed with lead plates, and pots of tin, lead, iron, and wood.

The cat slipped around the buffet, heading straight toward the hearth. Sirona followed him. There was still some warmth from the banked fire, and he settled himself in the precise spot on the flat hearthstones where it would be most intense.

The night was drawing on toward dawn. It would not be long before the kitchen boys, the lowliest of the cooking staff, came stumbling in half-asleep to fill the cauldrons with water and stir the banked fires of the kitchen and its nearby bakehouse into life. They would be followed by the bakers themselves, who would start the daily task of shaping loaves for the household from the dough they had left to rise overnight.

But there was still enough time for the two in the deserted kitchen to speak. Sirona sat down on the hearthstones near the cat. Warmth seeped up around her, and suddenly she felt terribly sleepy. She struggled to keep her eyes open, to focus her thoughts.

"What did I see?" She fixed her heavy eyes on the animal. "What did we all see?" In spite of her exhaustion, she listened intently to the answer.

"You saw a Goddess." The cat's voice was flat and expressionless.

"A Goddess." Sirona looked at him, amazed. "That"—she shuddered at the vividness of her memory—"was a Goddess?"

"Bast's Sister, to be exact. Her name is Sekhmet."

Sekhmet. Sirona rolled the alien-sounding word over in her mind, but did not attempt to pronounce it. "So that is why She helped me? Because She is Bast's Sister?"

"I doubt it." Cats were not physically constructed to show human expression, yet Sirona could have sworn that this particular cat was frowning. "Helping is not Her way," he went on. "Especially when it comes to the women of your line. She had Her own reasons for doing what She did, and helping you was not among them. Even so, She could not have come tonight, if someone who acknowledged Her memory had not called Her. She has been asleep a long time."

"The way Bast would be, if . . ."

Sirona did not finish. There were still those who believed in Bast, and so She remained awake. Now that terrifying being that Mau had called a Goddess had awakened as well, because someone knew of Her, and not only knew of Her, but *believed*.

"No one believes in Her anymore." The cat's slit gaze rested on Sirona's face. "You did not even know She existed. But," he added thoughtfully, "some mortal obviously does, else She would not have come."

"Bathilde," Sirona said suddenly.

The cat looked at her, and his orange eyes grew wide. "The noblewoman of this place? Ah. It could be."

"It is. It must be." Wide-eyed, Sirona met the cat's gaze. This had to be the noblewoman's doing; she was certain of it. Somehow, Bathilde had discovered the existence of the sleeping Goddess and had called to Her. But had Bathilde truly understood what she was doing? She had not seen, as Sirona had, the power of what she called up.

Her tiredness forgotten, Sirona wheeled around, involuntarily ready to seek out Bathilde with the shock of her realization. "She spoke of secret knowledge, of finding her way back to the old gods. I thought she meant our gods—the gods of Saxony—not"—she shivered again— "not that dread thing."

"She," the cat corrected. "Remember, we are speaking of a Goddess."

"I don't care. Goddess or not, She is evil."

The cat eyed her. "You are paying too much heed to the fears of that trader. Evil is a word mortals have always been fond of, and these days they use it more than ever. Yet not one in ten thousand understands the true meaning of it."

Sirona fell silent. She had a keen sense that Bathilde understood the meaning of evil: all too well. Sekhmet might have had Her reasons for saving her, but Bathilde had her reasons for calling Her in the first place. What was more, the noblewoman must have known the Goddess would come.

She was not the only one who was pondering these thoughts. The cat was crouched motionless on the stones, only the tip of his tail moving reflectively. "I think," he said, "that you had better talk to this Bathilde."

Sirona nodded. "I think so, too. At once."

She jumped to her feet, leaving the soaked wolf fur in a heap next to the hearthstones. Slipping around the buffet, she was about to open the outside door when it swung wide on its own. The first of the kitchen boys to arise from his bed stepped through. He was rubbing his eyes sleepily, but he stopped short when he saw Sirona standing there.

"Christ's Cross, who might you be?" he demanded. Startled and suspicious, he blocked the doorway, his eyes darting around the kitchen to see if anything had been disturbed. "Have you been stealing food?" His voice rose and fell unevenly, betraying his youth, but his age did not make him afraid. He had every right to be here, and she was most likely a beggar who had slipped in to take shelter from the storm.

Sirona drew herself up to her full height. "You do not recognize me?" She affected a pose of irritation. "I am but the wisewoman who brought your mistress's new baby into the world. Step aside, boy. I must speak with Lady Bathilde at once."

It worked. Hastily, the boy moved. If he had other questions, such as what she was doing in the kitchen house in the first place, he was sufficiently intimidated not to ask them. Two other servant boys were trudging drowsily up to the kitchen, and the first boy ran to meet them. They stopped in their tracks, listening intently as he whispered to them. Their eyes all followed Sirona as she started back to the manor.

None of them noticed the departure of the cat. Like a flitting shadow he slipped around the buffet, darted through the door, and followed the woman toward the manor.

8

Haganon was not a man given to waiting. Patience was a quality seldom required of a man in his position. The two assassins he had hired were the best; he had used them before, always with great success. They should have returned already. The task he had set them was an easy one: how difficult could it be to slay a lone woman? Yet they had not returned. That meant the woman was not dead. If she were, the men would have shown up to collect their fee.

Haganon slammed his goblet of morning ale down upon the table. The action drew curious glances from his house folk. The kitchen staff had brought in breakfast, and Haganon's seneschal, the servants, as well as the men-at-arms were helping themselves to hunks of bread, bowls of barley gruel, and ale dipped from a common barrel. The family sat at the high table with their lord, where they had been served their meal first: Haganon's wife, the Lady Judith, and their two living sons. The boys were gulping down their food rapidly, eager to get outside and see what damage the storm had left.

Lady Judith put down her own goblet, regarding Haganon with concern. "What is it, lord?" she asked. She was a round-featured woman of pale skin, light brown eyes, and red-gold hair coiled neatly about her head. Her manner toward her husband was always gentle, but her gentleness was belied by the firmness with which she ran her household. "Did you rest poorly last night?" she went on conversationally. "Small wonder if you did. It was a dreadful storm that visited us. Praise God we came through it safely."

"Praise God," Haganon responded automatically.

He gave his wife a brief glance. She had never been particularly attractive, and childbearing had coarsened her features, thickened her waist, and caused her breasts to sag. Still, the marriage had been advantageous; Judith had brought him rich farmlands as her dowry, she had given him sons, and she kept to her place, not interfering in men's business the way that cursed Bathilde did. He supposed he was as fond of her as a man could be of his wife, when he thought of her at all.

A servant appeared at Haganon's elbow with a flagon of ale. Irritably, the noble waved him away. He was weary of sitting at his board doing nothing. He had done it too long already. He was a man of action. It was time to take action again. He jumped to his feet.

"Husband?" Judith queried again.

Haganon ignored her.

"Arn," he shouted. "Attend me."

The seneschal leaped up. His mouth was full of bread, and hastily he sought to chew and swallow. "Lord," he mumbled through his chewing.

Haganon swept from the hall. Of course, he could have ordered everyone else to leave instead, but eaten up with impatience, he was the one who wanted to move. He had to be outside, pacing back and forth and staring into the distance for the first sign of approaching horsemen. The seneschal gulped down his mouthful of bread, took a last deep swallow from his mug of ale, and hurried after his lord.

The rain had stopped, but the morning had broken pale and watery, as though the storm still hovered. Haganon strode toward the stables. Around him the normal hubbub of a new day had begun. Those in charge of cooking and baking bustled back and forth between the bakehouse and the kitchen, bearing wood, loaves of bread, screeching chickens, armfuls of greens, and haunches of venison. The regular thunk of axes rose on the air as servants hacked into one great log after another. Voices chattered, mingling with

laughter and singing as people went about their tasks. The
head groom popped his head out of the entrance to the first
stable building, saw his master approaching, and ran out.

"Will you be wanting your stallion, lord?" he inquired.

Haganon jerked his head. "Not yet. Return to your duties." He bent a stern look upon the groom. "And make certain all your workers do the same. I want no one using his
ears instead of his hands, listening to things that do not concern him."

He strode on, with Arn following along behind. Around
the side of the stable he finally stopped. The men inside
were mucking out stalls, adding to the great heap of dirty
straw that lay to the rear of the building. The odor was
heavy, but the spot afforded privacy, as well as a good view
of the narrow track that coiled and wound its way through
the manor fields. If horsemen came down it, they would be
seen at once.

Haganon glowered into the distance. In the clear colorless light of this washed-out morning, he could see the
tiny figures of his peasants and their livestock, but the
track itself was empty. "There has been no word," he said
without preamble. "The assassins must not have succeeded, else they would be here with their hands out for
the payment."

Arn was a tall man, almost as tall as his lord, although he
was as lean as Haganon was burly. The seneschal was completely aware of what his lord was referring to. He had been
with Haganon for years and was fully in his master's confidence. But Arn was a cautious man, a quality that had stood
him in good stead during his years of service to the fierce-
tempered Haganon.

"Perhaps," he suggested, "it has taken longer than they
intended. The storm last night was indeed a bad one. It
could have delayed them."

"No." Haganon took several impatient strides back and
forth. "Those two are professionals. They would not have
let a storm interfere; instead, they would have used it to
their advantage. Something happened. It had to, else they

would be here." He paused, glaring out at the distant road. "It is time for me to take action of my own."

Arn regarded his lord in puzzlement. "But what can you do, lord, other than wait for some word?"

Haganon glared at him. "You will soon see. Fetch Ambrose the priest to me. It's time he paid a visit to Bathilde."

Arn was a cautious man, but he was also a highly clever one. He caught on to Haganon's thoughts immediately. "Ah," he said with a sudden smile. "The baby. There has been no baptism, has there? Bathilde would have invited you and the other nobles for feasting if there had been."

"Precisely. The priest will go to Bathilde's hall. What better reason can he have than to demand why the baptism has not been held? And at the same time, he can find out what is happening. He should be able to discover if the woman is still alive, and if she's not, he should discover some sign of that, too."

Arn's quick smile faded. "Would it not be better to send word to the abbot? Remember, my lord, the priest has never truly allied himself with your cause. He may not wish to be a party to murd"—he caught himself as Haganon's eyes narrowed— "to the deed you hired those men for, even if the one they were after was a heathen."

"I remember." Haganon's tone forbade further comment. "And you remember, Arn, that the woman was more than a heathen. She was evil, a *stria*. Certainly the priest would not countenance murder, but the slaying of such an evil creature? An enemy of the true faith? That will not only meet with his approval, but Bathilde will pay more heed to him than she would the abbot. Her dislike of the abbot is well-known, and the priest has a winning way about him. I will explain the situation, and he will help us."

When Arn said nothing, Haganon's strained patience snapped. "Well?" He turned his pale angry gaze on the other man. "What are you standing there for? Go have the groom saddle a horse so you can get the priest. Jump to it!"

He continued to stand beside the stable as his steward leaped to obey. He listened to Arn's voice passing on orders and heard the head groom reply. A short time later hoofbeats announced a horse being led out. Haganon glanced around, watched Arn swing onto a rangy brown gelding and nudge the beast into a quick walk. The seneschal passed through the confines of the busy manor, headed for the track, and set the horse into a canter.

Haganon stared grimly at the figures of horse and rider. They diminished in size, steadily growing smaller as they galloped toward the horizon.

"What have you done?"

Bathilde stirred in some astonishment at the tone of the woman who had addressed her. The house folk had rolled up their sleeping places and stored them away so that breakfast could be brought into the hall. Servants were setting up the long eating boards as others brought in bread and ale and porridge. Only the still-recovering Bathilde lay in her box bed by the hearth, alone and undisturbed, except for Sirona, who stood before her, dark eyes blazing, her face haggard as though she had slept not a moment the whole night through.

Levelly, Bathilde met the wise woman's furious gaze. "What have *I* done?" she repeated back to Sirona.

Sirona stepped closer to the bed. "Play the innocent with others," she hissed. "But not with me, not anymore. The time for that is over. You called upon a dark magic, Bathilde, and last night it answered you."

Bathilde gave her an odd delighted smile. "I suspected it," she exclaimed softly. "I dreamed that She had come."

"Oh, She came," Sirona said grimly. It did not surprise her that Bathilde already knew of the Goddess's appearance, but it did make her angrier. She glowered down at the smiling noblewoman. "And others saw Her besides me."

Bathilde's smile vanished at once. "Who? Who saw Her?"

"The two men She killed, to start with."

"The assassins?"

At Sirona's nod, Bathilde relaxed against the bolsters. "Ah. Then it's as it should be. I wanted Her to kill them." Puzzled, she looked at Sirona. "And that is why you are so upset? They needed to die. They meant to murder you. Have you forgotten?"

"I have not." Sirona spoke through gritted teeth. "Nor have I forgotten what is driving you, lady. So this is how you return to the old ways? By calling upon Goddesses from another land?" Her voice was rising and she caught herself, realizing she must be careful. She was already drawing curious glances from the servants as they went about their morning duties. "Goddesses Who have never set foot in Saxon before now?" she went on in a tone that was quieter but no less intense.

Bathilde drew herself up, staring steadily at the other woman. "I will use whatever tool comes to my hand in order to achieve my purpose." In spite of the fact that she lay in bed as an invalid, an aura of power and determination glowed from her. "This was a weapon I would have been a fool not to seek out."

Sirona regarded her in disbelief. "Weapon? Tool? You are speaking of a Goddess, Bathilde, an old and very powerful Goddess."

"I know that," Bathilde said impatiently. "Would I have called Her up otherwise? She is only here to help the true gods of Saxony regain their power. When that is done I will send Her back whence She came. Unless I still need Her, of course."

"And you think you will be able simply to send Her back? You speak as though you are casting a spell to rid someone of warts. No mortal can control a Goddess."

"You can." Bathilde leaned forward. "I know about you, child. I know far more than you realize, perhaps more than you know yourself. This Goddess is no stranger to the women of your clan. She would be no stranger to you, but for the fact that you and your mother before you have removed yourselves from your heritage."

Sirona grew pale. "How do you know this?"

"From your own mother."

Silence fell between them, a silence shocked and dark with pain. Memories of the woman Bathilde spoke of sprang up before Sirona's inner gaze. Raimond. Lean and dark with sparkling black eyes, as graceful as the cat that seemed so adamant on accompanying Sirona everywhere she went, who was in fact peeking at her now from an unobserved corner of the hall. The image of Raimond was vivid, yet wavering before the flood of remembering.

She had been a distant figure in Sirona's older years, but as a small girl it had not been that way at all. Then Raimond had laughed and held her, had whispered stories of the foremothers and begun to tell her about magic. All of that had changed when her father died. He had been beaten to death, his battered body found in the grove where he often went to pray. Many claimed that Christians killed him, for he was an outspoken man, devoted to the old gods and fiercely critical of the new religion and its influence. He was equally proud of his wife's ancient duties and boasted extravagantly of her powers, particularly if the listeners were Christian.

Whoever the murderers were had never been discovered, but one thing was plain: the change in Raimond. The stories of the foremothers had stopped; the gentle introduction to the arts of magic had dried up, vanishing like dead leaves in a winter wind. The strong and cheerful mother the little girl had known grew silent and withdrawn, a distant figure clothed in fear, and what Sirona later came to recognize as guilt. She continued to teach Sirona about healing, but when she spoke of magic, it was to speak of warnings, of premonitions dark and bloody. She would stare at Sirona, her once-bright eyes dull and haunted. "There is power in you," she would whisper, more to herself than to her daughter. "Too much power . . . but the new is stronger than the old."

The warnings grew along with Sirona. And Sirona took them in, the mother's fear stamping itself upon the child's impressionable mind. By the time she became a woman she believed what Raimond did: that power was not a gift to be used, but an unwelcome secret to be hidden from the eyes of others.

"Do not be angry, child." There was sympathy in Bathilde's tone. "Your mother and I spoke years ago. We were drawn close by what we both planned to do."

"You mean betray the customs of the mothers," Sirona said harshly.

"Yes," answered the noblewoman without evasion. "We spoke of it before she departed with her new husband and I became Erchinoald's lady. And that is what we did, she and I. At the time, my decision caused me to prosper. As for hers, well, I cannot say; I have not seen her since she left these lands. She was a sad woman, your mother, but she was wise. We talked a good deal in the days before she went away."

Sirona turned abruptly away to stare into the flames that crackled merrily about the great hearth logs. The memory of the last conversation with her mother resounded in her ears, each word ringing clear as though it had just been spoken. It had always been the custom in Sirona's family for the position of wisewoman to pass to the firstborn daughter upon her mother's death. Raimond had broken with that tradition. In Sirona's nineteenth summer, she had married again and left these lands to bide with her new husband in his home in Gaul. Thus had Sirona inherited her position, through default, and a painful leave-taking between mother and daughter. Raimond had not only left her duties as wisewoman; she had left her heritage, abandoning forever the Goddess and the traditions of her foremothers.

Watching her on that last day, Sirona had been a jumble of bewilderment, anger, and sad twinges of love. Raimond gazed upon her daughter, her eyes deep and troubled. Try to understand, she had finally said. It is too hard for me to stay. And now that you are grown you can take over my duties. But take care, sweet daughter. Act only as a healer. They will not harm you for doing that. But do no more. Remember what they did to your father for boasting of us. Do not give them the opportunity to do the same to you. The new is stronger than the old. Promise me you will remember that, Sirona. Promise me!

Sirona had promised. She had not seen her mother since. The pain of that day still brought the sting of tears to her eyes.

Bathilde broke in on her reverie. "It was a hard thing,

leaving you as she did. But she is not strong, not in the way you are. She had powers, though, and that was what she was afraid of." The noblewoman paused. "She was the one who told me of the Goddess with the head of a lion, and of Her powers. Sekhmet." She pronounced the name with only slightly less awkwardness than Sirona, but there was deep satisfaction in it.

Sirona's gaze jerked away from the hearth. "My mother told you to summon Her?" she asked in disbelief. "No, it is not possible. She knew nothing of that Goddess." Only Bast had been mentioned in the stories Raimond had told in early, happier times. Young as she had been, Sirona would have remembered any description of such a being.

"She did know about Her. She did not want you to." For the first time Bathilde grew uncomfortable before the wise-woman's dark-light gaze. "Perhaps she should have told you, that is between you and her. But I can tell you this: she was afraid."

"Of Sekhmet? She should have been. As should you."

"She was afraid of Sekhmet. But she was more afraid of you. No," Bathilde corrected herself. "For you." She fell silent, flinched a little at the direct glare that told her Sirona was waiting for her to continue, and went on.

"Your mother was a good wisewoman, though in spite of her skills she did not possess the powers of your ancestors. She knew this. And she also knew enough to recognize real power when she saw it. Especially when it resided in the daughter she had borne and raised. She thought"— Bathilde's eyes looked into the past, remembering her conversations with Raimond— "that the less you knew of the Goddesses of your ancestors, the safer you would be. She sought to protect you, my child."

"I know." Sirona spoke sharply. "She had good reason."

She thought of the cat and the temple he had brought her to. The sacred place of Bast, the Goddess to Whom she was supposed to be dedicated. But her mother had chosen not to serve Bast; she had stepped back in fear, and she had passed that fear on to her daughter. For Raimond, the dedication had lost its luster when her husband had lost his life.

Bathilde shook her head in negation. "She feared the power of Sekhmet; the stories she could remember tell of such terrible things. She thought that if you did not know of Her, you would never be tempted to seek Her out. But what she did was wrong. She kept you in ignorance, told you to throw your birthright away with both hands."

The odor of new bread grew more insistent; breakfast had been laid out, and house folk were pouring ale and helping themselves to hunks of bread and cheese. One of Bathilde's servingwomen approached with a platter of food. She frowned when her mistress waved her away, but obediently went back to the others.

Sirona scarcely noticed the servant, save as a reminder that she must not shout, as she dearly wanted to do. Her attention was fixed on Bathilde. "And the risks? Or do they not matter to you."

"I did as I must." The noblewoman's answer was equally stubborn. "Yes, there are risks, but the rewards are just as great."

Sirona felt her eyes drawn suddenly to the corner. The cat still sat there, unnoticed by the ever-present dogs, who were either too preoccupied with snatching bits of food or under some spell the creature had cast. She stared into the brilliant orange gaze for a moment. "Why did you not call upon Bast?" she demanded. "She is the Goddess of our line, not Sekhmet. My mother surely told you so."

Bathilde's dark eyes burned. Her jaw set with the same stubbornness as her voice. "I needed power instead of kindness," she said.

Sirona looked at her until the other woman's fierce gaze faltered. "You might have had both. Now it is too late."

She turned on her heel and strode from the hall. Still unnoticed by human or animal, the cat leaped after her.

Father Ambrose was young and earnest. In reality he was not as young as he appeared, but his faith gave him a youthfulness that would likely stay with him even when silver wreathed his head. It would be a long while before his hair whitened, though. Now it was a pale brownish blond that blew about his head in wisps. His eyes were bright blue, and his body was as wispy as his hair, though his priest's robes made him look more substantial. The expression on his face was deeply serious.

That day the priest had finally succeeded in being admitted to Bathilde's presence. He had tried before, half a dozen times over these last three weeks, but always without success. Each time he presented himself, the seneschal and one or two of the lady's servingwomen had been there to block his way. The mistress was still not herself, they had explained. The rigors of her ordeal had left her too exhausted to receive visitors, even ones as important as a priest. She was far too weak; she must first regain her strength.

Patient at first with this reasoning, the priest's forbearance soon grew strained. His was God's work, and these many excuses were interfering with that. He had been Erchinoald's priest, and the souls in this manor had been placed in his charge by no less than the bishop who ministered to Charles the Great himself. Under Count Erchinoald that task had been easy; the count was a devout man to whom the Christian well-being of the folk in his charge was as important as it was to his priest. The two men had been close, bound by their loyalty to the king and to their faith.

By contrast, Ambrose had never particularly warmed to Erchinoald's nearest neighbor, Count Haganon, whose lands bordered those of Erchinoald. The big arrogant-tempered noble was not an easy man to warm to, especially when he professed his devoutness. He made a great show of this—too great a show for Ambrose's taste. The abbot of the wealthy monastery endowed by the king seemed to approve, but Ambrose had often thought that the abbot himself was far too fond of the rich life.

The priest preferred to live simply, and he felt that he knew real faith when he saw it. Erchinoald, for instance, was a man whose belief was genuine. Haganon's devotion, on the other hand, was to power and influence, goals which these days, were only achieved by good solid Christians.

Erchinoald's death had been a tragedy, the import of which Ambrose was only now beginning to realize, and not only because of the friendship he had shared with his lord. Death—whether it came at a boar's tusks or in childbed—was commonplace. Baptized and properly Christian, each man or woman could count on going to their reward in the City of Heaven. The priest had said masses for his friend's soul and was confident that Erchinoald was safely residing in Heaven. It was those whom the count had left behind that Ambrose was concerned for.

Things had changed in the manor after Erchinoald's died, far more than they should. The Lady Bathilde held sway now, and while this should have only increased the Almighty Lord's influence, for she was a Christian and a woman, weak and in need of guidance, it had not. Indeed, the opposite seemed to have occurred. Daily prayers were not being held in the manor chapel. This was Bathilde's responsibility, and she was not attending to it. Ambrose knew this because some of the house folk had secretly complained to him.

Ambrose had not needed the counsel of Count Haganon to arouse his concerns; he was uneasy enough as it was. He had accompanied Arn back to Haganon's manor that morning with reluctance. He had to go, of course; it was his priestly duty, not to mention the fact that Haganon's position demanded it. But in spite of his dislike, Ambrose had to agree with everything Haganon had said. There was more than sufficient reason to suspect that the Lady Bathilde was allowing evil influences to overtake her.

The priest brooded on these thoughts as the plump seneschal conducted him through the manor gates and into the hall. He had intended to insist that he see Bathilde, regardless of her excuses, and to force himself into her presence if necessary. It had come as a surprise, even a relief, when his horse was taken off to the stables, servants bowed him inside, and he was ushered to where the lady waited to receive him.

It had not rained again, but the pale light of early morning was darkening as a cool breeze blew clouds over the sky. The clouds had been tattered rags when Ambrose had started out, but by the time he rode up to his destination, they had walled out the colorless sun. The priest hoped any downpours would hold off until he returned home, and if they did not, that he would be invited to stay on. He followed the seneschal into the great hall. Warmth reached out to him from a merry fire of huge logs blazing in the hearth. Ambrose went toward it gratefully, his gaze fastened on the figure in the high seat.

The noblewoman had apparently decided to leave her bed. She was nearly recovered, blooming with the triumph of her motherhood. Her handsome features were bright and glowing, her dark eyes grown vivid again, even the silver in her hair served only to enhance her returned beauty. She wore a rich tunic embroidered with silver threads that blended with the subtle strands of her hair, and she sat in the high seat as if she belonged there, as if she had always belonged there.

The priest, however, was quite oblivious to the lady of the manor's striking appearance. He was bent on his mission; no womanly charms would dissuade him from it. Servants had strewn fresh rushes over the floor and scattered sweet-smelling herbs among them. Ambrose strode through them, rustling the stalks and sending up fragrant odors with every determined stride. His long robe swished about his ankles, and the jeweled cross that hung to his chest gleamed, in spite of the gloomy day.

Halting before Bathilde, Ambrose stared at her with bright blue eyes. "Lady," he said without preamble, and there was both authority and disapproval in his voice. "My congratulations on the birth of your son."

Bathilde inclined her head and started to reply.

Frowning, the priest barreled on, brushing aside the greeting she had started to utter. "But why have no plans been made to baptize him?"

9

BATHILDE HAD BEEN LEFT MORE troubled by the talk with Sirona than she wanted to admit. This was not the way that she had planned things to go with someone she wanted so badly as an ally. Strength she had expected, but not the sweeping anger and sense of warning the wise-woman had exuded. Bathilde had felt herself not in control of the situation. She was not fond of the feeling.

For that reason, she deliberately chose to receive the priest. Sirona might present difficulties, but Father Ambrose was another matter. Him, Bathilde could handle, and she anticipated the meeting almost with relish. She decided to sit in the high seat to receive him. Once that place had belonged to her husband; now it was hers, and she was pleased at the prestige it gave her. The chair was made of precious ebony imported at great cost from far away. It was carved and burnished, and its height set her above the priest so that when he came in he had to look up at her, which pleased Bathilde still more.

She returned his gaze, her own expression carefully neutral. Her voice as she answered him, was neither welcoming nor openly hostile. "Has the church instructed its priests to forgo their manners?" she asked. "If so, then I have not. Good day to you, Father Ambrose, will you take refreshment? On a day such as this, some ale would surely be welcome, or mulled wine perhaps?"

"I"—taken off guard, the priest glared. "My thanks, lady, but no."

Hastily he sought to recover the advantage. Haganon had warned him of the woman's duplicity, but then, what

102

woman was not duplicitous? God had made them in that fashion and surely He had a reason for doing so. But this was not the time to ponder the puzzling aspects of women. The priest fixed himself anew to his purpose. His earnest blue eyes burned bright as the fire in the hearth as he strode closer to the high seat. He waited for Bathilde's dark eyes to drop before his. But the noblewoman's steady gaze refused to falter, a fact that caused the priest great displeasure, though he did not show it.

Instead he made his voice loud and sonorous, as though he were preaching in his church. "This matter is far too important to dilute with pleasant conversation and cups of ale. I am speaking of the immortal soul of your son." With a dramatic gesture, Ambrose touched the cross at his breast. "You have felt the touch of the holy oil and water yourself. Why in the name of our Lord have you denied this blessing to your child?"

Something flickered at the back of Bathilde's eyes. "Nothing," she said, cold and flat, "has been denied my son, nor will it ever be." Her voice softened, her expression resumed its careful serenity. "You need not have journeyed out on such a threatening day to concern yourself with our welfare, Father."

The priest's unhappiness was growing. He bent a deep frown upon the woman in the high seat. It dismayed him that he had to look up at her to do it, for that surely lessened the effect. "I must also bring up the matter of your prayers," he said sternly. "Or lack of them. Count Erchinoald, may he bide in the City of Heaven, faithfully attended mass every day. But since your lord's death, lady, the manor chapel has been silent. Why is this?"

Bathilde regarded him. Truth be told, she actually liked this man, which was unusual, for she had met other priests and found little, if anything, to like about them. But Father Ambrose was an exception. He was a Frank, not a Saxon; all the more reason to despise him, since he was one of the many priests brought in to maintain the forced conversions of Charles's initial campaign in Saxony.

Father Ambrose, though, had won many to him, and he

had done so through kindness, rather than force. He was good-hearted, generous, and devoted to his calling. The house folk, villagers, and farmers had all come to trust him. Many were the times he had brought food and clothes to those who needed them. Equally many were the nights he had sat up with people when they were sick, or attended them when they were dying. His ways were kind, and Bathilde knew that his concern for her soul, in spite of today's demanding disapproval, was genuine.

"I have been praying, good Father," she said honestly. "In my own way. You may believe that."

"And in what way have you been praying? I have spoken with some of your house folk, lady. There are faithful Christians in this house, and they have been forced to attend prayers in the village church because you have not called me to conduct mass."

The priest stepped closer, his blue gaze earnest. "Solitary meditations are all very well, lady, but you have a duty to your servants to keep them on the path of righteousness by your own example. A Christian's devotions must be offered up in a proper house of the Lord. A church, as your husband—blessed be his memory—built for that purpose."

"Else they will not be heard?" Bathilde asked the question softly. An undercurrent had crept into her voice, but Father Ambrose did not hear it.

"Exactly so," he cried, and gave her a pleased look. "I see that you are beginning to understand."

Bathilde gazed over the top of the priest's head. Thoughts pulsed through her mind: of the fierce Goddess she had called up but not yet seen, of the gentler Goddess Sirona had spoken of, and the centuries of devotion given to Them both. Then she thought of the gods and goddesses of her own people, drained of Their power and so terribly weakened by Christianity. They were still waiting, depending upon her.

"There was a time," she said in a musing tone, "when people prayed out in the open, under the trees and the sky. Oh, they gathered together, as they do now. But they were also free to speak with their gods on their own, in private, without the presence of a priest." She looked down, her dark eyes suddenly piercing those of her visitor. "For that is what you wish me to understand, is it not, good Father? That praying is not proper without you there to oversee those prayers?"

Father Ambrose's pleased look had been evaporating as he listened. "Take care, lady," he said in a changed voice. As kind as he was, this noblewoman was speaking in a way the priest could not countenance. "Your words hint of blasphemy. You are talking of older times and heathen practices. Superstition ruled the world then. Evil ran rampant. And yet I stand here listening to you speak of those times as if you yearned after them. What has come over you, lady? It is a priest's holy office to conduct the mass, to offer up the body and blood of Christ to the faithful. Must I remind you of that?"

A beat of silence dropped between them. *Take care,* Bathilde warned herself. It was too soon to start throwing priests out on their ear. She smiled. "Indeed not, Father. I am aware of my duty, and yours. But I thank you for reminding me."

Father Ambrose was not satisfied. "Then you will baptize the child and begin holding prayers in the chapel?" he pursued.

"I will perform the duties that have been laid upon me by the untimely death of my lord," Bathilde answered in a formal voice.

Now the priest was satisfied. "Good." He nodded to himself, absently touching his cross. "After all," he added in an attempt to regain his good humor, "people used to tie offerings to tree branches in an effort to appease their savage gods. But in these modern days, under the wise guidance of Charles the Great, we all know the foolish and dark superstition in that. The offerings blew away in the wind, or animals ate them, and the poor fools thought their prayers had been answered."

"Perhaps," Bathilde said.

The priest stared at her. Something still nagged at him. There was a quality to this meeting that was causing him to

feel vaguely disturbed. But he could also see that little more
would be gained from continuing the interview. He had
achieved the purpose for which he had come, and now
Bathilde was shifting in her chair, fussing with the folds of
her gown, definite signals for him to take his leave. In her
present position of power, there was nothing he could do to
gainsay her.

Irritation washed over his good-natured face, to be followed by a look of pity. "You need to marry again, lady," he
told Bathilde kindly. "Your duties press upon you too heavily, as they would upon any woman, for your sex is not bred
to bear the loads which the Lord has vouchsafed to men."

"I will consider it."

The undercurrent had not left Bathilde's voice. Yet the
priest had still not identified it as the source of his unease.
He was a good man, and as such his world was a simple
one. There was good and there was evil, and a Christian
sought always to stay on the path of good. Ambrose understood and reacted to the words a man spoke aloud, not the
subtleties that lay beneath one's tone of voice. This was one
of the reasons he did not like Count Haganon; the man was
far too subtle for his taste. Now he found himself reacting
the same way to the Lady Bathilde, a woman!

He bowed to the noblewoman, sketched the sign of the
cross in the air to bless her, and walked to the hall entrance.
Pausing in the entrance, he turned back to face her. "The
baptism must take place without delay. The babe needs a
name, and"—he crossed himself—"if some illness were to
befall the infant and he died of it, his soul would remain in
Purgatory forever. Make the preparations, lady, and summon me. I will come at once."

Bathilde inclined her head. "My thanks, Father."

Erect and regal in the high seat, she watched him leave.
The seneschal had been waiting outside at a respectful distance, and not until the voices of the two men and their
footsteps had faded away did Bathilde arise.

"You will have a name," she said to her absent son. "But
it will be a name given you in the old ways."

Standing by the chair, she thought of the foreign Goddess

she had summoned. There were more old ways than the ones that belonged to Saxony. The foreign Goddess was proof of that. The Goddess had promised that She would restore Saxony's ancient Shining Ones who had been forced into an enchanted sleep by the strength of the Christians. And all Bathilde had to do in return was render the lion-headed deity homage. It seemed a fair bargain.

But Bathilde could almost hear Sirona's voice demanding, "What homage will She require of you?" And in her mind's eye she saw the young woman's face, those strangely colored eyes blazing with suspicion and warning.

She smiled ruefully. The gods had truly sent the wise-woman to her after all. "As my conscience," she said aloud.

Closing her eyes, Bathilde pushed aside the image of Sirona, seeking instead an image of the Goddess she had summoned. Nothing appeared behind the veil of her closed eyelids. The fierce and murderous deity with the head of a lioness apparently had no wish to make Herself visible to the mortal who had called Her forth. Bathilde had only heard Her voice, knew of Her appearance only because the Goddess had described Herself to her. She found herself jealous of Sirona. After all, the wisewoman had actually seen Sekhmet, while Bathilde, who was responsible for awakening the Goddess from Her long sleep, had not.

The noblewoman wandered over to the table and helped herself from the tray of untouched refreshments brought in for the priest. It mattered little if she had not yet seen Sekhmet, she told herself. The important thing was that the Goddess was doing as She had been asked.

Bathilde took a goblet of mulled wine from the tray and left the hall. She walked through the corridor, pleased that while her strength was not completely back, she could still move with almost her normal briskness. The great outer doors stood open, and through them she could see the sky. She paused, sipping absently from the goblet of rapidly cooling wine.

Servants brushed back and forth on their chores, murmuring politely as they passed. Bathilde ignored them. Her attention was fixed on the outside. Clouds were boiling up again, and the wind was blowing harsh and heavy from the east. Bathilde smiled. East was the direction of Sekhmet's homeland. The Goddess was indeed listening. She saw the figure of the priest framed against the darkening day. He was standing in the courtyard, waiting for his horse to be saddled and brought out to him. Bathilde drew back so quickly the wine splashed from her goblet. That one she was through talking with. Between them there was nothing further to say.

Ambrose looked unhappily up at the sky. If the weather did not hold, he would be riding back to Count Haganon's manor in another downpour. He glanced impatiently toward the stables, hoping a groom would appear with his horse soon. Instead he saw a tall woman with unbound hair standing by the stable wall. At her feet sat a large black cat. The woman's head was bent toward the cat, and the animal was looking up at her. Both of them were very still, too still, it seemed to Ambrose.

The priest stared with growing intensity. Could this be the woman Haganon had spoken of, the one who had brought the taint of evil to a vulnerable Christian widow? It seemed to him that the two were talking together. But that could not be. Not unless—he touched the crucifix at his chest—the cat was a demon.

"She will not heed me." Sirona made no attempt to conceal her frustration. "She is set upon the idea that Sekhmet will help her and that *she* can control Her. A mortal, thinking that she can influence a goddess, and one not even of her own people!"

"Fool," Mau said. "But then I am not surprised. Mortals in general rarely act with any wisdom. You were unable to sway her at all?"

"I was not. Her ears are shut, and so dazzled is she by her ambitions she can see nothing else."

"Oh, she sees," the cat said darkly. "She sees Sekhmet. And those who see Sekhmet seldom see anything else."

"But that's just it. She has not seen Her." Sirona held

back a shiver. "If she had, I doubt that she would be so confident."

"Sekhmet would not have appeared to Bathilde as She did to you. She is too wise for that. She would tantalize and tease the woman, promise to deliver the things Bathilde desires most of all." The cat's voice had grown darker still. "Such has She done before, and too often, with the greatest of success."

"Then it seems that She will be successful again. Bathilde thinks that Sekhmet will wake the Shining Ones of Saxony." Sirona probed Mau's orange gaze. "Can She do that, cat? What will happen if She does?"

The cat did not answer. An instant later, Sirona saw why. A priest was bearing down upon them. His strides were jerky and purposeful, his eyes narrowed on both her and Mau. Sirona recognized him. He had been Count Erchinoald's priest, as well as tending to all the folk who lived upon manor lands. Obviously, he had come to see Bathilde.

Sirona watched the young priest hurry toward her. She had seen him often, though they seldom spoke. Oddly enough she respected him for that; he knew she was no Christian, but unlike other priests he had never berated her for not being of his faith.

Today that seemed to have changed.

Father Ambrose halted. His blue eyes swept from Sirona to the cat and back again. The wind stirred his wispy hair across his pale forehead. "Wisewoman," he started, "what is happening here?"

Sirona studied him. She was not of his flock, as Ambrose referred to the Christians who worshiped in his church. She owed him no deference, and certainly she was under no obligation to answer questions put to her in so rude a fashion. She was about to tell him so, when Mau rubbed lightly against her ankle. He did not speak, of course, but his meaning was clear. She should not antagonize this priest.

"What," she said bluntly, "are you speaking of?"

Ambrose pointed. "That cat. Where did it come from?"

Sirona gave him a frown, followed up by a shrug. "Why ask me? He is a cat. Doubtless there are many others beside him in a manor so large as this. The Lady Bathilde should be grateful; cats are very useful in keeping away rats."

"They are also of great use to the devil," Ambrose declared passionately. "For they are his agents."

Sirona was finding it difficult to keep her patience. Priests like Ambrose were the reason Bathilde's attendants had panicked when Mau had appeared on the night their mistress gave birth. On the other hand, she reminded herself, it was true that Mau was no ordinary cat. The priest had seen or sensed that he was a creature of magic, and to the priest that would be reason enough to fear him. In his eyes such creatures were always evil.

She looked Ambrose straight in his blue eyes. "Christians seem to find evil in a great many things that are natural," she pointed out. "I do not."

The priest blustered, not quite sure how to respond. "It appears," he said at last, "that you were speaking with this cat. Is that true?"

"Good priest," Sirona said, forcing patience into her voice. "Why are you asking me these questions? Cats are beasts. They do not possess the ability to speak as we do, and even if they did, why would that cause them to belong to your devil?"

"A beast who utters the speech of man is the work of demons!" Father Ambrose's eyes had gone wide with shock. "It is as I feared then. You were having unholy discourse with this creature." He crossed himself and stepped back, his horrified gaze on Mau, who stared back at him with the inscrutable expression any cat can call up at will.

"Priest," Sirona said. "I am not a Christian. I do not answer to you. But I will tell you anyway, that there are no demons here, or any other form of evil."

"We will see." Ambrose raised his hand at Mau and sketched a cross in the air. "Begone, demon creature!" he cried.

The cat did not move.

"Begone," Ambrose cried again. "In the name of the One God and His Only Son, I bid you!"

He was attracting attention. Several slaves who had been engaged in mucking out stalls peeped out of the stable door. A groom led out the priest's horse and stopped in confusion. His eyes darted back and forth between the priest, Sirona, and the cat.

"Father, what is amiss?" he inquired uneasily. The horse sidestepped, as if he, too, sensed the tension in the air.

"Pray with me," Ambrose exhorted him. He knew the groom; he had baptized him and his family three years ago. "Pray for the demon to depart."

Bewildered, the groom stared at him while the horse tugged again at the reins. "Demon?" The man's voice quivered in fear. "What demon?" He looked at Sirona. "Wise-woman, have you seen a demon—?"

"Why ask her?" exploded the priest. "She, a pagan herself, who has rejected the true faith."

The groom's expression turned stubborn. "She has delivered my wife of four healthy babes," he said mulishly. "I care not what gods she prays to. She is a wisewoman, and she has gifts."

Sirona smiled at the man. "There is no demon here, Osbert. Only Father Ambrose and me passing the time of day while he waits for his horse."

Ambrose started to contradict her, then looked about in consternation. The cat was gone. Perhaps he had taken advantage of the groom's appearance to dart away. That would be the obvious explanation—if the cat were only a cat. Ambrose squared his shoulders. There was no such thing as a cat that was only a cat. They were animals sacred to heathens. No good could come of such creatures.

He snatched his gelding's reins from the hands of the groom and swung up into the saddle. Forming the sign of the cross in the air again, he said to the groom, "You have my blessing, Osbert, despite your disobedience. But take good care, and do not neglect your devotions again. You are a simple man, of a simple station. It is for you to listen to those who possess greater wisdom."

He turned his gaze to Sirona. "Reject the temptations of old evil, woman," he said earnestly. "Send the demon from you. Come into the light."

Sirona returned his gaze, not with rancor, but with a genuine and sad wondering. "And who are you," she asked softly, "to decide what the light is?"

Ambrose did not answer. He pulled the gelding's head around and set him into a fast trot toward the manor gates. As horse and rider reached the road the skies opened, and it began to rain.

Haganon yanked a cloak about him and strode out into the courtyard of his manor. "Well?" he demanded. "Did you see her?"

Father Ambrose pulled up his tired horse, and both he and the animal stood drooping under the weight of the storm that had pounded them from the time they left Bathilde's manor. He had not planned to return to Haganon's hall. His dislike of the nobleman had not lessened, and he had not intended to obey the man's order to bring him news of his meeting with Bathilde. But the incident at the stable had changed that.

Wearily, he dismounted, giving his horse a pat on the neck. "I did," he said, his low voice barely audible above the drumming rain.

Haganon squinted at him through the wet gloom of late afternoon. "Speak up, then, priest. What was discussed between you?"

Ambrose frowned. "I will tell you that when you tell me what has happened to the laws of hospitality, my lord. My beast and I are tired. We have spent a good part of the day slogging along muddy tracks, and we are drenched to the bone. He needs a manger of grain and oat hay and a warm stable, and I need bread and meat, a large cup of mulled wine, and a seat close to the hearth-fire. Must I ask for what should be offered without question?"

Chastened, and doubly annoyed because he had been, Haganon roared for grooms. "Can you not see we have a guest," he shouted. "There you all sit, lazing in piles of straw, shaming me, while he stands in the storm. Tend to his horse, or I will kick each of you harder than any horse in my stable!"

The grooms hurried to do his bidding, and Haganon led the priest into the house, where Arn awaited. Other than giving orders to the seneschal for Ambrose's comfort the count said nothing else. Food and drink were brought, and the nobleman sat with a goblet of wine, watching as the priest satisfied his hunger and thirst. Finally, when Ambrose appeared warm and contented, Haganon set down his goblet.

There were always house folk in the hall of a great manor, and Haganon's was no exception. At a word from his lord, Arn went about the hall ordering those clustered around the fire to leave. When the last man-at-arms had gone, Haganon looked at Ambrose and raised an impatient eyebrow.

Ambrose understood. "Bathilde has agreed to have the child properly baptized." He took a deep swallow from his cup and held it out for Arn to refill. "In that I was successful. She will call upon me to perform the rites."

This was not what Haganon had wished to hear. He caught Arn's glance, but quickly turned back to the priest, studying the latter with narrowed eyes. The tale was not fully told yet, Haganon reminded himself. "Yet you do not look pleased, Father," he remarked. "Why is that?"

"I saw something else as well." Ambrose paused, and even Arn could see that he was troubled. "There was a woman by the stable at Bathilde's manor. Mayhap she was the woman you warned me of—"

Haganon leaned forward at once. "Describe her."

Ambrose shrugged. "She was a woman, my lord, as any other." His jaw clenched. "Well, not quite as any other. She was a wisewoman."

"Ah." Haganon slapped his thigh, a gesture of confirmation, as well as rage. The assassins *had* failed! But how could that be? Were the *stria's* powers so great? "Of course," he snarled. "She is a witch."

Ambrose gave him a look. "I would not have named her so from her appearance," he said in a critical tone. "One should not make judgements from appearance alone." He fell silent, thinking. "But there were other signs," he said at last. "And they trouble me deeply. This woman had a beast with her, a cat." He paused again. "Or at least, it had the appearance of being a cat."

Arn broke in. "What else could it be? A spirit—"

Haganon glared the steward into silence. "Go on, good Father," he said to the priest, and motioned for their goblets to be refilled.

"In truth, your man has the right of it." Ambrose nodded at Arn as the seneschal poured more wine into his cup. "Spirits appear in a multitude of forms and shapes to tempt the unwary. I believe this has happened in the house of Lady Bathilde. Darkness has spread its shadow over her and this babe. I did not realize it until I saw what I saw today. You did well to warn me, lord," he added to Haganon, a touch reluctantly. "In God's truth, cats are known as harbingers of evil. And black cats are the worst of all. It was a black cat that the wisewoman had with her."

"And what was she doing with the beast?" Haganon demanded.

Ambrose made the sign of the cross. "It seemed to me," he said very slowly, "that she and the cat were having speech together. The woman as much as admitted it to me. But such a thing cannot be, unless there is great evil in it. Only demons come to men in the shape of animals and speak with human tongue. This is well-known."

Arn promptly crossed himself.

Oddly enough, Haganon had begun to smile. "A demon?" he mused, and set his silver goblet down with a clank. "Yes, I believe you are right, Father. And there is only one way to deal with demons and those who countenance them."

Ambrose regarded him frowningly. "Indeed. And that is to banish the demons while praying for the deliverance of those who have fallen under their spell."

"Yes, yes," Haganon agreed at once. "We must all pray for that. In the meantime, you are tired, Father. Please, accept the hospitality of my hall. The afternoon draws on toward dusk. It makes little sense to ride on. I would be honored if you would lead my household in evening prayers. After the supper meal, my servants will make you a comfortable pallet in front of the fire."

The noble's words made Ambrose aware of how tired he was. He nodded wearily. "A kind offer, my lord, and I thank you for it." He emptied his cup, set it down, and pushed himself to his feet. "With your permission, I must excuse myself to use the privy."

At the count's nod, the priest started out of the hall, bound for the outdoor latrines, but as he reached the wide archway he turned back. His good-natured features were twisted in lines of worry. He had made the long wet ride from Bathilde's manor sunk deep in thought. His conviction that Sirona was having dealings with a demon had not lessened, yet Ambrose was not a man who liked to be used. He had become all too aware that for some reason Count Haganon bore a grudge against Sirona, a grudge he intended the priest to help him satisfy. That did not sit well with Ambrose. To use a man of God in pursuit of one's personal animosity was to misuse God Himself.

The priest fixed his gaze on Haganon. "Wisewomen are not evil," he said firmly. He addressed his words to both master and servant, but his attention remained focused on the nobleman, ignoring the fact that Haganon was suddenly regarding him with narrowed eyes. "Their duty is all-important: that of bringing life into the world. But we must keep in mind that they are women. And though it is fitting that birth be women's business, women are notoriously vulnerable to pagan influences."

The count shifted in his chair and seemed about to speak, but with uncharacteristic assertiveness, Ambrose overrode him. "Far better would it be were all wisewomen good Christians, but they are not. We must help them find their way to God's grace—"

Scowling, Haganon shook his head, no longer willing to be gainsaid. "Be that as it may, Father, this wisewoman is evil, and dangerous, as all evil is dangerous. She must be destroyed." His voice was steely with determination, and he turned a penetrating gaze on Ambrose. "Would you, a servant of God, deny the punishment that must be visited upon all heathens?"

"Beware, my lord." Father Ambrose met the noble's eyes with a cold blue stare of his own. "You tread upon God's ground now. It is not your place to level judgement or punishment; nor is it mine. Heed me when I say this to you: do not meddle your mortal man's affairs with those of Heaven."

He turned on his heel and strode from the hall.

Haganon watched the priest's departure impassively. Arn, however, was not so sanguine. "Lord," he said nervously, "perhaps it would be wise to consider what he says. He is a man of God, after all—"

"Silence," Haganon thundered. His impassive mien was a veneer put on for Ambrose's benefit. With the priest out of earshot the veneer split apart like shards of weak pottery, allowing the simmering rage to blaze forth. "Presume you to do my thinking for me? The priest is a tool, a means to rid me of that accursed woman and cast a pall over Bathilde and her ambitions, as well."

He leaped to his feet and stomped over to the fire. "A pox on those fools I hired; may they both roast in hell. Had they done their job rightly, that bitch of a wisewoman would have been pulled from my side like the thorn she is. And yet"—his anger was slowly cooling as he spoke—"mayhap it is better this way." He stared into the flames, and a tiny smile lit his craggy face. "There is a certain elegance to bringing our Lord into it." He blessed himself. "Yes, better indeed."

Arn, too, crossed himself. With the change in his lord's mood the seneschal felt emboldened to speak. "In truth, we must do the will of God," he murmured. Privately he was not at all convinced it was the will of God rather than the will of Haganon that was being discussed, but he had no intention of voicing that sentiment aloud.

Haganon gestured for Arn to follow him and paced swiftly from the hall to the doorway. Peering out at the slanting rain and gloomy sky, he nodded. "There is still enough daylight left for messengers to be sent out to my allies. See to it, Arn. Tell the riders to inform the nobles that they are to attend me tomorrow after the bells ring for morning prayers."

Father Ambrose had concluded his visit to the privy and was returning across the yard, head down against the driving rain. Haganon watched him approach. "We are good and loyal Christians," he said. "Not only my household, but all the nobles who have allied themselves with me. That will be important."

"Why?" asked Arn.

The slight smile came and went again. "Because," Haganon replied, "there is not a more devoted Christian in Christendom than Carolus himself."

The next morning Haganon informed the other Christian nobles of all that had occurred. They listened in silence, a few blessing themselves as Ambrose's encounter with the wisewoman and the demon cat was described in florid detail by the count.

"There is only one other thing to do now," he told them.

"And what is that?" asked white-haired Aelisachar.

Haganon smiled. "It is time," he said, "to pay a visit to the king."

10

I WILL BRING DARKNESS OVER THEIR land.

Sekhmet's voice was spoken flame. Her red-sheathed form was a swirl of flame and purpose. She stood atop Bast's mountain, Her golden eyes burning up into the silvery sky. The long fangs in the lioness's mouth gleamed ivory as She widened Her jaws in a delighted smile.

Her Sister's temple glimmered pink; brighter than it had been when Sirona had been there. Its graceful columns danced, casting and drawing shafts of light from the Cat-Headed Goddess, Who had left Her sanctuary to stand beside Sekhmet. From within the courtyard the many cats were wakeful, staring at the two deities with fascinated, unblinking eyes. Not in living memory had the Sisters met together in anything other than discord or outright enmity. This new peace, though wary on both Their parts, was astonishing, and much to be watched.

Unlike Sekhmet, Bast was not smiling. Her long green eyes were deep and glowing with thought. Yet, though She was not gloating with exultation, Her demeanor was no less purposeful than that of Her Sister.

You have done that before, She said dryly. *Or have You forgotten?*

I have not. Sekhmet's voice was suddenly heavy with anger. *But that was a different place and a different time. We were at war then.*

She bared Her teeth in a soundless snarl and fell silent. Memories scalded Her as She remembered the island of Eire and an angry, grief-stricken priestess. Daughter of Bast, She growled in Her thoughts. A Daughter who had forsaken Bast for Her Sister and had then betrayed that new loyalty for the old.

She caught Herself, snatching back Her exultant mood. *Well*, She said in a changed voice, *that, too, has changed. No longer are We at war, Sister. The sleep that came over all of Us Old Ones showed Me that We have a common enemy. Allowing ancient grudges to stand in the way of that is a luxury none of Us can afford.* Her yellow eyes blazed into the jewel-green eyes of Bast. *You agree, do You not, My Sister?* She pressed.

Bast looked at Sekhmet until the giant lioness head turned abruptly away. *Know this,* She said quietly. *It was not My doing that You were awoken from the Sleep of Being Forgotten. But what has been done cannot be undone, and in truth, I am not terribly sorry. I can see the sincerity in You, Sekhmet; not since the day Osiris called upon You in a fit of rage to destroy all humankind in the Black Land have I seen You so sincere.*

Sekhmet let out a hissing growl that in Her passed for a laugh. *Indeed. That was a joyful drink of blood, until You all tricked Me with that lake of wine. By My head, those were the good old days. Dare I hope they come again?*

No, Bast said shortly. *You dare not.* Suddenly She seemed to loom over Her Sister. *Do not mistake Me, Sekhmet. Over the ages You have forgotten that it was I Who slew the snake that menaced the world before the days of the first Pharaohs. I, too, have warrior strength in My blood; I always have. But unlike You, I have possessed too much wisdom to use it. I only turn to it now because I see that there is no other choice.*

No other choice? Sekhmet's whiskers curled. *There has ever been a choice and You have ever chosen wrong. You have finally achieved wisdom by realizing that We are in a battle for Our lives. We have been from the first moment that new God declared He would tolerate no Immortal Ones save Himself in the world of mortals.*

He is not new, Bast said reflectively. *But the Christians have made Him so. It is unfortunate that I did not understand that before.*

Sekhmet looked at Her curiously. *Why? Would You have done differently? Allied Yourself with Me sooner perhaps?*

The Cat-Goddess's gossamer-clad shoulders raised in a shrug. *I doubt it, for there was too much history between Us. But the reasons no longer matter. They are the past. It is the future We must concern Ourselves with.*

Indeed. Sekhmet's joyousness promptly returned. *You and I are only the beginning, Sister. Soon all the Ancient Ones will be awakening. When We are done, the Christians will be forgotten, and their God will be the One Who sleeps. Only We will take care to see that He never wakes. Now, to start with I will—*

You will act with care. Bast's melodic voice rang with warning. *We all must. This strife is between Gods. Mortals will be hurt; sadly, that is unavoidable. But I will not see more of them suffer than is necessary.*

Sekhmet pretended to ignore this. *The curse I brought to that foreign land of Eire did not work as I had expected,* She said pointedly. *But for a time it was very effective; even You will admit that, Sister. Without You to oppose Me, it will be effective again. Indeed, I have already begun. Since the mortal Bathilde called to Me I have been sending rain down upon her country. She asked for something to bring discredit upon the Christian God—*

And what better means than to devastate the growing season. Bast gazed upward at the sky of Her realm. Darkness was spreading spidery fingers over the silver shimmer of that broad tapestry. It was subtle, but to Her eyes unmistakable. Not since the long-ago days of the first Pharaohs had She seen that shadowy hue. It presaged the decision She had already made: that Sekhmet would not be alone in bringing disaster on the mortals of Sirona's land. Unlike the Lion-Headed One, though, the prospect gave Bast no joy. She brought Her gaze back to Sekhmet. *Yes,* She said. *I see.*

I am pleased that You agree. Sekhmet gave Her Sister Goddess a toothy grin. *But My powers are not what they were. The Sleep weakened Me, else I would have brought ice and snow instead of rain, and summoned My Bau as well.* Her grin widened. *That will come in time, as I recover My strength.*

I will add My powers to Yours, Bast said, and then cautioned, *remember this, though, My Sister, You may love death, but I do not. The season of ice and snow will come soon enough in its own time without Our interference. The storms We wreak upon the land will bring famine, and in its wake, anger toward the Christian God. That will be enough.*

And Your latest Priestess? A sneer hid itself in Sekhmet's voice. *She, who has forgotten so much, she has not the wisdom to be priestess to any goddess, much less to You. What are Your plans for her?*

Bast ignored the other Goddess's tone. *She will join Us,* She said calmly.

You sound very certain of that. Sekhmet regarded Her with dubious anger. *But so far the woman has shown no inclination to do so. And the mortal Bathilde needs her.*

A brief silence fell. What Sekhmet said was true. Bast knew there was no point in contradicting Her.

We need her as well. Sekhmet was no longer sneering. The expression on her leonine features was grim. *It is through her that the other gods will awaken. Bathilde has not the strength to do it alone. She is only one part of the link. Your priestess must complete the chain. Only when she combines her powers with Bathilde's can the gods of Kemet and the gods of Saxony join forces. Without her, Our own awakening will have been for nothing. You know this.*

I do, said Bast. Her green eyes wandered back to the sky. The dark fingers had thickened and grown longer. Once begun, how swiftly it spread, She thought. *The deeds are already set in motion,* She said aloud. *Mau will see to the rest.*

Mau. Sekhmet's fangs shone in disgust. *You place too much faith in that creature. But very well, I will wait to see what success he has with that mortal of Yours. In the meantime, let Us go to work, Sister. The mortals of this Saxon land have seen little of Our power as yet. Together We will bring rain and cold wind so great that the crops do not sprout and the newly born beasts die in their byres. No harvest will there be, for the grain will never have grown. Let the people go to their churches and priests then, and pray. It will avail them nothing. Their God will not hear them. He cannot. He has grown lazy and confident.*

As We once did. Ceasing Her perusal of the sky, the Cat-Goddess brought a stern gaze to bear on Her Sister. *We must not make that mistake again. It was Our complacency that allowed Christianity to sweep over the world in the first place.*

Sekhmet returned Her stare. *You would do well to listen to Your own words, Sister. Always have You loved mortals too dearly. Now do You see what it has cost You.*

The same as it has cost You, Who have never loved them, Bast retorted.

And yet, truth was there in Sekhmet's words, burning cold and inescapable as the Lion-Goddess's anger. Compassion, healing, the joy of life, those were the hallmarks of Bast's worship. And those were precisely the things She must set aside. It would be a task as difficult as anything She had ever faced in the uncounted eons of Her life.

But when the Others awoke and Their powers aligned as they were meant to, then would the balance and harmony of old return. This laying aside of Her nature would only be for a short time.

Or so the Cat-Goddess told Herself.

She hoped that She was right.

Driven from his attempt at finding cover, the exhausted stag darted into the wide meadow to run for his life once more. Sensing that the chase was almost at an end, the hounds pursued their quarry with wild eagerness. Behind them the hunters broke through the trees and thundered onto the meadow, driving their lathered horses forward. In the lead, mounted on a nervous big bay stallion, rode Carolus Magnus: king of Gaul, Saxony, and most of the Christian world.

The stag was close to being brought to earth. Carolus, experienced huntsman that he was, scented it as keenly as the dogs did. His teeth gleamed white through his light brown beard as he raised his spear in readiness. A laugh of pure joy burst from his throat, a roar that broke over the sound of the dogs. The nobles riding with him held back their horses. With the exception of a few honored guests, the majority of these men belonged to the king's favored war band. They knew that their lord must, as always, be the one to make the kill.

The end came swiftly. The hounds had formed a circle around the stag, bringing him to bay at last. Within that ring of snapping, barking dogs the stag defended himself with the determination of the doomed. His crown of antlers was impressive, and he used them with formidable skill as he spun and whirled to keep those fierce jaws from hamstringing a hind leg and thus bringing him down.

Carolus brought his plunging stallion in close to the desperate commotion. He was no longer laughing. His hazel eyes were narrow as he sighted along the spear and watched for the moment to strike.

The stag was panting, his pink tongue revealing itself in quick glimpses. Grimly, he swiped at two dogs with his antlers, spun about, and lifted his head high as though to get his bearings. The spear sliced through the air. The stag gave an oddly human shriek as the point buried itself deep within a sleek reddish brown flank. The graceful strong legs that had carried him so bravely on the long chase suddenly were as clumsy as those of a newborn fawn. He toppled to the grass, and the eager hounds swarmed over him, concluding the process of death with far less finesse than the single well-thrown spear.

Now it was the turn of the hound-master and his assistants to ride in and whip the dogs away from their fallen quarry. It was no easy task; the pursuit had been fierce, and the blood of the hounds was up. But soon enough they drew back, and the assistants dismounted to truss the stag, cut down a stout sapling, strip it of its leaves, and prepare a pole to carry the prize back to the king's hall.

Surrounded by his nobles, Carolus sat his panting horse

and waited for the task to be done. He was marvelously content. Few things were more deeply satisfying than a hunt that had ended well. He flashed his familiar merry grin at the customary cries of "well done," and "good clean kill, my lord." Such compliments were customary and expected, but in his case, they were also true. Carolus was an excellent huntsman, and he rode out on the chase often. Aside from his passion for war, hunting was the king's favorite pastime.

Carolus glanced about, and his hazel gaze lit upon one of the nobles. "Fine sport, eh, Count Haganon?" he shouted. He had to strain to make himself heard above the din of barking dogs, for his voice, though imposing, was not naturally loud and did not carry well. "It's not every day you see a stag die as bravely as that one did. What think you of our forests and game here in my fair lands of Aachen?"

Haganon smiled the broadest smile he was capable of, delighted at this opportunity to display his most courtly manner. "A rare chase, indeed, my lord," he replied loudly. "Gaul is a fine country, and your royal estate is the fairest of all. Its forests are deep, and its game fleet. I thank you for allowing me the opportunity to ride with you this day."

"Hmm." Carolus studied his guest thoughtfully. "Yet the hunting in your own lands is fine as well, as I know, having visited you there. You did not ride all the way from Saxony to hunt our Gaulish stags. Something is preying upon you."

His voice was still raised and the other nobles were listening. Haganon was not concerned about the other guests hearing; they were part of his own war band, allies he had carefully chosen to accompany him to Aachen. But he had no wish to discuss his business in front of the king's personal war band, men who all had secrets and goals that might run contrary to those of Haganon.

"My lord," he said carefully. "There is."

Carolus was famed for his shrewdness, as well as his tact, and he displayed that quality now. "Then come," he said. "Ride along with me back to the palace. We will talk."

It was a high honor to be singled out for the king's attention in such a fashion, and no one was more aware of that than Haganon. He hid his satisfaction beneath a calm, respectful exterior as he waited for Carolus to trot forward.

The huntsmen were almost finished with the task of trussing the stag and tying the carcass to a long carrying pole. Dogs milled around, sniffing the air and whining hungrily at the scent of blood. The other nobles were grouped together, discreetly sharing drinks of wine from several small flasks drawn from their saddles. Each man kept an eye on the king and was careful not to take too many swigs, for Carolus did not drink heavily himself—and did not approve of it in others.

The king waved a hand at them. "Follow us back with the stag, my lads," he shouted. "All of us will feast heartily on fresh venison this night."

He expertly put his stallion into a canter and headed back across the meadow toward the trees. Haganon threw a meaningful look at the nobles who had come with him from Saxony, and cantered after the king.

By the standards of his time Carolus Magnus was the very image of a ruler. He towered over most other men, a broad imposing figure whose muscle was slowly beginning to turn to fat. But Carolus's steadily increasing girth only added to his kingly appearance, though he himself sometimes favored his belly with rueful glances. He did so now, as he led the way into the trees and slowed his horse to a walk.

"I despise physicians," he said conversationally. "They tell me that my stomach ailments are caused by too many roasted meats. I must stop eating the flesh of the game I kill roasted and take it boiled in stews. Pah. What sort of man eats his meat boiled in stews? Women and children and the old and sick eat sop food like that, not kings."

Haganon started to agree, but then it struck him that here was the perfect opening to draw the conversation toward the reason he had come. "I eat only roasted meat myself," he declared. "And I always have. Physicians rarely know of what they speak." He lowered his voice. "But there are those, my lord, who profess to heal who are far worse than any physician."

The king's light-colored eyes fixed on him. "What are you trying to say, Count Haganon?"

"Well"—Haganon cleared his throat— "at least the physicians who attend you are all good Christians. I am speaking of those who are not."

Carolus nodded sagely. "The pagan evil is everywhere, waiting to rear its hideous head whenever we of the true faith grow lax. I have spent my life bringing the light of Heaven to those who dwell in darkness, and I will continue to do so."

Haganon crossed himself. "Well do I know it, lord. That is why I traveled all the way from my manor to beg for your attention." He paused dramatically. "I need your help, great king." And he paused again.

Dramatic pauses had little effect on Carolus; he was too much a master of them himself. "Speak up, man," he said impatiently. "We'll be back at my hall and the venison roasted to a crisp before you get to the point."

Haganon hastily sought to regain the ground he might have lost. "You know that your man Count Erchinoald has died," he began.

"Yes, yes," came the answer. "A good way for a man to die. Almost as brave as if he had died in battle. I have approved his widow to rule over those lands in his stead, at least until she finds herself another husband. A husband," he added, "whom I will approve, of course."

"That," Haganon said heavily, "is the problem. The widow."

"Problem?" The king's eyes grew more piercing. "There is nothing unusual in a widow managing her husband's lands. I have allowed it before. And from all reports, the Lady Bathilde is a fine Christian woman. I would have had my doubts otherwise."

"But that is precisely the point." Haganon leaned forward in the saddle. "Bathilde is not a Christian."

"She is." Carolus did not like to be contradicted. "One of my own bishops baptized her. Erchinoald insisted on it. He knew full well that I would not give permission for them to wed unless Bathilde found salvation in the true faith."

Haganon responded hastily. "That is true, my lord. However, it was also Erchinoald who held her in check and influenced her in the ways of the true faith. Now that he is gone, so is his influence." The count warmed to his subject. "Women need the control of men. Without it they are prone to all the evil forces of paganism. That is what has happened to Erchinoald's widow. She has gone back to the old ways. Worse: she has taken a priestess of those old ways into her house."

Carolus slowed his horse. Turning in the saddle, he fixed the other man with his piercing stare. "A *stria*?" The king's voice was low and dangerous. "Erchinoald's widow has welcomed a witch into the Christian household of her husband?"

Haganon smiled inwardly. This was going exactly as he had hoped. Carolus Magnus's passion for bringing the word of God to the heathen—by force if necessary—was legendary; it went hand in hand with his enthusiasm for war. Stamping out paganism was the king's personal obsession. There was no better way to arouse his anger than to warn him of former pagans who had slid back into the ancient paths of evil. He met Carolus's penetrating gaze, summoning up an aggrieved expression, as though it pained him to have to speak of these matters.

"I am sorry, my lord," he said with feigned sincerity. "But I fear that Bathilde's faith was never strong to begin with. Many believe that she accepted Christianity only so that she might better her position in the world by becoming the wife of a great lord. You will recall"—he paused delicately—"that she was naught but a slave in Erchinoald's household when his eye fell upon her."

"By the blood of Jesus," the king exploded. "The stubbornness of these heathens is like a brushfire. You stamp it out in one place, only to have it spring up in another."

Startled by the sudden loud voice, the stallion lunged forward. Carolus let him gallop down the narrow track for a few strides before pulling him back into a walk. Haganon urged his own horse to catch up, and when the two men rode side by side again, he started to address his king.

But Carolus made a sharp gesture for silence. The look he bent on Haganon was shrewd and cold. "I do recall that the woman was a slave. That matters not. All who come to the Lord's grace are equal in His eyes. The question I have is this: why are you so interested in bringing this matter to my attention?"

Haganon sought to look affronted. "I, lord? It is my duty."

Carolus waved this aside. "All men act according to duty, or their idea of it. But all men have their interests, as well. Tell me, Count Haganon, what is yours?"

Haganon hesitated. He was nonplussed. Things had been going so well, and now all of a sudden they were out of his control. Should he answer honestly, or dissemble? And whichever one he chose, to what extent should he carry it? He decided to compromise. He had known better than to underestimate Carolus, yet he had almost fallen in the trap of doing so. The man was far too skilled a ruler to be so easily led.

"Yes, I have my own interests," he said at last. "But they are not incompatible with yours, my lord. Bathilde has betrayed the true faith. In her hands the holdings of Erchinoald have taken on an air of ungodliness. She recently bore a son, and despite the pleas of Father Ambrose, the priest you yourself sent to our area, she has refused to have him baptized. Worse, there is the priestess, as I have told you. She is indeed a *stria,* the very embodiment of evil. Something must be done about her."

"And about the Lady Bathilde, who has taken her in." The king's eyes had lost not one whit of their shrewdness or their coldness. "You have a grudge against them both, don't you, Count?"

Haganon's pride was stung. "They are women," he said shortly. "Only men are worthy of grudges."

Carolus chuckled. "You have not met my wife or daughters." His merry features sobered. "Yet you have spoken the truth. The situation must be dealt with. I thank you for bringing it to my attention."

He thought a moment, as the horses slogged through a streamlet that ran across the track. "I am not without compassion," he said at length. "Bathilde has lost her husband, and that is a grievous thing, especially since she has now borne his son." He glanced sharply at Haganon. "The child is Erchinoald's, is he not?"

Haganon considered. It would have given him great pleasure to answer in the negative, but that would not be wise. Bathilde's behavior as far as marriage vows went had always been irreproachable. He could try to plant the seeds of doubt; however, there was not one man he could single out. "Yes," he said reluctantly. "I believe he is."

Carolus nodded. "It could be that she is undone by her grief. In such a state she could be easily influenced. Women are creatures who are governed by emotion. Yes." He nodded his head emphatically. "That is surely what has happened. We must give her a chance to return to God by removing the evil that has swayed her."

Haganon saw where this was going, and he was not entirely pleased. "But my lord, it was Bathilde's doing to take the *stria* into Erchinoald's household," he protested.

"Not if the *stria* compelled her to do it. Remove the influence, and the Church may find a precious soul restored to Her fold. That must be our first task."

The king's voice was firm. He had made up his mind, and, as was his habit, once he had done so, there was no changing it. Haganon resisted the impulse to argue further. After all, he told himself, he was still gaining part of what he had come for.

"I am at your command, my lord," he said, and loosed one hand from the reins to cross himself with a pious gesture. "How may I and my men serve you in freeing the Lady Bathilde from the evil that has overcome her?" He knew, of course, but he judged it better to allow the king to tell him.

Carolus threw him an impatient glance. "Need I explain the obvious? Go you to Erchinoald's hall and drive the *stria* forth. I will send additional men, along with Alcuin, my wisest bishop, to strengthen your force. Allow nothing to dissuade you. It is certain that Bathilde, and likely the witch herself, will try to prevent you from accomplishing your task. You must remain strong."

"I will," Haganon assured him with a fierce grin. "I will."

Carolus frowned. "Do not treat this lightly," he warned. "It is dangerous work I am setting you. The powers of the old ways are strong. The *stria* will not release Bathilde easily. She will probably seek to harm you and your men, even kill you, if she can. Your own faith must be strong; stronger than the dark magic wielded by this witch."

"We will be strong, I promise you. The *stria* will not defeat us."

"Good. You are brave to accept this task, Count Haganon. You have the gratitude of your king."

Haganon's mind raced, thinking ahead to the future. The gratitude of Carolus the Great was no small thing, and both men knew it. But Haganon had journeyed to Aachen with the hope that he would be given permission to dispossess Bathilde and take possession of her lands. This talk had not gone quite as he had anticipated; yet it was far from a failure.

Once Sirona, that troublesome wisewoman, had been disposed of, Haganon could make another journey to the royal palace. He was already planning it in his swift-moving thoughts. He would inform the king of his success, and of Bathilde's continued betrayal of her husband's faith. The next step could then be taken, and Carolus would grant him what he desired. What else could he do? He would not only be grateful for the destruction of yet another heathen priestess, he was also canny enough to realize the wisdom of supplanting a fallen Christian woman with a strong male ally.

The horses broke out of the forest. Ahead lay the neatly laid-out fields and gardens of the palace estate. Dusk was falling, and the palace was beginning to glow through the hazy light as servants lit candles and oil lamps. Carolus's stallion tried to break into a canter and jerked his head in annoyance when the king kept him at a walk. Normally, Carolus would have allowed the horse to gallop back to the palace stables, but the king's attention was on his companion.

"What other guidance may I offer about what lies before you," he inquired. "If you have more questions, Count, now is the time to ask them."

"I have only one." Catching the irritation of the king's bay, Haganon's stallion jigged impatiently, and with equal impatience, Haganon checked him. "What do you wish me to do with the *stria?*"

Carolus looked at him in surprise. "Kill her. What else does a man do with a pagan witch?"

Releasing the reins, he gave the bay his head and let the stallion gallop down the path toward home.

Haganon paused a moment before allowing the eager chestnut to follow. "What else," he repeated, and smiling, sent the stallion racing forward.

11

THE COLD WET WEATHER CONTIN-
ued, all the more fearful because it
was unseasonable. Winter was all
but over. It should have been a time
of warmth, sun, heat, and the smell
of newly growing things. Instead the
heavy damp odor of rain predomi-
nated every crack and fissure in the
land of Saxony. The storms came and went without letup.
They were accompanied by winds that slashed at the tender
stalks of barley and oats, rye and pease until the exhausted
plants lay flattened and lifeless in fields of mud, their roots
torn from the rich soil.

The new grass that should have been nourishing cattle,
sheep, horses, and all their young became submerged under
puddles of water that slowly widened into ponds. The animals grew thin, their ribs protruding from scrubby coats
and their hooves soft from standing in water and mud.
There was no hay to give them: it had all been used up in
the winter, and the newly planted hay had met a similar fate
as the other crops, drowning in the steady onslaught of rain
long before it was ready to be harvested. Only the pigs that
ran semiwild in the woods managed to find food, rooting in
the forest floor as they always had. They alone thrived, but
cattle, sheep, and horses could not eat pork, and the meat
that would eventually be gotten from the pigs would not be
enough to sustain all the people who needed it.

"The old gods have sent this weather," Bathilde said to
Begga, watching as the wet nurse gave suck to her son.
"They are angry at being forgotten, and this is how they
show their displeasure."

A frown creased the nurse's good-natured face. "Lady,"

she said nervously, and blessed herself with the Christian symbol of faith, "it is not meet to speak of such things."

"Is it not?" Bathilde's dark eyes were unblinking. "Things will get worse," she said. "Wait you and see."

Things did.

New storms lashed the fields of Bathilde and all other landholders, driving the people who made their living from those lands into increasing dismay. Begga the nurse had conveyed her mistress's words to the rest of the house folk, as Bathilde had known she would. The majority of the folk were Christian, and those who were not had learned to keep that knowledge to themselves. But as the rains continued they began to grow bolder. Famine loomed on the near horizon, and in the face of such a nightmare, speaking of the old faith no longer seemed to carry the threat it once had.

Bathilde did not need to hear her servants talking to know that others were echoing her words to Begga. As the rain pelted down, she became the only person in her hall to go about her duties with a slight smile upon her face. It made people, who were already uneasy even more apprehensive, to see their mistress so serene. Given the circumstances, it was unnatural, as unnatural as the circumstances themselves.

Bathilde's serenity was remarked upon in detail, though not to her face. It was her joy at having borne a healthy boy child, folk whispered. And why should she not be joyful, when it had seemed that both she and the babe would die? The loss of Count Erchinoald was balanced out by her having produced an heir. Surely, that was why she smiled.

And adding to that, the Christian servants insisted, was the visit from Father Ambrose a few days ago. A baptism would be held for certain, and then the world would return to normal. The rain would stop. Crops could be salvaged, perhaps even new seeds sown and harvested in enough time to save the land from famine.

But other voices contradicted them, in increasingly bold tones. There is another reason for this rain, they said. And it will not be set right by the baptism of a Christian child.

Caught between Christian voices and pagan, Isaac the

trader allied himself with neither. As a Jew he could accept the Christian version of God no more than he could the pagan. As a trader he could not continue on his travels, for the constant rains had turned the roads into a sea of mud. Delayed in Bathilde's manor with all his goods, he was still regarded as a welcome guest. The house folk bartered with him, eager to obtain shimmering bolts of cloth, finely crafted tools, exquisite jewelry, soft leather shoes, and an assortment of other marvels. They listened eagerly to his tales of the many places he had seen during his journeying. He, in turn, listened to them murmur about their worries and fears, made a fine profit, and kept to himself the dark magic he had seen.

Why he did so was not clear: not to him, and especially not to his young nephews. Nevertheless, in spite of their protests, he sternly demanded of them the same silence he maintained himself. Privately, he was convinced that the strange weather had been brought by the evil he had witnessed. How could it be otherwise? The memory of that hideous apparition with the body of a woman and the head of a beast would scald his mind until the day he died. But what would happen to him and his kin were they to speak of it? These were foreign matters. They had naught to do with him.

On the other hand, he was certain that God had directed him to save Sirona from the assassins and had then brought him to this manor. Was there another purpose for him to serve? There must be, else, why would the Holy One have allowed him to see what he had on that dreadful night?

The questions gnawed at Isaac, hovering just below the surface of conscious thought, as he made his morning prayers, discussed the day's business with his nephews, and went about his trading. As for Sirona: the woman had disappeared. Two weeks and a day had passed with no sign of her or the unnatural cat that had accompanied her.

"Thanks be to God," said Avrum, the eldest of Isaac's nephews. "She must have gone back to the place of the demon that appeared that night, and the cat with her. The evil is gone. Let all of us pray that the woman does not return, for she will surely bring that terrible creature back with her."

Isaac regarded him. "The woman may be gone, Avrum, but the evil is not." He gestured around him. "Where has this rain come from? The crops die in the fields, the pastures lie under mud and water, drowning the grass for the beasts, and the people here speak of famine. None of these things were happening before. What else do you think could have caused them?"

Avrum was only sixteen. His understanding of such matters had already been taxed to the limit. But his memory was sharp. "If that is true, Uncle, then why have you sworn us to silence about what we saw?" He shivered, and for a moment the terror reflected in his eyes was vivid, as if the apparition were still standing in front of him. "We must tell others, the Lady Bathilde, in particular—"

"No." Isaac himself was not sure why he was so adamant. It made him think, made him want to explain, to himself as much as to his nephew. But he found himself fumbling for words, uneasiness stirring within him as he, too, remembered that hideous and towering figure. "You must say nothing, Avrum," he muttered at last. "As your elder it is for me to decide when, to whom, and, indeed, even whether that night will be spoken of. Now come, it is time to lay out our goods for the day's trading."

He marched off, beckoning Avrum to follow. But though he refused to speak of it any further, the conversation stayed with Isaac all that day. The rains stayed, too, driving and slashing at the battered fields and pastures. People came to peruse the remaining trade goods, but their voices were subdued and their faces creased with worry. By dusk, when the last customer had gone and the bells were ringing to announce evening prayers for the Christians, Isaac had come to a decision.

Leaving his nephews to pack up, the trader went in search of the Lady Bathilde. Ordinarily he would have gone to the chapel, where the house folk always gathered at this time, but Isaac had listened well these last few days, and he knew that his hostess had stopped attending prayers, at least the Christian ones. He found her in the solar, gazing out at the darkening sky. To his relief, she was alone; they could not have this talk were it otherwise. She was standing in profile, and Isaac saw that there was an odd smile on her lips. Knowledge was in that smile, as if her eyes could pierce the wind-driven clouds, and what she saw pleased her.

A curious chill ran through Isaac. He spoke hesitantly. "Lady."

She turned at once, the smile vanishing into an expression of polite courtesy. "Ah, Isaac the trader. I hear your business has been very good."

Isaac inclined his head. "Lady, it has. At this rate, my stock of wares will soon be depleted. I fear that when it is, and if this evil weather does not clear, I may no longer be a welcome guest in your hall."

His use of the word evil was deliberate. He watched the handsome face of the woman before him carefully to see her reaction.

"All guests are welcome in my house," Bathilde said. "It is not your doing that the roads are impassable because of this rain."

There was a silence.

"Do you know whose doing it is, then?" Isaac asked at last.

Bathilde looked at him. "Do you?" she countered.

The moment had come. Isaac could not contain his shivering. Would the apparition blast him into ashes for speaking of it, as it had those two unfortunate men, or perhaps even more frightening, would Bathilde summon her men-at-arms as soon as she heard his tale and call for his death? He swallowed hard, drawing upon his courage, and above all, upon his faith in his God.

"Lady," he began, and swallowed again, "I think I do. But I fear to speak of it, for I am a stranger here, and it is all too common that strangers are held to blame when misfortune befalls a place. I have traveled widely, and I know this to be true."

Bathilde regarded him with piercing black eyes. "And

yet, you have sought me out. Either you are very foolish, trader, or very brave, to take such a chance."

Isaac sighed. "Likely I am both. But I am here, and so I will speak."

He plunged into a description of what he had seen on that fearful night. The words were awkward, halting, filled with echoes of the terror he had felt. He was not a man given to flowery and vivid explanations; those were not his gifts. But he was an honest man, and neither did he exaggerate. Not that he would have needed to. The only thing he left out was the presence of his nephews. He had an obligation to protect them. If Bathilde turned her anger against him, they might at least be allowed to depart with their lives.

"And then it—the thing—disappeared," he finished. "As if it had never been there at all. Only—only the rain was left."

Finally, he looked at the noblewoman. He had avoided her gaze as he spoke. Now that he was done he did not know what to expect. Terror, disbelief, anger? He saw none of these things. But what he did see gave him no comfort. Awareness was in Bathilde's eyes, burning and bright, as if she had known all along what he would say.

"The rain is still left," he made himself say. More words rushed out, unbidden, called up by his fear. "None of what I have said surprises you, does it, lady?" he asked in a whisper. "How could you do this?" His voice grew louder. "They are your own people!"

"Peace, good trader." The words were conciliatory, but the tone was not. "Think you that I would do aught to the folk of my land? You saw with your eyes, but you understand nothing. Nor should you. As you said yourself: you are a stranger."

"One can be a stranger and still recognize evil," Isaac shot back. "What you brought you must send away—"

The hard voice cut him off. "This is not your business. You would do well to forget everything about that night"— she paused, adding meaningfully—"and this conversation, as well."

"By the grace of God, lady, I wish I could!" Isaac glared at Bathilde, angry and frightened, but gripped still by the unaccountable determination that had led him there. "But I cannot. The vision of that demon burns me like fire. From the day I came to your hall I felt . . . as if some purpose was holding me here. At first, I thought it was the woman Sirona"—he caught himself—"but she is part of this, too. As much as you are, lady!"

Bathilde said coldly, "The men who were killed that night were sent to murder the wisewoman. And do you know why, you who think you possess such wisdom? She refused to bring about my death and that of my babe. She was offered a great deal of gold to do it, but she would not. Her reward was those men seeking her life. Would you have had them succeed?"

"Of course not." Isaac was indignant at the thought. "I would wish such a fate on no one." But that gave him another thought. "Someone sought the death of a mother and her innocent babe? A sin so great cannot be countenanced. Who would do such a thing?"

Bathilde looked at him. "The sin was not countenanced. Was that not what we are talking about? As for who sought it, the less you know about that the better." Her eyes seemed to widen and darken. "You have told no one else about that night, have you?"

"No one." Isaac did not question how she knew this. Power burned in this woman; even he could sense it. And he sensed something more: danger. His skin prickled with sudden fear. He felt a strong desire to step back, and it took every shred of his will to stay where he was. "You are not a Christian, are you," he asked in a near whisper.

She shook her head. "Not any longer. But why should that matter? Neither are you."

"Lady." Isaac took a single step closer. The power burning here was a dark power; he was certain of it. To deal with such matters was within neither his province nor experience, but he tried anyway. "It is true that I am not a Christian, but we Jews still know evil when we see it. I beg you, lady, turn from this course you have set yourself on."

She gave him an ironic smile. "You sound like Sirona."

"The wisewoman sought to warn you? But it was she who called up the apparition that night!"

"No," Bathilde said. "She did not."

Shaken, Isaac stared at her. The expression on the noblewoman's strong handsome features left no room for doubt. All this time he had been holding Sirona responsible, wavering between whether or not she was possessed of evil powers. Could he have been wrong? It seemed so. Inwardly, he writhed at memories of the storm, the flames surrounding the horrific figure of the demon, and worst of all: of how he had driven Sirona out into that terrible night, straight into the arms of men waiting to kill her.

"God forgive me," he muttered. "I called her a demon. I drove her out to those men. Have I caused her death, then? After saving her life on the road that day? But I saw her appear out of the air! Who can do that other than a demon? Was I wrong?"

The questions were directed more at Isaac's god than at Bathilde, but it was the latter who answered. At the stricken look on his face, she took pity. "Be at ease," she said more gently. "The wisewoman is alive and well, and she is no demon."

There was a long pause. Bathilde stared at Isaac, seemingly deep in thought. Abruptly she appeared to come to a decision. "Heed my advice, trader," she said. "Stay out of this. There is far too much that you do not understand. I wish you had not seen what you did that night, but it's done, and there is no undoing it. The best thing you can do now is pack up your goods and your nephews and leave my hall when the weather clears and the roads dry out enough for travel."

"The—the weather will clear?" Isaac cast a distracted and disbelieving eye at the shuttered windows of the solar. "It does not seem so."

"It will clear," Bathilde assured him. "For a time. And

until it does," she added in a grimmer tone, "you will say nothing of what you know to any man, woman, or child in my house. Give me your word as a man of honor that you will not."

Another handful of moments passed, each one lengthening and growing into the next, until the silence was as heavy as the rain outside. Isaac studied the woman before him. The warning in her voice was echoed in her face. Power was there, and death—or the threat of it—he was no longer sure. And yet, glimmering out from amongst those dark emanations, was a strange sort of compassion.

It was bewildering. But no more bewildering to the trader than the answer he heard himself make. "Very well," he said. "I give you my word, lady. I swear it in the name of Yahweh, the God of my people."

Bathilde perused Isaac's face, then favored him with a slow nod. "It is a good oath. Neither pagan nor Christian, but a good oath nonetheless. I accept it."

Isaac was still wondering why he had done it. But mingled with that wondering was an odd sort of peace, as if deep inside he knew what he had done was correct, though outwardly he was not so sure.

"And Sirona the wisewoman," he asked. "What of her? I have not seen her since—since that night."

Bathilde said nothing. The expression her handsome face wore had suddenly become unreadable.

"Lady?" Isaac pressed. "Know you where she has gone?"

"I do not." The noblewoman's reply was curt. "She left my hall the next morning. She has not returned."

Sirona had not run far enough.

She had tried. Indeed, she could not have tried harder. She had left the manor on the heels of Father Ambrose, although, unlike him, she had gone on foot and in the opposite direction. The confrontation with the priest had set the seal on her desire to leave Bathilde's house. She had talked with Bathilde, and it had availed her nothing. Sooner or later, the trader would speak of what he had seen. Clearly, the wisest course of action seemed that she should be gone when that happened.

Thus had she told Mau. The cat had disagreed, but Sirona had ignored him. This was not his decision; it was hers, and she would brook no opinion save her own. He could come with her, she told Mau, or return whence he had come in the first place, but either way, she was leaving.

Under a slate-gray sky she had set out for home. Sitting in the stable yard, the cat's orange eyes watched her depart. Sirona had felt his gaze upon her, but she refused to look back. Eventually, as she went on, the strength of those eyes faded.

However, those who followed her did not fade. Voices coiled about Sirona as she slogged along the track. Mud oozed over her ankles, so thick that her legs were aching before she had traveled a quarter of the way home. No one else was about; no one else was foolish enough—driven enough—to attempt an already impassable road with the threat of more rain looming in the dark skies. Yet the voices were there, for they belonged to no man or woman born of this world, but to goddesses.

Come back, the voices urged, soft and compelling. *Do not flee from Us. There is no need. We are your destiny. You are Ours. Come back, come back . . .*

Sirona recognized both of them: the rich melodic tones of Bast and the living flame of the apparition she had seen that Mau had called Sekhmet. Pulling one foot after the other out of the sucking mud, she tried not to listen to either one. She wanted to go home; never had her small hut with its bunches of dried herbs and cozy hearth and well-tended garden, beckoned to her as it did now. No longer did she have to fear the assassins; what she had to fear now was much greater.

But the going was so accursedly slow, and the weather— perhaps sent by one of the very goddesses urging her to stay—conspired to delay her. The wind freshened steadily, blowing into her face from the east. The clouds thickened. Soon the rain began again, slanting sideways across her cheeks like thousands of tiny needles.

Other things delayed her, as well. Slowed by the rain, she was forced to seek shelter before nightfall. Immediately she found that her healing skills were needed. A young woman had just been brought to bed for the birth of her first babe. The labor was an easy one, but when Sirona resumed her travel, other folk came out to hail her. Children had fallen ill with fevers. A farmer had broken his foot after an ox stepped on it.

And the rain continued to fall, harder and ever harder. The journey, which should have been a two-day walk, stretched instead into two weeks and several days.

Stubbornly, Sirona kept on. Each morning she started out, her mantle pulled tight around her, but the rain soon penetrated even the densely woven wool. And the rain had not quieted the voices. Music and flame, they continued to press at her through the drumming rain. As she trudged through the mud, the anger that had been smoldering within her since she had left Bathilde intensified, warming her against the rain with its heat.

"I am tired of this," she growled. She slogged on, and then shouted even more loudly, "Stop calling to me. I will not listen!"

They would use her no longer. Not Bast and not Sekhmet, Goddesses though they might be. And certainly not Bathilde, with her fevered desires and the power she had used with such a stunning lack of wisdom.

"None of you!" she shouted. "Do you hear?"

Including that cat, she added to herself, though she had seen no sign of him. Apparently he had not changed his mind about following her, most likely because he had known that it would begin to rain, she thought sourly.

Resentment burned deep inside Sirona's belly. Bathilde was sitting in her warm hall. Bast was in Her magnificent temple, and Sekhmet . . . well, that frightening deity was wherever She was. Even Mau, wherever he had disappeared to, had surely found himself a dry comfortable place out of the rain. Only she, the mortal woman they all claimed to need so badly, was out in this wet miserable weather, drenched to the bone, and up to her ankles in mud.

The anger burned hotter. Sirona's fists clenched. She took a dragging step, and a second one, and tiredly struggled to pull her foot up out of the muck for a third. A sudden gust of wind almost tore the mantle from her head. The anger gusted, too, straight into fury. Still fighting with the mud, Sirona raised her fists to the sky.

"Enough!" she screamed. "Enough!"

The rain stopped.

Sirona stumbled to a halt. The pounding rain was gone. A few lingering drops landed with loud splats on her head and around her feet, and then they stopped, too. The harsh breezes still blew, but their harshness no longer ushered in a downpour. Instead, it was thinning out the clouds, creating flashes of blue through the thick blanket of gray.

Standing frozen in the ankle-deep mud, Sirona gaped up at the sky. In another instant the sun might actually appear. Had she done this?

"Yes," a familiar dry voice said. "And about time, too."

Sirona yanked her gaze down. "How did you get here?" she demanded. She peered at the new arrival more closely. "You're not even wet." She shook out her drenched mantle. "Unlike me."

The black cat leaped aside to avoid being splattered. "So you must soak me to make up for it? Is stopping that storm not enough for you?"

"I did not"—Sirona forgot about her mantle, forgot even Mau—"I did not truly do that. Did I?"

She was asking the question of herself, rather than Mau, but it was the cat who answered. "Oh, you did," he assured her. "Do not tell me you did not feel the power pour through you."

Sirona stared up at the sky. "All I felt was anger. I was so weary of being wet, of fighting my way along this miserable track. I thought of—of others being warm and dry, and I grew angrier and angrier. Then the wind hit me in the face and I shouted and"—she made a bewildered gesture at the clearing sky—"this."

"Anger, power." The cat's voice was ironic. "So often they are one and the same."

Sirona glared at him. "And that is good?"

"What has good to do with it? Power simply is." Mau started to sit down, glanced distastefully at the muddy track, and thought better of it. "If you had been schooled at all in the heritage of your mothers," he added, "you would know this."

"My mother," Sirona reminded him grimly, "left the ways of the mothers behind her."

"Your mother did not have the gifts. You do. At last, you have used them. It's a good beginning. Late perhaps, but better than nothing. Of course, weather is one of the easier things to control. You have yet to learn about the more challenging aspects."

"Mayhap," Sirona snapped, "I have no desire to learn of them."

Unperturbed, the cat regarded her. "Indeed. Mayhap you will come to feel differently, in time."

"We'll see," Sirona replied through gritted teeth.

She resumed walking. The winds had completed their task of scattering the clouds, and a weak sun was revealing itself. Water and mud still clogged the road, but somehow the going seemed easier. As the sun's rays strengthened, it became easier still. The mud grew less clinging. The pools of water shrank to puddles, and birds suddenly began to stir and chirp from the dripping trees.

Sirona glanced suspiciously at the cat. Without explaining where he had been these last weeks, or asking whether or not he would be welcome, he was calmly accompanying her. Tail high, he was scampering along, seeking out the best places with light-footed skill. "Is this your doing?" she demanded.

His orange eyes were wide and innocent. "What? That this road is less abominable? No, human one. It is yours. You wished it to stop, and it has."

Sirona stomped along in silence. After a time, she said, "I could not stop those men from trying to kill me."

"Actually," Mau said mildly, "you could. You just did not know it at the time." He executed a beautiful leap over a rather large puddle and darted ahead. "You did not need the trader at all," he added over a sleek black shoulder.

Anger rustled in Sirona's belly again. "How unfortunate that neither the trader nor I understood that," she called after him. "For he and his nephews saw the Goddess slay those two men. What do you plan to do about that, cat? Or have you already done it? Have you asked Sekhmet to kill them, too, because of what they saw? A fine thanks it would be for having aided me, when, as you say, I did not need his help."

Mau turned back to face her. His long full whiskers went straight and stiff. "I have lived a great many lifetimes, woman, more than you can count, and in not one of those lifetimes have I ever asked Sekhmet for anything. I do not plan to start now."

Sirona was unimpressed. "Then you want me to ask Her, don't you? That is what this has all been about, is it not? They witnessed something they should not have, and Bathilde wants them removed. Their loyalty cannot be counted upon, for they belong to neither the new faith nor the old."

"Their faith is a great deal older than you might imagine," Mau said. "Although it makes no difference to the situation at hand." His whiskers relaxed, and he arched gracefully over another puddle. "So you think the noblewoman wants the trader and his kin dead?" he asked so conversationally that he could have been inquiring about a rut in the track.

"I know she does." Brooding on the disturbing talk she had held with Bathilde, Sirona did not notice the glance Mau gave her from the corner of his eye. "I saw the intention in her."

"You did, eh?" The cat's tone was more interested. "Does she know that?"

"No. She is too busy exulting over her own power and her success in summoning Sek—that Goddess. She sees nothing else but the purpose that drives her."

Mau slipped closer to her. "And is that not a good reason

to stay close to her? To prevent harm from coming to her purpose by seeing beyond what she does?"

"That," Sirona snapped, "is why I left. I do not care about her purpose."

This was not entirely true, but having said that much Sirona fell silent. There were too many thoughts tumbling around in her head for her to say more. Unbidden, the power had surged from a place she had thought well hidden. The vanished rain, the warmth of the new sun, were due to her, or at least, according to Mau, they were. Sirona would have liked to contradict him, but there was no point. He knew the truth, and so did she.

"Power or not," she finally said, speaking to herself, rather than Mau, "I do not like the idea of things happening beyond my control."

The cat slanted her a look. "Would you prefer slogging along in the rain with mud up to your eyeballs?"

"Yes," Sirona said shortly.

If a cat could sigh, Mau did so, then. But wisely, he did not seek to argue. They went the rest of the journey in silence, winding their way to Sirona's hut along increasingly dry paths, under a sun that grew brighter and brighter, even as afternoon advanced toward evening.

Only later would she learn that the gentle sun and drying track were sheltering her and Mau alone. Everywhere else in Saxony it was still raining.

12

THE SKY BEGAN TO CHANGE AS Haganon and his party neared the border between Gaul and Saxony. In Gaul it was the bright pale color of blue-glazed glass. Toward Saxony it was dark as old iron, and clouds tumbled over each other, obscuring the horizon. A moist gray wall that bespoke rain hazed even the clouds. The difference between the two lands was so striking that several men crossed themselves as the horses broke through the last of the woods that marked the delineation between one territory and the next.

Haganon guided his stallion over to the man whom Carolus had promised he would send along on this mission. "You see, my lord?" He gestured with his whip in the direction of Saxony. "There is evidence of the evil that has taken over our home."

The man turned a mild gaze on the rain-soaked land they were traveling to. "I see that foul weather is bound to attend us as we enter your land," he said in a deep, cultured voice. "But such is not always a sign of evil, good Count."

Haganon snorted. "It is in this case." He was about to say more. Indeed, he was about to chastise his companion for being so ignorant of the very task his king had set him. But the man of God was now looking at him, rather than the drenched landscape ahead, and something in those mild eyes made Haganon think better of voicing his sharp words.

Carolus had been as good as his word. He had not delegated a mere priest to attend Haganon, but his own religious advisor and close friend: the famous Alcuin of York, a scholar and man of letters nearly as well-known as Carolus himself.

Alcuin was of noble blood, though he was not a Gaul. His homeland was Albion, or Britain, as it was often called those days, and his fame came not from warfare but from his passion for scholarly pursuits. Coupled with that passion was a deep and abiding love for Christianity, along with a talent for teaching that was nothing short of brilliant. In the Church Alcuin was only a deacon, but his ability to educate had so impressed Carolus the king had lured him to Aachen to open a school in the royal palace. This he had done, and with such success that Carolus himself had, at times, been a pupil, and had bestowed the title of "Master of the Palace School" upon Alcuin.

Carolus had many advisors. He had no fear of listening to the counsel of others, for so great was his own strength of will that his ability to make decisions was unquestioned. Alcuin, however, was much in his confidence, more so than anyone else at court, except, perhaps, Carolus's beloved wife, Hildegarde. The two men were extremely close. Indeed, some nobles whispered—out of hearing, of course— that Alcuin knew every step that his lord was about to take, before the king had even raised his foot.

At first, Haganon had been pleased and honored that Carolus had ordered his most treasured comrade to accompany him. But as the party made its way east he found himself beginning to have second thoughts. In Haganon's view, religious men—whether they were bishops, priests, monks, or deacons—were greatly lacking in worldly knowledge. God was their province. It was up to other men—of noble blood, of course—to explain to these devout innocents where and when their holy guidance was most needed.

This Alcuin, though, was a different sort entirely. He was so worldly that it was downright irritating. For a man who had entered cathedral school as a child, it was astonishing. Yet it was so. Each conversation he had with Alcuin left him more and more uneasy. Haganon could not manipulate him as he could Father Ambrose, a most unpleasant discovery. It was becoming increasingly evident that Carolus had not shared all his reasons for insisting that his prized advisor ride along to Saxony to rid it of the evil that festered there.

Haganon saw that the Master of the Palace School still regarded him with that shrewd knowing gaze, as if he were reading the thoughts in Haganon's head. Unnerved, and angered because he was, the count forced himself to give the other man a courteous nod of dismissal. They had gotten ahead of the rest of the party, and the noble started to turn his horse away to rejoin his men, but Alcuin's mild voice stopped him.

"Evil is of great importance to you, isn't it, Count?"

Haganon strove not to glare. What an odd question! Yet this lowly deacon, who had risen to such prominence in Carolus's court, had a habit of asking such questions. Haganon strongly suspected that he did it on purpose, to throw men off so that he could discern their true motives.

Well, he would not discern *his,* the nobleman thought resentfully, and said aloud, "Of a certainty, it is, or rather the fighting of it. Is that not the task of all Christians, to fight heathen evil wherever they see it?" That was a safe, as well as politic thing to say, he told himself. The rooting out and destruction of paganism was the driving force of Carolus's life.

Alcuin rode along looking thoughtful. He was not a robust man as Haganon and Carolus were, but his features were round and his eyes merry, an odd appearance for one so learned and scholarly. "Indeed, the Lord has enjoined us to bring His word to the heathen," he murmured. He cast a sidelong glance at his companion. "But there is much to see. And we have not even reached Saxony yet."

"We will soon," Haganon told him. "And what you will see when we do, my lord, is rain, the accursed rain that has been plaguing us when the sun should be shining and the crops ripening in the fields." He went on, warming to his subject. "And you will see something else, as well: people slipping away from mass to whisper prayers to demon gods, and all of it brought on by the curses of that *stria.*"

"Ah, yes, the woman."

Haganon waited for Alcuin to say more, but the deacon

had gone silent, watching him with that knowing look the count found so irritating. *"Stria,"* he finally corrected with more asperity than he had intended. "The king himself has named her so."

"And ordered her death because of it. Yes, I know. You believe her responsible for all the troubles you have described."

"She is responsible." Haganon was bristling, his legs tightening around the sides of his horse. "Why would you think otherwise?" he demanded, as the animal sidestepped. "Do you mean to impugn my word, lord schoolmaster?"

The insult in his use of Alcuin's title was obvious, yet the other man took it in stride, giving no sign of offense. "I impugn no one, Count," he said easily. "Least of all you. To do so would cast doubt upon the wisdom of my lord, the king, who has set me the task of aiding you. That I would never do."

Haganon was not mollified. "Then why all the questions? You are a man of God, deacon. I'd have thought you would be more eager than any one to do the Lord's will."

"I am."

A change came over Alcuin's merry features as he spoke. Suddenly he was no longer the good-natured scholar, the man Haganon had become increasingly tempted to discount. Power now stamped itself upon him, burning in his mild blue gaze and hardening his jaw, until Haganon saw with irrevocable clarity how he had misjudged this man who carried only the unimportant title of deacon. In his own way, this advisor to the king was as formidable as Carolus himself.

He had better take care, Haganon cautioned himself. Already he had overstepped his bounds, perhaps irrevocably.

Alcuin gave him a cold little smile, as if he had again read his thoughts. Then the smile was abruptly gone. "Doing God's will is my sacred obligation," he said. "But heed me, Count, it is God's will and not man's that I obey. Even my lord king may not presume upon me in that regard. What makes you believe that you may?"

"I was not—"

The cultured voice, now gone as icy as the eyes, cut off the noble's protest. "You were, and I warn you now that I will not allow it. If the Lady Bathilde has truly fallen from the paths of righteousness, with the Lord's help, I will bring her back to the fold. If this woman—this *stria,* as you call her—is responsible for the lady's fall, and all else that you blame upon her, then she will indeed be punished. But the woman's ultimate fate lies in God's hands, as does the fate of us all. I, as His servant, merely carry out His will."

"Of course." Haganon was chastened and uneasy. If he were to succeed in his ultimate goal of discrediting Bathilde and gaining power in Saxony, then Carolus must continue to view him as an ally. If he were to alienate the king's closest advisor, he would do so at his peril. "Forgive me, my lord," he said humbly. "My words were ill chosen."

The aura of power that had made Alcuin appear so formidable was suddenly gone, dissipating as swiftly as a puff of wind. Before Haganon's eyes the Master of the Palace School became the easygoing man of letters again. His point had been made. He knew it, and so did Haganon. There was no need to belabor the matter any further.

"Ah, well." Alcuin's cold voice had regained its geniality. "Put it from your mind. All of us misspeak now and then. Only God in His wisdom is perfect. We, as mere men, can only aspire."

Hastily, Haganon agreed; he had little choice if he was to remain in the good graces of the royal advisor. It was a relief to know that Alcuin was not fatally offended, but that could not prevent Haganon from seething inwardly at this turn of events. It was not in his nature to give ground to other men so easily, particularly these churchmen, who he viewed as being of such little account. Alcuin was clearly an exception. Haganon now saw that the man was unpredictable. He had made it quite plain that he would make his own decisions about the state of affairs in Saxony. Worse: he was clearly doing so with the knowledge and approval of Carolus.

This might not be as easy as Haganon had thought.

A raindrop splattered down on the neck of the count's

stallion. Another drop hit Haganon in the face. Within moments the entire party of riders was being pelted by a flurry of icy rain. Alcuin looked up at the sky. However, he was the only one. The nobles around him rode on, heads lowered, their faces wearing expressions of resignation and dread. It had been raining when Haganon led them out of Saxony to Gaul; it was only to be expected that it would be raining when they returned. A few of the men muttered to each other, blessing themselves as the horses plodded east.

Alcuin pulled his finely embroidered woolen mantle up to his neck. "By the City of Heaven," he expostulated cheerily, still retaining his good humor, "we are riding into the ugly weather you spoke of indeed."

"Yes." Haganon looked across at him. "We have left Gaul and entered into our lands. Now, my lord, you will see the evil for yourself."

The fire snapped merrily in the hearth. Outside the open door the sky was darkening, but not with rain. Evening was coming on, and it was a clear evening, soft with colors from the sun that Sirona had so unwittingly summoned. That gentle sun had followed her and the cat all the rest of the way home. It had spread its warmth over and about them, making the travel swift and easy. The track seemed to dry by the same magic, the deep muddy ruts filling in and hardening even as Sirona approached.

She had marveled at these changes, though she had stubbornly refused to speak of her wonder to the cat. The paths that led to her house, branching off from the main track into the woods, were similarly dry. Water droplets still clattered from the trees, but long rays of fading sunlight were slanting through the leaves, gilding the drops and evaporating them before they could hit the ground.

In the center of its clearing, Sirona's house stood waiting, weathered and dry under the sun, gleaming with welcome. She had gone toward it gratefully, able to forget, at least for the moment, magic and power and her part in both. The door had swung open, its leather latch undisturbed. The interior was redolent with drying herbs and the mustiness of a closed hut whose occupant had been absent for some time. The pile of wood she had chopped before she left still lay beside the hearth. It was short work to kindle a fire, draw water from the nearby spring, and hang a kettle with stew makings over the hearth.

Mau watched all these preparations from Sirona's sleeping place, where he had made himself comfortable while he groomed his fur. "A meal will be welcome," he observed. His black nose wrinkled, sniffing appreciatively as Sirona cut up part of a smoked venison haunch—payment from a patient—to add to the pot. "Particularly one I don't have to hunt for."

She glanced at him over her shoulder. "I did not know that creatures of magic felt hunger."

"Yet another of the many things you do not know." He watched her gather up the chunks of meat and toss them into the simmering kettle. "It's a very cozy home you have here, human, but you cannot hide from the power, not even here."

Sirona chopped harder. "I am not"—she said between chops—"trying to hide. Do not presume to tell me what I am thinking." Setting down the knife, she snatched up handfuls of onions, peeled them with practiced jerks, and flung them into the pot. From a sack hanging on the wall she took out dried peas and threw them at the stew with more enthusiasm than was strictly necessary. She did not look at Mau, but her jaw was set, and her dark eyes were narrow.

Mau did not seek to contradict her. "You said you did not like things happening beyond your control," he pointed out instead. "Well, there is a simple remedy for that. Learn about your power and thus will you learn how to control it."

Sirona's expression did not change. She took up a long wooden spoon and stirred the bubbling mixture, then set the spoon aside. "This must cook for a while." She spoke blandly, as if she had not heard a word the cat had said. "I will go out and see to my garden until it is ready."

Mau curled up on the furs covering Sirona's pallet, as if he were about to take a nap. His eyes followed the wisewoman as she straightened up and walked to the door. He said nothing more.

Outside, Sirona knelt between the rows of young plants. Weeds had grown up in her absence, and she pulled at them savagely. Elsewhere the gardens were drowned, but this one, despite the weeds, was thriving. The rows of vegetables and herbs dripped with moisture, as if rain had drenched them, yet they stood happily, stretching their heads up to the sun. The sun that she had summoned. She felt pleased and angry at the same time, and not at all inclined to examine either feeling too closely. Instead, she rested her knees in the soft wet dirt and yanked up weeds, tossing them into a steadily growing pile behind her.

From the open door of her house the rich odor of cooking stew wafted out, reminding her that she had not eaten since early that morning. The growling in her stomach was welcome; it was a predictable and familiar sensation, exactly the opposite of any feeling brought on by magic. She pulled harder at the weeds, even though her knees and back were beginning to ache. The focus of her vision narrowed down to the living plants beneath her hands, those she wanted, and those she did not. Like a goddess herself, she showed them favor or condemnation, deciding which to save and which to tear out by the roots.

She never knew the exact moment when the scene in front of her changed. It came on gradually, a profoundly different scene slowly overtaking the familiar landscape of vivid green shoots and sprouting leaves. Weeds grew in this place, too, but they were tall, with stalks as thick as saplings. Instead of an earth that was dark and moist, the ground was dry as long-dead bones, covered with red sand.

Sirona stared and stared, feeling a sudden urge to weep. An air of abandonment sat on this desolate spot, heavy with the ancient grief of centuries, yet fresh and throbbing with a pain new as yesterday. Rubble lay everywhere: broken columns tumbled with pieces of marble and masonry. A building must have stood here once, massive by the size of the ruins, and beautiful. Remnants of gold still shimmered on the shattered columns; faded paintings could still be

seen on the broken stone blocks, though their outlines were
blurred, and their colors had long ago lost their brightness.

A steady wind blew, scattering the sand, and sending it in
drifts over a row of enormous statues. They alone had been
spared the ravages of time and neglect. Erect and proud,
they stood as if they still guarded this place and what it had
held. Layers of gold had once encased the statues, but it had
been hacked away by robbers, defacing their beauty, if not
their presence. The harsh fingers of blowing sand had fur-
thered the destruction, obscuring the features of many of
the figures, though others had somehow remained as clear
as the day they had emerged from the living rock under the
hands of stonemasons long since dead.

Sirona caught her breath. She recognized the form those
massive carvings depicted. In no way could she have forgotten the snarling half animal, half goddess that had
leaped out of flame and lightning to help her on that night
filled with magic and terror and death.

"Sekhmet," she breathed.

Her sense of grief was suddenly overlaid by dread. This
was a vision, but if she had been standing in this place in the
flesh she would have taken a step backward; even so she felt
herself take that step in her mind. This was a temple built to
that horrific being, She, Who was Bast's Sister.

Yes. A great voice boomed out in agreement. *This was the
greatest of the temples built in My name. Look upon it now.
See the devastation that has fallen over My place. Look
upon it well, so that you may understand My sadness, and
My anger.*

The deep powerful tones seemed to issue from the ruined
statues themselves. They rose up over the drifting sand,
drowned out the eerie whistle of the wind, vibrated in the
belly of Sirona herself. A new shape was forming, looming
above the ancient limestone statues. The Goddess was appearing in Her ancient temple. Shafts of crimson light
darted about Her. Flames burned from within the folds of
her clinging red sheath.

Do not fear Me, mortal, She said. I will not harm you. A
bitter growling laugh rippled through the air, and one enor-

mous hand clenched and unclenched about a fistful of seven arrows. *Indeed,* She added. *You have My thanks.*

"Your thanks?"

You have come to My temple. Thus have you called Me. A brave deed for one who must still go in terror of Me, as you did on the night I first came to you.

Iron rippled through Sirona's spine. She recalled Mau's dry voice advising her that mortals who refused to show fear of Her perversely pleased Sekhmet. "I thought," she said boldly, "that it was You Who called me. I was minding my own business, weeding my garden and cooking a stew."

The growling chuckle resounded again. *We have called each other, mortal.* The laughter vanished; the voice grew dark and flaming. *The souls that once filled My holy place have ceased to come long since. I have been banished, from this, My own house, by the forgetfulness of all the folk who lived in the Two Lands. They feared Me; they revered Me, and now they have forgotten Me. Only if a mortal speaks My name, or thinks it, as you did, do I have the power to appear.* There was a long pause. *Not even I,* the dark voice added, subdued and sad, *Goddess though I am, could have imagined that My worship would have one day come to this.*

Fierce the aspect of this goddess was, and yet Sirona felt a pang of sympathy at Her words. Such was the fate that had befallen the gods and goddesses of Saxony as well. Cerwidyn, Odin, Anu, the Great Mother Goddess, all the smaller Sacred Ones of water and wood, had been forgotten, and where They were not forgotten, They were hated. Only the great Mother Tree, whose arms held up the world, remained. The Christians, with all their power, still dared not touch so holy a shrine, even though few visited it these days, at least not openly.

The thought of the Mother Tree, almost as abandoned as this temple, made Sirona speak. "But I did not mean to call You. I—I do not worship You, Lady." She said this cautiously; the need for honesty vying against the wisdom of not angering this being whose mood seemed as volatile as the flames that surrounded Her.

I do not ask you to. Worship your own goddesses,

*woman, or worship My Sister, as your mothers did before
you. All I desire of you is to see.*

Without warning the scene before Sirona's eyes began to
change. The outlines of the temple hardened, growing
bright and whole, agleam with lamplight and incense. The
drifts of sand disappeared; the wind became a soft breeze,
and the statues of Sekhmet suddenly shone like flame, encased with the layering of gold of which they had been
robbed.

Look. The voice of the Lion-Headed Goddess throbbed
with rage. *Gaze upon My temple and see how it once was.*

Water lapped at a sandy shore. A lake had been there
once. Sirona saw it as it had been in the days of its glory;
resurrected, it glittered under a full moon, crescent-shaped
and holy. And that was not all. Lights danced on the surface
of the lake. A flotilla of boats was moving across the water.
Long paddles swept up in stately unison, shedding droplets
of water like a rain of jewels in the moonlight before they
dipped back down to the surface of the lake. The boats were
large and covered with gold. The one in the lead was bigger
and brighter than all the rest. As it and the rest of the boats
drew closer, Sirona could see a great golden statue in the
prow, as well as the people themselves. Somehow they
were familiar, and at the same time, profoundly alien to her:
bejeweled, dark-skinned, and gaily dressed in sheer linen
and glittering headdresses.

The music of their voices touched her ears, rising and
dropping in the measured cadence of sacred chants. Their
tongue was not hers, yet she grasped the meaning of every
word.

> *Come, oh Golden One, who feeds on praise,*
> *Because the food of her desire is dancing,*
> *Who shines on the festival at the light of*
>   *lighting the lamps,*
> *Who is content with the dancing at night.*
> *Come! The procession is in the place of inebriation,*
> *That hall of traveling through the marshes.*
> *Its performance is set,*

Its order is in effect,
Without anything lacking therein.

Do you see? The Goddess's voice had softened to a deep resonance. *Thus would they sing, as they carried My sacred image, in the most beautiful of barks back and forth across the lake, and then to My resting place in the temple.*

Sirona understood. Just as in the ancient ways of her own people, the religious festivals in this foreign land were held at night, when the glow of innumerable lights could direct the Goddess to the place where She would be honored. She thought of the rituals she had seen as a child, rituals that had grown scarcer and more secret as the influence of King Carolus's commands and the priests sent by him to enforce those commands took hold. But the old ways of Saxony had not yet gone the way of Sekhmet's worship; they still lingered, stubborn as unfulfilled dreams, refusing to die.

You deceive yourself, Sekhmet said, and Her voice had lost its softness. *Even now the goddesses of your land fade and wither, waiting for the strength that only you can bring them. But to bring them that strength you must first ally yourself with Me and with My Sister.*

Sirona gazed out at the flickering lights. Holiness resided in this place, deep and unassailable, or so those who worshipped here had thought. But they were wrong, she thought sadly. The lake, the worshippers, and the temple were long gone, swallowed up by the beliefs of a new way. They would not return. Sekhmet was showing her a dream. The reality was dust and sand and crumbling ruins.

And indeed, as if her thoughts possessed the power to affect the dream, it began to fade before her eyes. The voices broke apart; the lights were swallowed up by blackness. The fertile lake spun away, back into the memories from which it had been created. Even the burning presence of Sekhmet was suddenly gone.

Alcuin jolted upright. Had he been dreaming? For certain he had speedily dozed off in the bed of this comfortable chamber the abbot had insisted he occupy when Haganon's party cut the day's travel short and sought shelter at his monastery for the night.

"No." Alcuin spoke aloud, and the words rang out in the quiet room. "No dream was that, but a vision, a warning from God."

Images leered up in his memory. Once more he saw the pagan temple gleaming in evil splendor under a full moon. He saw the pagans themselves, dark-skinned and garbed in linen so sheer he could see the women's breasts, chanting in an incomprehensible tongue as they bore the image of their heathen idol over a glittering lake. He saw the idol itself, a hideous statue with the body of a woman and the head of a snarling lion. He heard it speak. The words were indistinguishable, but the sound was pure evil.

Blackness. Alcuin moaned and blessed himself. Blackness, as deep and impenetrable as the soul of a demon. That was what he had seen. Shivering set upon him, stabbing with icy nails, as though he still bounced on a tired horse under the driving rain. He pulled the furs up to his neck, but it did no good.

"Evil," he whispered. "I saw evil."

But from what source had it come? Was it so powerful it could penetrate the walls of this place of God, or was there something within the monastery itself that had called to it?

Alcuin thrust his feet out from the covers and stood up. Instead of cold stone, his feet encountered a thick bearskin. The chamber even had a brazier to fight off some of the night chill. The royal advisor looked about him with appreciation. He would have been content to stay in the common guesthouse, but this luxurious chamber was far more to his preference. In any case, Abbot Wala had insisted.

Count Haganon, the advisor had noted, had been quick to avail himself of the abbot's hospitality. Alcuin frowned. He had seen at once that Haganon, despite his outward words, was not a godly man. At first this had not overly troubled him; many powerful men were lacking in godliness, and Alcuin was worldly enough to know it; that was what made a man like Carolus so remarkable, the fact that he was truly godly.

Alcuin's grim expression deepened. His bare feet whispered back and forth through the coarse, soft bear fur. And then there was Abbot Wala. As the king's most trusted advisor, Alcuin knew many churchmen, men whose faith was true, and men whose love of God was tempered by their love of power. He had only met Abbot Wala for the first time this evening, but he had seen at a glance that the abbot fell into the latter category. He had also seen that between the abbot and Haganon there were glimmers of bonds, of words understood but left unspoken, and most of all, of plots that twined about both men.

Alcuin paused, then strode to the door. He pushed the heavy oaken slab open. The corridor was dark, lit at long intervals by torches guttering low. Alcuin called out. There was no response, and he called out again, louder. This time, he heard the sound of flapping sandals and a monk came running through the darkness.

"Send the abbot to me," Alcuin ordered. "At once."

"Now?" The monk was very young, still a novice. He had also just awakened. His sleepy eyes blinked at the request. "Everyone has retired, good sir. We retire early here. The abbot is surely abed—"

"Then wake him." Alcuin was startled by the curtness he heard in his tone; normally he was soft-spoken to all. But it worked. The monk pattered off down the hall, all trace of him, save his footsteps, soon swallowed up by the shadows.

Within a short time Abbot Wala arrived, his way lighted by a candle held by the novice. The abbot was rumpled. Obviously he had just gone to sleep, and was struggling without a great deal of success to hide his irritation at being summoned so abruptly. "Honored Advisor," he began, as the young novice peeped in behind him. "Brother Harvold tells me you are troubled. Is there some comfort lacking in your chamber—"

Alcuin waved this aside. "I have had a vision," he said without preamble.

The young monk's eyes widened as the abbot's eyes narrowed. Both men blessed themselves. "What sort of vision?" Abbot Wala asked.

"A premonition of the pagan evil that is ever waiting to defeat we who bring the true faith to the unknowing." Alcuin studied the man's features in the darting candle glow. He was more convinced than ever that his first impression of the abbot had been correct.

For an instant the irritation on Wala's lean face flashed sharper, though he was more awake now, and better able to conceal it. "Indeed," he agreed, nodding sagely. "The evil ways of heathens are ever watchful for weakness." Behind him the novice monk hastily crossed himself again.

"Weakness, yes." Alcuin had seen the irritation on his host's face. "We must all strive against weakness." He cast a glance about the richly appointed chamber. "Particularly when we are surrounded by comfort. I am as weak as any man, yet God has still seen fit to favor me this night. I believe He means to favor you as well, Abbot. That is why He sent me this vision."

Abbot Wala's hazel eyes had turned watchful. "I am humbled." His voice was soft, belying the caution in his eyes.

"Are you?" Alcuin's voice was also soft. "Then you will be pleased to accompany us tomorrow, when we seek out the *stria*."

Yes, he said to himself, watching the abbot's guarded expression, *perhaps God has sent me here to defend against more than a pagan witch.*

The garden sprang into focus around Sirona. Darkness had fallen. The neat rows of plants nodded their heads in the night breeze, at eye level, for she was lying with her cheek pressed into the damp ground. Dazedly she stared at them. For a span of breaths it was the dream that was real and familiar and not the familiar lines of vegetables. She pushed herself to a sitting position, stayed there for some moments, then rose unsteadily to her feet and made her way into the house. Her eyes fell upon Mau. He was sitting by the hearth where the fire had burned low beneath the kettle. The stew was long since done, having simmered and bubbled itself to a savory turn.

"Well?" The cat spoke as if Sirona had been sitting here all along, as perhaps she had been. "I believe the meal is ready, and I am hungry, if you are not."

Stiffly Sirona climbed to her feet. She was exhausted; wherever she had been, there had been no rest in it. But knowing she must have food, she dipped out a bowl for herself as well as Mau, and made herself eat. As the cat hunkered over a second helping heaped with chunks of venison, she crawled into her bed. Images of what she had seen filled her mind. She saw again the distant array of lights bobbing and glimmering on moonlit water, heard once more the chanting of voices whose owners had long since turned to dust. To the sounds of the cat's chewing and satisfied purring, she fell asleep.

13

THE LADY BAST HAD LEFT HER temple. Eons upon eons the glimmering corridors had been Her refuge from a world that had forgotten Her. But now She had risen from Her throne of silver and gold and departed from the peace and beauty of her ancient sanctuary. Only her four-footed children in the pink stone courtyard saw Her go, watching with bright eyes, as their Goddess set out by means of dark magic to travel to a place that was darker still.

From the lofty heights of Her sanctuary Bast flew downward. Deep and deep into the ground She went, diving far beyond the ancient breast of Mother Earth. Her destination was a place known only to the dead: the realm of the Duat.

In all Her countless millennia Bast had never visited this world below the world. She was a deity of the living. Life in all its abundance was Her province; the dark landscape of the Duat was a universe inhabited by those who had departed from life, as well as by those who had never been a part of the upper realms. The route to the Duat was tortuous and filled with dangers, even to an immortal. Slowly, Bast descended through a series of twelve caverns. A host of beings, any one of which would have terrified a mortal, guarded each cave. They flapped batlike wings, hissed and spit with deformed serpentine heads, as the Goddess passed them.

Bast ignored the gaping jaws that darted at Her. She had taken precautions and girded Herself with the appropriate spells. Properly protected, the safest way for a Goddess to deal with demons was to pay them no heed. She sailed past the guardians of cavern after cavern. Her long green eyes were distant; Her goal lay at the end of the forbidding shafts of the dead, in a place more vast and fearsome than anything She had yet encountered. But the deeper She went the more horrible the creatures became. Some had human bodies, as Bast Herself did, but their heads were those of hideous birds, reptiles, or insects. Others possessed two heads, or a head that faced backwards.

They screeched out their names, names as grotesque as they were themselves. "Blood-drinker who comes from the Slaughterhouse." "Backward-facing One who comes from the abyss." "One who eats the excrement of his hindquarters."

The voices strove with each other in the effort to be heard, clashing in discordant echoes against the sensitive ears of the Goddess Who was feline as well as divine. To the immense frustration of the creatures, Bast still took no notice. Names were significant, particularly in these realms. Were She to acknowledge the beings that called to Her, they would promptly entangle Her in their coils. They could be dangerous to humans, even to gods, and yet, these guardians were not intrinsically evil, despite their hideous appearance. Their task was to act as guards and sentinels, to delay and turn back any who sought to pass them.

Cries and groans arose from the souls of the mortal dead who had not been able to withstand the guardians. But these piteous sounds Bast also ignored. The destinies of their *kas* had been recorded; neither She nor any other god not of the Underworld could do anything to change that.

At last She came to the twelfth cavern. It opened its gaping mouth before Her, as black as Anubis, the God of the Dead Himself. And, indeed, the familiar voice of Her kinsman spoke to Her from the gloom. "Greetings, Sister," He said. "What has brought You here? The realms of the dead are not Your province."

Bast's eyes glowed with the light of the world above. Their green power picked out the form of Her kindred God, and She dipped Her head in greeting. He sprang forward out of the darkness, a giant jackal, whose body swiftly shape-changed into that of a man. All but the head. Atop the mighty shoulders the jackal head remained. The yellow eyes watched Her, and they were as long and slanted and filled with knowledge as those of Bast Herself. Anubis knew why the Cat-Goddess had come, but He waited for Her to say it.

You know why. Bast gazed around Her, then spoke the name with great solemnity. *Apep.*

A tremor ran through the vast cavern. The only light came from the eyes of the two deities, and in that light the walls shivered, as if they were made of flesh and not stone. From the caves above, the shrieks and calls of the guardians intensified.

Ah, the Jackal God said without surprise. *You wish to summon the Earthshaker.* He paused. *Are You certain, My Sister? It is a grave request.*

Bast regarded Him in silence. *I must,* She said at last. *And that, My Brother, You also know.*

Anubis returned Her gaze. For a moment something like sympathy burned in the yellow eyes. Suddenly the lines of His giant body wavered and shook, as He took again the shape of the jackal. He bounded forward, into the mouth of the cavern, where the black was as deep and dense as that of His own coat.

Very well, then, He conceded, looking back over a furry shoulder. *I will take You to Him.*

Bast glided after Him. The two deities passed on into the darkness. No light attended them, not even the hint of a shadow to illumine Their path. Fortunately They did not need any. Anubis's yellow eyes glowed with the flames of death, showing Him the way. Bast followed Him easily, Her own green gaze shining with the flames of life.

This last of the twelve caverns appeared to be endless. On and on went the God and Goddess. Finally, when the darkness had grown so deep it threatened to defeat even Their immortal eyes, something ahead of Them stirred.

First Anubis, and then Bast halted. In the faint light provided by Their glowing eyes the great Chaos Serpent slowly began to reveal himself. The process seemed to go on and on. There was no estimating his size; he was beyond such mundane reckoning. Coil upon coil wound in upon each other in layers; above them the head swayed in a rhythm older than the pattern of moon and sun. Eyes as flat and black as the cavern stared unblinkingly at the visitors.

The Chaos Serpent was as ancient as Ma'at, the force that held all things in balance. He was older than the earth itself, vaster than time and space. He was Apep, the greatest of all demons. His thunderous voice could terrify Ra, the Sun God Himself. His slithering through the Underworld caused tremors in the earth above. He was the very symbol of chaos, his movements able to reduce temple buildings— the equally potent symbol of order—to ruin within seconds.

Bast moved forward again, until She stood directly before those flat black eyes. She was well familiar with Apep's powers. There were times when this terrible serpent known as Earth-Shaker had slid out from the darkness to confront Ra, sometimes even daring to trespass along the celestial river upon which the Sun Boat sailed. The danger he presented was like the sandbanks that lined the Mother Nile and were the main hazard to navigation. He lurked beneath the surface of life, sometimes in his other shape, that of an enormous crocodile, ready to draw the unwary down to a terrible death. To the mortal folk of the Two Lands, he was the very symbol of fate and the awful blows it could deliver.

But Bast was no mortal; nor was She unwary. She waited while the archdemon surveyed Her. Demons, even one as beyond age as Apep, loved to frighten those who sought their aid; it was part of what made them demons, after all. One of the best ways was to appear in their most terrifying form and then be silent, allowing the visitor to stew in evergrowing fear, while he or she stumbled for a way to begin the conversation and ask for help.

Knowing this, the Cat-Goddess remained silent. She needed Apep's help, but it was unwise to start out letting a demon think it had the upper hand. Anubis knew that as well. The Jackal God sat down on His haunches, stretching His jaws in a toothy grin as He watched and waited.

Eventually His Sister's patience bore fruit. The Earth-

Shaker's scaly coils shivered in irritation. A flickering tongue shot forth, so long it would have overreached Bast and Anubis Themselves, had They stretched Their great forms end to end, and the Serpent spoke.

You seek me out, Daughter of the Sun, it said. *And why is that? You have ever been the enemy of serpents. Have You forgotten the time when You took Your cat form and slew my sister because she had threatened Your Father Ra?*

The voice appeared as vast and endless as Apep's endless coils. Bast suspected that far above the earth itself was shuddering. *I have not forgotten,* She answered. *But times have changed, O Chaos Serpent, and so has the world above. Long and long have you been in this cavern. It is no surprise that you do not know.*

She said this last deliberately, waiting to see if the Serpent responded to the mild jab. He did. A lurid glow glistened from the masses of his coiled length, and the voice seemed to growl like thunder drawing close.

But I do know, serpent-killer. The words appeared as in a long vicious hiss. *I am aware of all that goes on above or below. And why should I care that Your temples lie in ruins? I have stirred myself a time or two to accomplish that very thing. The demise of Osiris and Isis and all Their Children means nothing to me. I should rejoice in it.*

Then you would be making a mistake, O Apep, a lack of judgement unworthy of you. As the greatest of all demons, you should care most of all.

The gigantic head swayed a bit faster. Against his will the great serpent was growing intrigued. *Why?* The question was softer now, like the mutter of a fading storm.

Bast showed Her teeth. They gleamed like polished alabaster in the eerie light. *Because you thrive on chaos, Apep. It is why you were made, the very reason that you exist. What will become of you when I and My kind cease to be even a memory in the minds of mortal folk?*

The Serpent gave a vast sinuous shrug. His interest was waning as quickly as it had been piqued. *I will go on, of course. Chaos is eternal, and so am I. Never will there be a shortage of it in the world above.*

Bast was unruffled. *You are wrong*, She said calmly. *Do you think that new ways will not bring new forms of chaos? Such shortsightedness is unworthy of you, O Apep. Those who call themselves Christians are not content with driving out old gods. They would destroy Ma'at. They would drive out the very foundations of the world, and you with it. They have created a new demon to fear, they call him the devil, and even as I speak he is causing you, Chaos Serpent, to be as forgotten as I.*

Apep's head went very still. The flat black eyes glittered like obsidian, then flamed red. The jaws gaped wide, and a hissing roar bellowed forth. It was a sound that shook the ancient rocks to their fossilized bones. Wind and screams and toppling boulders rushed through the Chaos Serpent's roar of anger. Below Bast and Anubis's feet the ground trembled. Up through the twelve caverns the shaking went, until the entire underworld shuddered, and the voices of the guardians stilled in fear.

I, forgotten? Words seemed to form out of the rush of sound. *I will never be forgotten. These mortal scum will learn what it means to ignore the power of the Chaos Serpent. Many are the works of men that I have seen rise and many more that I have helped fall. These new times will be no different.* Silence dropped, heavy as stone. The shuddering of the caverns stilled. *Now tell me, serpent-killer. What do you want of me?*

Bast allowed Herself to smile. She drew closer to the massed enormity of the ancient serpent. *Your might, O Apep. I see far, but you can see farther. The days when You and I were enemies are swallowed in the blackness of the past. Lend Me Your power, Apep. Make Me stronger. That is what I ask.*

The giant head had resumed its hypnotic swaying. *You are strong enough, Daughter of Ra. Strong enough to kill a great serpent, though now You say that the day when You did so is nothing more than mist drifting up from these caverns. Well, and well, so You want my help. I will tell You this: You have grown soft since You slew that other serpent. You were a warrior then, but no longer. You desire my might, which is the heart of all disorder and upheaval. To have Your desire You must grow hard again. Are You willing?*

The Cat-Goddess's answer came without hesitation. *I am.*

The glittering black eyes studied her. The patterned reptilian head, an enormous and horrific distortion of the heads of more common snakes, lifted higher. *Well, then,* Apep responded, *we must call Your Sister.*

The black eyes closed; the huge head swayed in a new rhythm—and within the time it would take for a mortal to draw three breaths, Sekhmet arrived. The smoke of Her coming swirled about Her, briefly painting the cavern in streaks of crimson. Slowly it dissipated, revealing Her to the gazes of the others. The Lion-Goddess was wary, as well as curious, and each emotion strove with the other as She came to stand beside Her Sister and Brother. She turned Her yellow eyes upon Bast and Anubis, then stared at the Serpent.

You came. Apep's inner voice betrayed his satisfaction.

Sekhmet's eyes narrowed. *A summons from the Chaos Serpent is strange as moonrise in the middle of the day. It would be ill done, even for a Goddess to ignore it.*

You are wise, said Apep. *But then You have ever been so. You understand chaos. You always have.* The black eyes slanted at Bast. *Unlike some.*

Bast narrowed Her eyes back at him. *Understanding a tool and knowing when to use it are separate things, O Serpent. Do not mistake the one for the other.*

The mighty coils shivered angrily. A rumbling came from the heart of the stone walls. Just as suddenly, the cavern grew still as Apep calmed himself. *Well and well*, he said. *It does not matter. You seek my help, and that is enough.*

You. The swaying head turned to Sekhmet. *Once You were a deity of fate. I give that back to You. The Tablets of Destiny are in Your rule. But,* the Serpent continued, as Sekhmet's eyes burned, *you may act only in conjunction with She Who is Your Sister. For you, Lion-Goddess, are as pitiless as the sun, while You*—the inner voice took on an odd tinge of gentleness as it addressed Bast—*are the Mother. Your heat brings life. You are the source of all growing things. Together You will temper each other's gifts, and in doing so, You will both grow in power until none can stand against You.*

The Goddess Bast stood in silence, bathed in the eerie light of the tunnels. Long and long had She waited for this moment, for the time when She and Her Sister could finally make peace between Them. But there were drawbacks to such unity; She saw that as well. The opposing sides of two natures could not be joined without each drawing upon the qualities of the other.

Yes. Apep knew what She was thinking. Such mental reflections were as clear to him as colored stones sparkling through limpid water. *It is a high price to pay. Be certain that You wish to pay it.*

Bast stood silent, turning inward upon Herself. Already She could feel the stirrings of Sekhmet's fierceness within Her. But it was not an unfamiliar feeling, for it did not issue from Sekhmet alone. Far, far back, when the ancient past was made of mist, She, too, had indulged in savagery. In Her incarnation as a great cat, She had slain the serpent that menaced Her Father, Ra. Even after the passage of all these endless eons, She could still recall the pleasure of wielding claw and fang, of slashing and tearing with no purpose other than to kill. Long and long had She been revered as a giver of life, but once She had brought death. That capability had never left Her. By the act of drawing Her Sister to Her, She would be drawing the willingness to bring death, as well. It was a grave decision.

But Sekhmet had been doing Her own reflections. *I am Sekhmet,* the Lion-Goddess snarled. *You said yourself that I rule over the Tablets of Destiny. Do you wish Me to become soft and weak in the exercise of My will?*

Apep's voice seemed as stone again, solid and implacable as the black walls. *Do you wish victory? Then You will do as I say. And the Tablets of Destiny no longer lie under Your rule alone. They belong to both of You. I see the crav-*

*ing for power that lies within You, O Sekhmet. If You truly
desire that power, You will not forget my words. Acting together, You will be strong enough to defeat this new god and
restore the world to what it should be, to Ma'at. I will help
You—no new demon will I allow to bring chaos into the
world—that is my province! But You shall have my aid only
so long as Your alliance holds."*

The massed coils began to unwind with an enormous
echoing slither. The lurid glow that came from the snake's
flesh began to fade. Apep's head stopped its swaying and
dropped to the stone floor. *I have finished with both of You,
O Sisters of Fate. Go from here. Seek out the Goddesses
from the north. They are not as old as we, but they are old
enough. They, too, will wish to see the balance restored. But
then, You already know that. Go back into the mortal world
and be content that chaos will visit in plenty. I will see to it.
Go now. Anubis waits to conduct You.*

The voice seemed to draw itself farther and farther into
the tunnel, sending back faint reverberations as it went. *The
Jackal-Headed One always waits.*

From the gleaming black walls the God of the Dead took
shape. *Are You ready to accompany Me, O Kindred?* He
asked.

Sekhmet stalked forward, but Bast remained in Her pose
of still thoughtfulness. *My priestess daughter,* She murmured. *We did not speak of her.*

What matters that? Sekhmet's inner voice flamed with a
burning mix of scorn and admiration. *We no longer need
her. We have the Chaos Serpent. It was a brilliant of You,
Sister, to seek him out. With his aid Your mortal daughter is
of no consequence.*

Bast stared at Her. *The tablets of Destiny are in both Our
keeping. Look at them, Sister, and You will see that We do.*

The green eyes glowed into the yellow ones of Sekhmet,
each set of eyes burning with its own light. But as Anubis
watched, the separate flames seemed to meld and dance together. Sekhmet's broad feline features grew thoughtful.
Her whiskers twitched. For an instant the pitiless glare of
Her gaze softened, while at the same moment, the enig-

matic gentleness of Bast's eyes hardened.

The Jackal God leaped forward. *Come,* he said. *It has already begun.*

Sirona woke suddenly. A cold wet nose was touching her face, accompanied by the tickle of long whiskers. She opened her eyes. Mau's orange gaze stared into hers.

"Get up," the cat said. "We are about to have visitors."

14

"THERE DO YOU SEE?" HAGANON pulled up his horse and gestured savagely. "That is her house. And where is the rain, my lord Alcuin? Where is the rain?"

It had been a long ride since leaving the monastery, with a miserable midmorning camp made under the trees in a futile attempt to seek shelter from the rain. There was little dry wood to be found and the fire they started had stumbled into smoky life and then died, refusing all attempts to revive its flames. Wearily the men ate cold food and rolled up in their mantles to rest, but the sodden ground penetrated even the heavy wool, making rest, much less sleep, well nigh impossible.

As the afternoon crept in, bleak and blurred by the downpour that had continued unabated, Haganon gave the order to move. The men rose, relieved to have a reason to get up, every one of them in a humor as foul as the weather. They saddled their equally miserable horses and rode on.

Haganon led the way, Abbot Wala and the royal advisor directly behind him. The Count knew where the wisewoman lived; he had made it his business to find out, when he had thought that he could hire her to work his will upon Bathilde. What he was not prepared for as they neared the place of Sirona's hut, was the sun. Without the least warning it seemed to appear from nowhere. Golden and sweet as honey, it poured down over him and the members of his party, warming and drying them with its heat.

Men and horses alike slowed their pace, basking in the warmth, staring around in surprise and delight. Haganon was the lone exception. The sudden brightness only lent heat to the fires smoldering unceasingly within him. Of course, there would be sun where the *stria* lived. Was it not her unholy powers that kept her safe and called down ruin upon those who sought to destroy her? Until now, he reassured himself grimly.

His harsh voice battered at the royal advisor. "Look for yourself. *She* is not suffering in this weather as everyone else is. Our people will face starvation in the winter, but her little garden thrives!"

A smile, as thin and fleeting as the blade of a knife, cut across Abbot Wala's face. But it was gone before Alcuin brought his gelding up. He stopped beside the count and stared thoughtfully through the grove of oak and ash trees at the small hut standing alone in the clearing. The small plot of earth planted with herbs and vegetables waved green and healthy under the blue sky. The royal advisor's gaze wandered over the plants. His face was pensive. He said nothing.

"Look at us." Haganon's tone was explosive. "Man and horse, we are drenched to the bone. The rain is everywhere. You have seen for yourself the drowned fields and pastures, the crops unable to grow and the beasts unable to graze. Yet we come here, and it is *dry*. The morning dawns bright. God's blood, the very sun is shining!"

Alcuin's mild gaze narrowed, though whether from the count's comments or his oath could not be said. "It is indeed," he said quietly.

"And so?" Scenting triumph, Haganon was determined to press him. He could not have asked for better proof than this. It was almost as if the wisewoman was cooperating in her own destruction. "What would you call it when it rains in all places but one?"

"Magic," one of the nobles said, ignoring the glare Haganon gave him; the count had wanted Alcuin to answer, not one of his own allies, who already knew what was afoot. "It is magic," the man repeated stubbornly, and blessed himself.

"Cast by a *stria*, my lord." Abbot Wala stepped in, swiftly bringing the matter back to Alcuin. "She called up this spell. Just as your vision of last night warned you."

"And do you know why?" Haganon caught the abbot's eye. Wala had come to his chamber last night and told him of Alcuin's vision and subsequent insistence that he accompany them. The count had had little chance to speak with the abbot privately since then, but Alcuin himself had made no secret of last night's events. "To make the people lose their faith and pray to pagan gods to stop the rain," he went on. "For she is a heathen herself, sent by demons to corrupt our people."

To his immense satisfaction, Haganon saw that the royal advisor was listening to him closely. On the long ride from Gaul, it had become evident that Alcuin was a man used to his comforts, and from the moment they entered Saxony, comfort had been in short supply. The monastery had been the one exception, but its luxury had swiftly fallen into the dimness of memory after this long, drenched morning. They were all of them wet and miserable, and the Palace Schoolmaster, unhardened to rough travel as he was, had to be more wet and miserable than anyone else. He sat hunched over in his saddle, the rich embroidery on his cloak blurred and darkened by the constant rain. As Haganon watched, he let loose with a sneeze, looked a little embarrassed at its loudness, and promptly sneezed again.

Sneeze away, schoolmaster, Haganon thought, and bit back a laugh. His mood had been ugly, but suddenly he was finding himself in a much better humor. A chill and a stuffed nose in the king's advisor would surely work to the advantage of his plans as much as anything else.

Shivering in his dripping woolen cloak, Alcuin's round merry features were pinched and no longer quite so merry. He was also too intent on his own thoughts to notice Haganon's satisfaction. "There can be no denying that something ungodly is taking place in this land," he said gravely, speaking more to himself, than to the count, the abbot, or the other nobles. "It may be that the woman who bides in this house is responsible. How else to explain why the sun shines here, and here alone?"

"Yes, yes," Haganon agreed eagerly. "How else? You are

a scholar, Master of the Palace School, a man of letters, trusted by the king to educate his own sons. If there were some other explanation for what our eyes tell us, you of all men would know it. Of this, I have no doubt."

Alcuin glanced at him. "A wise man knows his limitations," he said coolly, adding, "and yet, there seems no other recourse but to confront this woman."

He murmured a prayer, sketched the sign of the cross in the air, and nudged his gelding forward.

The nobles watched in fear and admiration. "He is brave," Aelisachar whispered. "The hand of God goes with him."

"And so do we," snapped Haganon. "Come on."

They rode toward the hut, Alcuin in the lead, Haganon and Abbot Wala at his mount's shoulder, and the rest of the party close behind. Steam was rising up from all of them: horses' coats and men's cloaks alike, in the warm sunlight. It seemed certain that the thud of the animals' feet, the jingle of harness, and occasional snort would awaken the house's occupant. But there was no stirring from within. The sun grew warmer, and breezes rippled through the trees, as if this were any morning in summer. Vivid green and fragrant, the herbs in the garden rustled in the soft wind.

Yet Haganon was not deceived. He was not a man who was sensitive to worlds beyond his own; however, he was a warrior, with senses keenly attuned to survival. "Listen," he muttered sharply. "There is no birdsong."

Alcuin looked at him questioningly.

"Birds always sing on a clear morning," Haganon snapped impatiently. "If they do not sing in this place, it must mean they are afraid and have fled. And why would they do that? Because they sense what men do not."

Alcuin nodded thoughtfully. "The lower creatures have ever possessed a keener sense of the unholy than mere men. Do not forget, though, that many heathens hold birds sacred to their false gods. The absence of birds may not necessarily indicate the presence of pagan evil. It could mean the precise opposite."

Must the man be so eternally a scholar! Haganon clenched his teeth to keep from shouting his thought aloud.

Abbot Wala threw him a warning glance. "We are almost at her door," the abbot said calmly. "I suggest that you call to her to come out, my lord Deacon."

"Perhaps," Haganon could not resist adding, "you will then see that this is not the time for splitting scholarly hairs."

Alcuin did not reply. He walked his gelding forward until the horse stood directly in front of the closed door. "Whoever dwells in this house," he called, "arise and come out. You have visitors who would speak with you."

There was no sound from within. The advisor's voice had been strong and clear, and the nobles had glanced at each other admiringly as he spoke. But when the silence continued their admiration turned to unease. Several horses stamped fretfully, trying to pull the reins from their riders' hands so they could crop the first dry grass they had seen in several days.

Alcuin loosed the reins of his own mount, and with the stiffness of one unaccustomed to long hours in the saddle, he began to climb down.

"Lord, what are you about?" Aelisachar cried in alarm.

Alcuin's feet thudded into the grass as he landed. "Why, what I must, of course." He caught his balance and straightened up. "If she will not come out to me, then I must go in to her. Mayhap she can still be saved and brought to God's grace, as the Lady Bathilde will be." From the folds of his robe he withdrew an ornate crucifix.

Not to be outdone, Haganon slipped off his stallion, dismounting with far more grace than had the deacon. But his blunt features were suffused with rage. "The king, who is the lord of us all, has decreed that she must die," he hissed, and swung around to the abbot. "Father," he appealed.

"My lord Deacon," Abbot Wala said in his unruffled way. "Has God Himself not sent you a sign of what He desires to happen this day? We must not waver in interpreting His Divine Will."

Alcuin turned around to meet the abbot's gaze. The two

men stared at each other in silence. Wala's face wore its customary expression of cold control, but Alcuin's light eyes were suddenly piercing, seeming to measure and examine what lay behind the other man's cool exterior. At length, the schoolmaster spoke.

"I have no intention of wavering," he said serenely. "But no man can truly know Divine Will. We may only aspire to do what is right in His eyes. It is my hope that this woman's pagan soul can be slain, and she herself given a new soul, as she is reborn in Christ. Be at peace, good companions. I have confidence that it shall happen thus."

Haganon watched the scholar's erect figure stride toward the little house. "To the pits of hell with her soul," he growled. "As long as her physical body dies, I will be content."

"Then we had better make certain this goes as we wish," the abbot replied, low-voiced. "Alcuin is a godly man, a worthy quality to be sure, but ill-advised in circumstances such as this. I had thought he would be more pragmatic, given his high position, that I could explain matters to him and he would understand, but he is not. It will not go well for us if the woman speaks of how we tried to buy her services. He may very well believe her."

"He will not," Haganon said through his teeth, "have the opportunity. She will burn long before then." Stomping back to his horse, he swung himself into the saddle.

Alcuin reached the hut and raised a fist to pound upon the barred door. He had already composed the words that he would say to the one within, calling upon the Lord to summon her forth. But before his hand touched the wood, indeed, before he could open his mouth, the door swung open instead.

The wisewoman stepped out of her house. She looked first at the royal advisor, his hand still raised foolishly in the air, and then at the mounted nobles gathered behind him. "I must be very frightening," she observed casually, "for so many great lords to ride unbidden upon my house, armed as if for war."

"And so we are." Swiftly Alcuin sought to recover his

aplomb. Lowering his hand, he bent an intent gaze upon
Sirona. At first glance she was not at all frightening:
younger than he had expected, and dressed modestly, her
long dark hair neatly braided. But her eyes gave him pause.
They changed color even as he looked, appearing dark
brown one moment, then lightening to a startling shade of
amber the next. They were shifty eyes, Alcuin decided, not
the eyes of a good Christian woman but of a pagan, a witch.
"We are here to do battle on behalf of the one true God," he
declared.

The woman's neutral expression did not change. "Your
god is not here," she said. "And unless you have come seeking hospitality or else my skills in healing, you need not be
either."

"Well do I know that God is not here." Alcuin stared hard
into the woman's strange eyes, regarding her with great
earnestness. "That is why I have come, to bring Him to
you."

"And these others?" Sirona's gaze veered to the abbot
and the nobles. "What is their purpose?"

"To help me," Alcuin explained. "Or rather, to help me
help you."

Sirona said nothing. Not one of the men on horseback
had answered her. Sirona's stare traveled over each face.
She noted that these fierce noblemen, bristling with
weapons and mounted on their fine horses, dared not meet
her eyes.

However, two men did not look away. One wore the
robes of a monk. He was lean and tall, and he watched her
from the back of his rangy bay mare with an icy detachment, as though she were already dead. The other man was
mounted on a restive chestnut stallion. By his dress and
bearing, he was clearly the group's leader. He glared down
at Sirona, his light-colored eyes burning with hatred and anticipation.

Sirona's gaze fixed on this man's face and stayed there. A
ripple went through her, composed of anger and a strange
shock of recognition. Her muscles tightened, and she shivered at the same moment, yet her eyes did not drop from

his. She knew this noble, or at least knew who he was. His name was Haganon, and he was a Christian. And she grasped something else: the man was her enemy.

Yes, Mau said behind her. *He is the one. It is he who has set in motion all the deeds that were meant to cause your death.*

Sirona's eyes narrowed. She knew at once that he spoke the truth. A haze surrounded this noble on his restless horse, a nimbus of malevolence, directed solely at her.

The cat corrected her. *It is not only you he hates. Do not forget Bathilde and the man who tried to bribe you with gold to see that both she and her baby left this world.*

"Ah." Sirona muttered the exclamation aloud, seeing at once how everything came together.

Alcuin misunderstood. "Do not be afraid," he said. "The purpose of these men is the same as mine, to bring you to the light of God."

But Haganon had heard enough. "Let us get on with it," he snapped. "We all know what we came here to do. The woman is a *stria.* She has no interest in turning from her ways."

Alcuin swung on him. "I," the smaller man snapped, "will be the judge of that." He looked from the angry nobleman to the abbot. "There is much here to judge, and not all of it to do with the woman."

"And what do you intend to judge?" Abbot Wala's voice was loud. A rift of anger ran through his cold exterior. It was calculated, but no less lacking in impact for all that. He thrust his hand out. "Evil? Look, she carries on with her evil before your very eyes. Do you not see the cat?"

Alcuin paled. And yet the truth of it was standing before his eyes. There was the creature Abbot Wala spoke of. It had appeared without warning, as if it had indeed been conjured, stepping up alongside the woman to stare at him with eyes the color of flame. The royal advisor gazed at the animal and felt a shiver go through him. An unfathomable expression resided in those blazing eyes, a look that should not belong to a cat that was only a cat.

Alcuin was well versed in the theory of magic; he had

written and spoken much on the subject. There was natural magic and there was demonic. The latter relied on invoking demons to carry out the magician's command, and it was pure evil. Dealing with such beings as demonic magic required inevitably led to the moral corruption of the one who summoned them. Natural magic, on the other hand, simply utilized the phenomena of nature, and could therefore be used by Christians without doing harm to their eternal souls.

Alcuin had been hoping that the allegations made against this woman involved natural magic. Many wisewomen practiced that particular art, and though a number of his fellow clergy had begun to condemn "woman's magic," Alcuin himself did not. He saw little sense in such a step. Natural magic was as old as the world and grounded deep in the hearts of the common folk. To eradicate it would be nearly impossible, and Alcuin himself had seen wisewomen accomplish much healing with their arts to really wish to.

Neither did the royal counselor possess Carolus's ease of mind about shedding blood, even when it came to matters of the faith. He had not spoken of this reluctance to his king, much less to Haganon, but his hope had been that he would be able to declare the woman's practices not harmful, after converting her to Christ, of course. The vision sent to him last night had made him fear that this would not be possible. Now he knew it was not. The cat was incontrovertible proof.

His inner senses still prickled with warning over what lay afoot between the cold-eyed Abbot Wala and the hot-tempered Haganon. But this must take precedence. It still might be possible to save the woman's life, as well as her soul, if she recognized the peril.

Raising his hand, he made the sign of the cross. "Woman," he shouted in a strong voice, "you are surrounded by evil. Free yourself from its clutches. Renounce this demon that has sunk its claws into your soul." He gestured fiercely at Mau.

Sirona's face did not change. "I see no demon," she said. Her calm tone was an odd contrast to the advisor's shouting. "And if there is evil, you have brought it, not I." She stared pointedly at Haganon. "As for the cat," she added, "he is only a cat."

Haganon bristled, but Alcuin spoke before the noble could. "No. He is more than that, far more. Yet there is still time. Send the creature from you, and no harm will come to you. My word upon it."

"What?" Haganon exploded with outrage. "That is not what the king ordered. His command was to—"

"Peace, good Count," Abbot Wala broke in. "Deacon Alcuin knows what the king's command was. And he knows his duty."

Alcuin's mild gaze was suddenly hard. "I am Carolus's most trusted advisor, my lords. I fill that position, lords, not you. Do not forget that." As Haganon glared, struck momentarily speechless, Alcuin turned back to Sirona. "Young woman, do as the Lord in His wisdom bids you." His voice was deep with compassion and urging. "Turn from the demon. Save yourself. I will help you."

Sirona looked at the cat. Mau returned her gaze. *The Christian is right about one thing*, he said quietly. *There is indeed time, some anyway. But you have to make a choice.*

Using my power, you mean. Sirona's mouth turned down.

Yes. But other choices are open to you. You can repudiate me, as this Christian wants you to. You can send me away.

And what will happen to you if I do?

The cat's gaze was steady. *They will kill me.* His tail flicked up over his back. *Or they will try.*

That makes no sense. Anger flamed up within Sirona. "It makes no sense." She repeated the words, this time speaking them aloud, as she turned back to Alcuin. "This cat is no demon. And I am only a wisewoman. I practice healing, not spells. And how many folk keep cats to catch rats and mice? The number is beyond counting. Will you go to every house in Saxony looking for cats, and then accuse the people there of harboring demons?"

"No," Haganon shouted. "There is no need. We know where the evil is, and how to root it out."

He spurred his horse forward. But Alcuin blocked his

way. "Hold!" the advisor cried, his pale eyes blazing with fury. Wheeling back to the doorway of the hut, he pulled a flask from beneath the folds of his cloak and flung the contents at the cat. "By the power of this holy water," he cried, "begone, demon."

An expectant hush fell on the observers. The effect of holy water was well-known; when cast upon any creature of the devil it would shrivel and burn the demon, causing it to disappear. The sacred liquid had fallen squarely on the cat and everyone waited for the sizzle and smoke, followed by the shriek of vanquished evil. Even Sirona was surprised. Cats did not like water, and Mau was surely quick enough to have leaped aside to avoid the splashing.

Yet he had not moved. Nor did he sizzle and smoke and disappear.

The watching nobles exchanged glances. Several blessed themselves. Haganon's bearded face split in a grin of triumph. Alcuin, however, did not cross himself. Nor did the abbot. Instead, both men stared at Mau, glancing slowly from the cat to Sirona. The look on the abbot's austere features was grim and satisfied. The royal advisor's expression was thoughtful.

"Could it be," he asked in a soft troubled tone, "that the woman speaks the truth? That the cat is indeed only a cat?"

Haganon's triumphant grin vanished. "No," he snarled. "It could not. Both of them stink with evil. They reek of it, and you are too much of a fool to see it."

Alcuin wheeled on him again, but the noble plunged on. "The king entrusted you with doing what is right—"

"The king," Alcuin shot back. "Not you!"

"Then do as you were bidden. Because of your dithering and blithering the woman is gathering her powers even as we stand here. Think you that the cat is no demon? I'll wager that she is preparing to call upon worse than that beast!"

Haganon threw a glance at the abbot and fell silent. There was no need to say anything more. His words resonated with his men as nothing else he had yet said. Exclamations broke out, each man raising his voice to make himself heard above the others. Some yelled that the cat was indeed a demon, others that he was not. Regardless of what they thought, all of them backed their horses away in anticipation of Haganon's prediction of what the wise-woman intended to do.

Sirona watched the men argue. She watched the faces of Haganon and the royal advisor, in particular. Animosity roiled between the two like smoke from an untended fire. They reminded her of two ill-tempered dogs, ready to leap at each other's throats. It may be, she thought to herself, that she and Mau need do nothing but wait for that to happen.

But she had not reckoned with the abbot. Alcuin's scholarly face had turned stern, yet it was Abbot Wala who spoke. "Wisdom can sometimes issue forth from the most unexpected of mouths," he said, and leveled a pointed stare at Haganon's bearded face.

The noble flushed with rage and glared back, but the abbot had already turned to Sirona. "Mayhap the Lord Haganon is speaking the truth. The answer lies with you, young woman. But take care how you answer, for grave matters are at stake. Demons will seek you out if you speak falsely. They will tear out your liver, burn it in living flame, and scatter its ashes to the eternal winds."

Sirona took a single step forward. She observed with an irony composed of irritation, anger, and impatience, how the mounted nobles pulled on their reins, forcing the horses back from her small approach. "And how is that fate any different than the one you and these other good Christians will visit on me?" she demanded.

Beside her, Sirona felt Mau stir. *Well,* the cat said silently, *you are determined to make them angry, aren't you?*

She knew he was right, but suddenly she was too angry herself to care. "You ride up to my house—my house, not yours—making demands, telling me I must do this and that. Well, king or no king, you have no right. I do not recognize his authority or yours. The Lord Haganon you praise so highly is a Christian who would have murdered a woman, her innocent babe, and me. Yet he is the one accusing me of evil."

A change swept over Alcuin's face. "What is this talk of murder?" His eyes were suddenly intent, focused in a new direction. "Well?" he demanded, staring at Haganon. "What does she mean?"

"It is the demon speaking." Abbot Wala spoke quickly and smoothly, his voice revealing nothing. "To utter such words against a man of Count Haganon's character could only be the work of a demon. And she in its grip."

"Indeed," Alcuin answered. His gaze, however, had not faltered from its intense scrutiny of Haganon, and now the abbot. "And yet there is much here that has been left unsaid. Woman," he said kindly to Sirona, "why do you charge this nobleman so gravely? Tell me of things I do not know; I beg you."

"Ask her to make her charges as a Christian." The abbot's voice was deadly. "And then ask her to explain why it rains everywhere in our land but here. If she is not a *stria,* and if that demon beside her is in truth only a cat, then she will be able to swear in the name of Our Lord Jesus Christ. But if it be not a cat, then it will stop up her tongue with its claws."

Alcuin could not dispute the wisdom of this, despite the fact that its source was a man he had started out distrusting and whom he now distrusted even further. He held up the flask of holy water. The silver metal flashed brightly in the sun. Only a few drops remained of the precious fluid, but it was still enough to bring the woman safely into the fold. "Let me baptize you, child," he said gently. "Accept the true faith. Then you may speak of truth, and you will be believed."

It was a box with no openings. Sirona was all too aware of it. She would not become a Christian, and since she would not, she was condemned. The abbot knew that, of course, which was why he had proposed it. She turned her gaze toward him. He was watching her, and his face, Haganon's, and those of the other men seemed to close in about her, gloating and tight with anticipation. By contrast, the face of the king's counselor was earnest and hopeful; in his own fashion he truly did want to save her. But it was he who had placed her in this trap and then closed the door.

Her anger flared like oil boiling out of an overheated cooking pot. Whatever she said or did made no difference. These men wanted her death, and they would not be satisfied with less.

"Perhaps I should not disappoint you, my lords," she said acidly. "Perhaps I should give you my answer by putting a curse on all of you if you do not leave my house!"

She thrust out her hands, forefingers extended in the classic, ancient gesture of cursing.

Out of nowhere a cloud suddenly cloaked the sun. There was no sign of wind, but the trees around the hut shuddered briefly, as if something far below the surface had grabbed hold at their roots and shaken them.

15

A **TERRIBLE** **SILENCE** **CRASHED** down. Men blanched, made the sign to protect against evil, wheeled their horses about, as if to flee.

"Hold!" Haganon and the abbot roared together.

"What is upon all of you!" Haganon was fairly spitting in fury at the ease with which this woman seemed able to rout his own allies. "Would you run from this creature's threats like a flock of gabbling geese? You are men; get your bellies back!"

Slowly, the nobles turned their horses. Their faces blended into one giant stare, but their courage was returning, shamed upon them by Haganon. However, he was not alone in his temper. Sirona's own temper had swept words from her lips the way one sweeps ashes from her hearth. They had scattered in the air, and it was too late to sweep them back. Yet her fate was sealed in any case. The cursing gesture could scarcely make things worse.

It was Alcuin who finally broke the silence. "You have given your answer, indeed," he said sadly. "And would I that it be otherwise. Yet I asked for the truth, and now I have it."

He turned away. There was an air of finality about the movement, as if he were closing the door on any further attempts to reason with this stubborn woman. Among the group of men he was the only one who had shown no fear at the *stria's* threat. Abbot Wala had reflexively crossed himself, and even Haganon, despite his rage and frustration, had found himself yanking back on his stallion's reins at the witch's threat of a curse.

187

But now both men were triumphant. They saw the expression on Alcuin's face and knew they had won. With the satisfied expression of men who had accomplished a difficult task, they listened expectantly as the advisor spoke.

"A pagan this woman was born and a pagan she will die." There was no satisfaction in the scholar's modulated tones, only deep regret. "We can only pray that as the holy flames cleanse her she accepts the gift of God's grace, so that her soul be saved and she not burn in the fires of hell for all eternity. The demon, too," he added in a harder voice, "must be burned. The flames of righteousness will destroy it, as the holy water did not."

"It shall be done." Haganon beckoned to the other nobles. "Take her. Then gather wood for a fire." He was in charge again. The power had passed from this mealy-mouthed churchman to Haganon, and the count relished the transition.

But his companions had not entirely regained all of their courage. Haganon heard mutters, and he swung around. "I said take her!" His voice rose to a bellow. "She is but a woman and outnumbered at that!" Still, the nobles held back, driving Haganon to roar even louder. "Do you fear her curses? Then bind you her hands so she cannot work her evil! No, wait. I shall do it myself."

Leaping from his stallion, he strode toward Sirona. His face was set, his eyes narrowed with purpose. Sirona watched him approach, and the hands he had ordered bound clenched at her sides. Anger swirled behind her eyes. She would be a fool to allow him to succeed in his plan of killing her.

He will not. Mau's silent voice startled her. He had not moved from her side. *Let him do as he desires*, the cat went on. *It does not matter.*

Sirona cast him an astonished look. *You want me to stand meekly so these Christians can slaughter me, like a calf about to have its throat cut?*

The cat's eyes were steady. *Let your hands be bound, it makes no difference. And do not worry about the fire. We need it. In order for the magic to work, there must be a fire.*

Magic? Sirona asked.

But Mau did not answer, for the rest of the men had begun to follow Haganon's example and dismount. One after the other, they dropped to the ground. As they did so, their courage rekindled. They drew toward Sirona, flanking her like wolves closing in on a deer.

Alcuin had withdrawn to one side. He was praying, his eyes closed, and his face sad. Abbot Wala, too, was praying, though his eyes were open and his face wore a look of contentment. Haganon had drawn out a length of rope from somewhere and was holding it out in preparation as he approached the woman. He eyed her warily. She did not appear to be offering resistance; perhaps this would go well, after all.

He reached out for the *stria's* hands. For an instant that seemed to last forever she stared at him. The air quivered. The woman's eyes blazed. Without realizing it the nobles held their breaths. But in an odd contradiction to the burning look in her eyes, the witch allowed Haganon to loop the rope about her wrists.

His action released the men from the last remaining shreds of their caution. Shouts broke out, and they leaped to the task of building a fire. Alcuin alone paid no heed. Eyes closed, he continued to pray.

One of the afrites has already been called. Mau's silent voice sounded in Sirona's head. *Water. That fool of a Christian threw it on me without the slightest idea of what he was doing. Now they will make their fire, all unknowing that by doing so they are bringing us the afrite of fire, thus helping us in our working. You must call upon earth and air, and the spell will be done.*

Sirona heard him with only a part of her mind. From the moment Haganon's hard hands had touched her, the aura of a dream had descended. The rough bite of the rope about her wrists, combined with the scene before her, was even more unreal than the wind-driven trip Mau had taken them on to Bast's temple in the realms of magic.

The men had become eager now. Excitement had welled up in each man's breast, and the feeling was contagious; it passed like an illness between them. Each tried to egg his fellows on. It bothered them not that they were doing the work of servants. This was a holy task, and they would be blessed for performing it. The pile of wood rose rapidly, seized from within and around the witch's hut.

The men trampled through the neat house. They tore apart the bed, pulled down the rows of dried herbs, and scattered the contents of the two chests. One or two kicked at the cat, who dodged their feet with a snarl and resumed his place by Sirona's side. Several more devoured the stew as they urged each other to search for signs of evil. Left untended, the men's horses wandered into the garden and went to grazing busily on the budding herbs and vegetables.

Sirona stood impassively as her garden and house were ravished. Coming in and out of the hut the nobles kept turning from their work to watch for her reaction. None was forthcoming, and they were clearly disappointed by that. But as the task of laying the fire neared completion, there were those among the men who began eyeing her with a far different intention in mind.

"We should enjoy her," one of them finally muttered to Haganon, when the bonfire was stacked and ready to be lit. "She's not bad-looking, and she'll soon be cast into the flames. It would be a shame to waste her."

Alcuin's eyes flew open. "No!" he roared in a voice that rivaled Haganon's. "Not one among you will lay a hand on her. We are engaged in God's work, not pleasures of the flesh. We must take no joy in this deed, and any man who seeks to find any will feel the full weight of the Church's displeasure!"

The sudden furious response startled everyone. Even Haganon jumped. However, he made no attempt to contradict the advisor. Had Alcuin not spoken up, Haganon himself would have. The woman was a witch. Only a fool would couple with her, thereby making himself vulnerable to her evil powers.

"There is no time for that," he said aloud. "And if there were, a man would have to be mad to prong a witch." He narrowed his eyes at the waiting bonfire. It had been hastily prepared, but it would serve its purpose. He pointed. "Light the fire."

The faces of some of the nobles grew serious. Others grinned. Three of them ran into the house; a moment later, they emerged with brands lit from the hearth-fire. The wood that had been used to lay the bonfire was dry. It caught rapidly. Curls of smoke sizzled up from the bottom of the pile, quickly giving way to deep spurts of orange. Crackling filled the air as the fire found its voice.

The men stood in expectant silence, listening while the wood sang its burning song. The flames leaped up at the blue sky. Its light caught at the men's faces, painting them in shades bright as blood.

Haganon and the abbot stood apart from the others. They exchanged glances, then stared at Sirona. Their eyes gleamed, lurid as the fire.

Are you ready? Mau asked.

"Are you ready, child?" Alcuin's question came in an eerie repetition. "There is still time. Repent, confess, and save your eternal soul."

There are four afrites. The cat's voice was as calm and unhurried as if Alcuin had not spoken. *Water, Air, Earth, and Fire. They are the elements of nature, of what makes up the world. No true magic can be worked without them. They are friendly to you, human one; they always have been. Call upon them now, and they will protect both of us.*

Alcuin was still waiting for Sirona to reply. Bewilderment, anger, and compassion all warred in him at the way in which this woman was ignoring her fate. He had seen other pagans die in the same way, with that stoic indifference, and it baffled him, drove him to despair at their determination to so stubbornly refuse salvation. He strode up to Sirona, thrusting his face close to hers, taking her urgently but gently by her bound wrists.

"Answer me, woman," he said in a voice that grated with

pleading. "Will you not accept the true faith and save your-self?"

Sirona's distant gaze focused on his face. Its quality of changing from light to dark had gone; only the darkness was left. "I will not," she said.

Alcuin's shoulders sagged. Slowly he released the woman's wrists and stepped away. "I consign her to the flames." His voice was heavy. "Her and the demon familiar with her."

Haganon nodded with deep satisfaction. "Let it be done."

Two of the braver—or crueler—nobles came forward. A third followed with a spear held at the ready. He would impale the cat upon it and then thrust the creature into the flames.

Mau's light voice was still calm. *Use your power. Draw on it. Call it to you. Do you want us both to die?*

She did not. And the knowledge was borne in upon her like a blow. Death was flaming before her; if she did not act now, she would be consumed, and Mau, along with her. Sirona shut her eyes. For the first time in her life, she tried with full consciousness to summon what lay deep within her, so strong and so unwelcome. But pain immediately slashed at her, sharp and stabbing, crushing her with its intensity. Her eyes came open. There was a barrier in the pathways of her mind. Reluctance lurked within her, and it was a potent force in itself, as deep as the magic she was supposed to possess. And now it had become her enemy, allying itself instead with these men who meant to kill her.

Think about why you are reluctant, Mau said. *When you find the source of that reluctance, it will free you. But think quickly. Time is growing short.*

Hard hands seized hold of Sirona. The men had lost whatever fear they had ever held of the witch. It had been swallowed up by the reek of impending death and the witch's own lack of resistance to it. The man with the spear aimed and jabbed at Mau. The cat leaped aside, dodging the sharp point with ease.

The two men pulled Sirona forward. She closed her eyes

again. Smoke and the crackle of flames drifted toward her. Alcuin was chanting prayers in Latin. A few of the more religious nobles were joining him. But this time something happened. Behind her closed lids an image suddenly leaped up. It was formed entirely of fire, a huge figure of living flame that paused in its cavorting to gaze at her with eyes that burned more brilliant than the sun. It spoke to her in a voice that burned.

I am here, it said. *What magic do you choose to work?*

Above the fiery image another figure came swirling and dancing. It was clothed in water, shimmering and soft as spring rain, hard and driving as a winter storm. Its voice rippled over the heated words of the flame image.

I, too, am here, it said. *Work your magic. I will help you.*

The two voices burned and flowed in a strange unison. Call the others, they said. They are waiting.

Call them, Mau said. He had danced up behind her, mocking the efforts to stab him. *Earth and Air. Call them.*

The man with the spear thrust again at the cat and missed. He cursed and yelled for the others to help him. The two holding Sirona kicked at Mau, also missed, and added their curses to his. Prodded by Haganon, several of the nobles ran up. Surrounding the cat they poked and stabbed at him with long sticks, trying to force him in the direction of the blazing fire.

How? The question was torn from Sirona as the men pulled her forward again.

Summon the afrite of Earth from the east and the afrite of Air from the west, Mau said. This time he spoke from beside her. *But you must open your eyes to do it.*

Sirona obeyed. The flames were directly in front of her gaze. They filled her vision, snarling with power. But it was a power of its own making, completely removed from the control of the men who had lit the fire and now stood about it with long sticks, ready to push the witch into the heart of the flames and keep her there until she was reduced to ashes.

Yes. The flame afrite spoke in its giant sizzling voice. *You*

*shall see, after all. These puny creatures have no power to
make us do their will. Neither do you, but it does not matter.
We have decided to help you, not them.*

"Throw her into the flames." Haganon hurled out the
command in a voice that sounded scarcely less human than
those of the afrites. "Do it now!"

Alcuin's chanting grew louder.

Look with your inner eyes. The cat's voice was very
close, as if he were whispering in her ear. *See the source of
your hesitation.*

Sirona looked. An image was forming behind her eyelids. Her mother's face gazed out at her. The eyes, so like
her daughter's, stared into Sirona's soul. But there was
no magic in the depths of Raimond's eyes, no power,
only fear. Her mother's voice rang in her ears. The countless warnings against using her powers jarred and
pounded at Sirona. *The new is stronger than the old.* She
felt the force of the promise she had made on that last
day with Raimond dragging her toward death. Pain welled
up inside her, and from it sprang anger. Sirona felt the
distance between them, a distance of faith as well as
space. Raimond had left her behind, abandoning her and
their heritage to an uncertain fate. And yet, as Sirona
gazed into those sad, well-known features, she felt her
mother's love.

Finally, she felt the power. It surged through her, clean
and fierce, singing songs she had never heard. She called to
it, and there was no hesitation in her call. The barrier of her
reluctance was gone, as distant as her mother was, with her
love and her fear.

A voice beat at her ears, seeming to come from a great
distance. "The cat," Alcuin shouted. "Do not seek to slay it
with your spears, for it cannot be killed that way. You must
burn it. The devil's creature must be purified in the Lord's
flames."

Momentarily diverted from the larger entertainment of
seeing the witch burn, the crowd of nobles leaped to the
task of chasing the cat into the fire. Mau's great orange eyes
flashed at Sirona's, then, to the men's surprise, he stopped

leaping this way and that. Meekly he seemed to allow himself to be herded toward the flames.

Time froze. In that endless instant, Sirona's eyes whirled to the west and to the east. "I summon thee," she cried. "Air and Earth, come to me."

Far below, and far away, in a realm none of these men, or Sirona for that matter, knew anything about, the Chaos Serpent stirred its massive coils.

Sirona felt the ground tremble beneath her feet. The horses jerked up from their grazing, eyes rolling. The men holding her arms staggered, crying out in sudden fear.

The Serpent lifted its head, tongue flickering.

A gust of wind slapped the faces of everyone present. It howled as it buffeted the men, its voice sounding almost human. In response, the flames whooshed and then hurled themselves up at the sky with a deafening roar.

The voices of the nobles who had been praying along with Alcuin wavered and fell away. Alcuin himself continued, not pausing even as Haganon bellowed, "Quick, throw her on the fire! Fools! Can you not see she is trying to cast a spell!"

The cat let out a yowl that raised the hair of every man present, save for Haganon and Alcuin. The horses whirled as though they had all joined themselves into one beast and fled, reins trailing and leathers snapping in the wind. The men gripping Sirona's arms made a feeble attempt to thrust her at the fire. But the wind howled again, and the two men jerked away from her with yells of pain.

"She burned us," one said in horror. Wide-eyed, he and his fellow stared at their hands, at the red welts already swelling on their palms. Blessing themselves frantically, they backed away, scrabbling so fast they nearly fell down.

Haganon let out an oath and sprang forward. "Blast your eyes, I'll burn the witch myself then!"

Free, though her wrists were still tied, Sirona turned to face him. "Will you?" She raised her bound arms, and her eyes blazed light and dark. "*Will you*?"

Alcuin opened his eyes at last. "Lord God of Hosts," he cried. "Sanctify this evil in Your holy fires!"

But he was too late. Perhaps the new god was not listening; in any case, the power of the afrites overrode the royal advisor. An explosion of light burst over Haganon, Alcuin, and the men-at-arms. Sparks shattered and snapped. The intensity was so brilliant that none of them could see. From the fire, smoke swirled and thickened in a great choking cloud. The wind howled, and so did the terrified men. Even Haganon cried out and covered his eyes. Alcuin continued shouting out supplications to his god, but they were swallowed up by the wind and dampened by the smoke.

It stopped.

The wind fell silent. The smoke wafted into gray wisps, and the blazing light vanished. The flames of the bonfire gave a feeble sputter and went out.

For a span of heartbeats the screaming men were not aware that now the only noise to be heard was issuing from them. Haganon was the first to realize it. He swung around in a circle, his face suffused with blood so that he looked nearly black with rage. "Where is she?" he bellowed. "Blood of Christ, where is she?"

Rain began to fall, drowning out his words.

Sirona herself could not have told him. All she knew was that she was in the woods, in a grove of beech trees. She saw that much, but where? And how had she gotten there? She had called upon magic, and it had answered her. But now she could not remember what it was that she had wanted of the magic. She leaned against the trunk of one of the beeches and thought. Slowly she remembered. Mau. She had wanted to protect Mau.

"You succeeded," a voice said. "They will be looking for a large black cat with orange eyes and a white mark on his chest. They will not find him."

Sirona turned. The voice was familiar—too familiar. It could not be, she told herself. She stared. Her eyes felt as if they would keep growing wider until they bulged out of her face and toppled to the ground.

A man was standing behind her. Naked, lithely muscled and lean, sleek black hair and sharply defined features.

He smiled, and his eyes suddenly gleamed orange.

Sirona swallowed, struggling to speak. Finally, she got out a whisper that was more of a croak.

"Mau?"

16

THE MAN CONTINUED TO SMILE. "Who else?"

Sirona stared at him, speechless. The voice was stunningly familiar, deeper, but with the same light dryness peculiar to Mau. The man himself had the same quality of familiarity. The hair on his head was sleek and black as an animal's pelt. It grew less thickly over his arms and legs, but on his chest there was a fine soft mat of black starred with white, in the exact shape that the cat had borne.

"I suppose," the man continued, glancing down at his naked body, "that I will have to find some clothing. It's been so long since I've shape-changed that I'd forgotten." He frowned. "One of the more troublesome aspects of taking human form."

"Did I do this?" Sirona heard her voice as if it belonged to a stranger, stumbling and croaking like a frog in a marsh. Whatever magic she had used to call this man-creature forth still seemed to hold her in its grip, freezing her to the ground in a holding spell of disbelief. She gestured at him dazedly.

"You did. And you saved me from a most unpleasant experience, for which I thank you. Although it would not have been the first time." An expression of ironic distaste flitted over the human features. "Never will I understand the fascination your kind has with burning creatures that disturb them. The Christians have only imitated those who came before them. Fortunately, you and your foremothers have a talent for keeping me out of fires."

"But—but how?"

"How did you do it?" The man smiled. "By magic, human one. How else?"

In that moment he was Mau, unmistakably so. Sirona stared incredulously at the enigmatic expression in the orange eyes, noting the sly twist of the mouth that almost made her expect to see whiskers twitch. The reality of what she was witnessing crashed in on her with numbing force. She took a backward step and stumbled, her knees going suddenly weak.

Mau looked irritated. "Do get hold of yourself," he said impatiently. "We haven't time for histrionics. I thought you had discovered your strength at last, and long enough it took, too, I might add. Please, human one, do not begin acting as foolishly as those men who tried to burn us."

Sirona's stunned look hardened. "And well it was," she said coldly, "that those men were such fools. Else you and I would have both been ashes in their fire long since."

A sound rang out. It took Sirona an instant to recognize what it was. Laughter. This astonishing creature was laughing, and it sounded no different from the laughter of any man who was truly a man. She gaped, no doubt looking as foolish as the men Mau had just compared her to.

He laughed harder at her expression. "But I *am* a true man," he said, seeing the thought in her mind. "At least, to those who look upon me. Put clothes on this body and none of your mortal folk will see me as anything other than one of them. It's the beauty of magic, you see. And you, my human one, did it."

He started to thread his way through the beech trees. The sun was shining, and his pale skin glimmered through the dappled shade of the grove. Naked and beautiful, he was a creature of magic, indeed. Unable to take her eyes from him, Sirona followed. She had created him, or at least that was what he claimed, but as she walked and stared Sirona knew he spoke the truth. The knowledge was as powerful as the magic itself. She was astonished and enthralled. That she had done this made her feel larger than herself, and at the same time, smaller, dwarfed by this magic she and she alone had called up.

Mau's first few steps were awkward, as if he were a child learning how to walk. But he soon fell into the rhythm of maneuvering on two legs rather than four, and the grace that belonged to him in his true form began to reveal itself. As Sirona caught up with him, he looked down at himself.

"To be sure there are aspects of this form that are disconcerting," he said ruefully. "And these man-parts swinging about is one of them. It's a pity your magic wasn't powerful enough to call up clothing."

Sirona continued to stare at him. Of all the emotions roiling her, astonishment gained the upper hand anew. It left her speechless, and his bright laugh rang out again. Finally, she managed to find words. "Where are you going?"

He threw her a brief glance. "First, to find some clothes. Then . . . well, that is up to you. Where do you wish to go?"

Sirona paused. Mau stopped, too. Turning around, he rested his glowing eyes upon her and waited, with feline patience, for her to answer.

She stood there and thought. The face of Haganon rose up in her mind's eye. She saw the hatred in him, the desire for her death, and a smile that had nothing of humor in it curved her lips. "Perhaps," she said, "we should find Count Haganon and show him your new shape. I have a bone to pick with him after all, and so do you."

Mau watched her. "Is that wise?" he asked mildly.

"No," Sirona said, and sighed. "I suppose not. What is wise would be turn you back to a cat and put aside the memories of Haganon, as well as Bathilde, but that is no longer possible. Nor," she added, "is it wise, since they have not forgotten me."

Mau said nothing. His silence was an agreement in itself.

Sirona, too, fell silent. "We must go to Bathilde," she said at length. Her tone was an odd mingling of unwillingness and determination. "There is no help for it. Haganon and that abbot of his may go after her next. Indeed, they are sure to." She eyed him uncomfortably. "Although, as you said, we had better find you something to wear first."

Mau nodded without surprise, as if he had known all

along what her answer would be. "My thoughts exactly," he remarked, and set off again.

Sirona fell into step beside him. They passed from the grove of beech trees. A deerpath crossed a small meadow and wound off into dense oak woods. They followed it, moving faster, as Mau grew more and more accustomed to his human form. The sun accompanied them, slanting so bright and warm through the leafy canopy overhead that Sirona realized the magic she had unwittingly called up to banish the rain on the walk home from Bathilde's hall was still with her. It made her wonder if back at her hut a downpour was now drenching the men who had tried to kill her.

They walked for some little distance before the man who had been a cat spoke again. "Bathilde is strong," he said quietly. "And growing stronger."

"That sounds like a warning." Sirona slung him a glance. The shock of seeing him this way still struck her every time she met his orange eyes, but it was even more shocking to realize how rapidly she was growing used to him.

Mau nodded. "Therefore you must be stronger."

Sirona's glance lowered itself into a frown. "It was your wish all along that I join with Bathilde," she said sharply.

"No," Mau said. "It was the wish of my Mistress."

The man who had been a cat gave Sirona a long look from eyes that suddenly seemed dark. She could not fathom what she saw in those eyes, and she was not certain that she wanted to. But she listened to the somber words he spoke next.

"So be strong, human one. If you are not, blood will soak this land, and not the blood you wish."

They walked on in silence.

Bathilde had tired of waiting. Two weeks and more had passed; the rain had never once stopped, and there had been no sign of the wisewoman. It appeared that she had gone and was not going to return. The realization made Bathilde angry. Sirona had proved a great disappointment. Worse, she had jeopardized Bathilde's carefully laid plans. Yet, an-

gered as she was by the wisewoman's disappearance,
Bathilde could no longer afford herself the luxury of brooding. It was time and long past time to act.

She began by praying to the foreign goddess. At first, no
answer rewarded her pleas. This did not entirely surprise
Bathilde; that was why she had needed Sirona, after all. But
she did not give up. She was nothing if not stubborn. The
dark of the moon crept in, made even darker by the ever-
present rain, and late that night, as Bathilde lay in her bed
box, her baby son nestled against her, surrounded by the
snores and stirrings of her sleeping house folk, the voice
came.

You have been calling to me, it said, and the words were
like fire and thunder, hissing and rumbling through the
great hall.

Bathilde's eyes flew open. The familiar night darkness
had not changed. Shadows cast by the banked hearth-fire
played across the walls and rafters. The sounds of her slum-
bering house folk went on undisturbed. Not even the baby
had moved. The Goddess intended that only Bathilde
should hear Her.

"O Great Lady," she whispered. "You have come." Her
eyes probed the shadows. This strange power she had summoned had revealed Herself to Sirona, but not to Bathilde.
Would She do so now?

But the dimness of the sleeping hall remained unchanged. Only the voice spoke. *I have come,* it told her. *To
tell you this: seek out your own goddess. Go you out into
the land and honor Her with a sacred procession, as your
people used to do.*

"Freyja." Bathilde breathed the name with reverence.
Freyja was the Holy Mother of Life, the divinity of fertility
and death. She was sacred beyond all others. Ah, how She
had once been loved and worshipped. Once, Bathilde reminded herself. "But that was long ago," she whispered
sadly. "She has turned Her face from us. She will not heed
my prayers, O Lady. That is why I sought You."

She will heed you now. The fiery voice was rumbling off
into the distance like departing thunder. *Set out on your*

*procession and you will see. But above all, remember this:
if you would please Me, give Me blood.*

"Wait," Bathilde called out. "Lady, return, I beg You.
There is more I must know."

She was no longer whispering, and her voice awoke
Begga, the nurse, for that good woman ever slept with her
ears cocked for the sounds of a fretful babe or mother.
"Mistress," the rotund servant mumbled, shaking herself
out of sleep. "What's amiss?" She rolled clumsily off her
pallet. "Is it the child?"

"No, Begga." Bathilde lowered her voice. "A dream
woke me, nothing more. Go back to your rest."

Still mumbling to herself, the nurse obeyed. No one else
had stirred, save for a few dogs kicking and whining in their
sleep. As Begga's snores joined those of the others,
Bathilde lay staring wide-eyed into the darkness.

A sacred procession. Sekhmet had set her a task and
given no advice as to how it would be accomplished.
Bathilde had seen those colorful holy cavalcades often, but
Carolus, in his passion to conquer as well as convert Saxony, had banned all such rites. And yet they were still vivid
to Bathilde's inner eye; the missionaries sent by the conquerors could not control memories, after all. She saw
again the sacred cart in which the Goddess and Her priestesses were pulled about the countryside, heard the noisy
pounding melodies of drums, bells, and bull-roarers, and
smiled as if she were once again that wide-eyed little girl of
long ago.

The Christians hated Freyja; they called Her a goddess of
witchcraft, and Hers had been the first Shining One's worship to be banned. But Freyja's priestesses were soothsay-
ers, not witches. Through the power granted them by their
Goddess, they could predict the future. They journeyed
from village to village and feast to feast in their beautifully
carved and ornamented wagon-carts, traveling alone or in
groups, their wanderings an imitation of the moon, which
was sacred to them. The magic of these consecrated women
was great: they foretold the success or failure of coming
crops, healed the sick, divined the hidden, and could even

control unseen events in the life of the community. Small
wonder was it that the conquerors had been so anxious to
ban them.

And as she lay there remembering, a thought came to
Bathilde. Of course, she told herself. She would start here,
in her own hall and on her own lands. If Sekhmet spoke
truly and Freyja was indeed ready to heed Her people once
more, that first ceremony would set everything else in motion. And there would be blood for Sekhmet, for sacrifice
was always a part of ritual to the Goddess.

She looked down into the face of her son, smoothed a
hand softly over a tiny velvet cheek. She had already decided on a name, though she had said nothing of her choice
to Father Ambrose. "Widikund," she whispered. "A strong
name for a strong son, a child who will grow into a man
who serves the old ways. Freyja." She said the almost forgotten name, and tears sprang to her eyes. "In Your name,
do I dedicate my son."

In front of her bed box the banked hearth-fire suddenly
blazed up. For the span of several heartbeats the embers
flared high, reaching out to kindle a kindred light in
Bathilde's dark eyes. Then the flames subsided, leaving
only a warm glow that enfolded the noblewoman and her
babe in their embrace.

Bathilde smiled. Her eyes closed. She cuddled her son
close against her breast. She slept.

The next morning Bathilde sent word to all the folk who
farmed her lands, carried out their trades in the village, and
served in her house. The lady of the manor would speak to
them as well as their families, the messengers said, and all
must attend her before the gates of her house.

And so the people came. They walked, even those who
could afford to ride, for no cart or animal could make it
through the thick clinging mud that had once been a road.
Well before the hour the messengers had called for, they began to arrive. Those who lived on the manor itself assembled first, drifting up from their huts to gather in the open
space before the great house. The house servants finished

with their morning duties and hurried out, pulling mantles over their heads against the rain. They watched as the folk who lived in the village and on Bathilde's holdings came slogging through the mud.

Most were farmers: burly stern-faced men accompanied by women with muscled arms, tired faces, and children hanging onto their skirts. The village craftsmen—and a few craftswomen—were among them; weavers, dyers, cobblers, carpenters, brewers, and the highly regarded smith, who was believed to possess magical powers in order to work the secrets of metal. The workers of trades and their families were cleaner and better dressed than those who worked the land. But regardless of their station in life, all the people gathered together in a single mass that sprawled ever larger with each new group of arrivals.

They huddled close, as if that would keep them drier, murmuring softy as they waited patiently for the Lady Bathilde to appear. Under the relentless rain they stood, stolid as the animals in the fields. The weather and its effect upon their lives were taking their toll. Coughs and sneezes issuing mostly from children and the old, interrupted the steady beat of rain. Mothers pressed their sniffling youngsters against them, watching their own mothers and fathers with deep, worried eyes. Their husbands stared into space, many stamped with the pinched exhausted face all too common to peasants, a look they wore that bespoke despair in a year where the harvest would be bad.

At last a stirring went through the crowd. The heavy bars that held the huge oaken doors closed were being pulled back. Men-at-arms strode out, their weapons and their grim demeanors causing the people to go silent. More and more of them came, forming themselves into a wedge that would protect their mistress from this assemblage of common folk.

Then Bathilde herself appeared. She had scorned wearing a mantle and was dressed in her richest tunic, a flowing garment of red wool trimmed with gold. A corded belt of gold intertwined with silver encircled her waist, and heavy earrings, also of gold, dangled from her ears. Her iron-streaked black hair hung unbound about her crimson-clad shoulders, held back from the broad forehead by a gold fillet. She looked noble and fierce and exalted with a purpose so powerful it seemed to have set her whole body on fire.

Begga followed behind her, carrying the swaddled infant in her arms. Bathilde's women trooped along in a flurry of bright green, blue, yellow, and red tunics and mantles that contrasted with the more somber hues of the gathered people. The servingwomen were nervous. Many were Christian, not blind to the recent bent their mistress had been taking, and they were apprehensive about this summons and what she intended to say to the people of her holdings.

Bathilde, however, was throbbing with excitement. The crimson folds of her tunic swept about her ankles as she strode boldly forward. She pushed past the men-at-arms, ignoring their worried exclamations. Several of the bolder ones stepped forward in an attempt to block her way, and she waved them impatiently aside.

"Folk of my lands," she cried. "Am I your lady?" Her voice was as deep and burning as her eyes.

There was a murmuring pause among the people. "Yes," a man called out. "You are our lady." Others took up his assent, until the entire throng of farmers and tradesmen and house servants was shouting their acclamation of Bathilde.

Bathilde looked upon them. Rain dampened her thick gray-streaked tresses. Her strong features were stern and unsmiling. "Then, tell me what has happened to your fields," she said.

Silence. Men and women glanced uneasily at each other. Accusations hung on the dank air, yet, in spite of all the arguments between new faith and old, no one now wished to voice those debates aloud.

"Well?" Bathilde demanded, as the silence lengthened. "Has no one among you an answer to give me?"

"The fields have been cursed." The one who spoke was a woman. She was slightly past middle age; her face was lined and her graying hair was tumbling out of its untidy knot, but her arms were strong and knotted with muscle.

She looked around defiantly, daring others to contradict her. "A great evil has cursed them."

"Yes!" Bathilde leaned forward excitedly. "And I will tell you who has brought the curse among us." She paused, holding the crowd in her hands, in the dark flames of her blazing eyes. "The Christians have led us to this place, where our crops wither and drown in this rain, the fields lie barren, and our children cry for lack of bread and milk."

Bathilde's waiting women gasped and made the sign of the cross. Several of the house servants followed suit. Begga's plump features went white; convulsively, she clutched the baby closer as if to protect him. But she and the others were all behind Bathilde and so she did not see them. Her eyes were upon the people before her. She saw that her audience was stirring restlessly at her words and held up a commanding hand. "I know that many of you have accepted the baptism of the priests. I, too, have accepted the water being sprinkled upon me. But why have we done so?"

This time her authority could not still the crowd's uneasiness, and she raised her voice to a shout. "Because we had no choice. Did Carolus not send out his commands that we accept his religion or die? Well, we have done as he ordered, and look what it has brought us."

"But what can we do?" someone called.

Bathilde's gaze singled out the young man who had spoken. "The answer to that is simple. We should have known it all along." She paused again. This time when she spoke, each word rang clear and slow and strong. "We must renounce this new religion and return to the old ways, to the gods who have always nurtured and cared for us."

This time people joined the servingwomen in gasping. Others shouted out in approval or in shock. Here and there someone crossed himself, while the faces of others lit up with the bright flame of a faith kept hidden and suddenly welcomed into the light of day.

But there were those who were drawn neither one way nor the other, whose faces were stiff with dread as they glanced nervously about. They were wise, these folk; they could see the risk that attended the words of their lady. It was to them that Bathilde addressed herself, knowing that she must win them over to her cause.

She lowered her voice, forcing the people to grow silent in order to hear. "The Shining Ones of our ancestors are displeased," she said earnestly. "We have forgotten Them—nay, we have betrayed Them. In Their anger, They have cursed us, and rightly so. Our lands will not prosper again until we have gained the forgiveness of the true gods."

"And what about the forgiveness of King Carolus?" challenged the blunt voice of the brewer woman. "Think you, lady, that he will look kindly on our taking up the old ways? He will invade Saxony as he did before. What will happen then? At least one can be hungry and still go on living. Indeed, I would rather have my belly empty and whole than full but pierced by the swords of Frankish warriors."

"Would you?" Bathilde fixed the brewer with her stern gaze. "Consider carefully, good woman. You and I are both old enough to know what famine means. When children grow so weak for lack of food that they can longer cry, when aged mothers and fathers lie motionless in their beds, then will the swords of the Franks look better to your eyes. Death by starving is a slow and terrible fate."

She swept the rest of the people with her dark eyes. "Does any person believe that Carolus will aid us during a famine? That he will send wagonloads of grain to make up for our barren fields?Do any of you think the king of Gaul will be disturbed when our bodies lie in ditches, our bellies shrunken by hunger, trying to feed grass and sticks to our children because there is nothing else?"

No one dared answer. Even the strong old woman stood silent, her lined face looking thoughtful.

Bathilde nodded in satisfaction. "I do not think so either. I think that Carolus cares only that we are Christian; whether we live or die is all the same to him, so long as we remain faithful to the new religion." Her voice rose again. "As for me: I have turned away from Carolus's one god. I have returned to the Shining Ones, for They are the true gods. Only They will help us. All of you, my people, must turn away from the Christian god as well. Do this and the famine that threatens us will fade back into the darkness."

She paused. Her voice dropped. "I swear it."

A man stepped out of the crowd. He was well advanced in years, his white hair and dignified demeanor lending him a status that caused others to make way for him. "But what will happen when Carolus learns of this?" he demanded. "In truth, he will not come with wagonloads of grain but with swords. What do we do then, lady?"

Rain was pouring down Bathilde's face. Her strong features were fierce, transfigured. "We will fight. The gods will protect us. The warriors of Gaul will fall before us. This, too, I swear."

What she proposed was immense, and yet there was a power in this fierce red-clad woman that had begun to resound among her listeners. The broad and extensive lands of Saxony had always been free, until their bountifulness had caught the greedy eye of Carolus. Gaul had conquered, but the memory of freedom was still fresh, and few in Saxony had lost their taste for it. Physical hunger was a driving force; combined with the hunger for freedom it was well nigh irresistible.

The old man, however, had seen war before. "We are farmers and craftsmen here, lady," he said warningly. "We know how to use weapons, but none of us are the equal of professional warriors. I know that, and so must you."

Bathilde looked at him. "I do know it," she replied. "But I will provide a weapon that will defeat Carolus's army. Or rather, the gods will provide it. The warriors of Gaul will not be able to stand against this weapon. You will see." She swung her arms out wide, extravagant and exhilarated. "You will all see."

"What is this weapon," a man shouted from the back of the crowd. "We would see it, lady."

"Not it." Flames seemed to blaze over Bathilde's face. "She. And no, you cannot see Her. The time is not yet right.

In the meantime, let me tell you what will happen when we
have chased Carolus and his Christians from our land and
have won back our freedom."

Bathilde whirled around to the servingwomen, who were
frozen in appalled silence behind her. She strode to Begga
and snatched the swaddled bundle from the nurse's arms.
"Here," she shouted at the top of her voice. "Here is the son
I bore. Look upon him. He has been dedicated to the old
gods. He will rule Saxony, not some invader from the
forests of Gaul!"

Wheeling back to the crowd, she held him aloft so that all
could see him. There was a heartbeat of silence, and then
the throng erupted. People cheered, roaring their approval
in deafening bursts of noise. Disturbed by the sudden
clamor, the pounding rain, and especially by the unceremo-
nious way his mother had seized him, the baby began to cry.
No one paid any heed, or even heard, including Bathilde.
Smiling triumphantly, she held the shrieking baby higher so
that no one in her cheering audience would be denied a
glimpse of him.

It took some moments for the eruption of noise to die
down. When it did, Bathilde raised her voice again. "Go,"
she cried. "Depart to your homes and wait for the first sign
of the Shining Ones' power. It will come soon."

"What is it? What is it?" eager voices cried above the
shouting. "Lady, what will the sign be?"

"Ah," Bathilde said, and delight wreathed her features.
"Something that not even the Christians will be able to deny
is a sign. This rain that has been plaguing us will stop."

Gasps surrounded Bathilde and her crying son, mingling
with prayers to gods whose names had not been heard in
years. "When?" men and women yelled together. "When
will the rain stop?"

Bathilde's smile widened. She paused, as if she were listening to unseen voices. "Three days hence, my people."
She was still smiling, and now there was a quality of reverence about her. "Three is a sacred number, though so many
have forgotten it. Dawn of the third day will break clear.
And when it does you will see something else that has not

been seen in our land for long and long: a sacred procession to the Goddess Freyja!"

The roaring lowered to a fumbling growl of disbelief. People stared at each other, then raised their voices anew. The roar swelled in deafening bursts of noise: a wild cacophony of hope.

Begga and the waiting women exchanged horrified glances. The nurse drew a deep breath. Bravely, she stepped forward. "Lady," she said, making a futile effort to be heard. "Lady." She held out her arms.

At last Bathilde became aware of her baby's unhappiness, though she did not return him to his nurse. Cradling him to her own breast, she stood in the rain watching as the assembled crowd began to disperse. The people were going eagerly now, as if they had decided of one mind that the sooner they departed, the sooner the rain that had cursed them would depart as well. Within a short time, the gathering place was deserted, save for Bathilde and her house folk.

Bathilde gestured for Begga to hand over her mantle and swiftly used it to shelter her wet and wailing son. "Come," she said to her women, serenely choosing to ignore their expressions. They were Christians; all of them would probably have to be replaced, but she would not worry about that now. "This has been a good morning's work. Let us go back inside."

She led the way back to her house. Isaac was standing at the gates, flanked by his nephews. They had come out as inconspicuously as they could, staying on the outskirts of the crowd, watching all that had gone on. The trader's eyes met those of the noblewoman. Isaac's face was carefully expressionless, but there was a look of worry in his hazel eyes that he could not quite conceal.

Bathilde stopped before him. "I spoke the truth," she said so quietly that only he and his nephews could hear. "The rain will stop. Prepare your goods and your animals to depart. I will expect you to leave when the roads have dried enough for travel."

Isaac regarded her. "Lady," he said in a grave voice, "I think that is wise."

Bathilde nodded. "I think you are right."

She swept on, followed by her retinue. Isaac's eldest nephew stepped up in her wake. "Uncle," he murmured, "where shall we go?"

"Home." Isaac's reply was as sad as his eyes. "A storm of blood is approaching this land. We had best be gone before it breaks."

17

THE PARTY OF MEN THAT HAD COME to slay a witch found itself searching for the witch instead. First, though, they would have to search for their horses. The beasts were gone. They had fled when the cat let out its unearthly howl and were lost somewhere in the rain-dripping woods.

It was not an easy task. But then nothing facing the men left in the clearing in front of the wisewoman's hut was easy. The *stria* had left her would-be slayers in a state of near hysteria. They huddled together, frightened as children, looking around fearfully as the tops of the trees tossed in the wind and the rain streamed down.

Haganon was the first to recover. Shaking raindrops from his eyes, he stared about him in disbelief. Surely, he must have imagined it. But no, there was the fire—or what was left of it—and of the woman herself, there was no sign. His eyes leaped to his companions, and all around him he saw only panic.

The sight enraged him. To be sure, what had happened was terrifying and clearly the work of dark powers—in truth, Haganon himself had been frightened. But he and his men were warriors, hardened battle veterans. To see them whimpering and shaking like whipped slaves was intolerable. Order would have to be restored at once to these shaken cohorts of his, and it seemed that he was the only one able to do it.

Resolutely, Haganon set about calming everyone. His method was direct: he stomped about in the rain shaking shoulders and slapping and yelling into faces. Only Alcuin and Abbot Wala were not in need of such forceful tactics.

They stood silently on opposite sides of the soaked and ruined bonfire, and though it seemed that they were watching Haganon berate the others, both of them were in fact sunk deep in thought. The two clergymen were grim-faced and somber, but for different reasons.

The abbot had watched his plans go wildly awry. This woman had made a mockery of him, as well as the power of the Church. She was supposed to have died. Instead she had proved herself infinitely more powerful than he could have ever suspected. Abbot Wala was not a superstitious man; he left that to the common folk, but there was no denying what had happened here. His pragmatic idea that the woman be eliminated as a complication had exploded into something far greater. All at once she was a full-blown threat. A woman in possession of such power could not be allowed to act on her own. She must be under the control of the Church—which, in Abbot Wala's view was himself. Anything less posed risks he dared not contemplate.

Alcuin, on the other hand, was torn apart by what he had seen. His vision from last night swirled through his brain, and he was tormented with doubt. He had condemned the poor creature to death, believing there was no other way to save her. Had he done the right thing? Standing in the rain with Haganon's furious shouts ringing in his ears, he wondered. He had called out to God, and God had not answered. Or had He? Was the woman's disappearance a sign of innocence or evil?

"On with all of you!" Haganon's voice was closer, jarring Alcuin from his reverie. "Into the woods. We must find those horses!"

The nobles were gathering themselves together. Aelisachar came over to the royal counselor. The old nobleman's white hair was dark with rain, dripping in lank strands toward his sad worried eyes. "Deacon," he said hesitantly. "We must leave this place. It is not safe to linger—"

"I know, my lord." Alcuin gave the man a weak smile. "I'm coming."

Alcuin sighed and turned away from his contemplation of the fire. By now even the ashes had been washed away.

All that remained was the wood, a heap of blackened charred chunks dripping water into a widening pool. His eyes fell on Abbot Wala and Count Haganon. They had moved away from the others and were deep in conversation, their heads close together. Alcuin looked at them and frowned. As if he felt the counselor's gaze upon him, Haganon looked around and saw Alcuin staring at him. He raised an arm, shouting again that everyone must leave.

"My lord counselor." Aelisachar spoke more firmly.

"Yes, yes." Alcuin let the noble take his arm and guide him after the others.

The line of sodden, intimidated men went timidly into the forest. They were only too glad to leave the witch's hut behind. They tried equally hard not to let their thoughts dwell on the realization that the dark rain-drenched woods offered scarcely better sanctuary than the witch's abode. Yet they had no choice; the horses had to be found. With Haganon and the abbot at their head, they plodded through the trees, many of them muttering prayers and blessing themselves as they searched for the animals.

The forest spoke to them as they walked. Leaves whistled in breezes that seemed to spring up out of nowhere. Branches cracked and rubbed together, making the most nervous of the men jump. The rain pelted them, every drop a mockery reminding them of the sun that had shone when they passed through these trees such a short time ago.

At length they found the horses. The animals had remained together and were head down in a meadow, browsing on the wet grass, and oblivious to the rain. There was no sign of the fear that had stampeded them away from the witch's hut. Even Haganon's temperamental stallion barely lifted his head as his master walked up to him. The men mounted with relief. To be on horseback once more, to be able to move rapidly through the forbidding woods, made a tangible difference. The humans relaxed as much as their horses, and as they did, their courage began to return. Their voices began to compete with the rain as they rode on.

"Cursed *stria*," one of the younger nobles growled, and spit into the forest mold at his horse's feet. "By the wood of the holy cross, I felt the damned ground shake beneath my feet." He looked around. "How did she do that?"

"You know how," Aelisachar responded. "Indeed, you answered your own questions. The woman is a *stria*."

"And cursed by God." Abbot Wala spoke loudly, so that everyone would hear him, especially the royal counselor. "Do not forget that."

"How could we?" another man muttered. "When she came near to sending all of us to the maws of demons?"

Haganon intervened. He could smell the fear again. It was beginning to rise from the damp flesh of his fellows, reborn by this ominous conversation. It had to be stopped before it went any further. "Enough," he said sharply. "Whatever went on back there is over and done with. It's up to us to see that it doesn't happen again."

Silence attended his words. Metal jingled, horses blew softly, and harness leather creaked. The men glanced at each other. No one contradicted Haganon. But no one agreed with him either, a fact the count could not avoid noticing.

"Haganon," Aelisachar said at last. "Where are we bound?"

"Anywhere is fine with me," the young noble who had spoken before put in. "As long as it's out of these woods and this damned rain."

The count threw him a quelling look. "We'll return to the monastery," he said, having already discussed their destination with the abbot. "Abbot Wala has offered us his hospitality once again. We'll have need of it, while we decide what to do next."

His announcement was greeted with exclamations of approval. Men urged their horses forward, and now the murmurs were of a warm fire, hot mead, and a good meal.

The party broke out of the trees. The road lay before them, muddy and pitted with water-filled ruts. The sky was the color of Aelisachar's drenched hair. It was late afternoon, advancing toward evening, and the rain was as inevitable as ever. The riders sighed and pulled their mantles closer. The horses sighed, too, lowering their heads as they plodded forward.

Abbot Wala looked about him. The track they had followed through the forest was so narrow it would only permit them to ride single file. Out on the road, muddy and difficult as it was, they could spread out. The nobles grouped themselves in twos and threes, talking quietly. The expressions on their faces did a strange dance between fear, relief, eagerness, and apprehension. Haganon rode alone, at their head, as he had all along. His blunt features were carved into a rigid stare of rage and determination.

Abbot Wala could have ridden beside him, but instead the abbot was slowing his horse, looking over one shoulder. Plodding along behind everyone else, he saw Alcuin. The advisor had been the most silent of them all. He had joined the search for the horses without uttering a word, found and mounted his gelding in equal silence. While the others spoke of reaching the monastery, he still said nothing. And now he rode by himself, an awkward and yet somehow intimidating figure in his aloneness.

The abbot turned his horse's head and sent him back. Alongside Alcuin's mount, his dark eyes studied the smaller man. "You know," he said quietly after a moment. "Tell me you know, good Deacon."

Alcuin gazed at his horse's ears. "And what do I know?"

He did not use Abbot Wala's title, an omission not lost upon the abbot. "That what we sought to do was right," he said, more testily than he had intended.

"In the eyes of who?"

"In the eyes of"—Wala gave Alcuin a look of dumbfounded anger—"In the eyes of God, man! What else?"

"God," said the counselor, "may not have had as much to do with today's proceedings as I might have wished."

The abbot bristled. "What do you mean?"

Alcuin glanced up, and Abbot Wala saw the same quality in those mild blue eyes that had set Haganon back when the count, too, had sought to intimidate this good-natured scholar of the king. "I am not a fool," he said quietly. "Do not make the mistake of thinking me blind, as well as stupid."

A chill of warning laced along Wala's spine. "Good Deacon," he said cautiously, "I have no idea what you are talking about."

"Do you not? Well, then, we have no further need of this conversation, do we?" Alcuin returned his attention to the ears of his horse. "You may leave me," he said after a moment, and the note of dismissal in his formal, distant tone could have been learned from King Carolus himself.

There was nothing the abbot could say. Furious, but trying to hold on to his dignity, he nodded stiffly. Only the harshness with which he jerked at his mare's reins betrayed his anger as he rode away. He went to join Haganon, forcing the horse into a trot. She struggled in the thick gooey footing, her ears flattened in protest. Mud splattered from her hooves as she came up alongside Haganon's stallion.

The count looked over in distaste. "Have a care. You'll ruin my mantle as well as your mare. Only a fool would make her trot through this damned muck."

"Fool is it?" Abbot Wala's lip curled, though he allowed the mare to slow to a walk. "That seems to be a very popular word this day. But you, Count, had better concern yourself with more than your mantle and my mare."

Haganon scowled. "I'll find the witch. Have no fear on that score. I'll find her, and I'll see her burn."

"Your memory has gotten very short, my lord. You already found her, and look what happened." Wala brooded. "Air and water," he muttered, more to himself than to the count. "She called upon them, and they answered. This is bad, my lord, very bad." He looked over at Haganon. "And worse, we have that king's man to complicate things."

"We are all king's men," Haganon corrected coldly.

Wala snorted. "Save your sanctimonious chastisement, my lord. You are your own man, as am I. It's why we have this little alliance of ours, to serve both our interests. We see the future, you and I. And the future is Carolus and the Church. Above all, the Church must grow strong in Saxony, and if it does, since you have united yourself with us, you will gain in power and influence as well—"

"You state the obvious," Haganon interrupted irritably. He did not appreciate being reprimanded, much less reminded of how the *stria* had escaped him.

"I state the truth. And nothing is obvious, any longer. The woman is gone; we don't know where. However, I can make a good guess."

"So can I. She is hiding somewhere in these woods, hoping to escape us."

Wala shook his head. "No. I think she is headed to the worst destination possible: to Bathilde. And if she reaches her—"

"She won't," Haganon broke in again. "I will see to that."

As he spoke the witch's face sprang up in his mind. The wind she had called up howled into his ears, mocking him, and he realized how proud he sounded. Pride was a warrior's stock and trade, but too much pride could get a man killed. He had to prevent this creature from besting him again and not take foolish chances while doing it.

"What if she does skulk back to Bathilde?" he demanded. Caution was a sword with a blade that could be turned into a challenge, particularly against a man who was not a warrior. "I will gather more men, enough to outnumber Bathilde's men-at-arms, though I doubt they will interfere. And this time, I won't allow that royal schoolmaster to give her a chance to cast her spells while he's flapping his lips trying to make her a Christian. I see her; I run my blade through her before she can call up her demons. It will be as simple as that."

"Will it?" The abbot gave him a sardonic glance. "The woman has powers of which we know nothing." He fell silent. "Powers," he whispered after a moment, "that we ourselves may have been responsible for setting loose." Suddenly he crossed himself.

Haganon glared at him. "Superstition, Abbot? From a man as practical as you? We cannot afford it. Not if we would gain this future of which you speak."

"Superstition," Wala snapped, "has little to do with it. I am an educated man, and I see the world with the eyes of an educated man. This is more than the mindless fears of peasants. We were not prepared for what went on today, and we—no, you—dare not make the same mistake again."

"What do you suggest?" Haganon's temper was growing ever shorter. It seemed that the abbot wanted to lay the blame for today's fiasco on him, and the count was not about to allow it. "If it's blame you want to lay, my lord Abbot, there is more than enough to go around. Should we seek out another wisewoman and hire her to use magic to slay the first one?"

Tension crackled between the two men, stringing tight as drawn bowstrings. Abruptly, Abbot Wala sighed. "I wish we had never sought to hire the first one. We chose poorly, but it's too late to worry about that now. We have too much else to worry about. And that includes the king's advisor. Especially the king's advisor."

Haganon put up a dismissive hand. "Quarrels among churchmen," he snorted. "You handle the schoolmaster. You're better at such things. I will handle the *stria*." His teeth bared themselves in an expression composed of a snarl and a smile. "Magic or no."

The Ancient Shining Ones were not yet awake, but their presence was stirring in the land of Saxony. Being neither pagan nor Saxon, Abbot Wala could not have felt it. Being Saxon, Haganon and his cadre of nobles should have at least sensed it, but they did not. Christianity had taken most of that sensitivity from them. Ambition had taken the rest.

Others were not so blind. Rain was still falling, but people drew mantles over their heads and crept out into the downpour. In their hands they carried offerings wrapped in pieces of brightly colored cloth. Chilled by the wind and drenched to the skin, they went into the woods to search for holy trees. The birch tree, its white papery bark gleaming pure in the bleak light; the rowan, long known for its powers of magical protection; the elder, the hawthorn, and the most sacred of all, the oak.

Murmuring prayers, the people tied their precious, cheerfully colored bundles to the limbs of chosen trees. Some remembered the ancient prayers and incantations and tears ran down their faces, mingling with the rain, as they whispered the words forbidden to them by the Christian conquerors. Other people had forgotten the words. They had to make up their own, though it did not seem to matter, for their hearts and intentions were pure. Throughout the lands held by Bathilde, men and women watched their offerings swing from branches. The colors of the cloth soon darkened and ran in the rain, but despite the foul weather, those who had tied them there watched the small bundles and smiled.

But there was one who was not smiling—the priest, Father Ambrose. His church had quite abruptly become empty. The farmers and villagers, even the house folk of the Lady Bathilde, had vanished. Father Ambrose was not entirely surprised. He knew of Bathilde's summons, a summons from which he had been excluded. The exclusion had not sat well with him. He had seen the messengers going on their rounds, had seen also how they avoided his gaze. He had approached two of them, both Christians, to be met with embarrassed faces and eyes that refused to meet his. He would not be welcome, the eldest man had explained; the gathering was for Saxons only. Lady Bathilde, he added, shamefaced, had specifically forbidden that any Christian priest be present.

Ambrose had listened gravely and nodded to show that he understood. He had even blessed the two men. Afterwards, he had gone back into his church and prayed for guidance. He knelt there now, waiting for an answer. Silence attended his prayers. The cloth that draped the altar was white linen and it shone softly in the light from the wall sconces. The chalice atop the altar gleamed golden, even though it was only bronze. The walls, too, gleamed in the flickering light. They were finely built, but unadorned. The crucifix was the one ornate fixture and surely the most costly.

This place was a haven, and the young priest loved every stone and board that had gone into the building of it. That it had been built at the order of Carolus—a mortal man of flesh and blood, regardless of the fact that he was a king— mattered not all to Ambrose; the building of any church was a mandate from God, and therefore holy. He gazed up at the altar, opening himself to the usual quiet sense of reverence he felt whenever he looked at it. The altar was simple, as was the rest of the church. Ambrose had insisted upon simplicity, even though Carolus had authorized the sanctuaries built in his name to be costly edifices, impressive so that they would impress these uncivilized pagans, whose holy places were nothing more than groves of trees under the open sky.

But Ambrose was a plain man. Richly appointed churches were not what he was comfortable with. And young though he was, he understood something that his king did not. It was the faith of the priest inside the church that would draw the people to it, not gold-trimmed hangings, jeweled chalices, and silver candelabras.

Had he been wrong? Until now it had not seemed so. The people had come through the doors of the small church. They had been suspicious and wary, forced by Carolus's edicts, to accept the waters of baptism. But gradually Ambrose had won them over. He was a kind man, genuine in his faith and his concern for those God had placed in his charge. The folk of the village, the farmers, and the servants, craftsmen, and artisans of the manor, warmed to the gentle priest and the religion he preached, and he to them. In the five years he had been in this land, Ambrose had come to feel he had a place here, that the people regarded him as one of their own. What a painful thing it was to realize that the link between him and his flock had proved so tenuous, vulnerable to something so mysterious as the weather.

When the rains had begun they had at first swelled his flock. People had come begging for his prayers, for the blessings of the Christian priest. They had filled the church with their supplications that the rain would stop and their crops be saved. But neither their prayers for the intercession of Ambrose's god, nor those of the priest himself had any effect. And as that became apparent, the swell of parishioners had gradually slowed to a trickle, and then stopped altogether.

Ambrose knew why. Like Abbot Wala, he was neither pagan nor Saxon, but unlike Abbot Wala, he was a man attuned to the world around him. He stood in the darkness of his church, lost in thought. The christening of the Lady Bathilde's son had not happened. Instead, yesterday's gathering had taken place. Excluded as he was, Ambrose had still watched the people file past in silent groups. Later, he had heard their voices, roaring in anger and excitement. He could not make out words, but there had been a note in those voices that had sent chills down the priest's spine. A new force was abroad in this adopted land of his, and he knew instinctively that it did not bode well for the Church.

"No." Ambrose spoke aloud, his eyes resting on the crucifix. "Not new."

His voice sounded loud in the quiet church. He was certain that God had heard him. Yet he sensed that something else was listening as well. There was nothing new about what had surfaced. It was an old force that lurked in the shadows beyond God's holiness, older than time and part of an even older battle that must ever be fought anew if Christianity were to survive.

Ambrose remembered the way the people—his flock—had looked when they returned from the manor. Standing in the doorway of his church, he had seen them come back. Few would meet his eyes, and those who did threw him glares of open hostility. That also was new. There were pagans in this village, folk who refused to give up their heathen beliefs; Ambrose knew that, of course. But not until today had they dared to show their animosity toward him so personally.

Bowing his head, the priest returned to his prayers. Time passed, and lost in his reflections, he did not notice the stiffening of his legs as he knelt before the altar. Nor did he hear the voices at first. Finally, they grew loud enough to break in upon his concentration. Frowning, Ambrose lifted his head. Yes, there were indeed people outside his church, he realized. He unfolded his hands and rose awkwardly, trying to shake the feeling back into his deadened legs and feet. Sensation returned in a flood of needle-and-pin pricking, as he walked the short distance to the doorway, threading his way through the wooden benches.

Dusk was falling, a swift dusk, brought on by the gloomy rain-drenched day, and the promise of another wet miserable night. Ambrose took a candle from one of the wall sconces and held it aloft as he pushed open the doors.

Firelight met his eyes. The torches were covered with leather hoods, which prevented them from being extinguished in the rain, though their light was weak and flickering. A handful of men stood holding them. Ambrose could not make out their faces in the wet and growing darkness, but somehow he knew they were not members of his flock. Yet he still endeavored to make his words hospitable.

"I bid you welcome to the house of the Lord," he said kindly. "Enter. Have you come to pray?"

They all blinked at him, looking rather like owls, though it may have been the dancing torches that made it seem that way. "No," one of them answered in a gruff voice. "We do not pray to your god."

Ambrose straightened. Unaccountably his stomach grumbled, reminding him that it was long past the hour for his evening meal. "Then why have you come?" His demeanor was still pleasant, revealing no sign that since these men had marked themselves as heathens with no apparent wish to change that state, he hoped they would depart as unexpectedly as they had arrived.

There was more blinking from his visitors. "To tell you to leave," said the one who had apparently been appointed their spokesman.

It was Ambrose's turn to blink. "Leave?" he echoed blankly.

"You heard us." The man was growing bolder, egged on by his fellows. They clustered around him, raising their torches and muttering comments indistinguishable to the priest, but not to their spokesman. "We want you to leave," he said, and his voice was louder. "There is no place for you here, you, or your church."

Ambrose realized something else: they had been drinking. The damp breeze wafted toward him, heavy-laden with the odor of honey mead. He saw also that the light from the torches flickered so wildly because the hands of the men who held them were unsteady. He sighed. "You are drunk," he pointed out mildly. "All of you have been dipping into the mead a bit too heavily by the looks of you."

"And what if we have?" The spokesman's tone was ugly. "What else is there to do, with our crops rotting in the fields and our livestock drowning?"

Father Ambrose looked at him with compassion. "Go to your homes," he said gently. "Take shelter from this foul weather and sleep off the mead. You'll feel the better for it."

He started to swing shut the doors. A gust of wind sprang up. Fistfuls of rain slapped into Ambrose's face and snuffed out the candle. His efforts to close the doors seemed mocked by more than the wind. He tossed the candle into the church's interior—candles were too precious to waste— and used both hands to grab the door handles.

"Wait," the pagan shouted, "we are not yet done with you, priest!"

Abruptly the wind ceased, allowing Ambrose to close the doors. "But we are done," he said. "There is little to be gained in trying to reason with men far gone in drink. Come back when you are sober, if you remember that you still wish to threaten me."

He shut the doors with a bang. The candle lay where he had dropped it, and he bent to retrieve it. As he straightened up the wick trembled. Flame leaped out in a streak as red as the heart of a fresh-killed deer. It widened and spread, and in the broad lurid glow two figures appeared. They were enormous, looming up taller than the walls, beyond the roof, so that it seemed the church could not contain them. They flickered as the flame did, shrinking themselves as if they wanted Ambrose to see them in their entirety.

A lesser man would have cowered in terror. But the priest

had his faith to strengthen him. He was not afraid; he was
furious. How dare these creatures invade the sanctity of a
church? "Begone!" he cried, and made the sign of the cross.
"This is a house of God!"

The trespassers stared at him. To Ambrose's eyes they
were hideous. They wore the bodies of women, clothed in
garments so sheer he could see their nudity. Atop each set
of feminine shoulders sat the head of a great cat. The eyes
of one head burned green, and the eyes of the other blazed
yellow. Ambrose ran toward the altar. He expected the
demons to try and prevent him, but neither of them moved.
Outside, through the pelting rain, he heard the pagans. They
were still shouting angrily for him to leave.

"You should listen to them," the demon with the green
eyes said. Her voice was deep and rolling and filled with a
music that made Ambrose shudder, so far beyond his understanding was it. "It is still possible for you to depart with
your life."

The priest reached the altar. Curving both hands about
the jeweled chalice, he swung triumphantly around. "In the
name of the True God and His only Son, I command you to
be gone. Go back to the depths of hell, whence you came!"

There was wine in the chalice, and he flung it with unerring accuracy. "By the blood of Christ, I banish you!"

The wine hung in the air, and then splashed to the floor.
The demon with the yellow eyes opened her awful fanged
mouth and laughed. The green-eyed one regarded him
steadily. "You are a fool," she said.

"As are all mortals," the yellow-eyed one hissed. "We are
wasting time."

"He could live," the other said, and there might have been
sadness in that strange ringing voice from another world.

"But he will not," the laughing demon snapped. "As you
said, he is a fool."

The demon with the head of a green-eyed cat lifted her
arms. Words rolled out of her mouth in a tongue Ambrose
had never heard. She turned her terrifying gaze back to him.
"I have called the Serpent," she said, and suddenly he could

understand her again. "You may still leave. It is your choice."

Ambrose himself felt as if he were on fire now, but it was a holy fire. He blazed with love, for his God, and his faith. "I will not," he roared. "This is my church. Never will I abandon it to such as you!" Wheeling back to the altar, he fumbled for the small precious cask of holy water. Tears of frustration and rage and disbelief stood in his eyes as he saw that the water had no more effect on these beings than the wine had. Yet he could not surrender to this evil. Surely this must be part of a plan. God must have a reason.

The pagan men had stopped shouting for Ambrose to come out. They circled the church in the darkness, their torches held high. Anger rippled and grew in each man's breast, as hot as the mead he had drunk, warming him against the rain. The outspoken one shifted his torch from hand to hand. Curses spit from between his teeth. "No wonder the gods have turned away from us," he growled, slurring his words a little. "The Lady Bathilde is right. We have betrayed them, and there"—he thrust his torch at the wall nearest him—"is the proof."

His first thrust had been experimental; the thought of actually trying to set fire to this church had not really taken root. But the anger was growing in him, helped along by the mead. He jabbed at the wood again, and this time he was more serious. His companions stared at him. The idea of firing the church had not occurred to them either. It was a daring and frightening act, one with unforeseen consequences frightening to contemplate. But frightening or not, it was an act that seemed doomed to failure. The rain was heavy, the church walls were soaked with moisture from days and days of such weather, and the torch flare was weak.

Then something happened. Beneath the men's feet the muddy earth trembled. None of them noticed; they were far gone in drink, and their heads were reeling anyway. But suddenly the spokesman let out an exclamation. The flame of his torch had started to sputter. All at once it hurled itself forward with a whoosh. The protective cover spun off and the flame roared louder. The man's eyes went wide. He made as if to drop the torch but could not. A will other than his own had locked his fingers around the wooden handle. All he could do was stare, as the flame reached for the nearest wall of the church.

The other men cried out as the rain-wet wood ignited. Thin orange tongues licked along the wall. The man holding the torch stepped back, still staring. His amazement suddenly turned to certainty. "It's a sign," he shouted hoarsely. "From the old gods, the true gods! They want this abomination gone from our land!"

As he spoke, the torch flames of his companions also whooshed and roared, striking out at the walls of the church. The conflagration was swift, too swift considering the drenched night. It was indeed a sign, the men told each other, and their excitement grew. They helped the fire along, jabbing again and again with their savagely flaring torches, yelling with glee as new flames raced up along the building's walls.

Inside the church Father Ambrose was alone once more. With the first rush of flame, the demons had vanished. Their task was done, he realized. The odor of smoke stung his nostrils. The men outside were shouting, and there was a hungry note to their voices. Ambrose lifted his head. His young face was old beyond its years, his earnest blue eyes deep and sad. He understood the note in those voices. Death was present, and it was coming for him.

"If this be Your will, O Lord," he whispered softly, and knelt before the altar once more.

The smell of smoke had grown stronger. Dirty gray wreaths were curling through chinks in the walls. In the rafters overhead Ambrose could see the first glimmers of orange. The crackle of flames, faint only a few moments ago, had grown louder. On this rain-wet night his church should not have been burning. But it was. Evil had set this holy edifice afire, and the shouting men with their flaring torches were its instruments.

Ambrose clasped his hands together. "O Lord," he prayed, "wash away this evil. Dissolve the stain of this dark fire in Your holy water. Show these heathens who abjure Your true word that they will not triumph."

He closed his eyes, concentrating his whole soul on his prayers. The instants fled by, as fleeting as the remaining heartbeats of the priest's life. The flames mocked him. They were crawling among the rafters now, dancing and popping. Rustling noises were racing along the walls, sounding almost like the feet of countless rats, though Ambrose knew that flames were making that ominous sound. Waves of heat wafted down from above and around. The candles in their sconces fluttered feebly, as if seeking to fight back the inevitable.

Ambrose opened his eyes. It is your choice, the green-eyed demon had said. And so it was. He could run before the fire grew too advanced, snatch up the holy articles and flee into the night. The smoke and flames themselves would shield him. The men outside were probably too drunk to see him, much less mount an effective pursuit if they did. He could take shelter with Count Haganon, and proceed on to the monastery of Abbot Wala in the morning. He would tell them of this desecration, and they would take a terrible revenge on the perpetrators.

"No." Ambrose lifted his gaze to the crucifix. The holy cross was glowing. Reflected against the lurid flames, it was beautiful beyond anything the priest had ever seen. Beyond the sad, tortured figure of Christ on the cross, magnificent visions wavered, lit in gold. The City of Heaven, he told himself, and tears of gratitude filled his eyes. "I understand," he told his God. "Evil must not beget evil. I will not be a part of taking their lives, for they are unknowing in their evil. Their fate is in Your hands, as is mine. I give myself up to Your care."

Father Ambrose's prayers rose into the rain-soaked night sky. The heat grew terrible. Sweat mingled with the tears on the priest's face, but he did not notice. He did not see the wooden beams overhead come alive with flame. Nor did he did feel them as they crashed down upon him, extinguishing his prayers at last.

The blazing pyre of what had once been a church illumi-

nated the blackness outside. Battle cries arose from the
men. They were the first to be heard in this land for long
and long.

They would not be the last.

18

DAWN OF THE THIRD DAY BURST clear and bright over the lands of Lady Bathilde. No rainstorms slashed down at the fields, no unseasonable cold froze the tender plants in their beds. Birds stirred themselves in the trees, fluffed and preened their feathers, spread their wings out to dry, and began to sing.

The trilling sounds awoke the people of Bathilde's holdings. They lay in their beds and listened to the music with uncertain ears. It seemed as though birdsong had been drowned beneath the pounding of rain for an eternity. Disbelieving, they crept from their homes and gaped up at the sky, blinking as if they were bears coming out of hibernation. They whispered to each other and pointed.

The sun was out. It seemed to smile down on the upturned faces, spreading fans of heat and light across everything it touched. Children wandered away, tentative at first, but growing steadily bolder. They began to splash in the puddles. Dogs ran to follow. Soon the familiar cozy sounds of barking and exuberant shouts of young ones at play were ringing out to join the trilling birds.

Smiles shimmered unsteadily over the faces of the adults as they heard them. Bathilde had prophesied truly, they told each other. Some wept, some laughed, and many prayed. And the heartfelt prayers that rose up to meet the sun were the same in one thing: they were being sent to the old gods, not the new.

In the great manor house, Bathilde was already outside. She had risen from her bed and left the hall long before any others were awake. Even the kitchen boys who stirred the bakehouse fires into life every morning were still rolled up in their pallets when their mistress slipped into the courtyard to meet the dawn.

Bathilde had waited, and she was not disappointed. The sign had come. Still wearing her sleeping robe, with a mantle wrapped about her shoulders, she stood in the glimmering light. The rays of the sun bathed her, and soon she no longer needed the warmth of her mantle. She dropped the heavy wrap and smiled fiercely.

"My thanks," she whispered to the unseen foreign Goddess Who had answered her prayers. The sound of her own breathing pounded in her ears. Excitement stabbed through her veins with such force she almost staggered. She thought of her son and the inheritance she would, with the blessings of the Shining Ones, build for him to inherit, and she laughed aloud. Yes, it would happen.

When the house folk began stumbling out to stare owlishly at both her and the sky, she raised her arms in triumph. "Look upon this dawn," she cried. "Did I not say that in three days' time the rain would stop? Now will the fields and pastures give life to our people and their beasts. And this is only the beginning." She directed her piercing gaze to the Christians among her people, singling out each one. "I promised the Goddess Freyja a procession. This, has She told me: that wherever we travel throughout the land the sun will shine and the rain will cease."

She glared, waiting for one of them to contradict her.

No one did.

Sirona smelled the smoke before she saw it: thin dirty streamers coiling up against the washed-clean blue sky. She glanced at Mau. Even in human form his senses were still keener than those of any true human, and from the look on his face it was obvious that he had been detecting the dark odor for some time.

"What have they done now?" she growled, meaning Haganon and the men of his war band. His hard face leaped up in her mind. Had he taken out his frustration at her having escaped him by firing some other pagan woman's home?

Mau's uptilted eyes returned her glance. He was no longer naked. He had spirited away a tunic and leggings from one of the farms they had passed, and that morning he had appropriated a brightly colored mantle dyed in shades of green and yellow for himself. Incongruously, he had at first refused to wear shoes; going barefoot, he claimed, was far more comfortable. But after a day and night of rain and damp he had grumbled that barefoot in the Black Land was one thing and barefoot in this unfriendly place quite another, and had stolen himself a pair of soft felt boots.

"Are you so certain it is them?" he asked mildly.

"Who else?" Sirona snapped.

In the two days they had traveled together, she was just beginning to grow accustomed to him. There were even moments when she found herself forgetting his true origin. It was easier, she had reflected, to accept a man who had been a cat, than a cat who spoke like a man. And in some ways it was harder. The nights had been cold and wet and they had huddled together for warmth. The rain would not permit a fire, but they had not needed one. Mau's body gave off heat like a brazier heaped with charcoal, and when he slept he made a deep rumbling in his chest that Sirona found oddly soothing.

But he was still Mau, which meant that he was still annoying. As he proved when they came upon the source of the smoke. The rain had vanished. They had awoken to it, but as soon as they crossed the muddy track that marked the boundary of Bathilde's lands, the downpour was gone, as if it had never been. The sky glowed, deep and vibrant as the freshly washed gown of a noblewoman. Mud and water still pooled on the track, but the grass beyond was already steaming in the bright morning, beginning to dry under the warmth of the sun. Only the wreaths of smoke cast an ominous stain over the beauty of this daybreak.

Sirona paused to stare up at the sun. When she lowered her eyes, Mau was gone. He had darted ahead. Just as he

did in his cat form, she thought irritably. It was a madden-
ing habit, one that shape-changing clearly had not altered.
She walked on, and heard him calling to her from a stand of
beech trees. She frowned. The coils of smoke were drifting
up from behind those trees. Beyond them stood the Christian church presided over by Ambrose the priest. She quickened her pace. Her footfalls raised a rhythm of splashes as
she trotted through the wet grass. She passed through the
stand of beech and saw that the papery white bark was
stained black with smoke.

"Oh no," she breathed.

Mau was standing at the edge of the trees. He gestured to
her as she came up. "Did Haganon do this?" he asked, and
his light voice was harsh.

Sirona's eyes wandered slowly about. The small church
had been burned to the ground. Charred stones and a few of
the larger beams were all that remained, and they lay in a
tumble so haphazard that a stranger would never have
known a church once stood here. A shiver ground through
her bones. Involuntarily she clutched the amulet about her
throat.

"I sense death," she whispered.

"You sense correctly." Mau pointed to a spot near a rafter
charred nearly in half. "There is where he went to his god."

"The priest?"

"Who else?"

Sirona wondered at his tone. In spite of the way he had
spoken to her at their last meeting, she knew Ambrose had
possessed a good heart. She felt genuine shock and sadness
at his death. But Mau was a creature of magic—an immortal. Surely the death of one man must be very like that of
another to him. And Ambrose had belonged to a religion
dedicated to sweeping him and his Mistress from the memory of the mortal world. Why should he be so troubled by
the mortal priest's passing? If anything, he should be
pleased.

"You never answered me," Mau said. "Do you think that
Haganon set fire to this place and murdered the priest?"

"I do not." Sirona let her gaze rest upon the charred

beams. For an instant her inner eye picked out the contours of a body, a skull. Then it was gone, leaving only a shudder in its place. The flames had been so intense that not even Ambrose's bones remained. "Not unless he were mad, and that he is not. As a Christian himself, even he would not dare such a deed as this just to blame it on others. He would be condemned to what they call hell for it. No," she added sadly. "Christians did not do this. Followers of the old ways must have come here, though it is hard to imagine they would have been driven to this."

"Is it?" There was an edge to Mau's voice and hardness in the gleaming orange eyes. "Men are easily driven to many things in the name of their gods."

Slowly they walked away from the ashes of the church and its priest. But they had not gone far before the stench of smoke assailed them again. This time voices accompanied the odor, and the crackle of flames. Sirona had been born in these lands; she knew every league of them. Her eyes flew to the source of the smoke, and her jaw clenched.

"The holy grove," she said to Mau. "They have set fire to it."

The stand of oaks was ancient. From time out of mind people had prayed there. In the old days of power rituals had been held within the sacred circle. The thick branches had been a riot of color from the constant multitude of offerings left by the devoted. Their numbers had grown fewer under the pressure of the new religion, but had never entirely disappeared. Bathilde's prophecy had caused a rush of new offerings, and, this grove had been one of the most frequently visited.

Now the sacred trees were in flames. The beauty of the clean-washed day was gone. Smoke writhed black and ugly against the sky. The sound of an eager fire devouring the living wood choked out the songs of the birds. It seemed as though the trees themselves were screaming, and the bundles tied to their branches sobbing.

Sirona ran. She had not the least idea of what she could do, but still she ran toward the fire. Mau called something out to her, but she paid no heed. People were leaving the stand of burning trees, an entire group of them. This was no band of warriors. There were half a dozen families here: silent women gripping the hands of wide-eyed children, white-haired elders leaning on sticks, and stern-faced men. They were driving their animals with them, struggling to keep the sheep and cattle in order, so they would not flee in panic from the flames. Placid oxen were pulling carts loaded with possessions. Dogs ran barking at their heels.

But the men held torches, leaving no doubt as to their guilt. The ends were wrapped with rags soaked in oil, to make certain the trees would burn. These people had desecrated a sacred place, and, having done so, it looked as if they were leaving their homes.

Sirona pulled up in confusion. The odd cavalcade moved toward her, and she went forward, more slowly, to meet it. As she drew closer she recognized individual faces. She had delivered babies for most of the women, had nursed various illnesses among the old and the young, had set broken bones and bound up injuries for the strong and active. They knew her as well, and yet there was no welcome on any of their faces, even from those whose lives she had saved.

"What is happening here?" she called out angrily. "What have you done?"

One of the men in the forefront answered her. Sirona knew him. His name was Ardo. Although he was but a farmer, he possessed age along with a natural air of authority that caused others to listen to him. She had saved his leg for him last autumn when a windstorm brought a tree limb down on him. Four winters before that he and his family had become Christians. "We have taken revenge," he said. "And it is no more than is due us. Have you seen the church, which is a church no more, but only ashes?"

Sirona realized something else. Every one of these folk was Christian. Pain wrung in her heart, for them, and for the grove. "I have," she said in a gentler tone. "But the holy oaks have never done you harm. They did not burn your church; men did that."

A low rumble went through the families. People glared at Sirona, and Ardo waved his torch savagely. The flame was nearly out, and it hissed weakly in the warming air. "You are wrong," the farmer cried. "These groves do us harm simply by standing! Heathens are going into them again, making offerings, practicing rites the Lord has forbidden. It was those rites that told them to set fire to our church with Father Ambrose inside. And all of it begun by Bathilde, who has fallen away from the true faith."

"Bathilde." Sirona stared at Ardo with her strange eyes that shifted color even as he looked. "Was the burning of the church her doing?"

"It might as well have been. She, with her speeches and her prophecies, calling us all together to say that the old ways must return. Who else but heathens would have done such a terrible thing? I pray that they themselves burn in the everlasting lake of fire for what they have done."

"You," Sirona reminded him, "were once a heathen yourself. It was a terrible thing, indeed. But you do not know who committed the deed, not for certain, and these heathens you speak of are your own neighbors and kin."

"No more!" Ardo's face was dark with suffused blood. "Old and new cannot bide as one. Even I, a poor farmer, know that much. Bathilde wants us Christians off her lands; she has said as much. Well, we will go. For now."

Sirona looked from him to the others. They looked back at her, and their faces mirrored the same fury reflected on Ardo's. "Where will you go?" she asked.

"To the monastery. Abbot Wala will take us in, until God returns us to our homes." Ardo stepped aside. "You are no Christian, wisewoman," he said with dignity. "But you have always been good to us. We do not forget the times you have healed our hurts and delivered our babies. For that reason you need fear no harm from us. But take care. Other Christians may not be so charitable." He lowered his eyes. "They say," he muttered more softly, "that you are *stria*, a witch."

"Let them say what they will!" Ardo's wife sprang forward. "I have five living children because of her. No one, Christian or otherwise, will harm her while I have anything to do about it."

"Peace, woman." Ardo rolled his eyes skyward. "Have I not just said we would not harm her?"

"It's not us I am speaking of, and you know it well. Wise-woman"—the farmer's wife said to Sirona—"my eldest daughter went for service in the household of Count Haganon. She is only a scullery girl, but she still hears things."

Sirona smiled at her. "So do I, Rona, and I thank you. I will be careful."

She stood in the mud of the road, watching the assemblage of bleating animals and grim-faced people move away. Smoke stung her eyes. The oaks were burning hopelessly, beyond all help, save that of magic.

Magic.

Sirona raised her eyes to the sky. It was becoming easier to summon the power. Each time she called upon it, the hidden place where she had kept it all these years grew weaker. And this time she was acting of her own will, entirely fixated on what she had decided to do. She raised her arms.

Directly above the grove of flaming trees the sky darkened. Within seconds an intense shower beat down at the leaping flames. The fire sizzled in protest. Smoke hissed and turned black, spun up into the rain, and was swiftly dissolved. The oaks waved their giant gnarled limbs in thanks.

In the near distance the procession of Christians stopped and turned back to stare. Hastily, Sirona lowered her arms, knowing it was too late. They saw her standing alone in the road. They saw the cloudburst raining down on the trees alone, drowning out the fire. They already feared she was a witch. What they were seeing now only confirmed it.

She watched sadly as mothers pulled their children away and men slapped sticks at the oxen to move them into a lumbering trot. The group of families fled as fast as their slow-paced beasts and disorderly flocks and herds would allow. The noise of the yelping dogs faded slowly, until only the patter of rain was left.

"That," Mau said beside her, "was not very wise."

Sirona sighed. "What would you have me do?" She gestured to the grove. "They are sacred. How could I let them burn? You wanted me to renew my bonds with Bast. Are trees not holy to Her?"

Mau did not answer.

"They are headed for the monastery." Sirona's gaze went back to the group of peasants. Their figures had receded into indistinct shapes on the flat horizon. The fire was out. The oaks were charred and burned, but the healing rain had spared their inner hearts, and they would live. Others, she reflected, thinking of Father Ambrose, had not been so fortunate. "I had to do it," she said again. "But you're right. They will tell the abbot of this, and he and Haganon both will know where I am."

"Along with what you did." Mau turned a somber look upon her. Abruptly, he shrugged. "Well, the mouse is out of the hole and there's no sense in trying to force it back. But"—he slanted his eyes at the rain still soaking the oak grove—"you may as well tell that to stop. It has accomplished its purpose."

Sirona found that she did not need to ask how. The knowledge was springing to life inside her, as vibrant and inexorable as the green hearts of the oak trees. She had only to picture the rain stopping for it to happen. As the shower slowed to a trickle that quickly ceased altogether, she said to Mau, "You never said whether trees are sacred to Bast."

Mau walked on ahead. "There are," he said over his shoulder, "few trees in the Black Land. And none like the ones here."

Ardo's family and the others reached the boundaries of the monastery before sunset. They were no longer alone. Other groups had joined them, swelling their numbers until an unwieldy line of wagons and people and animals strung itself out on the road leading to the monastery. It was raining again; it had begun the instant the refugees left the lands of Bathilde and entered those belonging to the monastery. As they arrived, wet and weary, Abbot Wala himself came out to greet them. The prior had fetched him in consternation at the extraordinary sight of so many travelers coming to seek refuge at their gates.

The abbot was not known for his generosity of spirit. However, his position and the Rules of the Monastery bound him to offer a night's hospitality to any person who asked it. All monasteries maintained a guesthouse where the weary could spend that night and be assured of both an evening meal and breakfast. The bounty of both the food and the accommodations varied from monastery to monastery. Some abbots saw to it that travelers who came within the gates of their domain were provided with soft cots and large meals; others provided the bare minimum. Abbot Wala fell into the latter category. Travelers at his guesthouse slept on hard pallets and were given black bread, oat porridge, and cheese before being sent on their way the next morning.

But generous or not, Wala was wise enough to know that something ominous had wrought this exodus. With the prior at his side, he went out to the gates to watch the first of the arrivals straggle through. All of them wore the universal dress of commoners: brown-wool tunics and crudely fashioned squares of cloth with holes for the head and arms to serve as mantles. Farmers and villagers, the abbot noted. There was not a man or woman of noble birth among them. The observation altered both his bearing and his voice.

"What is going on here?" he demanded. "What has caused all of you people to leave your homes? And"—he scowled at the bleating sheep and goats and lowing cattle—"bring your beasts with you? You should be tending them, and your fields and shops as well."

An older man, clearly a farmer, stepped forward. Rain was dripping off his coarsely woven mantle, and he looked tired and miserable. "My lord Abbot," he said diffidently. "I am called Ardo. We beg the protection of this monastery."

The abbot eyed him. "For what reason?"

"A good one, my lord Abbot." Ardo looked around at the faces of his companions. "It—it has stopped raining."

"And that is a reason? When the skies have cleared so

that you can sow your crops and turn your animals out to graze? You should be taking advantage of such weather, not roaming about the countryside seeking food and shelter for the asking."

The prior, who was a kindhearted man, gave his superior an appalled glance, to which Abbot Wala paid no heed. Ardo himself remained expressionless. Inwardly, he could have been shocked or angered, but he allowed no sign of it to cross his face. He was a peasant; a man of his station could not afford the luxury of showing his emotion to his betters.

"The rain has stopped, yes," he said haltingly. "That, my lord, is why we have come. We had no choice."

"No choice?" Although he did not show it, Wala knew full well where this was headed. The *stria* had used her arts to stop the rain around her house. She could as easily have done the same elsewhere. "Who is your lord?" he asked. "Where have you traveled from?"

"Not lord," Ardo corrected. "Lady. The Lady Bathilde is our mistress. She took over the duties of the manor and its holdings when the lord Erchinoald died." He dropped his eyes. "She is the one we are fleeing from."

Haganon had appeared from the cluster of buildings reserved for important visitors. Folding his arms, he listened unnoticed to the conversation. His blunt features grew grimmer and grimmer with every word he heard. But when Bathilde's name was mentioned, he glared out at the gathering and stomped forward, the sword at his side jangling, his boots thumping with every step. "What has she done?" he snapped out harshly. "Speak up!"

Ardo looked up, and then down again. He did his best to comply. He recognized Count Haganon, and worse, knew his reputation. He had no desire to incur the nobleman's wrath. Stammering slightly at addressing a man of such rank, he launched into a description of all that had happened since Bathilde called the folk of her holdings together. The rapt attention which Haganon and the abbot gave him soon emboldened the farmer. He was a man who loved to talk, and in all his life he had never been given an audience of this distinction. Daunted at first, he eventually grew loquacious.

"And so the heathens burned our poor little church," he declared. "To the ground, my lords! It lies in ashes, and with it lie the bones of Father Ambrose. The Lady Bathilde did not hold the torch that committed the deed, but she might as well have. We are afraid to stay in our homes. She has made threats against us. Once our neighbors who refused salvation hid their faith in the old gods. But no longer. They mock us, and their faces are dark. When the rain stopped, as Bathilde foretold it would, they grew worse. It was not safe to remain."

Haganon raised a hand. "There was a wisewoman called to attend Bathilde at the birth of her son? What of her?"

Ardo's face changed. It was an odd question, one that seemed to have nothing to do with the tale he had been relating. Instantly, he thought of Sirona. His last memory of her was of watching her raise her arms and bring rain down upon the fire that he himself had set. The sight had horrified him. But what did Haganon want with her? As fearful as he was of what he had seen, he did not trust Haganon. The count was a cruel man, and the wisewoman had helped him and his own too many times to count. Yet she was a pagan. She had used dark arts to save the oak grove from what was surely justified destruction.

"Wisewoman, my lord?" he asked hesitantly, bargaining for time while he thought of how to respond.

"Yes, you fool!" Haganon rapped out. "All of you know her. Was she with Bathilde when she called you together? Where is she now?"

Ardo faltered. "I—" he began.

His wife Rona stepped in to rescue him. "We have not seen her, my lord." To the abbot and the noble her voice was utterly humble; to those who knew her it contained a tone that dared anyone, her husband, in particular, to contradict her. "She was not present when Lady Bathilde summoned us all to the great house. Nor was she seen either before or after the church was burned. She must be far from these parts on some healing errand. It is often so with her."

She fell silent. After a moment, Ardo nodded. "Yes, it is so," he agreed.

Haganon regarded them both. His face registered his skepticism. "You are lying." He delivered the statement in a flat hard voice. "You are fools indeed to think I cannot see it."

Ardo faltered, but Rona refused to be intimidated. "That may be, my lord, but nevertheless, we do not know where the wisewoman is." She said this with confidence, for that much was true. No one had seen Sirona since the grove. She could very well be on a healing errand. "In truth," she added, being careful to lower her eyes, "we pay no heed to the comings and goings of the wisewoman. It is the Lady Bathilde who concerns us. For it is she and not the wise-woman who has driven us from our homes."

Haganon's eyes bulged. Though spoken with outward deference, the woman's speech reeked with boldness and disrespect. The count's ruddy features suffused with blood as rage rushed over him. But before he could give vent to it, Abbot Wala intervened.

"Well, there is little point in continuing this any further," he said, and motioned to the prior. "We must take these people in." He scowled, his eyes wandering over the sprawling group. "All of them. Until the evil that menaces their homes is destroyed, it appears that we have no alternative."

Haganon gave the abbot a single burning glance, spun on his heel, and strode abruptly away. Wala completed his instructions to the prior and hurried after him. A tall man himself, the Abbot had to lengthen his stride quickly to catch up. "Where are you going?" he asked in a low voice.

Haganon swung on him. "Impertinent peasant! Were the woman from my holdings, I would have her flogged bloody. I would have done it anyway, were I not a guest in your monastery. And you—you did nothing. That ragged hag has knowledge of the witch and where she is. I saw it in the eyes of that dolt of a farmer!"

"Keep your voice down," Wala cautioned. "Do you want to rouse the royal counselor from his meditations? It makes no difference what those peasants know or don't know. This is a place of God, and they have come here seeking refuge. I can hardly order them flogged, even if I agree that it might be a good idea."

Haganon made a contemptuous noise. "You are a fool, Wala, as big a fool as that farmer and his ill-spoken wife. As for me, I have no intention of staying here waiting to see what Bathilde and that witch plan to do next."

Wala repeated his question. "Where are you going?"

Haganon answered him, and finally his voice was lowered. "Back to my own holdings, as quickly as my stallion can carry me. Whatever those witches have set loose will surely strike at my lands as it did at the priest and his church."

Wala nodded. "And at this monastery as well," he said gravely. "We must close the gates and prepare."

"The *stria* escaped us," Haganon said angrily. "Now she will seek her revenge."

For the first time, a trace of fear darted through the anger on his face.

19

OVER THE LENGTH AND BREADTH OF
Bathilde's holdings the sun continued to beam. The face of a long-
delayed spring shone gently upon
the land, and the fields began to
bloom. Green grass sprouted in the
pastures so quickly it seemed like
magic. The livestock fed eagerly and
soon, the lambs and calves that were born did not die as the
others had, but thrived and grew strong.

As Bathilde had said she would, she set out on her sacred
procession. Sirona and Mau came upon it as the procession
headed toward the boundary of her holdings.

The noise of Bathilde's approach preceded her by a good
league. Even to Sirona's ears, far less sensitive than those of
her companion, the sounds were audible. Such rituals had
been banished, but she still recognized the singing and music that accompanied them. But the voices and the pounding
whistling instruments called to her, brought to life what had
long been buried and was coming to life more and more
with each passing day.

She and Mau stood in the road watching the procession
come toward them. How different it was from the train of
Christians she had seen not so long ago. A nimbus of anger,
sadness, and fear had attended Ardo and the others, shading
them gray with defeat and discouragement. By contrast,
Bathilde and her train glowed with the colors of joy. Confidence gleamed about them as brightly as the sun. Their
voices rang with it.

Three carts formed the body of the procession. Bathilde
had not had time to see them carved with the wondrous detail of the old days, but the pagan carpenters she had sum-

245

moned—some of them old enough to remember how things
had once been—had done their best. With the coming of the
sun, flowers had burst into bloom, and Bathilde had set
women to gathering them in order to weave scores and
scores of wreaths. The carts, as well as the animals that
drew them, were bedecked with the fragrant results of the
women's efforts. A team of white mules drew the first cart,
and white oxen drew the other two. Garlands and wreaths
of greenery hung heavy about the necks and harness of the
mules. More decorated the horns of the patient oxen.

Riding in the carts and walking alongside of them were
the worshippers. All of them were women, and they were as
gaily bedecked with flowers as the mules and oxen. In
Freyja's processions it was traditional for the chief priestess
to be accompanied by a host of other priestesses in her jour-
neys. Such priestesses should have vanished under the
swell of Christianity; indeed, it seemed that they had. But
not all of them were gone. Gray-haired and stooped, they
had resurfaced nevertheless. In joyous thanksgiving, they
sang and played their instruments, not only for their own re-
newal but that of the land.

A throng of younger women had joined them. Like
Sirona, they had not the years to remember the glory days
of the processions, but they had rejected the Christian God
or had never accepted him in the first place. Free now to
worship as they wished, they danced in joy, learning the
words of the ancient songs and prayers from their elders,
playing the sistrums and bull-roarers and flutes with un-
practiced delight.

Bathilde rode in the first cart. Reposing in state, she
rested on several cushions stuffed with hen's feathers. Sitting behind her a woman—not Begga—held the noblewoman's baby nestled in her arms. In spite of the
afternoon's warmth, Bathilde was elaborately bedecked in
animal skins. An ornately fashioned crown of fur decorated
her head, and on her hands she wore beautiful soft gloves
also made from fur.

The sight of the fur caused Mau to emit a sound that suspiciously resembled a hiss. "Cat fur," he growled under his

breath when Sirona glanced questioningly at him. "This northern Goddess belongs to cats as my Mistress does. But," he sniffed, "the folk of the Black Land would never have dreamed of killing and skinning my mortal brethren to wear as adornment."

Before Sirona could answer him, Bathilde caught sight of them. A smile bright as the wreaths of flowers colored her face. As the mules drew nearer, she waved and called out a command. The women leading the team halted. The music clashed into discordant silence and the slower carts drawn by the oxen stopped as well. Women came up curiously, some of them smiling as they recognized Sirona.

"Wisewoman," Bathilde cried. "You have returned."

There was such genuine welcome in her voice that Sirona had to respond in kind. "I am pleased to see you so well, lady," she said, and bowed.

"And who is this with you?" Bathilde caught herself, her dark eyes growing wide as she stared down at Mau from her high seat in the cart. "Magic," she whispered.

Mau inclined his head in a gesture of assent. He said nothing.

Bathilde stared at the man who had been a cat. The longer she looked, the more it seemed that she could not tear her eyes away. Mau returned her scrutiny as calmly and unblinkingly as the feline being he truly was. Bathilde's face grew blank. She appeared to be falling into that wide orange gaze.

"Lady," one of the older women beside the cart said at last. There was worry in her voice, and she glanced suspiciously at Mau as she spoke. "Is anything amiss?"

Bathilde jerked as if waking from a dream. She pulled her eyes away from Mau and looked back at Sirona. The elderly priestess had called her back to herself, and the expression on her face was both awed and thoughtful. "You have changed," she murmured. "I see the power in you." She nodded at Mau. "And its evidence. You have accepted your gifts at last. May the name of the Goddess be praised!" she cried to the other women. "Another priestess has come to join us, and great in magic is she!"

The women burst into a chorus of welcome. Those who knew Sirona ran forward to embrace her. Those who did not came, too. Almost all of them gave Mau a wide berth, an exclusion that bothered him not in the least; cats hate to be hugged unless they are the ones to choose it. Sirona, on the other hand, found herself in the center of a winding knot of affection and goodwill. The intensity and suddenness of it took her off guard. Yet it was pleasant, after having her life sought so relentlessly by cruel men, to be met with such warmth. She stood in the women's midst, smiling, and a little dazed, as they made much of her.

"Come," Bathilde called down. "Ride in my cart with me, Wisewoman, and let us be on our way once more." She moved aside on the cushions to make room for Sirona.

It was a great honor, and Sirona knew it. The priestesses moved aside so she could mount the cart, but she did not move. She glanced through the crowd of women at Mau; Bathilde's invitation had not been extended to him.

Bathilde followed her gaze. "You, too, stranger," she added. "You may ride with us, as well." Her dark eyes narrowed. "It is not usual for men to be a part of Freyja's sacred procession, but you, I think, are an exception. What are you called?"

Mau inclined his sleek head again. "Mau, my lady."

Bathilde gave a little start at the sound of his voice. From the expression that flitted swiftly across Bathilde's face, Sirona knew she had not expected him to possess the power of speech. "An odd name," she said. "You are not of Saxony, are you?"

"No, my lady, nor any other land of the north."

For an instant Sirona thought Bathilde was going to fall into the cat man's enigmatic stare a second time. But Bathilde had regained control of herself and was not about to relinquish it again. She looked at Sirona, then back at Mau. "Well, then," she said for the benefit of her priestesses, "since you are with the wisewoman, you are welcome among us. So, will you ride in the cart?"

He smiled. "Thank you, my lady," he answered with impeccable courtesy, "but I prefer to walk."

Sirona could see questions burning in the noblewoman's eyes; Bathilde's awe of Mau was slowly being overcome by intense curiosity about him. To forestall it, she made her way through the women and climbed up into the cart. As Sirona settled herself upon the soft cushions, Bathilde gave the order to move on. The mules walked forward. The oxen plodded after them. After a few moments the music began again. Instruments wailed and pounded and whistled. Voices rose to join them.

Bathilde smiled. "Beautiful, is it not?" She indicated the musicians and singers with a graceful hand. "Long and long has it been since the land has heard the sacred music."

"The land has heard other things as well," Sirona said. "Like the crackle of flames." She watched Bathilde's face and went on. "The church of Father Ambrose lies in ashes. Did you know?"

The noblewoman's dark eyes were burning. "And all across my holdings sacred groves have been burned by Christians fleeing the true gods."

"Yes, but the farms and houses of those Christians have been put to the torch as well. Is this well-done of you, lady?"

"It is the wish of the Goddess," Bathilde said flatly.

Sirona wondered which Goddess it was the wish of: Bast, Sekhmet, or even Freyja, Who had perhaps awakened. "Has She told you so?" she asked.

Bathilde's eyes glowed under her elaborate crown of fur. "We will burn the holdings of the Christian nobles who would have slain my babe and me, and you, too, wise-woman; do not forget that. And we will start with Haganon's manor house. Do you object?"

Sirona thought for a long moment. She knew her face had hardened at the mention of that name. Mau was drifting along on the outskirts of the procession. He seemed too far away to hear the conversation, but Sirona knew it was not so. From the corner of her eyes, she saw him pause and stare at her, but did not allow herself to take heed. "No," she said at last. "I care nothing for Haganon or his manor, so long as the house folk are spared. They are surely innocent and have naught to do with his plans."

"There are no innocents," Bathilde spit. "If they belong to Haganon, then they are traitors to the Shining Ones. And the same goes for any others who walk in the trains of powerful Christians. Men like Abbot Wala. I do not forget that he, too, plotted my death."

In that moment Bathilde sounded no different than the abbot had when he had exhorted the nobles to burn Sirona. The memory made Sirona stiffen. She had no cause to love that churchman any more than she did Haganon. If his rich monastery were burned to the ground, it would certainly make little difference to her. And yet she could not help thinking of the small homely church of Ambrose the priest. It lay a charred ruin, but she pictured it livid with flames, with Ambrose trapped inside. It was a thought so vivid she swayed in her mind, as if she had been there when it happened.

She knew Mau was looking at her, but she did not return his gaze. Instead, she stared at the noblewoman, until Bathilde dropped her eyes.

"Very well," the noblewoman growled. "Since you desire it so strongly, we will burn only the house and its outbuildings. Those within will be allowed to leave with their lives." She bared her teeth in a grin. "They will flee to the monastery, of course; they are doing so already. That place will soon be bursting at the seams. But it, too, will be burned. Mark me. All traces of Christianity will be torn from Saxony. They must be. The ancient powers cannot truly return until they are."

Sirona said nothing. In that, she agreed with Bathilde. It was the methods of that rooting out that concerned her.

The two giant cats awoke first, both white as frost, with pale gold eyes. They stretched and purred and smiled as their sleepy eyes caught sight of Bast. The Goddess returned the smiles, ran a caressing hand down the cats' long backs, and waited for Her northern Sister to awake.

Freyja stirred. She lay on a bed of snowy feathers shaped like enormous wings, nestled in between the two cats who served as Her guardians. She was naked but for Her golden white hair, masses and masses of it that clothed the curves of Her lush body like a shimmering garment. Panels of curved clouds and light surrounded Her winged bed, enclosing and supporting the feathers so that She appeared to be floating upon the light.

Raising Her arms, Freyja sighed deeply. The movement lifted the hair from Her breasts, revealing an amber necklace of wide golden circles. A smile curved Her beautiful mouth, and She opened Her eyes. They were beautiful, too: as deep and blue as the sky before dawn. Languorously, She stretched out an arm, stroked one of the cats, and looked up at Bast.

"Ah," She murmured. "It has been a long sleep, and Who is it that comes to awaken Me from My slumber?"

Although Bast smiled, Her reply was formal. "I am Bast: Eye of Ra and Defender of Osiris. I am She Who comprehends all other Goddesses." Her voice grew less formal. "My heart sings that You, My Sister, are awake at last."

"Bast, from the land of the burning sands. Of course." Freyja sat up against the feathers. "Forgive Me; I should have known You at once, as My cats did. Your own cat came to wake Me, but then I slept again. My head is still muzzy from dreaming." She sighed. "Such pleasant dreams they were."

"And now it is time for them to end," Bast said quietly. "It is time for You to rejoin the world, Northern Sister."

A shadow crossed the beautiful face. "The world," Freyja replied sadly, and with a trace of anger, "is the reason for My dreams. The world desires Me no longer."

Bast inclined Her shining head. "Once that was true. But things have changed. Have You not heard the voices calling to You?"

"Yes." Freyja spoke slowly. "I heard voices. I thought that they were only in My dreams."

"Some of them, perhaps, but not all. Where is Your chariot?"

Both cats opened their eyes wide at the question. They leaped up and rubbed eagerly against their Mistress. The purrs that rumbled from their chests were deafening as thunder. Freyja made a gesture. One of the curving light panels broke apart. A chariot stood in the space. It was white and gold and glowing, as brilliant as the hair and skin and necklace of the Goddess to whom it belonged.

"There is My chariot," said Freyja. "But it is bound by dreams as much as I am. The days in which My guardians and I flew upon the clouds are gone."

"Your guardians," Bast remarked, "know otherwise."

The two cats had leaped from the bed of wings and run to the chariot. They stood in front of it, looking at Freyja expectantly. Their tails waved back and forth, and they shifted their front paws as if they could barely wait to leap forward.

Bast smiled to see them. "They understand." Her melodic voice purred and the cats answered with even louder purrs of their own. "Indeed, they heard the voices and understood the calls long before You did, My Sister."

"So it is." Slowly, rippling with grace and beauty in Her nakedness, Freyja arose from the bed. "But My understanding is also returning. I did hear voices. I heard Your Sister Sekhmet, O Bast of the burning sands. She spoke to Me, but She could not reach Me, not as You could. For You and I are kindred. Time out of mind have the mortals worshipped Us. Our realms lie on opposite ends of the world, and yet bestow the same gifts upon those Who revere Our powers."

The Cat-Goddess's emerald eyes warmed. "Healing and love and the fertile fruit of that love, yes, those are Our blessings. Once My worshippers traveled down the Mother River to My city to celebrate the great festival held in My name, just as the sacred procession now travels across the land in Your name. You are the Mistress, O Freyja, the Ancestress of the elder gods of these northern climes."

"Yes," Freyja murmured. "The Vanir."

"They are asleep, as You have been. They will not awaken until You call to Them, as I have called to You."

Freyja's wondrous blue eyes regarded Her Sister Goddess. "And is it time for Them to awaken?"

"Your people think so." Bast's whiskered face smiled. "They honor Your name, and they wait for You to return."

"Then I will." Her decision made, a burst of light washed over Freyja. She laughed, a joyous riot of sound. Her cats let out thunderous miaows that would have deafened the ears of any mortal.

Freyja walked toward Her chariot. Her steps were as long and flowing as wind sweeping over the feathers of Her winged bed. "First I must call to Frigga, She Who is My Other Aspect," She said. "For She still sleeps."

Bast knew Whom She meant. Frigga was Freyja's counterpart, as venerable and ancient as the latter was lush and beautiful. Together They comprised the Great Goddess of the North. Together Their power was enormous. She nodded in agreement. "It is wise to do so," She said. "You are My Sister, indeed."

Freyja's smile was a thing of incomparable beauty. She crooked a graceful finger. From out of nowhere a cape of feathers appeared and swirled over Her shoulders. Clad only in the cape and Her necklace, She stepped into the chariot. "Thank you, Sister," She cried. Her voice was a paean of joy. The last remnants of sleep had left Her, and She was glorying in the change. "We shall meet again."

"Yes," Bast replied with a wondrous smile of Her own. "We shall."

The amber links of Freyja's necklace caught fire, and the cats surged up into the clouds.

Within an instant they were gone.

As the procession approached the marker that indicated the beginning of Haganon's holdings, the weather ahead began to clear. It was a startling sight. The three carts and the sprawling party of women were bathed in sunlight, washed in warmth and blue skies. But in front of them, beyond Haganon's marker, clouds roiled with dark menace and rain streamed down over the drowned land. Dank winds blew toward the sacred train, but as they neared the marchers they became soft breezes that touched faces as sweetly as the kisses of children.

Bathilde pointed toward the marker. "Look you," she

cried. "See how the Goddess is with Us. She lights our way with sunlight, so that the folk of these holdings will see and give thanks and join our numbers."

Her voice rang with triumph, and with good reason. As the cavalcade sang and danced its way toward Haganon's lands, its numbers had swelled steadily. People had flocked to follow the three carts and its priestesses. They maintained a respectful distance, but they were there nonetheless. A great many men were among them. Caught up in the excitement, they had left their work to see if Bathilde's prophecy would continue to hold true.

They were the beginnings of an army, Bathilde confided to Sirona, an army that had only just begun to grow. Sirona found the fervor in her voice as chilling as it was compelling.

The team of white mules trotted by the stone marker. Instantly, the rain stopped. People let out an enormous outcry that grew even louder as the clouds broke apart and shafts of sunlight lanced down toward them. The muddy track dried with dizzying swiftness, allowing the wheeled carts to pass with relative ease. None of Haganon's men-at-arms appeared along the road to block their way. No doubt they were all at the count's manor, Bathilde told her followers contemptuously. Cowering like whipped dogs as they awaited the coming of the Goddess.

By the time the cavalcade reached the first village, the clouds had turned white and fluffy. The sky gleamed blue as new-glazed pottery, and birdsong was filling the air. On the outskirts of the village, people were waiting for them. It was small wonder that they were. The cacophony of singing and instruments had heralded their arrival, but even more astounding to the villagers was the smiling weather that had appeared out of nowhere.

Old and young, the villagers stood and stared. As Bathilde's cart drew even with the first of the watchers, cries arose. The people standing there reaped the benefit of the sun that accompanied the mule-drawn cart, and their reaction to it was much the same as the folk of Bathilde's own holdings. Among the laughter and sobs of the adults and the sudden darting about of the children, the procession drew to a halt.

A man advanced in years stumped forward, leaning on his stick, his rheumy eyes wide. "Lady," he said, for he recognized Bathilde, and was old enough to recognize her garb as well. "For many long days we have been cursed. Now you appear"—his gaze traveled to Sirona, for he also recognized the wisewoman—"and the sun is shining down upon us like a blessing. How can this be?"

Bathilde gave him a brilliant smile. "The answer to that is simple, and you have lived long enough to know it. Are you going to tell me you do not remember the sacred processions of old?"

"I remember." The rheumy eyes brightened. "Freyja would visit in all Her glory, and Her priestesses would do the holy work of the Goddess." The old man caught himself. Such memories were not spoken of these days, at least not where others could hear them.

But Bathilde's smile only grew more encouraging. "That," she said with enormous majesty, "is why we have come. To do that holy work again."

People behind the man muttered uneasily. The man himself looked worried. "Lady," he explained more softly. "We are Christian here."

"Are you?" Bathilde fixed him and the people muttering behind him with an ironic eye. "And how has being Christian helped you? Has it prevented this rain? Has it brought you good weather so your fields and orchards are fruitful? Has it caused your pastures to fill with good grass so your animals grow fat?"

The old man did not answer. The people behind him fell silent.

"And," Bathilde pressed, her voice turning thin and sharp as a newly whetted blade, "has being Christian brought you a kind and sympathetic lord? Has your lord done anything at all to help you through this hard season?"

The silence grew loud.

Bathilde nodded. The look she threw Sirona said that she had her answer. There was not a person here who did not know how grimly unsympathetic Haganon would be to his tenants if the harvest were bad.

"Bring me an animal for sacrifice," she said. "Sheep or calf or ox, it does not matter, but the beast must be whole and unblemished. Do this and Freyja will see through my eyes and speak with my voice, as She did in the days before unbelievers drove Her away."

A few of the women stirred. They looked up at the glowing sky, whispered together, and moved as if they were about to do the noblewoman's bidding. But most still held back. A younger woman finally spoke. She looked to be about sixteen winters, perhaps less. A baby hung in a sling from her back, and her belly was round with the presence of another.

"Forgive me, lady." The woman's voice was as youthful and hesitant as her face. "I am young and do not remember these things as Harvold and the other old ones do. I have never seen a beast sacrificed. We are poor, lady, and our beasts are precious to us. What—what will it bring us to do this thing?"

Her fellow villagers gaped at the woman's daring. She was taking a great chance to speak so boldly to a lady of Bathilde's rank. Haganon, it was well-known, would never have tolerated it. But Bathilde smiled upon the young mother and answered her gently.

"It will bring you Freyja, my child." There was a hypnotic melody to her words; unconsciously, the women who had appointed themselves as her priestesses began to sway in rhythm to her voice, their eyes closing. "And Freyja will bring us who honor Her power: to heal the sick among you, to divine the future, and ensure a good harvest. But most of all, She will bring Her blessing."

Bathilde paused. The singsong melody of her voice changed, and her dark eyes seemed to pierce the gaze of each villager. "To those who wish it. To those who believe. Let those who do not leave, lest they profane the ritual. Let them go to Haganon and see if he will grant them shelter. Or let them go to the monastery. Either way the rain will return as soon as they leave the influence of the Goddess."

People looked around, at each other, and up at the gleaming sky. Sirona sat in the cart watching them. Christians were among them; she was certain of it. What would happen if they indeed left, as Bathilde was telling them to do, and went straight to Haganon? He would surely respond by descending with his men-at-arms to destroy Bathilde and her procession. Flute and drums would be of little use against swords and spears.

Bathilde, however, seemed oblivious to this fact. "Sacrifice to the Goddess. Hear the prophecy," she called. "And you will join this procession and follow as my own folk do." She waved behind her at the throng of people.

"And what of our crops?" a man shouted. "If we traipse along after you, they will rot in the fields."

Unlike her reply to the woman, Bathilde's answer this time was knife-blade sharp. "They were rotting already under the rain, weren't they?" Again, no one had an answer for this, including the questioner, and her next words were gentle again. "Fear not. Freyja is the Goddess of harvest. She will see to your fields. Without Her, you and your families would have starved in the coming winter. Now that She has returned your bellies will be full."

The few women who had stirred before came to life. "We will fetch the sacrifice, lady," the eldest of them, who had a large goiter on her neck, said loudly. She looked around, defiance in her gaze. "For your words hold truth. Four winters ago I let the Christian priest sprinkle his water on me; Count Haganon commanded that all of us on his lands do so. Well, I cannot see that it has done my family or me any good. I miss the old ways. I want to return."

Bathilde held out her arms. "Then come. Come back to Her Who awaits you."

The women ran off to the pastures.

"Look there, Haganon." Aelisachar pointed at the road ahead. "Traders are crossing your lands."

Haganon reined in his horse with impatient hands. "What of it? Let them pass. I must get to my manor, and I would think that you'd want to reach your own holdings as quickly as possible, too."

"I do," the old noble said. "But traders always have news; everyone knows that. They might be able to tell us what Bathilde is up to. They might even have seen the witch."

Both Haganon and his horse fretted, the animal as eager to race on as his rider. But there was too much wisdom in Aelisachar's words to ignore. He gave the stallion his head and raced to intersect the traders. Aelisachar followed, as did Haganon's two men-at-arms. This was all that remained of their numbers; the other nobles had already split off to their own holdings as soon as they had left the monastery. Aelisachar, whose lands adjoined Haganon's, would soon leave.

The trader saw the four men approaching and stopped his pack train of mules. There was no point in trying to outrun them; he knew that as well as they. Rain dripped off his mantle as he faced them. His expression was neutral, and at the same time, stern. Traders were allowed safe passage through any noble's lands. But unscrupulous acts could and did occur. Out in these remote reaches a noble and his men might pose as bandits, robbing a trader of all he possessed and slaying him in the bargain, with no one ever the wiser. Those who followed the roads with goods must ever be prepared to defend them.

Therefore, the man held his oaken staff in a protective manner as Haganon pulled up in a shower of raindrops and horse froth and clods of mud. "There is no need for that," the noble said, gesturing at the staff. "I am lord of these lands, and we mean you no harm. Where have you come from and where are you bound?" he demanded, as the trader lowered his stick. Four youths spread out alongside the mules. Armed also with staves, they stared up at the horsemen with wide nervous eyes, but stood bravely, ready to fight.

"I am called Isaac, my lord." The trader addressed Haganon politely, though there was caution in his voice and manner. "I and my nephews are headed for home. We go by way of Aachen, where we will seek to do more trading at the king's court."

Haganon eyed the loaded packs on the mules. "How have you managed to conduct trade in this weather? The roads are well nigh impassable."

"Not everywhere," the trader said evasively. "And we have had shelter."

"Where?" Haganon shot at him.

Isaac looked up at him. "A noblewoman offered us hospitality," he said at last. "And when the weather cleared we went on our way."

He did not need to say more. Haganon and Aelisachar exchanged glances. "The weather has not cleared," Haganon pointed out sharply. "Are you blind, man?"

"No, my lord." There was dignity in the trader's voice, and a touch, a very slight touch of annoyance. "But not until we left the noblewoman's lands and crossed over into yours did the rain begin again."

"Where is Bathilde now?" Haganon bared his teeth in a snarl of impatience when Isaac hesitated. "Come, come, we all know Bathilde is the noblewoman you speak of. Where is she?"

Isaac's dignity remained unshaken. But he had to answer Haganon. How could he not? Bathilde's meeting with her people was vivid in his mind, as vivid as the warning she had given him to leave. As much as he disliked this arrogant count, as a man of God, Isaac could not allow him to go into danger unwarned, much less the innocent folk who lived on his lands.

"Lady Bathilde gathered her people together in a great procession," he said. "She prayed to her gods for the rain to stop, and it did. I do not believe in her gods, so of course I do not credit them with stopping the rain. But many others did, and that is why they followed her. She spoke of drawing still more to her gods, to the pagan beliefs they once followed. I fear," he went on, "that they may be headed onto your lands. At least that was how it looked when last we saw them. The lady," he added after a moment's reflection, "seems to bear a great hostility toward you, my lord."

"And I her," Haganon snapped. He wheeled his horse around. "On to the manor," he roared at his men-at-arms. "We must gather a force to repel them. By the bones of Christ, I'll not stand by while pagan rabble flaunt themselves in my face, and on my own lands! They'll taste the metal of my Christian sword first!"

Isaac was appalled. "Surely not," he protested. "They are mostly women. I only wanted to warn you to look to your own safety—"

"And I intend to." Haganon bent a savage glare upon the trader. "If they are only women, then why were you so compelled to warn me? I will tell you," he rushed on, when Isaac made no answer. "Because they are *stria*, witches, intent on using their dark arts against me! Aelisachar," he shouted, "will you gather your own men and ride to our aid?"

"I will!" the elderly noble yelled.

Completely forgotten, Isaac watched the men thunder away. He shook his head. "If the lady and her women are witches," he said to his nephews, "then mayhap their magic will protect them." His voice was heavy. "I should have said nothing. For all their sakes."

20

THE SINGING HAD BEGUN. THE older women had taught the younger ones the chants, and the melodies rose into the sun-warmed air, twining about the ears of the listeners. Those who held instruments played them louder than ever, to drive off any evil spirits that might seek to taint and damage the ritual.

The villagers watched avidly as Bathilde's priestesses prepared the animal chosen for sacrifice. It was a young white bullock: selected after lengthy and vigorous debate in the village as to which beast they could afford to lose. The bullock stood placidly as every spot of mud was cleaned from his coat and wreaths of greenery and flowers hung about his thick neck and horns. He seemed mildly surprised by all the attention.

People whispered and muttered as they watched. Slaughtering animals was commonplace, but there were those among them who had never seen a sacrifice. Blood spilled in the name of a pagan goddess was not only blasphemous; it was titillating.

It would fall to Bathilde to wield the knife. "I have never performed a sacrifice," she confessed to Sirona, looking nervous. "Neither Sekhmet or Freyja instructed me."

"Use the blade swiftly." Mau was suddenly standing with them. "Make sure your women have sharpened the sacred knife until it can cleave a hair. Slice across the throat and sever the vein in the neck with the first stroke. It is of utmost importance for the animal to die without pain. Goddesses want gifts, not suffering. Oh, and catch all the blood in a basin or chalice. Do not let any of it touch the ground."

He caught Sirona's eye and gave her the peculiar smile that could fit on the face of a man or a cat. "I have seen it done many times," he said.

Bathilde stared at him. "What are you?"

"You do not know?" Mau's gaze was ironic and a bit amused. "You are strong, lady, but you do not have the powers of the wisewoman. I am a cat." He watched Bathilde's eyes widen. "And a very old one. In the land of my birth gods and goddesses expected gifts every day. I sat in the temples and watched."

Bathilde's eyes went even rounder. "Shape-changer," she whispered.

Mau nodded at Sirona. "With the proper assistance." He looked beyond both women to where the bullock and the singers had gathered. "Hold the knife well," he admonished Bathilde. "They are ready for you."

The elder priestesses had indeed turned to Bathilde, waiting for her. The tenor of their singing had changed. The voices had deepened, taken on a variety of new notes. They were chanting spells, incantations that would eventually lull her into a trance. But first, there was the sacrifice. The oldest woman was holding out the knife, balancing it reverently on both palms. She wore a smile that was eager and oddly gentle.

Bathilde gave Mau a wondering look and went toward the priestesses. As she walked her self-possession returned. "Bring me the basin," she said. "We must catch the blood."

The sacrifice was performed with ceremony: in the midst of chants and the playing of instruments. The bullock did not suffer. The mild look of surprise never left him, even as the life-blood gushed forth from his throat and his legs folded beneath him. Bathilde's arm was strong. Splashes of the animal's blood had stained her arms and face, though, in keeping with Mau's instruction, none of the precious fluid touched the ground. A large silver basin, positioned expertly by the older women, had caught every drop.

"She did well," Mau said approvingly. "Well indeed, for the first time."

Sirona did not answer. An odd sensation was stealing

over her. She realized with a start that the chants meant for
Bathilde were having an effect on her as well. She also
sensed that Mau knew this. From the corner of her eye she
saw him glance from her to Bathilde. His sharp-featured
face wore an expression both grim and thoughtful. He
seemed to be expecting something, Sirona thought.

Bathilde's eyes were closing. Arrayed in her furs, she
swayed back and forth in cadence with the singing. The villagers drew closer together. The ceremony of the bullock's
death had entranced them. Now they awaited the next part
of the ritual in utter silence. They stared as some of the
priestesses came forward to support Bathilde and guide her
to a stool. She was floating deeper and deeper into the
trance.

Time passed. The priestesses continued to sing. Clouds
swirled across the sky, and the sun heated the congealing
blood of the bullock, filling the air with its coppery scent.
The animal's corpse lay stiffly, waiting to be butchered and
cooked after Bathilde's part in the ritual was finished. The
eating of its flesh would be a sacred act, the priestesses had
said. A hungry child started to cry in anticipation of that
meal, and was promptly hushed. Dogs sniffed and whined
at the smell of blood and fresh meat, but kept their distance,
banished to the outskirts of the crowd.

Sirona herself was floating. In and out she drifted, rising
and falling with the voices of the singers. In one of those
moments she realized that she was leaning against Mau. No
one else had noticed. Bathilde was the center of attention
there. Through heavy-lidded eyes she saw the eldest priestess raise her arm. The singers fell silent. The people
strained forward, hanging on to what would happen next.
Only the whines of the dogs and the buzzing of flies attracted to the blood broke the stillness.

"She is ready," the priestess said. "The Goddess is with
her."

Bathilde sat upon the stool. Only the supporting hands of
her women kept her there. Her body was slumped, but her
head was disconcertingly erect. Her dark eyes were wide-
open, but blank, as though something possessed her. The

people stared, fascinated, fearful, and unable to take their gazes off her.

"You may ask questions of her now," the old priestess instructed the villagers. "She will answer."

"Who will answer," breathed a woman in the crowd, "the Lady Bathilde, or the Goddess?"

The priestess smiled. "That will depend on what you ask."

The silence held. At last a man summoned up his courage and spoke the practical question that most affected them all. "Will we have a good harvest?" he called in a voice that quavered slightly.

Bathilde's dark sightless eyes fixed on the speaker, and the man shrank back. He almost made the sign of the cross, but caught himself just in time. Bathilde smiled at him. "Do not fear me, O my people," she said. "I am Freyja. Do you not recognize me, I who am your Mother?" A profound change had taken place in her voice. It was deeper, more sonorous. Divinity rang in every word. As the people stared an unearthly glow surrounded the figure on the stool. In that moment, no one in the gathering doubted but that Freyja Herself was truly addressing them.

"Freyja." The name wafted like a sigh through the closely packed listeners. Tears ran down the wrinkled cheeks of the ancient woman who first uttered it. She wept silently as others took up the name. "Freyja. Freyja."

The glow around Bathilde shaped itself. The bedazzled eyes of the priestesses and villagers saw another form superimpose itself over the noblewoman's slumped body. It was a beautiful form, clothed in light and nudity and feathers white as new-fallen snow. The glorious face smiled. "Now You know Me, My children. I am pleased." The glowing eyes singled out the man who had asked the first question. "You wished to know about the harvest," she said to him.

Speechless with wonderment, the man managed a mute nod.

"Demons were poised to attack your fields and flocks," Bathilde said in that altered voice. "But that will not happen. My protection lies over your lands now. When rain comes again it will be only enough to help the tender plants grow and nourish them so that you in turn will be nourished by plentiful stores of grain. The sun will shine and the grass will grow green and your animals will thrive. These words I give you in truth. Know and believe them, for they are spoken by Her Who never forgot Her children, even though you forgot Her."

More sighs rustled through the crowd. People looked at each other in relief and exchanged smiles. But others looked shamefaced. They had forgotten Her, indeed, and there were many among the villagers who wondered if the terrible rain that had plagued them was the cost of that forgetting.

The old woman who had first whispered Freyja's name was driven to voice the question that was in the minds of so many. "Lady, was it You Who sent the rain, then? Out of Your anger at us?"

The glowing form threw its head back, and sad laughter bubbled from Bathilde's lips. "It was not I, My children. But other Shining Ones are more easily angered than I. To be forgotten does not please Them."

"We will not forget You again, O Freyja," another voice in the crowd promised. Others took up the pledge. A chorus of vows swept forward, beating at the ears of the priestesses gathered about Bathilde. They welcomed the acclaim with smiles of joy. As the people cried out, and the holy women beamed, the giant glowing figure superimposed over Bathilde grew larger and ever brighter.

But not everyone in the gathering took part in the shouts of fealty. After all, Christianity had been imposed on these people, and it had been imposed long enough so that for some of them it was no longer forced. These people who had become true Christians had been uneasy at Bathilde's arrival to begin with. That uneasiness had grown as they discovered how few in number they were compared to how lightly the new faith rested on the shoulders of their neighbors. They watched those neighbors reach out to a goddess they had learned to regard as pagan, watched them forsake the new for the old, and they trembled. The rain had stopped, and supposedly this Goddess had done it. Strange things were at work. They needed a priest, not priestesses and a noblewoman in a trance, to help them understand. But no priest was there, only magic.

One by one, they began to edge away from the gathering. Yet, despite the admonitions of their adopted faith, they could not quite bring themselves to leave. They lingered, held by an unwilling fascination, as the eldest priestess urged the people to ask more questions.

"Ask what you wish," she said. "The answers the Goddess gifts you with will not go unfulfilled."

After a brief hesitation the questions began.

"Will this plague of rain cease elsewhere as it has here, O Lady?" a burly man who held the important position of smith called out.

The divine voice was sweet and filled with promise. "If the people there welcome Me as you have, it will."

Additional inquiries followed. They were more personal, as the villagers, drawn into the ritual, lost their fear and grew bolder. Pregnant women asked if they would bear a healthy baby. Farmers asked about the planting of certain fields, and which of their animals should be bred and which slaughtered before winter. Craftsmen asked about the success of their business. Mothers asked about the health of their children, and grown children asked about the health of their parents.

To all of them Freyja, speaking through Bathilde, gave truthful answers. The truth of those answers was judged by the fact that some of them brought happiness and others brought pain. Freyja was a Goddess of life. But death was an inescapable part of life, and She ruled over that darker aspect as well. Agriculture, animals, and the health of the men and women who tended them, were Her province. Reawakened by Bast from Her long sleep, strengthened by the belief of the villagers, blessings flowed from Her lips, mingled with occasional pronouncements of sadness.

Throughout the ritual, Sirona had remained in her place beside Mau. Leaning against his lithe, sturdy frame, she had listened and swayed in the grip of her own trance. Images drifted across her mind. She saw fields ripening with grain: a wealth of barley, wheat, and rye, gleaming under the sun like a king's treasure. Glossy cattle and thick-fleeced sheep dotted pastures, grazing with calves and lambs at their sides. Rituals of ages past came to life once more. Freyja's processions were much larger then; dozens of carts traveled the muddy spring tracks, stretching out for many leagues. They were vivid with noise and color, and not just one village awaited their arrival, but many, the people thronging together in excitement as they waited for the first glimpse of the sacred carts.

Entranced, Sirona watched the tapestry unfold before her inner eyes. How beautiful those days had been. There had been an order to them, an ancient symmetry. Festivals had filled the lives of the people, a richness of change overseen by the myriad wonders of the old gods. It made her long for those days to be made real, not just pieces of dreams floating before her eyes, seen yet never able to be lived.

All at once the images began to darken. Slow at first, the darkness spread rapidly. It glistened black and red, like blood from a mortal wound, and it stained the brightness of the tapestry as inevitably as death. Sirona stiffened against Mau. She strained to see the images, but even the power of her inner eye could not pierce the swirling cloak of blood. A voice spoke to her, coiling out of the darkness.

Warn them.

The darkness lifted as abruptly as it had appeared. But now Sirona saw new images, and her heart froze with horror. Horsemen thundered down upon the ornamented carts and the priestesses around them. The faces of the riders were twisted with fury. They shouted incoherent battle yells, and their swords were raised in readiness to attack. The blades already seemed wet with blood.

Warn them. Freyja is too caught up in Her awakening to see the danger. It is up to you, My daughter.

Sirona's breath caught in her throat. She knew that deep ringing voice, and she knew something else as well. The horseman in the lead wore Haganon's face.

She jerked away from Mau. She heard someone speaking, and realized that it was her own voice. "Run." The word came out hoarsely, and she repeated it, still ragged, but louder. "Run!"

The priestesses nearest her and Mau turned their heads. A few of the villagers frowned. But most of them—priestesses, villagers, and Bathilde herself—were utterly caught up in the ritual and paid no heed, if they heard Sirona at all.

Sirona lunged forward. She grabbed the arm of the eldest priestess and spun her around. Outraged, the woman gaped at her and started to protest, but the wisewoman's words slashed her into silence. "Haganon and his men are riding upon us. Bathilde must be brought out of the trance and gotten away."

The woman's eyes widened. "How do you know—" She stopped herself. One look into Sirona's eyes left no doubt that the wisewoman was speaking the truth. Even so, she shook her head. "It is dangerous. The link with Freyja must be severed slowly and carefully, with the proper incantations—"

"Quickly," Sirona snapped. "There is not time. If they find Bathilde here, or any of you, for that matter, they will kill you."

Still, the priestess hesitated. "What about the villagers?"

By now, the attention of the other priestesses had been drawn. They still supported Bathilde on the stool, but they were listening to Sirona, and so were more of the people. The villagers were surfacing from fascination into apprehension. "What is she saying," several voices demanded. "Did she say our lord is coming?"

"The people will be safe," Sirona said to the elder priestess. She raised her voice so that the villagers could hear. "Haganon is not interested in you. He is not so great a fool as to slay those who work his lands for him. But we must take the Lady Bathilde and go. The ritual is finished. For now."

"Freyja will protect us," one of the village women who had helped select the white bullock for sacrifice insisted. "She is here. She has spoken to us."

"And She will continue to be with you." Sirona gentled her voice. "But we of Her procession must leave. It is not wise to remain."

The woman was eyeing her. "Freyja has shown you a vision?"

Sirona saw no point in trying to explain about Bast. "I have been given a vision, yes," she said.

Satisfied, the woman nodded. "Make haste, then," she ordered to the group at large. "We have to move the beast and clean up the blood."

A bustle of activity started. It was jarring, to be hurriedly cutting up the bullock and carrying it away, rather than lighting sacrificial fires to cook the meat as a gift to the Goddess. The sacred trance of Freyja's chief priestess was not supposed to end in such a fashion. The superimposed figure of Freyja wavered in surprise. Bathilde herself was so dazed she could not be brought entirely back to herself. She had to be lifted from the stool and into the cart, all the while staring about her in confusion.

"What is happening?" she asked over and over. Her glassy eyes fixed on Sirona as the latter helped maneuver her into the cart. "The Goddess . . . is She in danger?"

"Not the Goddess, but you, lady," Sirona told her. "And the rest of us, too. Haganon has learned of the ritual and is coming to attack you." She did not really think that Bathilde would grasp what she had said, for the connection had not been properly severed. But the noblewoman's dark gaze cleared momentarily, as if Freyja were speaking to her. "Yes, yes, we must go then." And she lapsed back into her communion with the Goddess.

Sirona darted over to Mau. The villagers had worked magic of their own. The evidence of the sacrifice had been removed in an astoundingly short time. "We're ready to leave," she announced. "Come on."

Mau had not moved. "For some of us it is too late for running," he said with an odd sort of calm. "I will stay here."

Sirona glared at him in frustration. "Are you mad?" she snapped, wanting to shake him. "Bast Herself warned me."

"And rightly so. You must leave, so that Haganon does not see you. But I am another matter."

"Speak plainly! You're a man now, not a cat."

"That," Mau said patiently, "is what I thought I was doing. And while we are on the subject of my being a man, have you forgotten why you changed me? That uncivilized oaf of a noble will not recognize me in this form. I will see that the people here remain safe, while you see to the safety of the others." He smiled. "It is really quite simple."

Not quite, Sirona realized grimly. The sound of hoofbeats drummed in her ears. The noise resounded strangely, leaving her uncertain as to whether she was hearing it through her ears or by some other means. She saw by his face that Mau heard it as well.

"They approach already," she said despairingly. "We won't be able to get far enough away. They will ride us down like hounds on a hare."

"No they will not." Mau's dry voice was calm. "You will not let them. Now go. You'll know what to do when the time comes. As for these others, leave the rest to me."

Sirona left him. She had no choice. The rhythm of galloping horses was inexorable. She ran toward the procession, only to find that moving this unwieldy mass of people along was like trying to herd a flock of geese. Indeed, she felt like a farm woman, chasing after this one and that, flapping her arms, futilely seeking to keep everyone together and moving. The priestesses, aware of the threat, did their best to help, but there were so many followers, and not all of them saw the necessity to leave. Younger men dragged their feet, and a number of women. Their blood was up. The three who had set fire to Ambrose's church were there; others had torched Christian fields and homes before joining Bathilde. The Goddess Freyja was with them, these restless folk muttered. The Shining Ones were rising again. Why should they run?

Power surged in the air. Long and long had it been suppressed and it would be held back no longer, even by a lord as fierce as Haganon. Sirona stared about her. She saw the angry faces of the men, the set faces of the women. She looked at Bathilde, dazed in her cart, and at the priestesses determined to guard her, though it be at the cost of their lives. The drum of racing horses was deafening.

She wheeled around. The land was flat and marshy, made even more so by the recent constant rain. The riders came over a low rise and descended into the flats. The pace of the horses slowed, their hooves showering the men atop them with clods of mud. The rain swept along with them, drenching man and animal alike.

But above their heads Sirona saw figures. Bast swirled there, and with Her, Sekhmet. Their eyes blazed at her, shining and fierce. Sekhmet, clothed in fire like the sun She summoned, raised a hand, and the rain stopped. The horsemen slowed, looking up in astonishment. Haganon, in the lead, urged them on; Sirona saw his soundless yelling. His features were contorted with rage. Bast looked directly at her. Her green eyes were enormous; they filled the world, and they lanced into Sirona's soul like javelins. The message they spoke was clear.

Sirona closed her own eyes, then opened them. "Hide us," she cried, and did not realize that the words she spoke were in a tongue far different than her own.

Bast stretched out Her arms. Light flowed from Her fingers, darting and sparkling like a river of stars. Shatteringly bright, it poured through the sky, straight toward the procession, flinging itself to the ground between Bathilde's cart and the crowd of villagers. Thousands of glittering shards coalesced, forming themselves into a wall that grew up and then out, elongating itself so that each group was shielded from the other. It sprang from nowhere, a marvel to Sirona's eyes, but only her eyes. She quickly realized that the others, including Bathilde still sunk into her trance, did not see it.

She alone watched, staring through the shining barrier that to her was transparent as precious glass, as Haganon and his men clattered up to the gathered villagers. Behind her the carts lumbered on their way as fast as the oxen could move. The followers went after them, even the combative young men, who had finally been persuaded to leave. No one looked back. Not even the priestesses, preoccupied with getting Bathilde to safety, noticed that Sirona was lingering behind.

The villagers stood in silence, watching as their lord drew rein. Haganon glared about him. "Well?" he grated without preamble. "What is on all of you? Why are you clumped together like ants on a honey cake when there is work to be done? You should be out tending my lands."

No one answered. The people looked at him stolidly. Their silence lay heavy on the air, filled with the respect they always showed to their lord. And yet, there was something different about them this day. Haganon sensed it. The faces of the adults were placid as ever, the children subdued, but things still were not as they should be. They looked at him and did not look at him. There was another presence here, and it was interfering with his authority. Haganon knew what that presence was.

"The witches have come here." He delivered the words like sword strokes. "Bathilde has trespassed on my lands spouting blasphemy. Did you think I would not discover it?" He punched a fist up at the sky. "Where the witches go, the weather clears. They have been here. You hide that from me at your peril."

Blank eyes looked up at him. They were as mute and stupid as sheep, Haganon thought contemptuously. More stupid, for sheep at least had the wits to bleat when they were in danger. "One of you had better answer me," he said, and his voice was low with threat.

Haganon's gaze was suddenly drawn to one of the men. He was standing off to the side, and the way he looked at the count was different from the others. There was no blankness in the man's expression, none of the docility Haganon expected when dealing with peasants. What was more, though he was dressed as a commoner, he did not look familiar. Haganon did not know the names of all the folk who worked his holdings, but he knew their faces. This man's face was not one he had seen before.

The count kneed his stallion forward, using the animal's body to shove the villagers aside. People jumped hastily out of the way, but the man Haganon had singled out did not move. He stood calmly as the noble halted before him. His eyes were a strange color, Haganon noticed. The observation added to his animosity.

"You," he said brusquely. "Where on my holdings do you belong?"

The man smiled. "What makes you think I belong anywhere in what you call your holdings?"

Haganon stared in disbelief. "What insolence is this?" he roared, and raised his riding whip to slash the man across the face.

The whip struck empty air. Somehow, in a move Haganon had not seen, the man had managed to avoid it. Now he was standing behind the count's stallion. "You should leave," he said mildly. "It would be very wise if you did."

Haganon's roar this time contained no words. He yanked the stallion's tender mouth, almost pulling the beast back on his haunches as he swung him around. He drew his sword with a ring of metal and let it sing through the air as he sliced at the stranger's head.

"But then, wisdom is not one of your virtues," the man said from another direction. "And I doubt that you will live long enough to develop it."

Haganon's face had turned the color of a ripe beet. Before his men-at-arms, and these humble farmers who must ever show him respect this stranger was humiliating him. It could not be tolerated. For days one bad thing after another had been happening to him, striking at his pride, embarrassing him before his inferiors. And it had all begun with the wisewoman, the *stria*.

To Haganon her death was no longer necessary for practical reasons alone. Somewhere on the long wet ride back from the witch's house, he had come to realize that she had cursed him. There could be no other explanation, and the only way to remove such a curse was by killing her. Yet she continued to elude him. The mockery of this stranger brought all the frustration and anger simmering within him to a head.

"Kill them," he bellowed at his men.

The villagers drew together. Dumbstruck, they stared at Haganon, not quite believing what they had heard. The men-at-arms were equally dumbfounded. They were warriors, highly trained in the art of killing. They had sworn oaths to Haganon that they would use those skills at his command. But not only were these people unarmed, they belonged to the very lord whose interests they were pledged to protect.

"My lord," one of them said. "Are you certain?"

Haganon nearly struck the unfortunate questioner down. "They seek to deceive me, and I'll be damned if I allow deceitful peasants to live on my lands. Now teach them a lesson, or by God, I'll teach you one! And we'll start"—he jerked his sword at the odd-eyed stranger—"with him!"

The stranger laughed.

In that moment Haganon's anger boiled over. Bellowing, he sent his horse charging forward. The villagers scattered in a dozen different directions. Mothers snatched up children, husbands leaped to shelter their families, and old ones unable to run stood bravely, waiting for death. Dogs began barking furiously, but the people themselves still kept their eerie silence, as if they were too stunned to grasp that their own lord meant to attack them.

Haganon slashed at the man, a blow aimed at cleaving his skull. His target slipped away from the charging horse, as maddeningly elusive as was the wisewoman. The sword whistled and sang. Haganon whirled it through the air and brought the blade down. This time it connected with more than empty air. The old woman with the goiter, who had foresworn Christianity, defiantly spoken in favor of Bathilde and led the other women in selecting the sacrifice, was in the way. Haganon did not quite know whether it was intentional; it happened, that was all. His sword split the old woman's skull, slicing it down to her shoulders.

There was a wet thunk, a spray of crimson, and the halves of the head neatly separated and fell. The body itself stood for an instant still pumping blood, then it, too, toppled over. The woman had made no sound, but those around her did. Screams broke out, and people ran now in earnest.

Half-heartedly the men-at-arms started to pursue them.

The stranger had gone very still. He looked at the woman's corpse and up at Haganon. His orange eyes caught fire, blazing so brightly that Haganon, even in his rage, had to glance away.

"Well?" The man turned away from Haganon, and there was a world of contempt in that single lithe gesture. He glared up at the sky. "Well," he said again, "what are you waiting for? More of them to die?"

Thunder rolled through the cloudless sky.

21

SIRONA HAD WATCHED THE WOMAN'S death through the glittering wall. Disbelief washed through her, then horror. This was not what she had dreaded. It was the safety of Bathilde and the procession she had feared for. With her own lips she had told the villagers that they would be safe, that Haganon would not harm his own peasants. How could she have been such a fool? She was stained with the old woman's blood as irrevocably as if she had wielded the sword along with Haganon. And more blood would add to that stain if she did not act at once.

She whirled around. "Come back!" Her voice was a hoarse shriek, so distorted she scarcely recognized it "Look upon what they are doing! Come back!"

Gone was the need that had urged her to get the procession to safety. Blind rage governed her. The sight of that good old woman's mangled body was like a vision sent by demons. And she would only be the first. Was this the price these villagers were to pay for welcoming the old ways back? In that moment she hated Haganon as she had never known she could hate another human being.

"Come back!" she screeched again. "He is killing them!"

The priestesses leading the carts stopped at once. The procession's disorderly retreat halted, growing even more confused as people spun around and hurried toward Sirona. The elder priestess led the way. Her eyes in their nests of wrinkles were huge.

"Killing, Wisewoman?" The priestess stared past her, and Sirona saw at once that she could not penetrate the

276

magic of the wall. "I see nothing," the woman exclaimed. "The villagers have gone."

Sirona cursed. She had not stopped to think that only she might be able to see through the wall. How could the people with the procession help prevent what they could not see? Worse, what if the wall—thrown up as protection—did not let them through?

The answer burst in her mind like a flame.

"Bathilde." She grabbed the priestess by both arms. "We must wake her."

"We cannot. She is still—"

Sirona pushed past the woman and her protests. In three strides she reached the cart and leaped up to where Bathilde lay on the cushions. She bent down, piercing the noblewoman's blank gaze with her own. Behind the spell wall the screams of the villagers shredded her ears.

"Freyja." The cry was an incantation and a summons. "Awake and let Your priestess Bathilde awake with You. Your children are in danger!"

The dark eyes stared up at her, and Sirona repeated her cry. "Freyja!"

The blankness began to clear. Bathilde stretched out a hand; the fingers trembled wildly, like birds trying to fly. Sirona seized it in her own. At the touch of their hands a shower of sparks flashed behind the wisewoman's eyes. Bathilde gasped, in the grip of a pain that was sudden and exquisite and terrible. So this was what real power felt like. It hurt.

But Bathilde's eyes were focusing on her. And above them the enormous shape was forming once again. *Who seeks to harm My children?* Freyja's voice was no longer warm. Threat rippled through the sonorous tones. The glow that surrounded Her was darker: shot through with sparks like the ones flashing behind Sirona's eyes. The voice grew louder. *Show them to Me.*

"Through the wall," Sirona managed to gasp. "Lower it, and You will see."

"What wall?" the elder priestess demanded. She and the

others were clustered about the cart. The rest of the people were jabbering so loudly the old woman had to shout to make herself heard.

Bathilde sat up. "Wall?" She stiffened, staring straight at the glimmering barrier. "Ah," she said. "I see it."

Of course you do. Freyja's voice was deafening. *You are My priestess. But look well, for now you will see it gone!*

An unearthly yowl split the day. Instantly, it was followed by a second equally chilling howl. Sirona saw a golden chariot come wheeling across the sky. It filled the upper reaches. Two gigantic cats drew it, both of them white as snow under a full moon. Bathilde saw it, too. She gasped and cried out in wonder. The noise of the people grew. They, as well as the priestesses, could not see as clearly as Sirona and Bathilde, but they all sensed Freyja's presence.

As light and airy as the snow their coats resembled, the cats flew toward Freyja, and in a motion that mortal eyes— not even those of Sirona and Bathilde—could follow, the Goddess flowed into the chariot. Straight as arrows, as unerring and precise as flesh-and-blood cats pouncing on prey, the sky cats leaped at the barrier. It shattered in an explosion that only the wisewoman and the noblewoman could hear. The chariot followed in their wake, and Freyja's voice clashed like a battle trumpet.

Sisters, I have come!

The people of Her procession could not hear the dissolution of the wall, but they saw what it revealed. And what they saw sent the men roaring forward in fury.

The headless old woman lay in a heap of blood and gore. Several more villagers had fallen near her. The rest were running for their lives. To Sirona it felt as if an eternity had passed, giving Haganon far too much time to wreak havoc. But apparently only a handful of moments had passed, enough time to do more murder but not enough time to implement the massacre that Haganon intended.

People were fleeing and shrieking and stumbling. Horses were lunging after them. Bathilde's men and a number of the women charged into the uproar. There were some men-

at-arms among them, but the majority of them were commoners, armed only with staves and cudgels. In their fury it
did not matter. They ran forward, to what looked like their
own deaths against the better-armed force of the count.

But they were not alone.

Voices thrummed in the air. They resonated like wind
tearing through clouds. Yet there were no clouds. Then
Sirona saw Them. Bast and Sekhmet, with Freyja riding to
join Them in Her golden chariot. All three Goddesses were
clothed in fire. Their eyes burned implacable as death. The
white cats yowled in anticipation.

Sekhmet's gaze glittered down at the mortals dodging
and leaping and crying in the flat, marshy field. Crimson
swirled about Her, staining the fangs in Her lioness mouth
like blood. She was smiling, and Her eyes were hungry as
death.

But Bast looked at Sirona. Flames leaped in Her green
eyes. She was beautiful and terrible at once. She raised a
mighty arm and pointed. Her voice pounded through
Sirona's being like a great drum.

Look.

Sirona followed the direction of the Goddess's hand. She
saw what Bast wished her to see.

Haganon.

When Freyja's cats smashed through the glittering wall
they had also smashed through a barrier in her. In the tumbled wreckage of that inner wall, something new bloomed.
It burned through her veins, hot as freshly spilled blood,
and left a hungering for more. She wanted death.

Haganon had seen her as well. He wheeled his stallion.
Froth splattered from the animal's mouth as he reared. Sitting atop his horse, Haganon displayed his teeth in a savage
grin. "At last," he yelled. "Now I will end this, once and forever! I will rip your head from your body, witch, and see
your curse die with you!"

He sent the horse lunging forward. His sword whistled in
eagerness for her blood to be added to the wetness that already stained its gleaming blade.

"I call on you," Sirona cried. The words burst from her,

and though she did not know who or what she was calling to, she had not the least doubt that she would be answered.

The thunder rolled forward again. But it was no longer just in the sky. It came from everywhere, the ground, the cerulean sky, and from far below the earth. Sirona caught a horrific image: a vast serpent in a cavern black as a burial chamber. It was lifting its head and shaking its massive coils. She glimpsed its eyes, infinitely worse than the flat black eyes of any normal snake. Coldness filled them, as far-reaching and merciless as an endless night. Awareness glittered in those eyes, and a knowledge older than time. The Serpent looked at Haganon. Its gigantic head darted forward.

The ground writhed beneath the hooves of Haganon's stallion. The horse let out a screech that sounded human and executed an astonishing leap backwards. Haganon slipped to one side, fought desperately to regain his balance, and would have succeeded had the earth not followed him and shook again. The stallion made a wild sideways leap and bolted, sending his rider flying unceremoniously through the air.

Other horses were bucking and rearing, throwing their riders as Haganon's had. As the men were flung to the ground they leaped to their feet—or tried to. The earth itself was attacking them. They got up, only to fall again as the Serpent shook its coils. Sirona saw an enormous black tongue flickering in and out, as though the creature was laughing.

The men of the procession had halted, watching open-mouthed. The ground was bucking and rearing as wildly as the horses, but only under the feet of the village's attackers. Where Bathilde's people and the villagers stood, it lay serene and still as it always had.

"Freyja is protecting us!" a man cried. He belonged to the small number of men-at-arms who had renounced Christianity to accompany Bathilde. His sword was already unsheathed. Running from the calm earth to the fierce earth, he reeled unsteadily, but still managed to decapitate one of Haganon's men.

His deed galvanized the others into action. Echoing his cry to Freyja, they ran forward. The ground was their ally. It seemed to actually rise to fling them at their targets, while at the same time it tripped the men-at-arms and sent them sprawling. Bathilde's men and women leaped on them with howls of anger, beating them savagely. The villagers had stopped in their flight. They beheld these people—peasants like themselves—defending them, and angry courage replaced their fear. Shouting Freyja's name, they joined in the attack.

Unhorsed, their weapons tumbled from their hands, Haganon's men-at-arms found the situation abruptly reversed. They were terrified. They had been against this deed of slaughter from the start. Now the very earth had turned against them, and they were fighting for their lives against a furious mob of peasants who normally would not even dare to meet their eyes. This was magic, magic that was clearly not in their favor. And the pagan goddess whose name the people were shouting had brought it on. They struggled to gain their feet and run from this accursed place.

The count himself had clambered up from his fall. His wide eyes were glued to Sirona. Terror and rage warred together in their depths. Never taking his eyes from her, he bent down, snatched up his sword, and ran toward her. The earth tripped him. He got up. Thunder rolled around him, so loud he was forced to drop his sword and clamp his hands to his ears.

Sirona pointed at him, unconsciously using the same gesture Bast had. Her voice pealed out, even louder than the thunder. "Haganon," she screamed. "I name you murderer! Slayer of helpless women! You are a man without honor!"

The words tore through the air. Haganon bared his teeth. "Witch," he bellowed. *"Stria!* You are misbegotten and a spawn of evil. God has cursed you, and I will send you to hell with my own hands!" He reached to recapture his sword.

Sirona laughed. It was a cruel sound. "I am cursed? It is you who are cursed, O Haganon. Your god is not here, but mine is. Look upon Her power!"

She pointed to the sword in Haganon's hands. He had raised it over his head and started a new charge at her. Thunder roared again. This time it was accompanied by a blast of wind. It howled out of the sky. To the ears of those present it sounded eerily like the yowling of an enormous cat.

'Freyja's cats," people whispered.

But Sirona smiled. She knew Who was howling, and it was not Freyja's cats. An instant later they all discovered what she already knew.

A giant figure was forming in the sky. The wind blew the lines and curves of it together so that it towered directly over Haganon. As its shadow fell over him, he looked up. And froze in his tracks. A demon was hovering over him. Its body was that of a woman, garbed in a clinging garment that revealed hips and breasts and thighs. But instead of a woman's face, the long slim neck ended in the head of a cat. An enormous cat with blazing green eyes and a savagely snarling mouth.

The creature fixed its lurid gaze on Haganon. Its fangs shone in a white and terrible smile. Raising an arm, it pointed at the sword in the nobleman's hands. Haganon let out a shriek of pain and fell. The weapon went whirling out of his hands. It struck the ground blade first, thrown there with such terrific force that it was buried up to its jeweled hilt.

It was the final straw. Screaming in terror the surviving men-at-arms fled. The earth helped them along, lifting and rippling and hurling them faster then their legs could carry them. Stumbling and falling and shrieking, they kept running. Weaponless, not daring to look above him at the demon in the sky or behind him at the *stria* who had called it forth, Haganon leaped to his feet and ran after them.

As the sounds of their flight faded into the distance, the earth and sky fell silent. The calm day that had smiled over Freyja's ritual returned. The change was so abrupt that the people standing there wondered if it had all been a dream. They looked up at the sky and found the glorious apparition gone. They looked down and counted the dead. Haganon and his men had left a number of dead in their wake, but they had left the dead of the villagers behind as well. Not as many as there could have been, but too many nevertheless.

Slowly, moving with tentative steps, people began to gather around Sirona. By unspoken consent they kept a certain distance, staring at her with faces that mingled awe, respect, and more than a little fear. The elder priestess pushed through the circle of staring faces.

"Wisewoman!" There was no fear on her lined features, only delight. "Who was she? How did you call her?"

Sirona hesitated, considering her answer. Then it came to her: so clear and perfect in its truth that She knew the Goddesses had given it to her. She smiled. "That was Freyja's Sister. She is a Goddess from a far land, come to help us restore the old ways."

The priestess embraced her. "You saved us all," she declared. "You are truly as Lady Bathilde said, a woman of power. You called upon the forces of earth and air to protect us, and they did so. Give the wisewoman your thanks," she cried to the assembled people. "We owe her our lives!"

"No, no," Sirona insisted. "It was not I—"

But no one was listening. They were too busy cheering and crowding in to try and touch her. Gone was the distance they had kept; the old priestess had in effect laid a blessing upon her, and all of them wanted to express their gratitude, and perhaps gain a bit of that blessing for themselves. Through the jostling bodies Sirona caught sight of Mau. He was watching her, and the expression on his face was unreadable.

At length the other priestesses cleared a path for Bathilde. She strode through them, and at sight of her the people fell silent. The noblewoman had fully recovered from her trance. Her dark eyes were clear and piercing. "Thank you," she said simply into the silence, and added with a meaning to her voice that only Sirona understood, "I knew you would not fail us."

People raised their voices again. Sirona bore the acclaim for a few moments, and then tried to make her own voice heard. Finally, she succeeded in getting them to listen. Her eyes blazed at them, shifting between the dark and light, turning at last to a steady burning darkness. "This is not meet," she said, looking from one face to another. "To celebrate in the midst of the slain. We must see to the dead." She indicated the bodies with a sweep of her arm. "They lie there, murdered by the orders of Haganon."

Bathilde responded at once. "The wisewoman speaks wisdom once more. We will see to their burial." Her voice became a shout. "And to avenging the sacrilege and death Haganon and his Christians brought here this day!"

People raised a fierce shout.

Sirona said nothing. She looked at the dead villagers, tumbled in the sad, awkward positions of violent death, and rage burned in her heart. She sensed Bathilde come up beside her but did not turn to look at her. The noblewoman gripped her arm.

"So," she hissed, "is this blood finally enough? Will you join your power to mine, once and for all?"

Sirona's gaze remained fixed on the bodies lying in pools of slowly congealing blood. Flies were already lighting to feed on this unexpected feast. The smell of spilled entrails was foul on the air. Slowly she raised her eyes. Bathilde had been about to speak, but at the look in those dark-light eyes she thought better of it.

"Yes," Sirona said, and her voice was as terrible as her eyes. "It is enough. We will work magic together, you and I. And the Goddesses will help us."

Why did You not slay him? Sekhmet's tone was irritated. *You should have. He was about to kill Your priestess.*

Bast smiled and did not answer.

Sekhmet's yellow eyes grew brighter. *Sister,* She said dangerously, *are you becoming soft again?*

Bast laughed. *You still do not see far, do You? She used her own strength to stop him. He fled from her, believing that she called up the shaking and the thunder. She is stronger now, and is that not what We want?*

He will tell others of what happened here, Sekhmet

growled. *We should have killed them all.* She licked her whiskers. *The blood was not enough.*

Bast laughed again. *Let them go. They will indeed warn others, and what of it? You are still thirsty, are You not?*

Haganon and his men were running, though no longer on foot. They had come upon most of their horses, for the animals had stopped and begun to graze as soon as they had left the fright of the shaking earth behind them. Being mounted gave the men back some of their confidence, but not even Haganon suggested that they return to confront the pagans who had driven them into such ignominious retreat.

In the midst of their flight Aelisachar met them. He had exhausted his horse in riding back to his own lands, but had taken only enough time to take a fresh mount and assemble his men-at-arms. Even so, he had been too late. That fact was immediately apparent as he caught sight of the bedraggled force riding toward him.

"In the name of God, man," he expostulated, pulling in his horse before Haganon. "What happened?"

The battered men-at-arms crossed themselves. Haganon let out a string of oaths, and when he had finished, he finally answered. "It was the *stria*," he snarled. His face was pasty white. Aelisachar had never seen his fellow nobleman shaken, much less afraid, and he was shocked to see both on Haganon's burly features.

"You look as if you have seen ghosts," he said. "What did she do?"

"She shook the earth," one of the men-at-arms cried. "She called up thunder and a great wind that blew the sword from my lord's hands. And—" he shuddered, unable to continue.

Haganon finished for him. "She summoned a demon. An enormous hideous creature with the head of a beast and the body of a woman."

Aelisachar's eyes widened. "Truly?" he whispered, and blessed himself. With an effort he got control of himself. "I should not be surprised. Not after what we saw when we tried to burn her. You are fortunate," he added soberly, "to be alive."

The men-at-arms voiced their fervent agreement.

Aelisachar looked at Haganon. "Should we ride on to your manor?"

Haganon cursed again. He looked at the faces of his men, saw the terror there, and knew what he must say. "No, we dare not. The evil she called up will surely attack us there as well. We cannot stand to fight when the earth shakes beneath our feet."

Aelisachar was appalled. "Your family is there," he protested. "You cannot desert them. Your honor—"

"My honor is not the issue!" Haganon's look was so savage that the older man stared at him in amazement. "Have you heard no word of what we have told you? This is magic, of the darkest kind. Swords and spears are as nothing against it."

Aelisachar looked grave. He blessed himself. "Then what shall we do?"

Haganon glared behind him, as if he were seeing once again what had happened. "We must slip away and get to Aachen and Carolus. We need a great force of priests, as well as fighting men. It is our only chance to stop a full-scale revolt of these pagans and their magic. If that happens, we will lose everything." He looked at the older noble. "Your lands are in as much danger as mine, and so are the holdings of every Christian noble who has sworn fealty to Carolus. Only he can save us now."

Haganon was soon to discover how prophetic his words were.

That night the fires lit up the sky as the great manor burned. All of Haganon's family and almost all of his house folk had fled. They had no choice. They were Christian and refused to turn away from the religion they had adopted. They were fortunate to escape with their lives, and they knew it.

Sirona watched the flames with cold satisfaction. She sensed rather than saw Mau glide up beside her. "You are quiet as a cat, even as a man," she said to him.

He ignored that. "The sight of this pleases you?" He jerked his head at the burning manor and outbuildings.

"Why should it not? He deserves no less."

"But he is not there."

Sirona shrugged. "He is a man who values his possessions. It's why he went after Bathilde, for her lands. He will feel the loss of his proud manor far more than the deaths of the men-at-arms who died fighting for him today."

Mau began to pace. His strides were restless. He stalked as gracefully and angrily as a cat with four legs instead of two. "That may be," he snapped. "But you have missed the point. You missed it entirely. I expected more of you, certainly more than I would expect of these other witless fools."

"Fools?" Sirona gave him an incredulous glare. "You think it foolish to restore the Ancient Harmonies, to call back the Shining Ones, your own Mistress among them? That is what you wanted! You were the one who first took me to Bast! I was content to be a healer, to have no doings with the heritage of which you told me. I wanted nothing of power and magic. But Bathilde would not be content with that, and neither would you."

Mau stopped pacing. "You still do not understand." He sighed. "Well, why should you, when My own Lady is as caught up in this as the Others." He looked at Sirona, and his eyes were deep and sad and beautiful. "They are following Sekhmet's way, the way of blood. But I am a creature of life. Bast Herself made me so, though now She has given free rein to the part of Her that links Her to Her Sister. I, though, have no other side. I am as I have always been, and, therefore, I see clearly, more clearly than any of Them." His gaze grew sharp. "Including you, human one."

Sirona regarded him steadily. "And what do you see?"

"I see"—the eyes of the man who was a cat grew deeper—"that power can heal and power can destroy. You must learn to know the difference."

Sirona looked back at the manor. Timbers were collapsing with tortured roars, sending flames shooting up at a dark sky lit with stars. Smoke stung the air. The moon in her full fecundity floated over the scene. She was as orange and glowing as Mau's eyes.

Voices drifted through the smoke, calling for the wise-woman.

"And you must learn before it is too late," Mau added.

Sirona turned to meet his gaze. Her face was troubled. The voices calling for her grew louder. She shook herself angrily, turned away and went toward them.

22

TWO DAYS LATER SIRONA AND
Bathilde and their procession, which
had swelled to the size of a small
army, marched upon the monastery.

By this time so many people had
taken refuge there that they resembled a small army themselves. However, despite the abbot's ungenerous
spirit, the monastery was capable of accommodating them.
For this was a showplace, built by Carolus to advertise his
power as well as that of his religion. Buildings extended
over three hectares. There were sheepfolds and quarters for
the shepherds; stables for horses, cows, goats, and bulls,
with houses for the goatherds, cowherds and drovers, farm
hands, and servants. The opulent church, along with the
cloister and luxurious abbot's house, formed the
monastery's heart. Nearby stood the kitchen, cellar, bakery,
and brewery. There were baths, a large infirmary bordered
by neatly tended gardens of medicinal plants, a school,
quarters for the novice monks, and more kitchens, bakeries,
and breweries. As in any great manor house, there were
dwellings for the domestic servants and artisans, kilns for
drying fruits and grain, a mill, and granary and the thresh-
ing floor.

Bathilde's procession went past the cemetery that lay just
outside the stone walls that enclosed this bustling complex
within. Fruit orchards stood there, and vegetable gardens.
There was a large close for geese and poultry, but it and the
dwellings nearby were empty, the occupants having either
fled or taken shelter inside the walls.

As with every other place the procession had gone, the
weather had cleared at its coming. By now the people were

almost becoming used to the miracle, but to the Christians peeping out, the smiling sun was an omen of ill portent, one that had appeared through forces alien to the new religion.

Row upon row of faces stared down at the sprawling convoy from the monastery walls. Curses rang out from some, along with imprecations from others. But most of the Christians were oddly silent.

"They are afraid," Bathilde observed to Sirona with satisfaction. "And well they should be."

As if to contradict her words, the lean figure of Abbot Wala suddenly appeared. If he was afraid, there was no sign of it in either voice or manner. The monks along the walls had seen the procession approaching along the flat plains for some time, and he had had time to prepare. Tall and lean, dressed in his richest robe, a silver crucifix on a heavy gold chain belted about his waist, he was the picture of religious fervor and indignation.

"Blasphemers!" he roared. "I pray that you have traveled here to ask forgiveness for your sins." His gaze singled out Bathilde where she sat in her place of honor atop the cushions, brilliant in her robes and furs and crown. "And you most of all, lady. You lead these people, and you have taken them down the paths of waywardness. The burden is yours to bear for their evil acts, and especially for their falling away from the Church."

Bathilde laughed. It was jarring for the monastery's faithful to hear mocking laughter in response to the abbot's fierce words. The monks blessed themselves; the people who had taken refuge there muttered. But Bathilde only laughed harder. "The one burden I bear," she finally replied, "is that I did not bring my people back to the true faith earlier."

The abbot drew himself up even taller. "You will throw yourself at these holy walls in vain." As he spoke he profoundly thanked Carolus for those walls. Walls were a new thing for monasteries and not yet common, but the king had insisted on them. Wala was grateful for his foresight. "God will protect us," he proclaimed.

"Will he?" Bathilde's gaze was ironic. "Has he protected the other churches we have burned?"

"Save your soul, lady." Abbot Wala put all the sternness at his command into his voice. "Send these people home. Renounce the evil you have embraced or"—He fell silent, for Sirona had suddenly stepped out to where he could clearly see her. "The witch," he breathed, and despite all the scornful words he had said to Haganon about her powers, he discovered that his hand was making the sign of the cross of its own volition.

Bathilde saw him blanch as he caught sight of Sirona, and to those gathered on the monastery walls her smile was a frightful thing. "My people are home," the noblewoman said to the abbot. "It is you who must leave, if you desire to go on living. Return to Gaul. Tell your king that Saxony has thrown his Christians out like a dog vomiting up rotten meat. We do not want you here. We never did."

Her followers set up a cheer at their lady's words. An ominous rattling went up, as they shook the unlit torches they carried. Abbot Wala narrowed his dark eyes. "I see naught here but a rabble," he said coldly. "And you, an insignificant woman dressed in outlandish pagan garb, as their leader. Even with that witch by your side you will not prevail against stone walls and armed men."

"Truly?" Sirona spoke for the first time. Her voice was piercing. "Then why are you afraid?"

And it was true. Abbot Wala was afraid, no matter how well he hid that fact from others. They both knew it. He had not forgotten how she had escaped the death he and Haganon had planned for her. Inwardly he cursed Haganon for riding away and encouraging his cohorts to do the same. There was a small force of armed men within the monastery, but if this pagan mob was truly bent on destruction, they might well be able to accomplish it, particularly if the witch aided them.

He sought to cover his apprehension behind the shield of religion. "Begone!" He lifted the glittering crucifix at his waist. "God will strike you down lest you depart this place dedicated in His holy name!"

It was an impressive speech, but neither Sirona nor Bathilde were swayed. Sirona stepped forward. Her dark-light eyes swept past the abbot, dismissing him as effectively as a slap. She addressed the people staring fearfully down from the walls, and her arresting voice and eyes were gentle.

"Many of you know me," she said. "And, therefore, you know that I bear you no ill will."

Behind her Bathilde frowned. "Wisewoman," she said sharply.

Bathilde wanted all Christians to leave Saxony, declaring that the Shining Ones would not be satisfied with less. Sirona tended to agree, but gazing at the faces of these people she knew she could not condone their deaths. She had tended to many of them—lancing boils, easing fevers, setting limbs and caring for all the other illnesses that beset mortal folk. The healer arose in her, and deliberately she disregarded the noblewoman's disapproval, just as she had Abbot Wala.

"Take your families and leave this place," she went on. "You will not be harmed. Our quarrel is not with innocent folk who have the misfortune to be caught between warring gods. Stand aside from what is to happen, and you will be safe."

"Where will we go?" someone called out.

"Be silent!" Abbot Wala was enraged. He was losing control of his own flock, and worse, it was at the doing of this witch. "No one is going anywhere!" he shouted. "I forbid it!"

Bathilde stood up amongst her cushions. "Then prepare to see your Christian Heaven," she called. "For this blight upon our land that you call a monastery is to burn. The Shining Ones have decreed it!"

She waved the torch holders forward. They obeyed eagerly, striking flints to ignite their torches and then quickly setting alight the torches of others. The people of the monastery watched in horror. Children began to cry. All along the walls men and women began to snatch up their youngsters, leap from their places, and rush off to gather their belongings.

Abbot Wala tightened his lips. Beckoning at his armed men, he ordered them to loose a flight of arrows at the pagans below. "And send the first arrows," he commanded, pointing at Sirona, "straight through her breast."

The men exchanged glances. "My lord Abbot," one ventured, "she be a woman, and unarmed."

"Do it!" the abbot shot back.

Reluctantly they obeyed. Pulling arrows from their quivers, they set them to their bows and sighted at the target their superior had ordered.

Sirona raised her arms and turned her gaze up to the clear sky.

At that moment, the pagan men-at-arms leaped forward raising their shields high over their heads to deflect the deadly rain of missiles. The torchbearers and the people of the procession shrank back.

"Lady," Sirona cried, "I pray You: take hold of these arrows and send them to where they truly belong."

Bathilde and Mau may have been the only ones to know to whom the prayer was directed. However, the answer was evident to all. Like a flight of birds taking wing, the arrows hissed through the air. In the moment before they met Sirona's flesh they froze, quivering in the air. Describing a complete circle, they swung back upon themselves with shrill whistles. Most clattered harmlessly onto the stones of the courtyard. But not all of them.

A shriek tore apart the fabric of dread that had taken over this day. People stared transfixed, Christian and pagan alike. Their eyes were fastened on Abbot Wala. He still stood upon the wall, but his tall form was wavering. Arrows protruded from all over his body, blossoming like grotesque ornaments on his rich robe. He let out another cry, though this one ended in a gurgle of blood. Spreading his arms, he fell. It was an oddly graceful flight; the folds of his robe spread out like wings. He wheeled through the air like a great bird, to land with a crash in front of the monastery walls.

For a terrible instant there was complete silence. Then pandemonium broke loose. The common folk who had taken refuge in the monastery fled. The monks ran, too, spreading in different directions to the church, the scriptorium, and various offices, desperate to seize the monastery's holy objects and get them to safety lest they fall into pagan hands. Only the archers stood in frozen silence, appalled at what their arrows had done.

The people of the procession attacked the monastery walls with frenzied howls.

Sirona continued to look up at the sky. Bast had answered her, but it was Sekhmet Who now appeared. Only Sirona saw Her. The fangs in the great lioness mouth shone, as, laughing, the Goddess pointed Her finger at the buildings within the monastery. One by one, with each point, the buildings caught fire. Flames leaped up with a hollow whoosh. Inside the walls the screaming intensified.

"Open the gates!" scores of terrorized voices shrieked. "Open the gates!"

"Yes, open them," the pagans echoed, but in their voices there was no terror, only bloodlust.

Groaning in protest the gates swung apart. Afterward, the survivors would say the gates had made such noise because the heathen gods had forced them open. The pagans would say the same thing, but with delight in their voices. In the end no one would ever know how the gates came to be opened, for the men-at-arms still stood frozen upon the wall.

Frantic Christians poured out through the entrance. Smoke followed them in ominous black billows. Sirona saw Bast join Sekhmet's towering image in the sky. With Her was Freyja. The three Goddesses were outlined in dazzling brilliance. They were limned with power. The power, Sirona realized, of the new giving way to the old.

Bathilde's followers allowed the common folk to depart in peace. Their sights were set on targets far more representative of the hatred that had bloomed in them during these last days: the monks. Blood resonated in their howls; a crimson sheen blossomed about them as they entered the burning monastery in waves. They caught the dark-robed monks, pulled them through the gates, and began to beat them in plain sight of the Christian men-at-arms. It was enough to bring the men-at-arms back to themselves, and in horror they leaped from the walls to defend the holy brothers.

Sirona heard the thunderous hissing laugh of the Lion-Headed Goddess. Sekhmet pounded Her massive fist through the air. Flames leaped from the conflagration and found a new home in the bodies of the men. Just as She had incinerated the assassins who had tried to kill Sirona on that rainy night that now seemed to have taken place in a distant past, Sekhmet did the same to the Christian soldiers. The men ran, letting out hideous sounds that no human throat should ever make. They fell, and before the eyes of the pagans they and their weapons became living towers of flame that charred with unnatural swiftness into ashes.

The people roared their approval. Their hunger for blood fed Sekhmet, and She, in turn, fed theirs, so that the killing became a stink upon the air. Through it all—the monastery in flames, the dead and dying monks, and the fleeing people—the sun continued to beam down as if in blessing.

It was noontime, and the day was bright and hot. The sky was as blue and sweet as a newborn's eyes, and golden sunlight poured over the violent destruction below. The images of the three Goddesses fairly glowed with gratification.

At length the violence began to burn itself out. There were no more monks or Christian men-at-arms to be killed. The great monastery complex was collapsing in on itself. Its many dwellings and buildings were of wood, and wood burned rapidly. Soon only the walls remained standing, an odd sight, now that there was nothing within them to protect.

As the sounds of destruction began to give way to quiet, Bathilde came up to Sirona. "This was well done, save for one thing. You should not have promised those peasants they could leave unharmed. They are Christians. We should have slain them along with the monks." Sekhmet's appetite for blood was mirrored in her gaze. The noblewoman's dark eyes were burning red as coals.

"They are also Saxons," Sirona said. "Clear the bloodlust from your thoughts, lady, and think. They will tell of what they witnessed this day. And who knows, some of them may be impressed enough by the power they saw to throw aside the new religion and return to the old ways."

Slowly the red mist lifted from Bathilde's eyes. She smiled and nodded. "Wisdom flows from your lips, Wise-woman. Mayhap Freyja will influence their hearts—"

"Look, look, another one!"

The man's voice rang out, followed by other calls, as a bedraggled smoke-stained figure darted wildly through heaps of smoldering rubble. The pagans gave chase, hooting and jeering. How he had managed to survive up to this point was amazing, but the fugitive's luck had run out. Now that he had been discovered, the unfortunate man had no chance of escaping his pursuers.

"Another priest," Bathilde said without concern. "They will do with him as they did with the others."

"Kill him, you mean." Sirona's glance strayed to the tumbled bloody heaps that had once been the monks of this Christian holy place. An uneasy feeling struck at her. She recognized it as prickles of regret, until her eyes fell on the arrow-pierced corpse of Abbot Wala. He had intended on seeing her die a horrible death, but he had died instead. She was not sorry. And as for these dead monks: well, she was certain that they would have assisted their abbot in throwing her upon the bonfire.

The sounds of the chase grew louder. Men yelled, and women laughed. Sirona saw that they had caught their quarry. Forming a circle about the monk, they were pushing and shoving him from one person to another, cursing as they did so. Steadily the manhandling became rougher. People raised their staves and clubs.

Sirona's eyes narrowed. The man in the center of the brutal circle was not a monk after all. She took a step forward.

"What is it?" asked Bathilde.

Sirona broke into a run. "Stop!" she shouted. "Leave off!"

It was hard to say who was more astonished at the interruption, the fugitive or the people that ringed him. Faces turned toward her, and the harassing of the man instantly stopped. He stood in the middle of his attackers, a slightly built man, wavering and exhausted, his fine clothing torn and dirtied. Wiping blood from his face, he slowly turned his red-rimmed eyes on her.

"You," Sirona said to him. "Of course, you would be here."

"And you," the man replied hoarsely. "You would, of course, be here as well."

Bathilde came up beside her, puzzled and displeased. "What is upon you, Wisewoman?" She stared coldly at the man in the circle. "Think you of showing mercy to this new mouse our people have cornered?"

Sirona did not answer. She studied the royal advisor. Alcuin, she recalled, was his name. Despite his ominous situation he did not seem afraid. His thin grimy features were calm, even serene. There was none of the arrogance and naked fear that had characterized the abbot.

"I do wish to spare him," she said abruptly.

Bathilde and the others stared at her in surprise; so did the captive. Sirona did not blame them. She was a bit surprised herself.

"Freyja's golden chariot, why?" demanded Bathilde.

Sirona tried to explain. "He tried to spare me when Haganon and the abbot would have burned me alive." She looked directly at Alcuin. "I cannot but return the deed in kind."

Alcuin returned her gaze. He did not appear relieved; indeed, the look on his face was one of deep unhappiness.

"Absurdity," Bathilde declared. "He is a churchman. He should die." Her people muttered in agreement.

Sirona shook her head. "There is kindness in him. It would change the good fortune that has followed us to shed his blood."

Kill him. Sekhmet's voice burned through Sirona like flame. *His blood must join the others'.*

Bathilde also heard the Goddess. Satisfaction lit up her handsome features. "You see? The Shining Ones know what must be done."

Not all of the Shining Ones. Bast's deep melodic voice joined that of Her Sister. *My daughter speaks wisely. Let the mortal live, for in truth, there is kindness in him. Not all of these Christians need die for Us to gain Our power.*

Bathilde's satisfaction had given way to displeasure. Bast had not chosen to address her, but Bathilde had gifts enough to know that another Goddess was speaking, and not to her. She scowled. "They speak to you as they do not to me," she complained.

Then hear Me. Freyja's lovely voice twined about both women. *Allow the man to depart in peace. There has been enough death this day.*

Bathilde was transfigured. The discontent on her face vanished as if it had never been. Sekhmet was a glorious presence imbued with power. But Freyja—Freyja was part of Bathilde's soul. She loved Her. "Ah," she said softly. "If it be Your wish, Lady."

Enchanted, the people watched as their lady communed with the Goddess. Unconsciously, they lowered their clubs.

Sekhmet let out a low growl. Yet She was outnumbered. She gave a vast, irritated shrug. It was only one mortal, after all, and She had drunk plenty this day.

Bathilde examined the advisor. "Your accent is not of Saxony, but of Gaul. Is that where you are from?"

"He is the king's chief advisor," Sirona said.

"Indeed?" Bathilde looked interested. "Well, king's advisor, if we let you go, will you scurry back to your lord and warn him of what has arisen here? Will you advise him to keep his army out of Saxony, lest we destroy it?"

Alcuin's pale steady eyes met Bathilde's dark ones. "I will, Lady," he said. "But that does not mean he will listen."

"Hmm." Bathilde's eyes hardened. "Well, that will have to be enough. Find him a riding beast," she cried. "Nothing too fancy. A mule will do for the likes of him, lucky as he is to be leaving at all."

Two men ran off to do Bathilde's bidding. Alcuin made

no attempt to move through the ring of his captors. He had been saved, yet he still showed no relief at his reprieve from death. "I do not deserve your mercy," he said to Sirona, and there was pain in his face. He had not heard the Goddesses speak; he only knew that the witch had granted him his life. "I condemned you along with Haganon and the abbot. I would have let you burn. It is not meet for you to give me this boon, not after the way I dealt with you."

"No." Sirona shook her head. "You are not like them. You were misled. Death is too strong a punishment for paying heed to bad counsel."

"And these others?" Alcuin's voice was gentle. He gestured to the bodies heaped haphazardly about. "What was their crime? What did they do that merited their dying?"

Sirona's eyes shifted color, turning as dark and hard as Bathilde's. "Perhaps no more than any believer in the old gods, the gods your priests rail against, preaching that those who do not forsake them must be put in fires, taking away our sacred ways by force, and threatening those of us who try to hold on to them."

She fell silent, realizing that her voice had risen in anger. She saw that Bathilde was nodding in approval. The people were glaring at Alcuin. The aura of hostility was flaring again, inflamed by the wisewoman's words. They shifted closer. The staves and clubs began to be raised again.

The sound of clopping hoofs broke the tension. The two men were returning, leading a bridled and saddled mule. "He belonged to the monastery," one explained. "We found him in the pastures outside. All the monastery beasts are there. They were spooked by the fire but otherwise unharmed." The man snorted. "So little did these priests fear us they did not even bother to bring the animals inside the walls for safekeeping."

"Fortunate for the beasts that they did not," Bathilde pointed out. "We'll take them with us. But first"—she crooked a finger at Alcuin—"here be your mule. Get on him and go on your way. Quickly," she added. "Before the Goddess changes Her mind."

The people parted to let the advisor through. They glowered, but none made a move to interfere with Alcuin as he walked up to the mule. Roughly the man slapped the animal's reins into the Christian's hands and stepped aside. Alcuin pulled himself up into the saddle. But rather than starting away, he looked at Sirona.

"You spoke true when you said I listened to bad counsel," he said quietly. "I will remember it. And if God allows me to return to Gaul alive, I will do my best to see that the King of the Franks does not receive the same bad counsel I did."

He clucked to the mule, nudged with his heels, and the animal set off at the slow walk common to all mules.

They all watched him go. Bathilde's expression had turned thoughtful. "Do you think he will really tell Carolus not to come to Saxony?" she asked Sirona.

"He said that he would." Sirona's eyes were on the advisor's lonely figure as he and the mule headed toward the horizon. "He also said that he would warn him not to pay heed to Haganon. Yet, in the end, that may mean very little."

Bathilde laughed. "In the end, it matters not what he does." She swept her arm out at the ruins of the smoking monastery. "The Shining Ones are with us!"

The route to Gaul had led Haganon, Aelisachar and their men to retrace their steps, and in doing so they had ridden near enough to see the smoke from the burning monastery. They did not go nearer. They could not, Haganon told them. It could mean their lives, and if they died, who would then warn Carolus of what was brewing in Saxony? Thus it was with astonishment that they heard a hoarse voice hailing them, and beheld the approach of a tattered figure on a tired mule.

Even then Haganon would not have stopped had Aelisachar not insisted. Impatiently, the count pulled in his horse as the rider begged the reluctant mule for a plodding trot that was scarcely faster than his walk. As man and animal came nearer, Aelisachar gasped.

"I knew there was something familiar about him," he exclaimed. "Christ's bones, it is Alcuin, the king's advisor."

Haganon had guessed that already. It made little difference to him. Alcuin had proved useless; it was time to move on to those who would be of use, namely Carolus and the great army at his command. Scowling, he gripped the reins of his restive mount and waited for the advisor to come up.

The mule stopped, more of his own accord than his rider's. Slumped in the saddle, Alcuin stared at the noblemen. His face was pale as milk; his blue eyes were sunk deep in purplish hollows. "Did you see the smoke?" He pointed back in the direction of the monastery. "You must have seen it. It hovers on the air like a miasma, even from this far away."

"We saw it," Haganon said shortly.

"And you did not ride to help?" Outrage warred with fatigue in Alcuin's voice. "The pagans came with torches in their hands and murder in their souls. You say you saw the smoke, and yet you did not—"

"We could not!" Haganon was not about to allow this puling scholar to cast aspersions on his honor. "The *stria* has joined those pagans, and she has called up dark forces so strong no mortal man can fight them alone." He jerked an arm at his men-at-arms. "Ask my men, and they will tell you. They saw what I saw." The men nodded in vigorous agreement, and the count went on. "We narrowly escaped death in our own encounter with the pagans. Had we ridden to the monastery, we would have cast away our lives for no purpose. Far better that we seek help from those powerful enough to render it."

Alcuin listened in silence. "Abbot Wala is dead," he said bleakly. "He told me that you had taken your men and gone to confront the witch. I thought it was a mistake. I thought you should have stayed to defend the monastery."

Haganon glared. "Are your ears plugged so you cannot hear me? If we had stayed, we would have died along with the abbot." He took care not to show his dismay at hearing of Wala's death. The abbot had been an important ally. It would be difficult to replace him. Although, he reflected bitterly, there were far worse things to worry about than his original plans to take over Bathilde's lands.

"My lord speaks the truth," one of the men-at-arms put

in. He and his companions blessed themselves. "What we saw, Deacon"—the man shuddered—"what we saw . . ."

Haganon silenced him with a brusque motion. He studied the royal advisor coldly. "Who killed Abbot Wala? No— you need not answer. The *stria* did it. I know she did."

Alcuin met his eyes. "You are wrong, my lord. The woman you name witch saved my life. The others wanted to kill me, but she would not allow it." He dropped his eyes, recalling the look in the woman's strange eyes as she had spoken to him. Her words still rang in his ears, though he had no intention of repeating them to these men. "It is due to her, and her alone," he finished, "that I speak with you now."

Aelisachar, who had been listening in silence, looked surprised. "Indeed? Has she had a change of faith then?"

"No, no," Alcuin said sadly. "She is far from Heaven's grace, which makes her kindness to me and my failure to save her soul all the harder to bear."

"Ah." Aelisachar looked relieved. If the witch had converted to the new religion, she would have been immune from further efforts to slay her with the king's approval. As the man who baptized her, Alcuin would certainly defend her, and Aelisachar was well aware that Carolus would listen to his advisor over Haganon, no matter how vociferous the latter's objections were.

The old noble glanced at Haganon. His confederate's hatred of the wisewoman had become intensely personal. Mayhap it was warranted; Aelisachar, after all, had not seen the horrors that Haganon and his men described. But he had seen enough at the witch's hut, and for his part Aelisachar was regretting ever being drawn into this coil.

He had been lured by the promise of additional land and influence; neither had materialized, and instead he found himself trapped between Haganon's grudges and the likelihood of a full-scale revolt, not to mention the menace of magical forces arrayed against him. He heartily wished he had never listened to his fellow noble's schemes, but now it was too late. He was bound by his honor to see this unfortunate mess through to the end. Even, he reflected grimly, if that end be his own.

Distracted, his mind still working over the difficulties presented by Abbot Wala's death, Haganon picked up his reins. "I thank God for your safety," he said to Alcuin in a perfunctory manner. "Ride with us, for we are headed for the king's court at Aachen."

Alcuin stared at him for a long moment. "Oh yes," he said at last. "That is where I was headed myself."

23

BATHILDE'S FERVOR SPREAD through the land, as high and hot as the flames that had devoured the monastery built by Carolus. People had been angry and frightened by the mysterious and devastating rain. They were eager to find a cause for it, and the procession's arrival, accompanied by beaming sunshine, was enough. People hailed the change as a miracle, one wrought by the old gods and not the new. Bathilde had said that if they returned to the old ways, the famine would be reversed. It had happened, just as she had promised, and the response was mighty. The people's rededication to the ancient paths began to reach a fever pitch.

For the majority of Saxons, Christianity had never done more than rest lightly on the surface. It was a garment easily cast aside. The ancient ways, on the other hand, were deeply ingrained, bred into the bones and blood of the people. Beliefs so much a part of Saxony's consciousness could not be forgotten in a generation or in ten generations. Carolus had enforced his religion on his subjects, but he was about to learn that force was never an efficient means of winning a people's heart.

Bathilde had already learned it. Flushed with exultation at her success, she sent out messengers bearing word that it was time to rededicate the sacred groves, beginning with the most sacred of all: *Irminsul*, or the World Tree. Her words traveled as rapidly as a summer fire in dry grass. People came flocking to her call.

Farmers raced to plant vegetables and grain in fields rich with silt from streams and marshes that had overflowed and now receded. They rebuilt fences from fieldstone tumbled by the flooding, and pastured their beasts. Freyja would look after the crops and herds in their absence, they told each other, and took their families to join the procession. Villagers went with them; so did innumerable house folk attached to the manors of the noble born, including those of the new religion.

The Christian lords could only note these defections with consternation. They were becoming more outnumbered by the hour. Abbot Wala was dead, murdered by the pagans, and Haganon was gone, no one quite sure where. His family had taken refuge with one of Haganon's allies, telling awful tales of the burning of his manor. It was rumored that Haganon had set out for Carolus's court for help, but with hostile pagans roaming everywhere, who knew if he had succeeded? The priests were of no use; once they had feared losing their influence, now they feared losing their lives. From all over Saxony, they left their churches to seek dubious safety with the few Christian nobles who still had the means to protect them.

As the sunshine spread across the land, the roads dried with magical speed. Once so empty, they became dotted with travelers again: groups of peasants looking for better lands and kinder masters; slaves in flight, taking advantage of the unsettled times to make a bid for freedom; clerks who had broken their vows to take up the old religion; and the occasional trader. Weaving through the various bands were the pilgrims: Christians who did not hesitate to travel thousands of leagues through the Empire or outside it to perform a penance or venerate a relic. In their eyes, the threat represented by heathens was of no consequence; it only made their pilgrimage more holy.

But looming over this burst of normal travel was the presence of Bathilde and her procession. Its numbers swelled daily, almost by the hour. Bathilde continued her march to the World Tree. It was a bloody progress, one that was charred with smoke. Bathilde ordered her followers to torch the churches they came across, and the people were swift to obey. Abbot Wala's monastery had been one of the first casualties, but it was not to be the last.

And over it all the Shining Ones rejoiced. More and more had awakened from their sleep. They were the Vanir: the attendant gods and goddesses to Freyja. Like Her, they were deities of fertility, but magic was their true province, and with their awakening it came bursting back into life. Christianity had dimmed the old magic, caused it to fade in the brightness of the new power. Now the balance had shifted. The gods had been in this land long before the priests sent by Carolus. Blooming across the sky, blazing in their new-found strength, they laughed and sang in the thunder of crashing clouds, certain that they would live long after the new god and his priests had fallen into dust.

There was Odin, the fearsome All Father, God of storm and harvest. Heimdall, the God of light, rode beside him on his horse with the golden forelock. Innumerable goddesses were coming out of sleep and stretching their arms out to the sun. Gefjun; Erce; Nehallenia; and a host of others joined their sister Freyja, and Her kin from across the seas. Bast and Sekhmet, allies as They had not been since before the time of Pharaohs, swept through the skies, delighted in what They had wrought.

The key to their success walked below them. Sirona had blossomed as the goddesses had done, and it was a fierce blossoming. She was the link, and she knew it. In combining her powers with Bathilde's, she had enabled Bast and Sekhmet to combine Their powers with those of the Saxon gods. It was she who had brought the power of these two distant lands together and melded them into a terrible force. There were no regrets or doubts left in her about her new place in the world; the image of the old woman cleaved by Haganon's sword had dispelled the last of them.

She strode beside Bathilde's cart and thought of all the times she had been driven away from her healings by priests who equated witch and wisewoman as one and the same. She thought of those priests railing against the old ways and how they must be stamped out. Memories of sacred groves burned to the ground scalded her, ancient customs hidden, until they began to be forgotten. Now she was traveling to the most sacred grove of all, a place the new religion had not been able to penetrate.

Irminsul, the World Tree, was older than the world of mortals. Created by the Shining Ones, her task was to bind the nine sacred worlds together with her roots. The stories that surrounded the holy tree were as sacred as the tree herself. Once there had been a war between two races of gods. The tree commemorated their truce, and she nourished all spiritual and physical life. Yet she was constantly under attack by evil creatures angered by the peace between the gods. Demons sought to chew on her roots; others tried to devour her tender buds and spreading green leaves.

Only the cult of priestesses that had always lived at *Irminsul* kept her safe. There were nine of them, for nine was a number of magic and mystery, a number of the moon. Even Carolus and his army in their initial invasion, and the king's more peaceful but no less zealous Christian missionaries had not been able to dislodge the guardians of the tree. The sisterhood remained as they always had, sprinkling the vast gnarled roots each morning with water from a sacred well to protect her from the rapacious demons.

Bathilde's army arrived at the holy site while the sun was breaking over the wooded hills that overlooked the River Wiser. Light poured over the tall stands of fir and pine, gilding the green branches so that the entire forest seemed to be wearing crowns. Hawks soared in the brightening sky, and wrens sang and fluttered among the trees. Foxes raced through the undergrowth, pausing to stare out at the great cavalcade with clever black eyes. Along the river, does and fawns lifted their heads from their morning drink, then bounded into the forest cover.

In a cleared space on the banks of the river stood the World Tree herself. She was a needle ash, and the cleared area she stood on was necessary. For she was enormous. Even in a land where giant trees were commonplace, the World Tree towered, making all others seem like saplings.

Sirona's eyes were dazzled by the sight. "The World Tree," she said softly to Mau. "It is said that she grew out of the past, lives in the present, and reaches to the future." She looked at him. "Do they have such trees in the Black Land?"

Mau's orange gaze wandered over the great tree and the forests rising on the hills. "The Black Land is a place of sun and desert and the ever-changing hues of the Mother of All Rivers. Trees are there, but none like this."

"I would not have thought so." Pride rang in Sirona's voice. "There has ever been only one *Irminsul*."

"Trees have ever been sacred to your people. Your fore-mothers worshipped them." A distant expression crossed his face. "Veleda, the first of them, found me among trees such as these. In those days, Gaul was a haven of the old gods, and the new religion was unknown. But that was in the past. Much has happened since then."

Sirona studied him. "How many ages have you seen, Mau?"

He shrugged. "Enough so that I lost count long ago. But remember this: you are of an old line, one that I think will survive the intolerance of the new religion. Veleda, and all the daughters after her, have been blessed by my Mistress. A blessing from the Lady Bast is no small thing."

"And Her blessing?" Sirona felt a comforting warmth beneath her breast, as if the Cat-Goddess were smiling at her. "It extends to me as well?"

"You know it does. But in these days that may not mean a great deal." Anger was in the cat man's voice, and sadness. "Heed me. In one way or another I have been a companion to Veleda and all the Daughters of Bast who have come after her. Some of them were fortunate and passed their mortal days in peace and serenity as they kept the shrine of my Mistress; others lived in hard, bitter times and suffered. But in all the lives of Lady Bast's priestesses that I have witnessed, there is one thing in your life that is different."

Sirona walked on beside him, waiting. "Well?" she pressed, when he remained silent. "What is different?"

Mau looked at her. "I have never doubted the wisdom of my Mistress's blessing." He paused. "Until now."

* * *

Haganon, Aelisachar, and their men, with Alcuin in tow, arrived at Aachen in good time, even though the stubbornness of the royal advisor's mule had held them back more than Haganon would have liked. The two noblemen and the advisor were promptly brought before the king.

Carolus sat in his audience chamber, on a throne of costly ebony inlaid with gold and mother-of-pearl. His war band stood about him, and his chaplain. The king of the Franks was a shrewd observer. He leaned forward in his carved chair, took one look at the faces of the men before him, and rapped, "What happened?"

Haganon took it upon himself to answer. On the ride to Gaul his terror over what happened at the village had faded. Anger had replaced it, and a calculated intent to turn those frightening events to his advantage. He had thought and planned carefully the words he would say to Carolus. Over and over he had rehearsed them in his mind, so that they would flow naturally to his tongue when he said them aloud.

"Lord," he said, and bowed deeply, "we were beset upon by evil, an evil so great it has taken over Saxony. We were lucky to escape with our lives. Many other good Christians did not."

They were dramatic words, spoken with all the flair Haganon had at his command. And they were true. Behind him Aelisachar nodded fiercely. Alcuin stood off to one side. His thin lips were pressed together, and his face was expressionless.

But Carolus was not a man impressed by flair. "Tell me what befell you, and do it plainly," he ordered. "I sent you to slay a witch. Did you succeed?"

Only slightly chastened by the king's tone, Haganon crossed himself with great piety. "We did not, lord. But it wasn't for lack of trying. The witch is far more powerful than I had supposed. She turned the very fire we built to burn her against us. She disappeared into the air, and when we tracked her down, she cast spells that made the earth shake us from our horses like leaves falling from an aspen tree. I can answer you no more plainly than that. Ask my companions, and they will tell you the same." He crossed himself again, and this time, remembering the scenes he had described, it was not a gesture made for show.

"What Count Haganon says is true, my lord," said Aelisachar. "I saw him after these things had happened. The look upon his face—the way he spoke—he could not have been lying."

The king's broad handsome features were grim. "And Erchinoald's widow? What of her?"

"Bathilde"—Haganon spit the name like a sour taste—"is completely under the influence of the *stria*. Both must be destroyed if Saxony is to be regained for Christendom. I appeal to you, great lord: assemble your army and march with us against this heathen evil. Bathilde and the *stria* have cast their evil over your province. They have restored pagan ways. They have burned my manor! And that is not the worst of it. Churches have been set to the torch. Your monastery has been burned to the ground and reduced to rubble. Abbot Wala is dead, murdered by the witch's dark magic."

Unable to refrain from more drama, Haganon flung out an arm at Alcuin. "Ask your counselor, for he was there. He saw the foul deed with his own eyes."

The count paused for breath, confident that his speech had achieved the desired effect. This was going well, he told himself. The men of the king's war band were muttering ominously. As for Carolus himself, the king's hazel eyes were on fire and his massive body was hunched in the great chair like a tiger about to spring.

As a devout Christian, nothing would heat the king's blood more than hearing that pagans were burning his monasteries and killing his appointed abbots. And the best part was that all of it was true. Alcuin would of a certainty confirm all that Haganon had said, and that would set the seal on the king's rage. Carolus would march into Saxony, lay waste to the heathens, and award Bathilde's lands, and perhaps the lands of others, to his loyal noble Haganon as a reward. Great as the *stria's* powers were, even she would not be able to prevail against the full might of the Franks.

Haganon nearly smiled. Abbot Wala had done him a great favor by getting himself murdered. Basking in success, he waited for the king to speak.

"Alcuin?" Carolus stared at the slight man. "Where are your words, good friend? I have heard nothing from you."

"That," said the other man with a faint bitter smile, "is because I have not had the opportunity."

"Well, you have it now," the king told him. "Was Abbot Wala murdered?" His voice was the low growl of an angry bear. His eyes were narrow and glittering.

Alcuin moved forward. He walked slowly past Haganon, sparing the tall noble not a single glance. He stopped directly in front of the throne and looked up at Carolus. "My noble king." His educated voice was suddenly loud. "The abbot was murdered indeed. And for that, Count Haganon must bear responsibility."

Blood rushed into Haganon's face. "You dare—"

"Be silent." Alcuin did not look at Haganon, but he spoke in a voice the count had not known that the scholar possessed. "The king has asked me to speak, and I will. My lord," he said to Carolus, as Haganon gaped in astonishment, "the mission you sent me on was ill-fated. The worst of it is that it took death and burning and the mercy of the very woman whose execution I was supposed to preside over to make me see it. I was granted my life, and in return I promised that I would tell you of bad counsel. I have come here to do that."

"Bad counsel?" Carolus's gaze slashed across Haganon like a razor.

Alcuin sighed, but his voice remained steady. "It is true that the woman is a witch. It is also true that heathens are committing desecration against the true faith, the greatest of which was the destruction of the monastery and the murder of Abbot Wala. But Abbot Wala and Haganon must bear the blame for the madness that is now sweeping over Saxony. They plotted together to deprive the Lady Bathilde of her widow's portion. They coveted her rich lands and were willing to blacken her name to gain them. I believe"—he threw Haganon a cold probing look—"that they tried to embroil the wisewoman in their scheming, and she refused. For that, Haganon convinced you that she was a witch and must die. Obviously, he wanted to quiet her, permanently."

"Lord!" Haganon would have struck the little counselor down, but he did not dare. "These are lies." His mind worked furiously. "I forgive him, though"—with a huge effort he calmed his voice—"his wits have been undone by all that he suffered. Aelisachar and I both noticed it as we traveled to your court."

Alcuin laughed. "If only that were the case. But it is not. I know all too well what I am saying. And I trust you, my lord, to be the best judge of it."

Carolus sat absolutely motionless in his fine chair. However, the men of his war band knew what that stillness portended. When the king grew tight as a drawn bowstring, it was wise to steer clear. All of them were glad that they were not Haganon. If the bowstring twanged, the Saxon count would be the target.

"Your trust becomes you, my friend," the king said. "And I see naught," he added with another quelling look at Haganon, "that indicates your wits are addled. But what of everything else you have told me? Witchcraft and paganism are serious matters that must be dealt with. The destruction of the monastery must be punished. And the murder of Abbot Wala must be avenged." He clenched a big fist on the arm of his chair. "Regardless of the machinations he may have been involved in, he was my man. To strike at him is to strike at me."

"I know." There was grief in Alcuin's pale blue eyes. Deep lines had carved themselves around his mouth, and he still sniffled from the cold he had caught from his long hours in the relentless rain. "But heed you this, my lord. I think that the Widow Bathilde and the wisewoman were driven to their desperate acts. It does not excuse them, and I agree that this heathen uprising must be stamped out before it spreads any farther, but I would also tell you that the

wisewoman spoke up for me when the other pagans would
have killed me. She showed me mercy when I had showed
her none, and she convinced Bathilde to do the same. Indeed, she showed more kindness than the count. He took
his nobles and men-at-arms and left the monastery before
the pagans arrived, thus leaving us unprotected—"

This time Aelisachar, as well as Haganon, sprang forward with shouts of protest at this challenge to their bravery.

"Silence!" thundered Carolus. He looked at Haganon,
and rage fairly seethed about his massive frame. "You," he
said dangerously. "You began this coil by drawing me into
your schemes. Me, the ruler of Christendom! To think, I
must now deal with rebellious pagans for no other reason
than your greed." His voice grew still more ominous. "You
sought to turn me into a pawn, to make a fool of me. That
will not be tolerated."

"My lord!" Haganon's ruddy complexion had gone the
sickly shade of curdled milk. The speed with which this had
all gone wrong was stunning. Yet there still had to be a way
to salvage it. "The *stria*!" he cried. "She has put a spell on
your advisor. Listen to how he speaks, defending witches as
though they were godly women. Are these the words of a
Christian man in his right mind?"

"They are my words," Alcuin said tiredly. "And I am under no spell."

Carolus jerked his head. "I believe you, my friend.
Whereas, you," he said to Haganon, "I do not believe." He
swept his fiery gaze to Aelisachar. "What have you to say in
all this? Do you stand with him?"

A heavy silence descended. Every eye fastened itself on
Aelisachar. The old man felt sweat trickling under his
armpits. Haganon's life was hanging in the balance, and as
Haganon's ally, so was his. But what good would it do to
declare that he stood with him? Haganon was going to die
regardless. And, truth be told, the count had made a number
of decisions that were ill-advised; Aelischar could remember every one of them, now that he stood ready to be
blamed along with Haganon.

He saw the stern impatience on the king's face, and finally answered. He did not meet Haganon's eyes. "I stand where I have always stood," he said. "With you, great king, to whom I gave my oath, as a noble and as a Christian."

"As did I!" Haganon shouted.

"No." Carolus's eyes were like shards of amber. "You stand for yourself, Count, and you always have. Your oaths are as lightly taken as wind through dead leaves." He raised his voice, calling for the guards. "I strip you of your titles and lands. Whether I strip you of your life as well will depend on what happens next in Saxony. In the meantime, you may sit in a cell and wait. Thus is the reward I grant to those who think the king of the Franks may be manipulated to their will."

The blood that had darkened Haganon's face had left it, leaving him pale as an old skull. Surely he had misheard. All his plans and successes could not be collapsing like this, with such devastating speed. "The *stria*," he said, looking from faithless Aelisachar to the king in horror. "These are not your words; they could not be. She has ensnared you."

Carolus motioned disgustedly at the guards. "Take him away."

Haganon raised his voice as though he were on the field of battle. "She has ensnared you!" he yelled. "She has ensnared you!"

The guards came forward, seizing the count by the arms before he could jerk away. His hoarse voice could be heard long after they had pulled him from the audience chamber.

The priestesses and their attendants had prepared lavishly for the ritual that would take place at the World Tree at moonrise. Bathilde would name her son there. Some whispered that she intended to present him to the Shining Ones as the king of the Saxons, pledged to restore the old ways, while she acted as regent until he reached an age to rule. The folk who whispered this thought it a good plan.

Sirona agreed. Night was falling, and as the ceremony began, she stood with Mau in the place accorded to the honored: a torchlit circle beside the great tree. More torches had been sunk in the earth to light the broad pathway leading to the World Tree. Flowers were strewn between the torches and all about the tree herself, perfuming the night. Half a dozen cattle and horses stood waiting for the sacrificial flint knives that would spill their blood. The scent of roasting meat and fresh bread made the air itself seem as if it could be eaten. An enormous feast of venison, pork, beef, bread, dried fruits, barley beer, and mead had been prepared for the sprawling numbers of people, who had gathered all about the approaches to *Irminsul* in the fading twilight, and were still jostling for the best view of the ceremony.

At last the wailing cries of horns wound through the air. Instantly, the murmuring and pushing of the restless crowd ceased. The music was sinuous and compelling, a call to prayer. The nine priestesses of the tree walked forward. Each of them held a curving four-foot horn, which they continued to play as they walked. They were garbed in the black robes of their order, their hair unbound, and long swords with amber handles belted about their waists.

Waves of movement rippled though the assemblage as the flaring torches revealed the priestesses. Men and women went down on their knees, raising their arms and chanting the ritual response to the call of the horns. Some remembered the ancient words, and some did not. But those who had forgotten listened with longing ears, and were soon praying with as much fervor as their companions.

In the wake of the priestesses came Bathilde. She, too, was garbed in a long black robe. She was alone. Her black hair was coiled elaborately about her head, and she walked with long stately strides. In her arms nestled her son. He had been given a wine sop to make him sleep, for it would be considered an omen of ill portent if he cried at such a solemn ritual. The sop had worked; the baby lay in his mother's arms, his tiny eyes closed, his little fists resting against her breast.

The people's voices boomed as the noblewoman and her baby came into view. Tears streamed down the cheeks of the older ones. The women standing with Sirona also wept. Most of them had accompanied Bathilde from the very start of her trek, and now they were witnessing its culmination. They grasped one another's arms in joy, crying out prayers of thanksgiving.

The priestesses gathered in a circle below the tree. The wailing music of the horns continued as they turned to await Bathilde. Darkness had spread out beyond the rows of torches. Above the massive roof of the World Tree the sky was clear and lit with stars. The full moon was rising, flowing up from the last purple bank of twilight, as if the night itself were giving birth to that orange glowing orb.

Bathilde and her baby joined the priestesses. The nine women lowered their horns. As the music fell silent, so did the people. Still kneeling, they were utterly silent, waiting, layered by anticipation. Attendants led up the first sacrifice, a two-year-old stallion the color of milk. The sacrifice of such a valuable animal held enormous significance and was performed only at a ritual as important as this. The oldest priestess took up the flint knife. In the heavy silence she raised the blade and then wielded it with flashing skill. The beast must die quickly, without suffering, or the act would be tainted and the life given unwilling.

Blood cascaded from the stallion's throat. A vast sigh flowed from the mouths of the watching people. The animal's brown eyes widened in surprise but no pain, as the spirit of his life fled. The strong white legs folded like those of a newborn foal. Two other priestesses followed the horse's fall, positioning themselves to catch the fluid in a silver bowl so large it took both of them to hold it. As the throat blood poured, two more priestesses took up a second bowl filled with water from the sacred well.

The oldest woman laid aside the knife. As her remaining four sisters took the baby from his mother, the elder dabbed her fingers into one bowl and then the other. Murmuring ancient words, she anointed the drowsy baby's forehead with blood and water. The infant yawned, wrinkling his tiny nose at the smell of blood. The priestesses smiled.

When the sacred women returned the baby to Bathilde

she held her son high, stretching the swaddled bundle toward the limbs of the giant tree. "I dedicate my son to the Shining Ones," she cried. "In Their honor, do I give him his name. May They look favorably upon him and give him Their blessings." She paused, then shouted, "Widukind! The king of Saxony!"

The assemblage took up the cry, roaring out the baby's name. "Widukind," bounced across the low hills and echoed from one side of the wide silvery river to the other. The moon glowed. The night seemed to smile.

Sirona watched with shining eyes. She shouted the child's name herself, and turned to Mau. "It is a good name," she told him, pleased. "A strong name for one who will grow into a strong man."

"Let us hope," Mau said, "that he lives long enough to grow into it."

"Why wouldn't he? Christians are fleeing Saxony from all directions. We will have our land back and the Gods to protect us."

"For how long? Where do you think these people of the new religion are fleeing? They will head to Gaul."

Sirona shrugged. "Let them. Most came from there, and as for those that did not, well, perhaps Gaul will be a better place for them."

Mau looked at her. His eyes had grown very wide, and the bright orange color had darkened. He said nothing. Sirona gazed into their depths for long moments. She stiffened. There were images in his eyes, and they were covered with blood. She drew back, staring at him. Around them the shouting went on. The rest of the sacrifices were being led forward. When that was done, the feasting would begin. The celebration would go on through the night. Only when dawn pinked the sky would the hardiest revelers finally stumble off to find a place to sleep. Sirona made a conscious decision that she would join them. Yes, there were bloody images in Mau's eyes, she told herself, but they were of defeated enemies, perhaps from ancient battles at some other time in his long, long life.

Thus it was that Mau eventually found himself alone next to the blood-soaked roots of the World Tree. Only he noticed a lone horseman cantering away. The rider was cantering west, in the direction of Gaul.

24

"KING?" CAROLUS ROARED. "THE pagans have named a *king*?"

No one dared speak. The man who had brought the news trembled and did not lift his eyes. It was not unknown for the bearer of bad tidings to be put to death for his efforts. Carolus appeared angry enough to do just that.

The king slammed a massive fist onto the jeweled arm of his chair. "There is only one king of Saxony," he bellowed. "And you are looking at him!"

"The Saxons," Alcuin finally said with his usual mildness, "would appear to have other ideas."

"Then they shall learn the danger of such thinking!"

"Their king is but an infant in swaddling bands. His mother will have to act in his stead, and she is but a woman. This was a gesture, nothing more."

Carolus shot his counselor a withering glare. "Gestures lead to actions, and for you to mouth such foolishness ill becomes a man as wise as yourself." The king's rage was still white-hot, but it was already giving way to the calculation for which he was justly famed. Armies and weapons and strategies were whirling in his hazel eyes as he went on. "Haganon was right about that woman, after all. I thought to offer her more mercy than I showed him. I see now that I was wrong."

"You were not wrong, my lord." Alcuin looked earnestly at his liege. "The hallmark of a great ruler is mercy."

"And another hallmark is knowing when to grant mercy and when to withhold it," Carolus shot back. He rose from his chair. "Now is the time for withholding." He began to shout orders to his nobles for assembling the army. The heat for battle was contagious, but when it was a battle to be fought on religious grounds it was sacred. The blood fever spread like flames from a great hearth-fire warming everything it touched. Eyes blazing, the nobles ran off to do their king's bidding, and Carolus turned to Alcuin.

"I do not understand." His intelligent features were baffled and exasperated. "The Lord Jesus Christ is the only true religion. Why will these heathens not realize that?"

Alcuin looked at him and his voice was somber. "Truth is many things to many people, my lord. There is good and bad in heathens and Christians both. 'Tis a simple lesson, but one that is easy for the wisest of men to forget."

"You, one of the most devout Christians I know, would speak so?" Carolus regarded the other man in astonishment. "What happened to you in that barbaric country that you defend these bloody pagans, the very ones that wanted to kill you?"

Alcuin sighed. "I am not defending them, lord. But things are not always what they seem. Haganon, a Christian, would have left me to my death, and it was a pagan, the very woman we went to execute, who saved me. I saw a great deal while I was in Saxony. I learned even more. The people there are stubborn and proud. You have enforced your will on them before with fire and sword, and still they rise against you. It may be that marching into their land with an army is not the way to bring them to the Lord."

Carolus snorted and refilled his wine goblet. "That is why you are not a king, my friend. Sometimes fire and sword are the only answer, particularly with the Saxons. I am tired of having to forever fight with these people. I have been gentle in seeking to extend the word of God. I have been gentle as their king! Well, that is ended." His voice had grown louder and louder, until he was shouting. "They think to set themselves against my rule? They think that they may burn my monasteries and kill my churchmen, and I will do nothing? Well, their memories are as feeble as their faith. By the blood of our Savior, they will learn that to their sorrow."

Goblet in hand, he stomped from the hall. Alcuin did not seek to follow him. He knew his king well, and he knew that when Carolus was in this frame of mind, there was no point in attempting to sway him. Alone, he walked to the hearth-fire. He stood for a long time staring down into the flames. There in the leaping orange light was the bonfire Haganon had kindled as a pyre for the witch. There, too, was the great monastery burning behind the arrow-riddled corpse of Abbot Wala. But by the same token, how many pagan sacred places had been put to the torch since Carolus first conquered Saxony? So many that the smoldering rage Alcuin had seen in the people on that dreadful day had finally burst free. Alcuin saw all these things, and he could have wept. Fire and sword. The words pounded in his brain. In all his years he had never seen those tactics lead to anything but more of the same. He blessed himself.

"Lord," he whispered, "is this truly how You wish Your teachings brought to the unsaved?"

There was no answer. Alcuin was not surprised. Mayhap there was no answer to give.

Will you show her the spell? Bast asked.

The Goddess's image floated in the moonlight, washed by silver. Beside Her, the World Tree stood alone, deserted by its mortal worshippers. Exhausted and content, the last of them had finally stumbled off to drunken slumber. Wrapped again in solitary peace, the tree sang its ancient songs, its broad canopy rustling gently in the night breezes.

Mau, still in his man form, showed his teeth. *I will not. This is a dark and dangerous magic, and I'll have no part of it.*

On the other side of the great tree Sekhmet appeared in a flash of crimson. *Coward*, She sneered.

Mau's eyes glittered in the moonlight. *Better a coward than a fool. And a Goddess Who is a fool is the biggest fool of all.*

Sekhmet made an enraged noise deep in Her throat. She raised a giant fist as though she would smash it down atop Mau, but Bast stopped Her.

Sister, the Cat Goddess said with deceptive mildness, *You would not want to harm one of My children, would You?*

Sekhmet lowered her fist. *He is insolent. My creatures would never speak to Me so. You should demand more respect from him.*

That, Bast replied, still mild, *is between him and me.* She looked at Mau. *There is need for this magic. The new god is gathering his followers. They bring destruction with them.*

Mau's eyes turned darker than the night. *And what have we brought?*

Sekhmet growled angrily, but Bast ignored Her. She stared searchingly at Mau, and when he said nothing more, She spoke. *Very well, I will give her the spell. But if you will not help, then do not interfere.*

I will not have to, Mau said bitterly. *The consequences of the spell will be interference enough.*

"Why have you summoned me at this hour?" Bathilde's normally strong voice was fretful. She was wrapped in her bed robe, and her handsome features were shadowed by fatigue. With a curt gesture, she dismissed the slave who had awakened her. "And to the kitchen of all places! By the nine sacred worlds, I am weary, Wisewoman. I have sung and eaten and drunk far too much. I would sleep, and so should you."

The celebration had lasted all that moon-silvered night and well into the next day. People had commemorated the naming of their infant king with joyous abandon. The huge feast had been reduced to piles of gnawed bones, tumbled platters, and empty beer jugs. Their joy finally overcome by exhaustion, the common folk had crowded into huts and stables or crawled off under trees and bushes to sleep it off. The wellborn had been welcomed into the manor house of a pagan noble and his family, with special places of honor given to Bathilde and Sirona.

Now Bathilde had been disturbed from a much-deserved rest in the comfortable bed that had been made up for her, and she was not at all pleased. Blearily, she saw that Sirona was smiling at her. It was not a pleasant smile.

Bathilde was not the only one who was weary; Sirona, too, had indulged herself, mayhap more than she would have, if not for the images she had seen in Mau's eyes. The voice of Bast had awakened her from her own sleep in the overcrowded hall.

Enemies will soon approach, the Goddess said. *They will be great in number. Combine your magic with that of the other so that you may stop them. Heed me well, and I will give you the means.*

Sirona had listened. Her blood had warmed under the touch of the Goddess. And when Bast had finished, Sirona had risen from her bed and slipped from the hall.

"You wanted magic, lady," she said to Bathilde. "Well, the time has come, and you and I must do it together. I chose the kitchen because it is more private. Once we have begun, we must not be disturbed."

Bathilde looked around the deserted building. Those who did the cooking always slept by the warmth of the banked hearth-fire. But tonight the pallets were gone, and the fire had been built up until it crackled and sang. "Where are the servants and slaves?" she asked.

"I sent them to sleep in the hall. The head cook is loyal to the old gods. She was more than happy to accommodate me." Sirona moved to the trestle table standing nearest the fire. "Come, lady. I will show you what we must do."

Bathilde's tiredness was instantly forgotten. She moved forward eagerly. Candles lay there, stacked in so many piles that they entirely covered the rough-hewn surface. Bathilde stared. "How did you come by all of these?" she asked in wonder.

Sirona did not answer. Picking up a handful, she carefully added them to the kettle that hung over the fire. "Help me," she ordered the noblewoman. "They must all be melted, and then allowed to cool."

Ignoring the peremptory tone that in other circumstances might have made her bristle, Bathilde took up a handful of candles. "Powerful spells can be worked from wax," she observed, turning back to gather up more and drop them in the kettle. "But these are a great many candles. They will make a greater amount of wax." She did not mention the other fact: that this would be a costly spell. Candles were precious and a luxury enjoyed mostly by nobility; there were enough candles on the long table to last an entire winter.

The contents of the kettle were beginning to bubble and spit. The odor of melting wax filled the air. Sirona took up a long wooden spoon and carefully stirred the kettle. Her teeth gleamed. "We will need a great deal of wax."

"Why?" Bathilde's eyes narrowed. She paused in the act of scooping up more candles. "What have you and the Goddess's messenger seen?"

"An army," Sirona said. "And we must stop them."

"Ah." Anger hardened the noblewoman's face. "How do you know—no, you need not tell me. I believe you. Of course, Carolus would march on us. You made certain of that when you insisted on letting his man go at the monastery."

Sirona stared at the other woman. "That is nonsense, and you know it. We have challenged both the power and the religion of the Franks. Think you that their king would not notice? If the advisor did not tell him, someone else did. Mayhap Haganon himself, or one of Carolus's other Christian spies."

"It is so." Bathilde sighed. Stretching out a hand, she clasped Sirona's arm. "Forgive me, Wisewoman. I spoke rashly. How foolish, to fault you for something as inevitable as the coming of dawn and the fall of night. Yes, Carolus would learn of Saxons taking back their sacred places. And yes, he would bring his warriors against us. It is fated."

Gently Sirona drew away. "Never mind; it is forgotten. Now let us get these candles into the pot. The spell must be finished before sunrise."

Steadily, the two women set to work. The candles melted rapidly, surging in the kettle until the liquid wax threatened to spill over. The kitchen sweltered with heat and the heavy wax smell. Sweat beaded the women's faces. Sirona's hair broke out of its braids and curled in tendrils about her face. Bathilde cast aside her robe and worked on in her shift. When the melting was finally done, it took their combined strength to swing the iron arm from which the kettle was suspended away from the fire so the bubbling liquid could cool.

Sirona beckoned Bathilde back to the table and took her hands. "The Goddess gave me these words," she said, quiet and solemn. "Say them with me, and the strength of the Shining Ones and the magic of my foremothers' Goddesses will flow together."

Carefully, she taught Bathilde the words that would call up the spell. They were strange words, hard to pronounce, tasting awkward on lips accustomed to the Saxon tongue. But they worked. A red haze sprang up in the overheated kitchen. At first Bathilde thought it issued from the fire. Sirona knew otherwise. Red was the color of power, Bast had said, the color of the most powerful magic. Now it came to show Sirona herself. Swirling and flowing, sweeping in circles of sparkling crimson, it took over the kitchen.

The women continued the chanting. With each moment the red haze took on strength. It grew thicker and thicker, swirling more frenetically as each musical alien word was uttered. Bathilde's dark eyes were alight. She felt the power coiling deep in her belly, an awesome sensation, as if she were making love and giving birth at the same instant. The heat radiating from Sirona's hands was so fierce it seemed as if the wisewoman's fingers had been transformed into living flames. Bathilde looked at her face and saw that the changeable eyes were glowing red, as red as the light sweeping through the room.

Sirona's voice fell away. Bathilde followed suit. The crimson power continued its swooping dance in a silence broken only by the crackling fire. It had been summoned, and it would not leave until it was bidden. The wisewoman released the noblewoman's hands, and together they walked toward the kettle.

"Come out." Sirona's voice was deep and musical, imbued with a quality that went far beyond this smoky wax-scented room and into realms that lay far beyond the night sky. "Come out and live."

She extended her hands to the kettle. Bathilde did the same.

Something stirred in the depths of the kettle. The wax rippled and spit. A blob hurled itself from the liquid surface and landed with a splat at the women's feet. Swiftly it took shape. Arms and legs shot out; shoulders formed; a head popped up. Before their eyes a tiny man stood. His face was featureless, but he tilted his head and looked up at Sirona as though he could see her. In his soft hands he gripped a sword and a spear.

The red fog dived at the kettle and surrounded it. The wax frothed like a lake stirred by storm winds. Balls of wax began launching themselves out of the kettle. By the score they landed on the packed-dirt floor of the kitchen, each blob taking shape as quickly as the first one had done. An army was forming around the women's feet. Hundreds of tiny waxen men, all identical, save for the fact that some were armed with swords and spears, while others held bows and quivers of arrows.

The numbers grew, until the hot soft figures pressed against the ankles of Sirona and Bathilde. And still they came. The kettle was large, and, as Bathilde had noted, there were a great many candles. Now she understood why.

Sirona waded to the door. Flinging it open to the night, she called out to the wax men in a low singsong tone. "Go, little soldiers," she sang. "Go, small warriors. Find our enemies and slay them. In the name of Bast, Defender of Horus, and Sekhmet of the Seven Arrows, I bid you. Protect us."

Words came to Bathilde's lips. She did not have to think of them; they were just there, and the saying of them was right and good. "In the name of Freyja, the Great Goddess; Baldr, the Bright One; Odin, the Sky God; and all the Vanir, I bid you." She trembled with the power of Their names.

The wax army obeyed. They swung about, formed themselves into orderly ranks, and marched for the door. Wave after wave passed into the darkness. But the kettle was not yet empty. More wax was splattering onto the floor, taking man shape and hurrying after its fellows. The night was far advanced when the last row of little men marched through the door and vanished into the darkness beyond.

With their absence, the atmosphere in the kitchen abruptly changed. The kettle sat empty, deserted of its magic. The red mist made one last series of swoops and circles, then vanished.

Sirona looked at Bathilde. The scarlet glow had left her eyes. She looked like herself again, grimly satisfied, though very tired. "We did well, lady," she said. "When Carolus and his men cross the border into Saxony they will encounter our little men, and when they do, you may be certain that they will run for home, screaming in terror."

"Those of them that still live." Bathilde smiled, showing her teeth.

"Yes," Sirona said, and her eyes were as cold as Bathilde's smile. "Those that live."

The Frankish army mustered with the speed of long practice. On a cloudy windy morning Carolus wrapped himself in a royal blue mantle, mounted his favorite warhorse and led his men toward Saxony. It was a great force that followed him. First came the king's personal war band, followed by the general cavalry, also composed of nobles, all of them mounted on fine warhorses. Aelisachar and his men-at-arms rode with them; the only Saxons in the group, but perhaps the most dedicated. Foot soldiers followed, each man carrying a shield and shortsword. Sturdy freemen marched after them, armed with pikes, axes, and spears. Trailing at the rear, in a far less disciplined manner, rolled the noisy caravan of loose cattle, servants, slave dealers, and camp followers.

The Franks made good headway. The skies remained cloudy, but no rain fell, and the tracks remained dry. By noon of their eleventh day of marching they were approaching the tall stone that marked the border of Saxony. As Carolus's stallion took the first steps into Saxony, the clouds abruptly gave way to sunshine and blue sky. The king looked up and frowned. Behind him in the cavalry, Aelisachar stared apprehensively up at the sky and crossed himself. His face was as gray as his hair.

The foot soldiers sweated in the unexpected warmth. As the infantry strode along in the rhythm of travel, a pikeman in one of the rearmost ranks let out a sudden yelp. "Holy Mary's paps, something bit me!"

The soldier's fellows glanced around. The pikeman yelped again, and all at once his legs buckled. Amazed, the man realized that he had been hamstrung. His wild stare swept the ground. A tiny waxen figure stood at his ankles. It was holding a spear, the point dripping with blood. The figure cocked its head in an oddly whimsical gesture. It seemed to be looking up at the pikeman, but it had no eyes. It lifted the spear, leaped up, and thrust the bloody point deep into the soldier's throat.

The pikeman's beginning scream ended in a gurgle and a spray of blood. As he went down the other pikemen stared in disbelief. The attack had happened too swiftly for any of them to grasp it. One of the men caught sight of the wax figure.

"Look," he started to exclaim. His voice was abruptly cut off. Half a dozen tiny arrows were protruding from his neck. The soldier dropped his pike and fell.

The rear guard of the infantry now found itself besieged. Eyes wide, they beheld a stream of little figures converging on them from all sides. It was all they had time for. The tiny men ran with unnatural speed and lethal aim. Before the soldiers could raise their weapons to defend themselves, they were being cut down. Screams rose. An axman swung his weapon, brought it down, and sliced one of the attackers in two. The wax figure split apart in two neat halves, then, before the ax wielder's incredulous gaze, they promptly came together. The soldier let out a terrified cry. Before he could do more, the reunited little man killed him.

All through the ranks of the infantry the scene was repeating itself. The waxen figures with their blank faces did not need eyes to plant their weapons. They were impossibly quick, and, as other men were finding out, they could not be crushed or sliced apart. Wherever they leaped they brought death. Within moments, terror was running as rampant as were the wax men themselves.

The cavalcade of camp followers stumbled to a confused halt. It took some time for them to see what the source of the confusion was. But as more bodies fell, and the orderly ranks broke apart and fled, the collection of servants, slave dealers, and women caught sight of what was sending them into such a wild retreat. Gasps erupted as they saw the army of tiny figures. Screams of "magic" and "witchcraft," burst from dozens of throats, and the camp followers joined the flight.

The wax men advanced their attack with methodical speed and skill. Up through the rows of soldiers they went, wreaking havoc, until the mounted nobles finally realized that something was amiss. They wheeled their horses, but they were already too late. Agonized screams tore the air apart. Riders lurched in their saddles. The awful sounds were coming from the throats of horses. Shrieking in agony, the hapless animals were toppling to their knees. The tiny attackers were using their spears and swords to hamstring and disembowel them. As the nobles were flung to the ground, their shock lasted only an instant, so swiftly did the same weapons open their throats.

Aelisachar saw the wax figures, and his face blanched. "Holy Mother of God," he breathed. There was no doubt in his mind as to the source of this attack. "The witch," he screamed hoarsely. "The witch has sent them. Run, run! They will kill us all!"

At the head of his war band, Carolus heard the old noble's screams. He and his nobles swung their horses around. Openmouthed they stared at the chaos behind him. The king's face went black as a thundercloud. "Stand!" he roared at the top of his lungs. "Stand, by all the circles of hell, or I will send you to hell! What the devil is going on here!"

From his position the king had not yet seen the wax men.

But the nobles not in the war band, the ones around Aelisachar, heard the old man's cries all too well, and they saw what he saw. With the tiny warriors darting and leaping before their eyes, flight was unquestionably the best option to those fortunate enough to still have horses under them. Aelisachar's terror was contagious as a plague, though it took little to send the cavalry and, indeed, the entire army into panic. Waging battle against rebel Saxons was one thing; but none of these men—either noble or soldier—had planned on encountering magic. They had not the stomach for it. Even a leader as charismatic as Carolus could not convince them to stand their ground once the impulse to flee had taken root in their minds.

And flee they did. Screaming, some of them even flinging away their weapons to run all the faster, Carolus's mighty army turned tail and ran.

To his rage and shame, Carolus found himself forced to retreat along with them. His war band surrounded him, yelling that he and they could not be left alone, that this was no normal ambush but the result of an evil spell.

"We cannot lose you, lord," one of his most trusted friends shouted. "I would die with you. All of your war band would. But what good would that do? This is magic! We cannot fight against it!"

It was that plea that persuaded Carolus. He set heels to his horse's sides and took off after the other nobles.

But even the king's retreat did not stop the deadly little men. The wax warriors dashed along with the army, creating more carnage amidst the frantic ranks of mounted nobles and running infantry. The border of Gaul was only a quarter of a league away. As the first desperate men stumbled through the line of trees, they slowly realized that their pursuers had stopped. Others followed, and discovered the same thing. Apparently whatever magic had called up the wax demons prohibited them from leaving Saxony. Panting and shuddering, staring fearfully behind them, the Franks began piling up on the blessed safety of their own ground.

Although the rear vanguard of servants and camp followers had seen the attackers, they were the only ones to have escaped the carnage. They could not know that the power of the little warriors did not extend beyond the borders of Saxony. All they knew was that they had witnessed something terrible. They clustered around the survivors, each one striving to make his or her voice heard, yelling out questions, grasping at the arms of the stunned and dazed soldiers.

Into this rapidly disintegrating confusion rode Carolus and his war band. At once they set about restoring order. They forced the camp followers back and drove the scattered ranks of the army back into a semblance of order. Only when that was done did Carolus and his nobles take counsel together.

The king was red-faced with anger. "Cowards," he raged. "I should have every one of you flayed alive. Starting with me, for letting myself turn tail and run along with you! I, the king of Christendom, running away from a battle!" Foam flecked his lips as he shouted, and his warhorse sidled nervously beneath him.

"My lord," quavered one of the nobles. "You are a great king. But you are a man. Those things were demons. They were not made of flesh and blood. No man could have fought such creatures and won."

Another noble spoke up. "Did you see them, lord?" He shuddered. "They could not be slain. I ran one through with my sword. My horse trampled several more. They sprang up as if nothing had happened and went after me." He shivered again and patted his horse's neck. "This beast and I would be among the dead now if we had not run."

Carolus's temper was cooling. "Witchcraft," he said in a calmer tone. "Haganon spoke of it."

"Mayhap it was one of the few things he spoke of truthfully," a third noble dared to say.

Carolus nodded. "Alcuin spoke of it as well. And every man here knows the veracity of my royal scholar." His eyes blazed. "If what happened here today was witchcraft, then there is only one way to fight it, through the word of God. We will return to Aachen; however, we will be back." He shook a fist in the direction of Saxony. "We will be back!" he shouted. "And this time, we will have priests who will call upon the true Lord. Thus will we triumph over pagan evil!"

The nobles set up a cheer. One of Carolus's great abilities was his talent at inspiring men, and even this setback could not dim his power and force of will.

"But first things first," he snarled when the cheering had subsided. "Bring me the Saxon noble. I spared him when I should not have. Fetch him here so that I can swipe his head off with my own hands. If not for his womanish cries, my fine war band"—he glared around him—"would have stayed and fought like men, rather than running like a bunch of virgins on their wedding night."

Privately, the men of the war band doubted that. However, not one of them was foolish enough to say so when Carolus was this angry. They went off to do his bidding, only to find that Aelisachar was not among the living. They could not find him among the other nobles; nor was he with the infantry or even among the camp followers.

That left only the piles of dead. No man was eager to search there, but neither did they wish to tell Carolus of their reluctance. Slowly they rode back to the stone marker. Beyond the trees all was eerily silent. The bodies lay sprawled where they had fallen. Crows and ravens and flies were arriving to feast, drawn by the smell of blood and spilled entrails, but of the demon attackers there was no sign. The nobles sat their horses in the trees for some time. They looked and listened with all their might, watched their horses for signs of fear, and noticed nothing to mar the peace of the dead. The demons had apparently gone.

At last, with many muttered prayers and crossing of themselves, they ventured out to the bodies. They walked their horses through the corpses; some of the braver men even dismounted to look more closely. Finally, after searching for some time, they discovered that the Saxon noble would escape their king's wrath after all.

Surrounded by the corpses of his men-at-arms, Aelisachar lay beside his disemboweled horse. His face was still white as chalk, though now it lay at some distance from his body. A pool of blood glistened under his chin. An expression of absolute horror was stamped on his features.

25

THE MESSENGER THREW HIMSELF off his lathered gasping horse and called for Lady Bathilde. She came outside at once, not waiting for him to be brought to her. Lord Notker, her host, hurried after her, and so did Sirona.

"The Franks have crossed the border with a great force of men," the man reported breathlessly. "But they were hardly past the marker stone, when they turned around like a flock of chickens and flew for home."

Bathilde went very still. "How do you know this?" She glanced at Sirona, who was standing at her elbow.

"A cowherd was watching from a hill some leagues away. He saw them come, and he saw them leave. Word of it was carried from mouth to mouth until I delivered it to your ears, lady."

"Did he say what caused them to run away?" Bathilde asked. She sounded as short of breath as the messenger.

"No, lady," he answered. "The herder was too far away to see what drove them. And he was fearful of venturing too close."

"Wise of him," Sirona commented softly.

The man glanced at her and nodded. "But he did say that it looked as if they left the bodies of dead men and horses behind them."

The tension left Bathilde's body. She smiled, as if at some secret joke. Indeed, she scarcely seemed able to keep herself from laughing. "You have done well," she told the messenger. "Freyja and the Vanir are pleased, and so am I."

Notker, the pagan noble gestured. He had never renounced the old ways. He belonged to an older generation, his shoulder-length blond hair was fading to gray, but his blue eyes were young again, bright and excited by these recent events. "Take your horse to the stables, then go to the hall," he told the messenger. "You deserve a good meal and a long sleep by the fire."

The tired man bowed and led his blown horse off to the stables. Lord Notker looked at Bathilde, paused as if to linger, then changed his mind and, with many glances back over his shoulder, reentered the manor.

Bathilde whirled on Sirona. "It worked! Freyja's golden chariot, how it worked!"

"Of that," Sirona said calmly, "there was never any doubt."

Bathilde clapped her hands together. "So the wax men of our magic sent the Franks scuttling back to their caves. Where are the creatures now?"

Sirona looked off into the distance. "They have achieved their purpose."

"Ah, but they haven't." Bathilde's eyes were like black coals. "Their work has scarcely begun."

Sirona's eyes flashed back to her. "Work, lady?"

Bathilde scarcely heard her. "There is so much to do. All the sacred groves must be rededicated and the Shining Ones welcomed with festivals and sacrifice. Sacrifice"—she smiled that secret smile—"yes, there will be many sacrifices. We must gather our people together and return to my lands at once. Come, Wisewoman, let us prepare for the journey home."

"You have not answered me." Sirona laid a hand on the noblewoman's arm, and her fingers were hard. "What work?"

Bathilde faced her. "The work of reclaiming Saxony for the Shining Ones, of course. And there is only one way to do that, by driving these Franks and their religion from our borders. That is the reason we called up the wax men, is it not?"

"It is."

Sirona stood for a moment, watching Bathilde. Power

had laid its hands about Bathilde, and she was fierce and flushed with the strength of it. But power had a will of its own; it could shoot off in unexpected directions. Sirona had been wary of it for that reason from the first. Her experiences, exhilarating as they had been, had also reinforced the need for caution. As she looked into Bathilde's burning eyes, it seemed evident that the latter had experienced only the exhilaration. Should she have involved Bathilde in that dark spell? The answer was clear. Bast had said that their powers must be combined, or the magic would not work. Still, the look in the noblewoman's gaze when she had spoken of sacrifices seemed to carry the glint of blood.

"I hope, lady," she added, "that you continue to remember that the reason we brought the wax men was for the defense of our people."

She saw the other woman's face tighten. "Do you question my loyalty to our task, Wisewoman?" Bathilde demanded.

Sirona waved an impatient hand. "Magic is an imprecise skill, lady. I warned you of that when first we met. We who ask for its help can never take its answers lightly."

"I remember your warnings," Bathilde said. "And I remember your fears. I thought you had gotten over both."

"I have learned wisdom." Sirona's voice was cold. "Magic is a gift and a weapon, but unlike a sword or spear, it has a mind of its own. It can turn in one's hand, with consequences not imagined. If you call that fear, then no, I have not gotten over it."

A glint of surprise rippled through her as she realized that her words sprang from the wellspring of truth. Somewhere during the days since she had left Bathilde's hall, she had not only learned to embrace the heritage of Bast, but also to respect it. Perhaps that was the difference between her and Bathilde. There was acceptance on the noblewoman's part, but no respect, and coupled with that was her eagerness. It was a dangerous combination.

The observation made Sirona uneasy. Currents were swirling between the two women; Sirona's flesh tingled with their touch. The bloody images she had seen in Mau's

eyes sprang up in her mind, so vivid that she almost murmured the question aloud. Whose blood? On the night of
the naming she had been certain it was Frankish blood.
Now she wondered.

Bathilde was frowning. Her body was as tense as her
face. "Tell me, do you regret what we did? Your magic and
mine sent the Franks away gibbering in terror. Would you
have rather had them slaughter us?"

Sirona looked at her. "I have no regrets," she said
steadily.

"Good." Bathilde's entire demeanor relaxed. She let out a
deep sigh of relief. "For there must be no ill will between
us, Wisewoman. The Shining Ones mean for our powers to
work together."

Only when Bathilde had turned away and gone back into
the manor calling out orders, did Sirona utter the word that
had been in her thoughts, the word that she had not spoken
aloud. "Yet."

Haganon found himself taken from the dungeon as unexpectedly as he had been thrown there. Indeed, the same
guards who had dragged him to the damp stone cell now
came to retrieve him. He had lost track of whether he had
spent hours or days sitting in this walled darkness with only
the scuttering of rats for company. But the isolation had not
cowed him; if anything, it had only fed his rage and sense of
injustice. The *stria* had done this to him. That thought
rolled over and over in his fevered mind like a log being
tossed through a swift-moving river.

He drew himself up, squinting in the light of the torches
the guards held. "Do not touch me," he warned, determined
to speak with the authority of his position. "I will walk to
my death as befits a man of noble blood, not be dragged like
a runaway slave."

"You are not going to your death," one of the guards said
brusquely. "At least not yet. The king has summoned you.
Come along."

Haganon fell silent. Astonishment washed through him,
along with no small sense of relief. However, he had no in-

tention of allowing these inferiors to see that. He strode forward with as much dignity as he could muster. The guards fell in beside him, one of them leading the way, while the others flanked the prisoner. Haganon discovered that outside the dungeon it was afternoon. The daylight was piercingly strong after so long in darkness. He blinked and stumbled, losing much of his hard-fought dignity as the guards reached out to steady him.

By the time they entered the palace Haganon's eyes had nearly adjusted to the brightness of day. Once again he found himself entering the royal audience chamber. The last time he had walked over that tiled floor he had felt himself invincible, utterly in control of his present and his future. Today he knew better. But still, he yanked his arms away from the supporting hands of the guards. He would not have the king see him as a prisoner, even though it was Carolus who had sent him away as one.

Carolus was enthroned upon his high seat, as he had been the last time. A cheerful fire blazed in the hearth, and Haganon's mouth watered at the spicy scent of mulled wine. The nobles of the king's war band stood in their accustomed places. Alcuin was present, along with the king's other royal advisors. There were also priests, a great many of them. Haganon stared. He had never seen so many churchmen gathered in one place before. Had Carolus called them here to pronounce sentence upon him? The faces of all the men—priest and noble alike—were grave, shadowed with something Haganon could see but not name.

The king was regarding him with narrowed eyes. "I had intended," he said without preamble, "to have you executed. However, God has seen fit to spare you. Do you wish to return to Saxony?"

Haganon was speechless. He was certain that he had not heard correctly. Carolus was looking at him impatiently, and it suddenly occurred to the count that if he did not answer quickly, this offer of life could be yanked from his hands. "With all my heart do I wish to return home," he declared fervently. "As a pledge of my thanks for your renewed trust, I would rebuild the monastery and offer up prayers in your name all the rest of my days, Lord King."

"Spare me your gratitude." There was ice in Carolus's voice. "And this has naught to do with trust. Certain events have made me see that killing you would deprive us of a valuable weapon in the fight to claim your land for the true faith. But make no mistake, you have not returned to my good graces. You have lost my trust, and you will not regain it. Be that as it may, I have a use for you, Count, and so does God. If it were otherwise, all your promises and prayers would be nothing more than chaff."

Haganon looked around the chamber. All at once he was able to name what it was that he had seen in the faces around him. Fear. "What has happened?" he asked. "What did the *stria* do?"

The circle of faces exchanged glances. "No one has said it was the woman," Alcuin pointed out, and his normally mild voice was hard.

Haganon stared at the advisor with genuine hate. "Who else?" he asked darkly.

"It may have been her," Carolus broke in. "In the end it makes no difference. Your countrymen have risen against my authority, and they have used a black and terrible magic to attack my army. My warriors and I will return, of course. And this time, an army of priests will march with us, carrying the blessings of God as divine protection against pagan evil. As for you, Count Haganon"—his stony gaze fixed on the noble's face—"I want you to tell me the most important place to the pagans in Saxony. I mean to go there and destroy it."

Haganon answered without hesitation. Christian though he was, he was still a Saxon, and there was only one response that he or any other Saxon would give. "Irminsul," he said. "The World Tree. It is the very heart of the pagan religion." Shivers pricked along the back of his neck. Irminsul was the heart of Saxony itself. He was betraying far more than a gaggle of heathens by turning it over to the Franks. What terrible curse would befall him for such an act? The *stria* had already sent a dreadful spell to attack the Franks; that much was obvious. What would his fate be?

He pushed his uneasiness aside. Superstition, he told himself. He was above the credulous fears of peasants. "Send the tree up in flames," he said strongly. "And the pagans will never recover."

Carolus looked contemptuous. "Only heathens would set such store by a tree. That will be the target then. I vow that I will set fire to it with my own hands. You," he ordered Haganon, "will come along and lead us to this tree. Afterward, we will see what becomes of you."

"Yes, my lord." There was nothing else Haganon could do but agree. This was a chance to keep his life, and, if all went well, he might even gain the rewards of land and titles he had looked forward to only a few days ago, before the witch had ruined all his plans. Yet there was a question nagging at him, and in spite of the risks that asking it entailed, he had to speak. "What of Aelisachar and our men-at-arms? You could have had this knowledge from any one of them. Then you would have had no need of me."

Carolus rose from his chair. Towering on the dais, he glared down at Haganon. "Your countrymen were slain when my army was attacked," he said shortly. "Every one of them. That is the reason you still live."

He stepped down off the dais and left the audience chamber.

"Bathilde is gathering sacrifices," Mau said. "Did you know?"

Silent as the cat he truly was, he stepped out from behind a beech tree to meet Sirona as she passed. She started at his sudden appearance. There had been no sign of him in days, not since the naming ritual at *Irminsul*. The sacred procession had set out on the journey back to her lands, and Bathilde had asked repeatedly where the man of magic was. Sirona had not been able to tell her. Privately, she wondered if he had returned to Bast. It would not have surprised her if he had; he had seemed so unhappy on that night when everyone else was so joyous.

Yet here he was again, looking no happier than when she had last seen him. "Well?" he prodded. "Did you know?"

She considered her answer. "Bathilde wants to rededicate the groves and holy places. She is probably asking folk to select animals to be sent to the Shining Ones."

"Not quite." Mau's sharp features were hard. "The souls she wants to send are of the two-legged kind. And she is not asking. She is taking."

The words landed on Sirona's ears like blows. "Bathilde is gathering people for sacrifice?" The idea itself was not what caught at her. Human offerings were a part of the old religion and always had been. But she remembered the look in Bathilde's eyes, and felt a cold fist squeeze in her belly. "Who are they?" she whispered.

Impatience flickered over Mau's face. "Do I really need to tell you?"

"Christians." Sirona muttered the word and fell silent. She thought for a long moment. "It could be that it is just," she said at last. "Have their priests not vowed to destroy us? They have invaded our country, forbidden the old ways, and preached that we must be stamped out. Is it not right that we stamp them out first?"

Mau simply looked at her. "I cannot answer that, just as I cannot answer why mortals must ever feel a need to slay each other in the name of their gods. But I can tell you this: Bathilde is not only snatching up those priests that have not already been killed. She is seizing your own people."

"Are they slaves?" Sirona hoped that was the case. Slaves were the common choice for offerings to the gods. Most of them went willingly, for to die in the name of a Shining One was to spend eternity in the embrace of the gods. But she saw the reply in Mau's face and knew what he would say.

Had he still possessed whiskers, they would have twitched in disgust. "Some perhaps. But most are freeborn. Farmers and their families, villagers, servants, whatever nobles who were too foolish to flee beyond her reach. Bathilde has taken them all."

The hand clenched around Sirona's vitals tightened its grip. "How?"

"Through the spell my Mistress gave you." The slanted orange eyes burned. "So far, Lady Bast has not seen fit to interfere. Freyja is content because these are Her own children who renounced Her for another god. And as for Sekhmet, She is delighted. She always is, at the prospect of blood."

"But the wax men cannot act without both our wills! That was the way the spell worked. It needed us both."

Mau shook his head. "The wax men cannot kill without both your wills. But causing terror, assisting Bathilde's men-at-arms in tracking down those she wishes them to find, is something else. I warned you that she had grown in power. You would not tell her where the wax men went after they chased the Franks away. She found out for herself." His voice went cold. "With the help of Sekhmet."

Outrage began to ripple through Sirona's shock. "I did not know." The anger grew. "How did she keep this from me?"

"It was easy," Mau said with a shrug. "You are a healer, first and foremost. You were busy with tending the ill, and thus distracted."

It was true, and Sirona wondered how he knew it. As the procession returned home, she had been drawn back into the work of a wisewoman. The usual illnesses and accidents that attend any large gathering had begun to surface, claiming her attention. By the time Bathilde's unwieldy train straggled past the stones that marked the first border of her holdings, Sirona was fully engaged as a healer again. Magic was potent and exhilarating, but to heal was her real calling. Caught up in the immediacy of its demands, she had almost forgotten that the land was still in turmoil.

But no longer. The shell of these last busy days was just that, a shell, an illusion that had been shattered by Mau's words as sharply as a skim of ice. Had she immersed herself intentionally, to avoid the reality of what was happening?

"I am no longer distracted," she said, slow and hard, and her eyes were flickering between dark and light so fast they seemed like twin candle flames caught in the wind. "I will speak with Bathilde. Now."

Mau watched her. "She will want to speak with you, too."

"Will she." Sirona swung around. She was tired; she had been up all night at a birth and was eager to go home and seek her bed. But all that was forgotten. "You can come along," she flung over her shoulder as she started back along the track. "I suspect Bathilde will want to see you as much as me."

Driven by Sirona's anger, the trek to Bathilde's manor was covered swiftly. Sirona marched past the men-at-arms and the steward, ignoring their queries, and sought out their mistress. She found Bathilde in the hall. More men-at-arms were clustered around her, and they were deep in conversation. Indeed, there were many warriors at the manor, more than Sirona had ever seen. The observation added fuel to what Mau had told her.

"Wisewoman!" Bathilde's eyes lit up with her smile. "I have not seen you in days. Where have you been?" Her gaze went to Mau. "Ah, you have brought the magic one with you." She stared at him hungrily.

"Send these men away." Sirona jerked her head at the other folk who always congregated in the hall of any great manor: servants, children, unoccupied men-at-arms, and the ever-present dogs sleeping by the fire or nosing among the floor rushes for bones. "Send everyone away, or else come outside. I must speak with you alone."

The tone in her voice ended the other conversations, and it wiped the smile from Bathilde's face. The noblewoman looked at Sirona thoughtfully, then stepped away from the men gathered about her. "Let us talk out in the sun," she said, and deliberately added, so that all could hear, "for it is a pleasant day, now that the Shining Ones are smiling on us once again."

Sirona spun on her heel and strode from the hall. Looking mildly amused, Mau glanced about him and followed. The house folk stared in surprise. The wisewoman's behavior was an enormous breach of courtesy, as well as a slap at Bathilde's rank. But if the noblewoman was angered, she chose not to show it. Under the eyes of her silent people she went out after her visitors.

In the clear daylight, Sirona confronted her. "You are taking Christians by force and holding them to be offered as sacrifices." She stated this flatly, proclaiming every word as if daring Bathilde to deny it.

And Bathilde did not. She regarded Sirona calmly. "If you had stayed by my side instead of taking up your healing arts, you would have known that," she said.

"Do you accuse *me*?" Sirona's anger was building as steadily as Bathilde's calm. "I am a healer, and I was caring for your people—*our* people. Little did I realize that you would be trying to kill them."

"They are not," Bathilde said curling her lip, "our people. They gave up the right to be called Saxons when they abandoned their oaths to the gods."

"That decision is not up to you!"

"Who better?" Bathilde's eyes were exalted and fierce. "And the Shining Ones think the same. We will rid the land of the new religion's foul influence in a river of blood. The Franks will learn of it, and soon they will be afraid to cross our borders again."

Sirona thrust her face close to Bathilde. "Killing warriors is one thing; driving invaders and their ways from our soil is another. Even slaying for revenge I can understand. But when you turn against our own people that is not only wrong, it is foolhardy!"

Bathilde laughed. "Foolhardy? Carolus and his war band will find themselves the fools if they set foot in Saxony." The laughter stopped. The handsome face changed. "And they will."

Sirona drew back. "You are building an army."

Bathilde glared at her. "Of course. We have need for an army. I am not so foolish to ignore mortal defense as well as magical. I have been waiting for you, Wisewoman. I would have sent a messenger to seek you if you had not appeared today." Her dark eyes went to Mau, who had stood silent all this time. "And I have been hoping you would bring this one with you."

"Why?" Sirona asked dangerously.

"He has powers." Bathilde gave Mau another searching hungry look. "Don't you?" she said to him.

The smile was back on Mau's sharp features, and it was sad and faintly bitter. "You believe that I do."

"Yes, yes. That is why we must work the magic again!" Bathilde wheeled back to Sirona, seizing her hands before she could pull away. "But this time, with the three of us. Think of it, Wisewoman. How strong would we be if we combined our powers in the sacred threefold number! There would be no need for a mortal army, after all."

"No." Sirona yanked her hands free. "I will not."

Bathilde's stared at her. The mad excitement in her dark eyes was giving way to annoyance. "Why this reluctance, Wisewoman? With the wax men, we would destroy our enemies—"

"What enemies? Farmers and their families? Villagers dragged from their houses and shops? All of them penned together like beasts waiting the knife? They are Saxons, lady, just as you are. I do not hold with their religion, but let them depart in peace if you would not have them bide in Saxony. Do not kill them."

"I must." Bathilde's face was suddenly like stone. "Their blood is demanded. Its shedding will be proof of my loyalty. The Shining Ones demand it." She swung to Mau. "Tell her! You know the Goddesses want blood."

Mau said nothing.

"Tell her!"

"They may, lady," he said. "But so do you."

Sirona took a step back. "Bathilde," she said, "you are no different than those of the new religion."

The revelation staggered her as she uttered it. But once said the words could not be taken back. And she would not have done it if she could. She remembered the look in Abbot Wala's eyes. She saw Father Ambrose railing against Mau. She remembered words, threats from other priests and other Christians since the new religion had come to Saxony, preaching that the old ways were evil and must be driven out. The memories haunted her. And she knew that in Bathilde the hatred had come full circle.

"Where are you going?" Bathilde cracked out the question. "Wisewoman!"

Her calls rang out on empty air. Sirona kept walking. She did not look back.

Mau started past Bathilde, and she leaped forward to snatch at his arm. "Wait! I need you." Her fingers closed on nothing. He turned to face her, and she froze at the look on his face.

"I am not here for you," he said.

When he walked on, she dared not follow.

26

"YOU KNEW." SIRONA WAITED TO speak until they were past the manor gate. She looked at Mau. The bloody images were in his eyes again, and now she understood them all too well. Pain wrestled with anger in her voice. "You knew all the time that it would come to this."

He shrugged. "And I know what you must do now. So do you."

Sirona stared into the distance. "Will She listen to me?"

Another shrug. "That, I do not know. She has not listened to me."

"Then I will not ask Her." Sirona's jaw tightened. "I will go where my path leads me."

An aura of death hovered about the mortals below.

Bast looked down at the people. Male and female, young and old, the reek of fear coiled up from the flesh of each one. Long and long had She been watching, since the first of them had been brought to this place, and the disquiet that had caused Her to appear there had kept Her from leaving.

A sinuous voice rolled up from the depths of the earth. *It is what you wanted, O Goddess. Chaos. The land trembles and the blood flows. I have brought these things as You requested. Do You regret Our bargain?*

Bast continued Her perusal of the mortals below. *So sad they are,* She murmured to Herself. *Mortals have never feared Me. Always have I brought joy and happiness to Their hearts.*

These mortals, the Chaos Serpent reminded Her, *do not even know that You exist. They are not of the Two Lands.*

*They have never heard Your name and would not care if
they had. Listen to them. Even as they wait for death, they
still pray to their false god. Why does it matter what becomes of them?*

It should not matter, Bast said. *And yet it does. Whether
they know it or not, they will be sacrificed to Me as much as
to the gods of this land. Human offerings have never been a
part of My worship. It troubles Me that it would start now.*

The Goddess felt the Serpent give a vast shrug. *The
world changes and does not. Mortals have been giving each
other to the gods since they began. Thus has it always been.
If not You, then some other Divine One will take their blood.*

Like Sekhmet. Images of the Lion-Headed Goddess's
worship rose before Bast. They bore the crimson tint of
Sekhmet Herself. In Her temple the priests would take the
blood of sacrifices and smear it across the lips of Her
golden statue so that She might drink and be appeased. That
had been in the past. But there were enough northerners
here to appease Her as at any ritual of old.

A warning hissed in Apep's great voice. *You have made
Your alliance with Her, and You have gained what You desired. Would You break that alliance because of a little mortal blood?*

Bast's farseeing green eyes looked beyond the enclosure
where the mortals were being held and guarded. She
watched two figures approaching through the forest of oak
and ash trees.

The Chaos Serpent knew they were coming as well. It
did not see them, but it felt their footsteps, as it felt everything that moved on the surface of the earth. *Your priestess
wishes to free them,* It said. *I can feel the intention in her
walk.*

Yes, Bast said. *I know.*

And Your cat child wishes to help her.

I know that, too.

Will You prevent them, O Goddess? The Serpent asked
the question with an ancient detachment. Its enormous age
had made it remote to mortal doings long ago.

Bast did not answer.

* * *

Sirona peered out through the trees. The afternoon sun revealed what lay in the meadow to her with merciless clarity.
A huge enclosure had been built. It looked as though it was
meant to house cattle, but what it held were people. Hundreds of them, with more still coming. She watched as a
cadre of men-at-arms herded at least twoscore prisoners to
the pen. The people were terrified; she could see it in their
posture, in the constant desperate Christian signings they
made. The men-at-arms, too, were frightened. They kept
glancing behind and around. Several were holding spears in
one hand while using the other hand to make the gesture
that protected against evil.

"There," Mau said. "Do you see?"

The group had reached the enclosure. The gate was
swung open by other men-at-arms acting as guards, and the
people shoved inside. Through the slats in the fence Sirona
saw them join the others. People were milling hopelessly,
some embracing and weeping on each other's shoulders,
some standing in silence or praying, while still others
cursed the guards and shook their fists. She tore her gaze
from the scene in the enclosure and looked at the creatures
her magic had called up.

They were everywhere. Tiny and dangerous, they stood
holding their miniature weapons, eyeless, yet aware of all
that went on. They outnumbered the men-at-arms, who
took care to give them a wide berth. Indeed, the warriors
appeared to be as frightened of the wax men as their prisoners were. It was these misshapen and mysterious beings that
were holding the imprisoned Christians, as well as their
jailers, in check.

Sirona swallowed. "I unleashed those things, Mau. I did
not care. I knew they would kill, and I wanted them to. But
I thought they would be killing Franks. Never did I think
something like this would happen." The heavy odors of cap-
tivity wafted through the air. She smelled excrement and
urine and sweat, all overlaid with the sour stink of fear. She
gulped again, feeling sick. "How can I stop Bathilde from
doing this?"

Mau smiled. "That is the easy part. Just tell the wax men to open the gate and let the people inside go free."

Sirona slanted him a disbelieving glance, but there was no mockery in the cat man's expression. "They will obey you, as they obeyed Bathilde. The wax men do not reason. They have no loyalty save to those who called them. Without the combining of your strength with Bathilde's, they will not kill for you, any more than they would for her. But just as the wax men gathered these people for her, so will they release them for you, if you command it. The hard part," he added, "is what Bathilde will do when she learns of it. Unless . . ."

He did not finish. Sirona did it for him. "Unless Bast gives the deed Her blessing."

Mau nodded. "My Mistress gave you the power to bring the wax men to the mortal plane, and She can take it from you just as easily. Only She has the ultimate command of their actions. If She does not wish you to do this thing, the creatures will not heed you." He paused. "The danger here is great. My Mistress could even order them to slay you, as they slew the Franks."

For a long moment Sirona was still. Breezes soughed through the budding leaves, and birds chattered in the branches. Children in the enclosure were crying. A man broke into a spate of cursing that abruptly ended when a guard slammed his spear against the wooden slats. "Bast says that I am Her daughter." Sirona spoke slowly. "Would She truly order my death?"

"Once I would have been able to answer you." Mau's voice was soft. "Now, I no longer know. She has allied Herself with Sekhmet. No one can say where that will lead."

"I can." Sirona stood up. "It has led to this, and it must be stopped before it goes any further." She looked up where the sky shone blue between the lacework of branches. "If you will not help me, Lady, then I beg you, do not interfere." Her eyes went to Mau. "All I have to do is tell the wax men what I want of them?"

He nodded. "Call out, and they will flock to you like sheep to the shepherd."

"Very well."

Sirona strode out of the trees.

The guards turned toward her curiously. Most recognized her. "Wisewoman," one of them called. "What brings you here?"

He gasped and stepped back. His companions followed suit. The tiny wax men were flowing toward Sirona, holding their weapons, and leaping with that awkward frightening speed. Under the astonished stares of the men-at-arms they converged from everywhere, an army of grotesque, hopping figures. They surrounded her, staring up with their sightless faces, waiting for her commands.

"Open the gates," she told them. "Free the ones inside and allow them to go on their way unharmed. When that is done, I bid you leave the mortal world and return to the darkness from which you came."

The men-at-arms strained to hear what she had said, but she had spoken the words too quietly. The wax men heard her clearly, though, and they rushed to obey.

Sekhmet swooped up before Bast in a swirl of outrage. *What is she doing?* She screeched. *She is going to free the sacrifices!*

Yes, Bast said quietly. *She is.*

The Goddess looked at the scene below. Sirona was facing the enclosure that held the captives. The wax men were streaming toward her, while the mortal guards stood clustered together, motionless and terrified.

Their blood is marked for Me. Sekhmet fairly spit flames. *And not only for Me, but for the old gods, the true gods, including You, My Sister. The mortal woman gathered them for Us with Freyja's consent. You knew this! Indeed, You helped. Was it not You Who gave Your priestess the magic for the wax warriors in the first place? To allow her to interfere now is to break Our alliance.*

Have You not drunk enough, O Sekhmet? There was no condemnation in Bast's question. *You had blood in plenty when the wax men killed the warriors of the new religion. And more blood will be flowing soon enough. Surely you do not need to drink from these women and children and old ones. The blood of men who are fighting and dying in battle is far more bracing, and when the warriors of the new religion return, there will be a great deal of it.*

Sekhmet's yellow eyes glittered with sudden thoughtfulness. The flames of Her rage lowered and dimmed a bit as She considered Her Sister's words. Below Her the wax men had swung open the gate of the enclosure. The priestess was exhorting the sacrifices to leave, reassuring them that they would not be harmed. Slowly, seeing that the wax figures were under her control and that the men-at-arms were too frightened to interfere, they were beginning to obey her. As the first people went out of the enclosure, others followed. The speed of their departure grew steadily.

Sekhmet watched this and growled deep in Her chest. Bast drew closer to Her across the swath of sky. *Do You not remember Apep's words when We formed Our union? He said that in allying with Each Other We would blend Our natures. Indeed, that has happened. I have taken pleasure in the shedding of blood, I, Who am a Goddess of Life. But You, My Sister, have taken on a part of My nature, as well. Take heed of that part. Is it You Who truly needs the blood of these people, or is it the mortal woman Bathilde?*

Sekhmet looked at Her Sister. The Lion-Headed Goddess was growing ever more thoughtful. The scarlet haze of Her presence whirled and darted with ideas She would not normally have concerned Herself with. They were not welcome ideas, but they were there, and She could not deny them.

Abruptly She reached Her decision. *Mortals have ever acted according to My wishes,* She said gruffly, *not I according to theirs.* She lifted Her arms, and the flames swirled high again. *Our bond holds. Let the humans go.*

She vanished with the flames.

Carolus regrouped his forces and struck with the fury of the religiously indignant. Accompanied by an even greater number of fighting men, as well as the army of priests he had vowed to raise, he marched again into Saxony. His warriors went with more than a little reluctance; many of them had gone on that first ill-fated expedition and were not anxious to return. But the charisma of their king and the divine protection afforded by the priests encouraged and drew them on. Still, despite the presence of the true God, when they reached the marker stone, the bravery of all them plummeted.

This was the place where the demons had leaped out to wreak their havoc. Putrefying flesh had laid its curse on the air. The corpses of the slain had eventually been given Christian burial, but the bloated remains of horses lay scattered where they had fallen. The Franks looked about, their eyes rolling white, their voices rumbling in mutters of trepidation. Haganon was with them, no longer a prisoner but not truly an ally, and no less afraid than the others. Only Carolus and the priests showed no fear. The king sat his warhorse with dignity and absolute serenity. The churchmen, including Alcuin, came in his wake, praying and waving censures that smoked with incense.

The army passed the marker stone without incident. It advanced into and through the trees, and still nothing happened. Alert as hunted deer, the men who had been there before watched the ground. The demons were tiny, they warned the others, no higher than a man's ankle. By the time one might notice them it would already be too late. Their whispered words could have stampeded the panicky soldiers, save for one thing: the dreaded little creatures did not appear.

Erect and powerful, Carolus kept his place at the head of the Franks. Unlike his men, even the proud nobles of his war band, he disdained to watch the grass beneath his stallion's hooves for signs of attack. His high voice rose to join the prayers of the priests, and as the army followed after his tall figure, it gradually became apparent that no mysterious assault would be forthcoming.

The king suddenly wheeled his horse. "Now do you see, my warriors," he shouted. "Our prayers are answered, and the Lord is with us. Did I not say that no creatures of the devil would dare to mar our path so long as we kept our faith?"

A few men set up a cheer. Others joined in. The voices swiftly became so thunderous they drowned out the chanting of the priests. A sense of invincibility swept over the army, carrying even the most apprehensive survivors along with it. Carolus took note of it. They were past the place where the ambush had occurred. Breezes were springing up, sweeping away the stink of death. The flat, marshy plains of Saxony lay before him. He would cross them to the forested depths, where he would lay waste to his goal.

"Ahead, brave warriors!" he bellowed. "We will ride through this pagan land, leaving destruction in our wake. And when we are done they will never challenge the might of the true faith again! Ahead, to the World Tree, where we will see it in flames!"

He sent the stallion into a gallop. The war band thundered after him. The main body of the army broke into a run, as if Irminsul stood right before them.

When the first reports of the invasion reached her, Bathilde did not believe them. She was cradling little Widukind, gazing at his dark downy skull with fond possessiveness, when the messengers arrived. Their faces were gray with exhaustion and dread. They could barely stammer out the words they had ridden so far to bring.

"Did not the magic stop them?" she demanded after they had finished.

The two men looked at her. "Magic?" the eldest asked.

"Yes, yes, the army of wax warriors I summoned with the help of the Shining Ones. They drove the Franks away not one month past, when they sought to cross our border. They should have met them again."

The man shook his head tiredly. "I have heard of those creatures; everyone in Saxony has. But there was no sign of them. Only Saxon warriors met the Franks, lady—mortal men who fought like mortal men, and died like mortal men. They were few, and the Franks far too many. King Carolus

himself is leading them. We were not prepared. Lords Ago-
bart and Rorigon gathered their men-at-arms and went out
to meet them. They were both slain."

Widukind began to fuss. Bathilde soothed him absently.
"Something is wrong," she muttered. "Why were they not
there?"

She had forgotten the presence of the two messengers
until the second one spoke. "Lady, you must gather the
army. It is early yet. The Franks only invaded five days ago.
We killed two horses each in our haste to tell you." He exchanged glances with his companion. "And there is something else."

Bathilde looked up sharply.

"We have learned the destination of the Franks," the first
messenger said. "Carolus means to march on Irminsul and
burn it to the ground."

Both men waited for Bathilde's reaction. Although many
noblewomen knew how to use weapons, females were, nevertheless, unsuited to war. The messengers had discussed
that at length during their brief rests on the ride to
Bathilde's manor. But they had also discussed the fact that
Bathilde was a powerful priestess and in the hand of Freyja,
the Great Goddess. The waxen men she had called up were
fearsome. They looked at her hopefully. If the waxen creatures were no longer in the world, mayhap she could summon some other magic that would defeat the Franks.

Bathilde rose from her chair. At once the nurse hurried
forward to take little Widukind. She turned to the messengers, and her bold features had regained their calm. If there
was turmoil roiling within her, she did not show it. "Refresh
yourselves and rest," she said. "The Shining Ones will have
need of your sword arms when we go to battle to defend
Them and the Saxon way of life."

The men bowed and left her. "What do you think she will
do?" whispered the younger man to the older, as they went
toward the hearth, where the kettle of beef broth that simmered all day in most manors sat waiting. The latter
shrugged. "She has to do something, else we are all
doomed."

They soon discovered what Bathilde intended to do. They had barely finished their first cup of broth and had just succeeded in cajoling a servant to bring them bread and stew left over from the midday meal, when the seneschal called out for everyone to attend the mistress. Setting down their cups, the messengers followed the rest of the manor folk outside.

Swiftly, the noblewoman strode to the platform in the curtis that her husband had once used for making announcements. "Make haste," she told the people of her household. "The Franks are bound for *Irminsul*, and we must reach there before them. We march at once. Messengers, attend me for instructions. The army must be gathered."

A flurry of activity surrounded her. As the house folk ran off to their various tasks, she stood by herself, alone and almost forgotten in the excitement. *The wisewoman*, she thought to herself. *I must find her, and quickly.*

Carolus and his army began a raging progress across Saxony. The flames of revenge had been lit in the king's breast, and blood, instead of quenching the fire, only made them burn hotter. Hundreds of Saxons died. Many gave up their lives in battle; others were taken prisoner and given a stark choice: baptism or death. To Carolus's bafflement and increasing fury, they overwhelmingly chose the latter. In his anger the king could not grasp the obvious, that this was not only about gods but freedom.

The seeds of resentment against Frankish rule had been planted long ago. Bathilde's call to remember the old ways was but the water that allowed them to burst into flower. Common folk and nobles alike watched this army of invaders march into their land, and, united by Saxon stubbornness, they took up arms. Even in defeat, that stubbornness could not be quelled. Battle after battle was fought and lost. Afterward, taciturn and bloodied, the prisoners would stand glaring at their captors and snarling oaths at the priests who sought to baptize the them. Locked in sullen defiance or chanting prayers to Freyja and Odin, they went to their deaths.

"Heathen to the last," exclaimed Carolus after the latest round of executions. "Why will they not learn?"

Alcuin regarded him. "They might say that you are the one who is not learning, my lord," he suggested.

The king bristled. "I have given them every chance. Another ruler would have killed such rebels out of hand, but I am concerned with greater matters. I fight on behalf of the Lord. I seek to bring Christianity to these barbarians who live in darkness. None of them need die. They are fools! I offer them life and the light of the true faith, and they spurn my gifts."

He broke off, studying his counselor darkly. "You are the only churchman who has not gone among the prisoners and sought to convert them," he pointed out. "Why is that, my friend?"

Alcuin sighed. "Because, my lord king, it would do no good. Trying to win souls by the sword is a bad business. It always has been."

"Indeed." Carolus's eyes, red-rimmed from the many battles, turned small and glittering. "The rest of my priests do not say so."

"The rest of your priests do not see the truth, nor would they speak it if they did. Your goodwill is far too important for them to gainsay you."

"And it is not important to you? Oh, never mind. Your loyalty is not in question, Alcuin. If there is one thing I may rely on, it is that I will always hear your true thoughts, whether I hold with them or no."

"Then hear my thoughts now." Alcuin drew closer to the king, his thin features suddenly intent. "You accomplished the purpose that brought you here. You say the Saxons have learned nothing, but I say they have. I think they have seen the futility of revolt. And surely, my lord, you have slain enough of them to realize that they will not accept our Lord willingly. Why not gather up our army and go home?"

Carolus gave the scholar a disbelieving look. "You talk

like a madman, Alcuin. I will have accomplished nothing until this entire land is Christian." He leaned down to the shorter man. "Know this: we will continue on to the place these heathen call the World Tree, and along the way, if I have to put every man, woman, and child to the sword, then so be it."

He spun on his heel and stalked away. Alcuin stood alone, left to his thoughts. Horses neighed, and orders rang out in the near distance as the army prepared to move on. Flushed by constant victories, the men had almost forgotten the horror of the demon attack. They laughed and joked and called out to each other, paying no heed to the piles of bodies still warm and steaming that lay off to one side. The air was rank with the odors of death. Priests ranged among the corpses, praying in sonorous voices for God to aid them in their work.

Alcuin watched angrily. His brothers in Christ were as hungry for death as Carolus. He looked down at the ground. It was soft and spongy, soaked with blood from that day's battle and the executions that had followed. The last time he had been in Saxony this earth had been drenched with rain. Now he would have to traverse it again and see it drenched with blood. He dreaded the prospect.

Unexpectedly, he thought of the wisewoman. *Would she be able to stay out of the army's path?*

27

MA'AT IS NOT BEING SERVED.

Bast's voice was as cold as the Caverns of Duat. She stood in the deepest of those caverns. She was alone, and Her long green eyes were fixed on the massive coils of the Chaos Serpent.

What of it? The Serpent flicked the end of his tail. *You asked for chaos and that is what I gave You. Chaos and Ma'at are opposites. You may only have one or the other, which You know, O Goddess. In any case*—the tail flicked again—*Ma'at is no concern of mine.*

But it is of Mine. And that is why I have come.

To restore the balance of Ma'at. You are dissatisfied so soon with my gift?

Bast continued to stare at the vast creature. An aura of grief clothed Her, and even in the darkness of the cavern it shone as vivid as the glory of Her form. *I meant for chaos to destroy the new religion and its followers*, She said. *And for a time that was so. But your gift has also turned on those it was not intended for. The old gods have awakened, indeed, but now blood flows from the throats of the mortals who worship Them, and They—We—are powerless to stop it.*

You are not powerless. Apep made a seductive stir that rippled all his coils. *Let chaos work as it will and You will be stronger than You have ever been. In time, chaos turns against all mortals. Eventually, it will attack these followers of the new religion, and their interloper of a god will fade to dust. All You need do is wait. What is the blood of a few mortals against that?*

Bast moved Her head in a sad gesture of negation. *I have*

thought of that, O Serpent, and I cannot go on. The price is too high. I have paid more than I should already.

What of the Others? Apep asked. Disapproval wound through his echoing voice as sinuously as the rippling in his coils. *Do They, too, want my gift withdrawn?*

The Chaos Serpent already knew the answer to his question, and Bast was fully aware of it. Freyja and the other Shining Ones were as troubled by the bloodshed as She was. But not Sekhmet. And, of course, Sekhmet would not be. The Lion-Headed Goddess had awakened from Her long sleep to a surfeit of blood. By now She was drunk with it. The gods of Saxony were grieving at the number of their children who were being slain. But Sekhmet would not have cared if every body piling up belonged to a worshipper from one of Her own temples. It was, Bast thought ruefully, what made Her Sister so strong, and at the same time, so weak.

Yes, She said to the Serpent. *They would rather return to Their sleep than see the land and people They watch over destroyed.*

Sekhmet does not belong to this land or its people, Apep pointed out slyly. *Remember how displeased She was when You insisted on letting Your priestess free those mortals.*

I remember, Bast said shortly. *But it was I who sought you out, O Serpent. I made the bargain, and now I am breaking it. I will deal with My Sister.*

The Serpent let out a vast rumbling hiss. *You realize that not all of it can be stopped? Once chaos sets certain events in motion, even I cannot halt them.*

Halt what you can, said Bast. *I will do the rest.*

The World Tree, serene and beautiful in Her ancient wisdom, stood as She always had, waiting. Every day her priestesses performed the ageless rituals in unchanging peace, and even on this day, they watched with a serenity as great as that of the tree they served, as Bathilde and her vast array of followers came pouring over the hills.

Death was sweeping across the land, and Bathilde, with all those who had come to join her, had raced to stay ahead of its reach. The noblewoman was enraged by the temerity of Carolus, but she was not desperate, not yet. The news that Sirona had freed the sacrifices added to her anger, though it did not surprise her. In any case, there were more Christian prisoners: people trying to reach the Franks rather than flee from them. The army had gathered them up, and they would serve Bathilde's purpose when they arrived at the World Tree.

Now they were there. They had reached *Irminsul* before the Franks. Waves of relieved sighs went through the pagan ranks as people caught sight of the nine priestesses assembled before the giant needle ash. Bathilde had spoken true. The weary hasty journey had not been made in vain.

Bathilde spun her mare around to face the throng. "You see?" she cried hoarsely. "The Shining Ones march with us. They will not allow this scourge of invaders to continue. In our most holy place, we shall sacrifice these Christians. Their blood will water *Irminsul*'s roots as an offering to Freyja. And it will be followed by more, by the blood of Carolus and his army if they dare to desecrate the World Tree!" Buoyed by cheers, she lashed her tired horse into a gallop and rode toward the priestesses.

"Lady," the eldest priestess greeted Bathilde, when she had dismounted, "your coming was foreseen. We have been awaiting you."

"And the Franks?" Bathilde shot the question out harshly, as the warriors began the business of setting up an armed camp. "I did not foresee them. Did you?"

In spite of her calm, there was an uneasy flicker in the priestess's blue gaze. Bathilde saw it and tensed. "We did," the priestess said. "They will come here, lady, but what will happen when they do was not shown to us." She paused. "Is the wisewoman called Sirona with you?"

"No," Bathilde snapped. "I have sought her with my arts, but she has left the path of the Shining Ones. Why do you ask if she is here?"

The priestess turned away and her sisters with her. "She will be," she said over her shoulder.

Bathilde stared after the retreating white-clad figures.

Abruptly, she called out for her men-at-arms. The nearest one answered her call. "Set out guards to watch for the wisewoman," she told him. "Pass the word among all the others that if she is seen, she is to be taken prisoner and brought to me at once."

The man frowned. "Lady, we must gird for war and prepare this camp against an attack. There is too much to do to worry about a wisewoman."

"Do it!" Bathilde hissed. "Fool. With her here, we need not fear an attack."

Sirona knew Bathilde was looking for her. She and Mau had traveled far, staying out of both the invaders' path and that of the noblewoman. Mostly they traveled across an abandoned landscape. People had left their homes either to hide or to follow Bathilde, and food and shelter were to be had with troubling ease. But Bathilde had not given up. She walked through Sirona's dreams, calling to her. Days and nights passed, and waking and sleeping the wisewoman used her own magic to hide from her. Bathilde's calls became demands that fairly screamed in frustration, and still Sirona did not answer.

"I cannot," she told Mau. "What she wants has not changed."

He nodded. "You are different, but she is not. Although," he added dryly, "she is consistent. I'll say that much for her."

That night another dream came to Sirona. They had stopped for the night at a deserted farmstead, where they had made a fire in the cold hearth and scavenged a meal from bags of barley and dried peas the occupants had left behind. Mau had picked at the food, complaining that porridge was not proper fare for a cat. But afterward he had quietly lain down before the fire. Sirona had joined him there. Since they had begun their travels they had slept that way, curled up together, keeping each other warm. Sirona took an odd comfort from his presence. Even in his human form he radiated warmth, nearly seeming to purr, as on this night she dropped off into dreams.

Daughter. The deep notes of Bast's voice rang through the corridors of sleep. *It is time to speak.*

Sirona stirred, smiling in her slumber. *I am listening, Mother.*

Ma'at must be restored. The world has gone out of balance. It is for you to set things right.

Awake Sirona would not have known what Ma'at was, but in the dream there was perfect understanding. *How can I do this, Mother,* she asked.

First: look upon what I show you.

Scenes began to unroll themselves across the night darkness. Sirona saw Bathilde shouting, and she saw the wax men. Small and terrible, they were dashing through ranks of Saxons and Franks alike, killing both with indiscriminate efficiency. Freyja and Sekhmet were watching. Freyja's magnificent face was carved in lines of ageless grief. Sekhmet was smiling, and her fangs were stained with blood. The killing continued until bodies lay heaped upon each other like cordwood. The land was empty, barren of life, for with humans dead, the wax men had started slaying the animals. And now Sekhmet was no longer smiling. Her yellow eyes were narrowed in dismay. She called out to Bast. Sirona could not hear what She said, but there was anger and dismay in the roaring voice.

Sirona wept in her sleep. Tears rolled down her cheeks, tears as heavy as the death that weighted Saxony.

You see. Bast's melodic tones thrummed over her tears. *Death upon death is an offense to the sacredness of Ma'at. It must not happen.*

Yes, I see. But what can I do?

Go to the World Tree.

The tears slowly stopped. *Will You help me keep* Irminsul *safe then?*

Bast's ageless breath seemed to beat through Sirona's entire body. *The time has come for the World Tree to live on another plane. Bathilde has no understanding of Ma'at. She would keep the World Tree safe at the cost of what I showed you.*

But if the World Tree dies . . . what of Freyja? What of

You, Mother? Does restoring Ma'at mean You will go back into Your sleep? Grief rolled through Sirona. She had discovered the presence of Bast. Was she now, after such a short time, to lose it?

The Goddess's voice was gentle. *I am awake now, and as long as mortals live who speak My name, I will remain awake. After the World Tree, you must leave Saxony. Go to My land, to Kemet. Recall My memory to those who were once My people. Keep My name alive.*

I will, Sirona whispered. *But . . . how will I go there?*

Mau will show you. The rest you will know.

The stark visions vanished. Mau stood before Sirona's inner gaze. He was in his other form, the mighty cat that she had seen in Bast's temple. There was another cat with him. The image of this second cat was vague, its outlines wavering and indistinct.

The World Tree. Bast's voice faded along with the image. *Do not wait. I will see that horses come to you so that you may go there all the faster.*

Sirona opened her eyes. The embers of the banked fire limned Mau's face. He had rolled up on one elbow and was looking at her. "You know," she said to him.

He inclined his head. "I would do better staying on a horse if I had four legs rather than two, but I will do my best."

She looked at him. "Tell me something, Mau. Why have you not changed back to your true form?"

He gave her a smile so odd she could not begin to define it.

"It was I who changed you," she mused. "Am I the one who must return you?"

"Something like that. But rest easy, human one. When the proper moment comes you will know what to do, just as you did when you changed me the first time."

His tone was as odd as his voice, and Sirona glared at him in annoyance. But he said nothing more.

They rose at first light. Less than a league from the hut, the stones that fenced a pasture had tumbled, and two stocky mares were grazing just outside, as if they were waiting for them. Mounted, the distance to the World Tree was little more than a day's ride. But for several leagues before they reached their destination, Sirona and Mau knew they must be careful.

Carolus and his army had arrived ahead of them.

There was no element of surprise in the approaching battle. Both sides had massed and for most of the early morning the screaming of curses and insults went on, as the warriors worked themselves up to fight. Carolus led his horsemen back and forth before the lines of his infantry in a splendid and threatening display. Saxons fought strictly on foot, and mounted cavalry had proved a valuable tool against them in past encounters. The priests encouraged the Franks' efforts, praying loudly, blessing and enjoining the men to fight well.

The pagans facing them were no less clamorous. If this battle were lost, far more than life would be lost with it. Every man—and the large number of women who had chosen to fight—understood that. Sacrifices had been made, prayers sent along with them to Odin, the God of War, and Frigga, Freyja's battle aspect. Now it only remained to join the battle and drive the invaders from this most sacred of places.

Behind the ranks of the two armies, the sprawling camps of the noncombatants waited. If either enemy broke through the lines of the other, all those in that particular encampment would be doomed. Sirona and Mau had entered the outskirts of the pagan camp. Their arrival went unnoticed in the tense atmosphere of preoccupation, and they slipped through the wagons and animals and darting children to a spot where they could see the two armies. A new wave of shouting went up from the pagan warriors. It was colored with fury, and as Sirona edged forward, she saw why. Haganon had appeared in the front ranks of the Franks. Before the outraged eyes of his countrymen he strutted and postured, insulting the Shining Ones in a reverberating bellow.

"I will thank Bast and Sekhmet both, if he dies in this battle," she said to Mau through gritted teeth.

"Have no fear," Mau said in a strange voice. "He will."

The sight of Haganon, coupled with the blasphemy he was shouting was the final tinder that lit the conflagration. The pagan warriors rushed forward. Carolus and his officers yelled out their orders, and the battle was joined.

Sirona had drawn off her magic cloak of concealment. With it gone, she sensed that it would take little time for Bathilde to find her. Metal clashed against metal, horses and men screamed, and the noblewoman came running toward them. Her long tunic was stained and torn; her hair tossed in disheveled waves down her back. In one hand she held a sword, its blade stained rusty red.

"Do you see what is happening?" Bathilde's eyes were wild. Her voice was nearly a shriek. "The Franks outnumber us!"

Sirona's calm was jarring by contrast. "How could I not see? I have been healing the hurts of our people since they came. Is there blood enough for you, Bathilde? Beware how you answer. It is our own people who lie bleeding on the ground."

"The blood of Franks is there as well. Join me, Wisewoman, and more of their blood will water the earth."

"That will not happen." The sounds of battle were growing louder, and Sirona had to raise her voice to be heard. "How many times must I tell you?"

"Even with this?" Bathilde waved her sword in the direction of the clamor. "Are you no better than our enemies? The Franks outnumber my warriors. We must summon the wax men. Only they can save us."

"They will not save us." The vision Bast had shown her burned in Sirona's mind. Tears burned her eyes. "Instead, we will be cursed. If we bring them back, Bathilde, more and more death will result. There will be no end to it."

"I do not care!" Bathilde's voice was as ragged and savage as her appearance. "All that matters is victory!"

Sirona stared at her. "For you, or for the Shining Ones?"

Bathilde's bloodshot eyes met hers. "I will be queen in Saxony." She snarled out every word. "And my son will be king after me. You"—she leveled the sword at Sirona's throat—"will help me, Wisewoman. We will summon the wax men, or you will die right here."

"So now you would kill me, the very one who saved both you and your son." Ignoring the sword, Sirona did not take her eyes from the noblewoman. "What have you become, Bathilde?"

"What you should be." Bathilde jabbed the blade closer. "You have lost your stomach for our task, and you must get it back before it is too late. The Red Goddess promised me Her aid when first I called to Her, if I sacrificed blood in Her name—"

Mau's light voice broke in for the first time. "Sekhmet will not aid you any longer, mortal woman. Yours has become a losing cause. Sekhmet is awake, and She has blood. But even Sekhmet does not countenance madness. She knows that in this case, it will avail Her nothing."

Bathilde's furious eyes went from him to Sirona. She uttered a hoarse incoherent cry and lunged at the wisewoman. Sirona jerked aside. Bathilde leaped after her. The madness Mau had spoken of was stamped clearly on her features. This time when she lunged, she released the haft of the sword.

"Strike her down," she shouted.

The sword flew to do her bidding, and Sirona reacted without thought. She threw up a hand. The weapon jerked to a halt just short of its target. It hung in the air for an instant, quivering wildly, then dropped to the ground.

Bathilde stood motionless. Her fury had not robbed her of all reason. She saw the power in Sirona and knew at last that the wisewoman could be neither persuaded nor threatened. "I will do it myself!" she yelled, and spinning about, she ran straight toward the fighting.

Bathilde ran desperately. The focus of the battle had shifted closer to *Irminsul*, leaving the encampment in ruins. The dead and wounded sprawled everywhere. Countless children lay among them. The lifeless forms of those children accused Bathilde; she saw the heads smashed in, the throats cut, the small bodies pathetic and broken. *Widukind*. She swallowed a sob and threaded a path through the disarray. She had to find him. Frantically, she screamed out the name of the pagan nurse who had replaced Begga.

"Ermengard! Ermengard!" Her legs were aching, her throat burned, and still she called. "Where are you?"

She scarcely believed it when a voice answered her. There was so much noise from the fighting that she thought she must have conjured it up from her desperate need. But a pile of bodies was moving. Bathilde stared in horror and then overwhelming relief, as the nurse crawled out from underneath. Clutched tightly in her arms was the baby. He was crying angrily, and with her chest heaving, Bathilde blessed her son's every sob of displeasure. She helped Ermengard to her feet, frowning as she saw how bloody the woman was.

She took Widukind from the nurse's arms, asking as she did so, "How badly are you hurt?"

"Only lightly, my lady. Much of this blood belongs to others, may they bide in paradise with the gods forever. I hid the child and myself beneath them." Ermengard shuddered. "If I had not, the Franks would have slain us along with the rest. Thank Freyja, there was too much commotion for them to hear the baby's cries."

"You did well." Impulsively Bathilde embraced her. "Know you if anyone else has escaped?"

Ermengard managed a shaky nod. "Many ran for the forest. I am certain that some of them made it."

"Then you must take my son and join them." Bathilde had already made up her mind, but as soon as she spoke the words aloud she felt the absolute rightness of her decision.

"Yes, yes." The nurse straightened. "I am strong enough to carry him. Come, I will show you the way—"

"No." Bathilde handed her burden back to Ermengard's arms. Never had she done anything so difficult; giving birth to the child had been easy by comparison. Pain ran through her arms, as though the sword she had tried to turn on Sirona had stabbed her instead. She forced herself to continue. "You must go alone."

Holding the squalling baby, the nurse gave her a bewildered look. "But you must come with us, my lady. How can you not? You are in the hand of the Goddess. The people look to you."

"No more." Oh, it was hard to say the words. The pain spread from Bathilde's arms to her throat as she said them. "The Shining Ones have left me. Otherwise"—she gestured around her—"this desecration would not be happening. No, Ermengard, the people must look to someone else, to Widukind."

She laid a gentle hand on the baby's damp forehead. His cries were fading at last to exhausted gulps. Terrible had been this day for such a young one, but he was strong, he possessed his mother's blood and will. He would survive.

"By Saxon law, my son has been named king," she said firmly. "Take him to the forest. Shelter him with any pagan nobles that survive this day. Let them foster him in the old ways, and when he is old enough he will claim his destiny. This task I lay upon you, faithful Ermengard. Do not fail me."

The nurse's blood-grimed face was solemn. "I will not. But you, lady, what will you do?"

Bathilde pushed her in the direction of the thick woods. "Go on. Hurry, before any of the Franks return." When the nurse still hesitated, she raised her voice. "I order you. Go!"

She watched Ermengard set off for the forest. The woman's first steps were hesitant, but they soon lengthened and grew faster. Bathilde's eyes strained for one last glimpse of the bundle the nurse carried. Only then did she stoop to retrieve a bloody sword that had been dropped by one of her warriors as he died. Holding it high, she marched gravely toward the World Tree.

"Death is on her," Mau said. "Did you not see it?

Sirona was still panting. "I see that she was trying to kill me."

Mau shook his head. "You are too strong for her to kill you. You proved that. It is she who is going to die. That is why Sekhmet has deserted her." He pointed. "But they are not done with you."

Sirona followed his gaze. A dozen Franks were charging

toward them. But not all were Franks. She drew in her breath. In the front rank there was a familiar face: Haganon. His face was blackened with smoke and blood, but Sirona could not mistake him. Nor could he mistake her. Whatever fear he had of meeting her again was gone. The earth was not shaking, a clear sign that the power of the Christian priests had prevailed against heathen magic. There would not be a better time to kill her.

"Now is your moment." Mau seemed to have no fear of the attackers racing at them. "Remember the dream My Mistress sent you, and you'll know what to do."

And all at once, Sirona did. The harmony, the balance of it was so perfect that she found herself laughing. Haganon saw it, and his face grew even darker. "The *stria* laughs," he roared to the Franks with him. "We'll see how she laughs with my sword in her mouth!"

Sirona closed her eyes. "Cat you were and cat you are, all in the same. Daughters of Bast were my mothers and daughter of Bast am I, all in the same. We are Her children. Bless us with Her aspect."

Sensation blasted over her like a wave. So intense was it that she wondered if the words had failed, and Haganon had struck her down after all. Her body seemed to be flying apart like leaves torn from a tree limb. But instead of landing haphazardly on the earth like leaves, her scattered parts were somehow reassembling themselves. Jarringly, she found herself on all fours, yet there was not a trace of awkwardness to the position. She opened her eyes. Everything sprang into focus around her: the blades of grass traced with droplets of blood, the flames leaping up from burning wagons, the tossing beards of the men as they ran toward her. Each detail was delineated, sharp and impossibly clear. Shocked by the clarity of such vision, she looked down and saw black paws.

It had worked, and so well that she was dazed by the success of it. Air flowed over her skin that was now clothed by velvet-dark fur. The ripple of powerful muscles was as heady as new wine. She shouted in exultation, but her voice came out as a deep rumbling purr.

Cries of horror rang in her ears, painfully loud in the new acuteness of her hearing. Haganon and the Franks had stopped in their tracks. Their eyes were enormous. One man blessed himself, but the others were too terrified to do anything but stare. Sirona paid no heed to them. Odors were being borne to her on the wind, and she tasted every one in her nose and tongue. The air was heavy with death and fear, and the fear was especially strong from the men facing her.

She had taken on Bast's aspect, but she was far from the hearth-size cat Mau had been. Here was no creature to curl up by a human fire. She was a giant animal, large as a bear, and just as formidable. She glanced to one side and saw that Mau had changed, though not back to his mortal feline aspect. He was the shimmering silver-brown cat of Bast's temple, as large as Sirona. His orange eyes watched her, seeming to smile.

A new scent came to her, vivid and harsh. The odor brought her attention back to the men facing her, for its origin was Haganon. The Franks with him had drawn back, but he stood alone, glaring at her, his eyes distended. At last, he managed to speak. The words were garbled and barely recognizable.

"I *will* kill you," he croaked. Clasping his sword in both hands, he raised it above his head and ran at her.

Now Sirona was able to put a name to the odor he reeked of. It was hate. *Do what you must,* Mau said in her mind. *Otherwise, I will have to.*

The sword blade flashed in the air like a shaft of sunlight. But its target was as elusive as sunlight. Sirona had already left the ground. The muscles of her new shape sent her surging up in a leap that Haganon had neither the time nor the reflexes to avoid. The sword flew from his hands. He crashed to the ground, already dead, his throat torn out.

Atop his body Sirona looked up. Her mind was awhirl with the life she had taken, with the taste of death and revenge and justice. Her eyes were blazing. Her fangs were bright with blood.

The Franks fled screaming.

* * *

Irminsul's death lit up the sky. The trunk of the great tree was solid and had resisted the flames, but Carolus had persisted. His men had to chop it partially down before the fire's bite took hold. The nine priestesses had fought like demons, defending Her to their own deaths. With them had fought a host of others. They, too, were dead. Indeed, the hundreds and hundreds of bodies covered the grass like a tapestry of sprawled limbs, twisted faces, and gore.

Carolus leaned on his sword, exhausted and satisfied. "The heathen tree will not rise again," he observed to his war band and the priests who stood with them. "And neither will the heathens who defended it."

"A worthy fight," one of the priests said above the crackle of flames. "The Lord is pleased."

Carolus blessed himself. "The unwomanly priestesses of this place are dead as they should be. But where is the noblewoman Bathilde? She, too, must die for her part in this."

"Already dead, my lord," one of his nobles said. "Haganon the Saxon saw her in the fighting and slew her." He spit reflectively and made the sign of the cross. "Then he shouted that he was going off to find the *stria.*"

"The *stria,* yes." The king looked up. "Where is the Saxon? I suppose I have to congratulate him for killing her. Well?" His voice grew louder. "Why are you all staring at me like frightened deer?"

"The Saxon is dead," another member of his war band said. "And the *stria* . . ."

His voice trailed off, and Carolus exploded in impatience. "Speak!" he roared. "What about her?"

"Talk is flying about. It is probably just battle talk, my lord. You know the sights that men think they see in the midst of hard fighting. But some of the soldiers are saying the *stria* slew Haganon—that she turned into a great cat and tore his throat out."

Instantly, the priest crossed himself. But Carolus snorted. "Nonsense. They must have been imagining it."

"I thought so, as well," the nobleman said, and hesitated. "But, my lord, the Saxon's body was found not long ago.

And his throat was indeed torn out. I saw it myself." Beneath the battle grime the man's face was pale. "It looked as if an animal had attacked him."

Carolus stared at him. He said nothing.

Well away from this discussion, Alcuin was standing by himself. The day's carnage was an abomination, and his brother churchmen's satisfaction in it, even more so. His tired eyes were watering from the smoke of the dying tree, but suddenly they caught movement. Amid all this death, life was still stirring. He peered sharply, trying to see more clearly.

Two cats were making their way toward the low, forested hills. They were very large; even at this distance Alcuin could tell that. As he stared, one of the cats turned and looked back at him. Alcuin felt a shock of recognition that staggered him. Then the animal turned away, loping with the fluid gait of her kind, to join her companion. Soon they were both out of sight.

Alcuin heard the voice of his king calling to him. Slowly he went toward the summons. He wondered if he should mention the two cats, but quickly dismissed the idea. The priests were declaring cats to be demons, and the warriors would find it great sport to mount their horses and hunt such large beasts down. Alcuin found that he did not wish for that to happen. Death enough had visited this day without adding more. He walked away, determined to say nothing.

After all, they were only cats.

Ma'at may not ever be restored. There was more sadness than anger in Sekhmet's voice.

Ma'at is eternal, as are We, said Bast.

Small good that will do either of Us when We are asleep again. I should not have listened to Your counsel about the mortal Bathilde. Mad though she was, she still brought Me blood.

A smile came and went on Bast's cat features. *You listened because Our aspects are joined, and You saw the wis-*

dom of My words. We will not go to sleep again, Sister. My daughter—Our daughter—will keep Our names alive.

She did slay that mortal well, Sekhmet admitted grudgingly. *Perhaps there is some hope after all.*

Yes, Bast said. *There is.*

Author's
Note

Carolus Magnus, known to history as Charlemagne, ruled Frankish Gaul from A.D. 768–814. Supported and backed by the Catholic Church, he embarked on a tireless campaign to bring Christianity—through force of arms—to the whole of Europe. An inspired leader, as well as a brilliant military strategist, he succeeded in controlling most of central Europe and northern Italy, in addition to his own native Gaul. His intense embrace of Christianity represents the early steps toward the development of the European culture, a culture synonymous with Roman Christian. So important was his influence that historians have named the period of his rule the Carolingian Renaissance.

Whether Charlemagne's devotion to his faith was genuine or a function of the fact that being a Christian was useful, is a matter of speculation. Certainly the Church condoned his wars of territorial acquisition, from which it took its share of the spoils. And those wars were terrible, a bloody series of aggressions against the pagan deities Charlemagne's own ancestors had worshipped. His Saxon Wars were legendary. In 782 alone he massacred more than four thousand men, women, and children, and destroyed the sacred shrines of Saxony, including Irminsul, the holy tree that was the "Column of the World." His methods of conversion for the survivors were straightforward: accept

Christianity or die. Those who accepted baptism were sent into exile and slavery.

Alcuin of York, Carolus's treasured advisor, was an actual historical figure. Carolus placed a high premium on education, and this was what drew the English scholar to the Frankish court at Aachen. Much has been written about Alcuin. He was a brilliant teacher, a gatherer and distributor of knowledge, and under his guidance Carolus's Palace School became a center of learning and culture for the whole of Europe. While Alcuin may not have been as sympathetic to pagans as I have portrayed him, from all historical accounts he was a man of deep humility who held that life had great sanctity. He is described as warm-hearted and affectionate and beloved by everyone who knew him. I like to think that he may have felt at least some compassion for the unfortunate non-Christians of his day.

My portrayal of the Saxons as stubborn pagans is based on fact. A warrior known as Widukind also did exist. He was a resistance leader of courage and determination who led the last of the Saxon revolts against the Franks. Carolus had to adopt increasingly savage measures, including the aforementioned massacres, before Widukind finally submitted and was baptized.

In thirty-three years of war Charlemagne built the Holy Roman Empire upon piles of bodies so vast historians have never been able to calculate their number. Indeed, his policy of conversion by the sword was so successful that the Church backed Christian rulers in this kind of military activity for centuries.

Sarah Isidore
Seattle